THE IRON SNAKE

THE IRON SNAKE

A Novel
by
John J. Gaudet

Brandylane Publishers, Inc.
Richmond, Virginia

ISBN 1-883911-72-9

Library of Congress Control Number 2006938550

Cover illustration from *The Lunatic Express* by Charles
Miller, 1971, courtesy of Macmillan, London, U.K.

Brandylane Publishers, Inc.
Richmond, Virginia
www.brandylanepublishers.com
www.TheIronSnake.com

To
my wife
Caroline Henrietta Broome Gaudet
without whose encouragement and help
this would not be possible.

CONTENTS

LIST OF CHARACTERS

In order of appearance, fictional characters appear below in bold regular; non-fiction characters appear in bold italics.

Kimani wa Kiruri – Kikuyu descendant of chiefs and leader of men
Muthuri – Young Kikuyu storyteller and aspiring witch doctor
Alice McConnell (*Dada dogo*, "little sister") – Daughter of George
George McConnell – Surveyor; father of Alice and husband of Rosmé by second marriage
Mary Kingsley – Explorer and author of note; Alice's adopted aunt
Roger Newcome – Son of Susan; trader and friend of the Kikuyus
Stephen Hale – Retired from the Indian Civil Service; District Commissioner of Machakos
Lady Susan Kingsbury (née Newcome) – Mother of Roger; former mistress of Stephen; later husband of Sir Godson Kingsbury
Rosmé McConnell (née Curtis) – Mother of Dorothy; wife of George; Alice's stepmother
Dorothy Hale (née Curtis) – Stepsister of Alice; wife of Stephen
Dr. Karl Peters (*Mikono wa damu*, "the one with blood on his hands") – Former High Commissioner in German East Africa; lately a businessman in London
Albert (*Kiboko*, "the hippo") **and Elise Shimmer** – German agents provocateur in Kenya
Franz Shimmer – Adopted son of Albert and Elise
Fritz Kohl – District Commissioner of Kilimanjaro in German East Africa
David McCann – Son of a Bishop; lately District Commissioner of Nairobi

Hon. Brian Stanford – Presumptive Fifth Baron of Manchester; friend of the Somalis

Jimmy Harris – Assistant to Stephen in Machakos

Capt. (ret.) Jeffrey Porter ("J.O.") – White hunter migrated to Kenya from Matabeleland

Lord John Allen (*Nge*, "the scorpion") – Fourth son of the Marquess of Wellstone; Supervisor of the Railway in Nairobi

Jakoby – Zulu woman of many talents; local agent for the Shimmer family in Kenya

Capt. Daniel & Mrs. Jenny Lloyd – He is seconded from the Indian Army and commandant of the garrison in Naivasha; his wife is Alice's best friend

Capt. (later Major) Bobby Curtis – Brother of Rosmé; seconded from the Indian Army; later commandant of the 1st Uganda Rifles in Mombasa

George Whitehouse – Chief Engineer Uganda Railway

Capt. William Bagley – Seconded from the Indian Army; Stationmaster Nairobi

Capt. Matthew Woodham-Stayne – Seconded from the Indian Army; Head of Railway Security

Karegi – Mkamba beauty; later the first qualified African nurse in Nairobi

Ian & Isabelle Burns – High Commissioner of the Kenya Protectorate and his wife

Kona – Somali servant of Brian's; later serves Alice as keeper of the cheetahs

Lizzie and Jane – Alice's pet cheetahs

Dr. Charles Sharpe, M.D. ("Charley") – Physician for the Railway; later Public Health doctor in Nairobi

Harry DeSuza – Former Stationmaster; lately organizer of resistance to the Railway

Zaliwatena – Son of Karegi

Lts. Bradshaw ("Gerry") & **Smythe** ("Smitty") – Formerly Indian Army; later 1st Uganda Rifles

Syonduku (*Mama mdogo, "Auntie"*) – Mkamba woman held in high regard by the people in Ukambaa villages

Kaiser Wilhelm II – King and Emperor of Germany
"Big Billy" Kirkpatrick (*Kifaru*, "the rhino") – Commandant of the Army in Kenya
Veejay Shah – Assistant to David in Nairobi

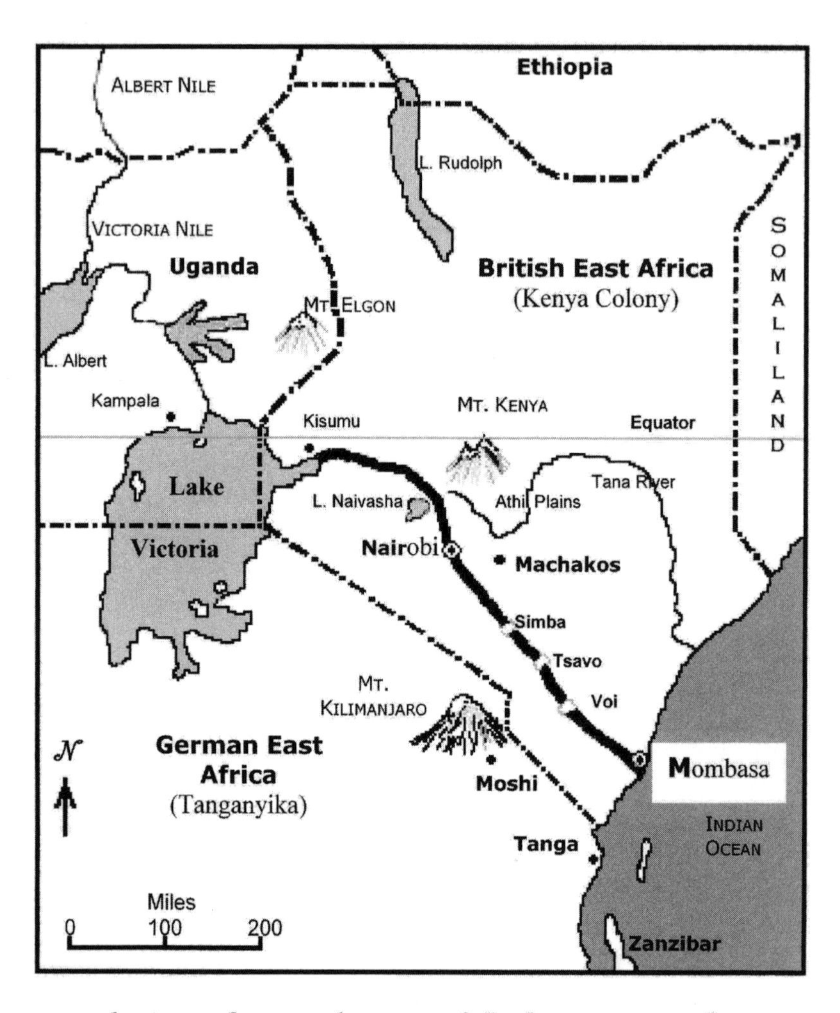

British East Africa at the turn of the last century, showing the course of the railroad and the lay of the land.

PROLOGUE

Kikuyuland, Kenya, 1890

The large, black rain clouds rolled down low over the slopes and seemed about to swallow him as he ran, naked and wet. His brown body glistened in the light that faded with each passing minute. He held his quiver and bow tight against his bare body and ran, trying to outrace the storm. Termite mounds, grass tussocks and tree roots disappeared as the black clouds took control of the sky making it seem like night descending in mid-day. Large raindrops splattered on the path, and then the breeze turned cold and sheets of rain began blowing across the grass and treetops along the trail. His goal was the slight rise on his right, where a small craggy overhang would provide shelter.

He slipped under the ledge just as the heavens crashed down and thunder rolled over the lush tropical landscape with a horrific roar. His breath came in gasps and he felt as if the ground were shaking as he lay peering out through the downpour. In sympathy with the earth, his body shivered at the cold display of nature's power sweeping over the land. The sweat and rain on his body felt chill, but did not distract from the spectacular display before his eyes; the dazzling light flashed and the thunder crackled and roared ominously. After a while he looked around his dry niche. He could stand only in a crouch as he moved about. At one end of the ledge was a dry log, the remains of burnt wood near it. With his knife he chipped kindling from the log, as others had obviously done before him.

Reaching out to one side of the ledge, he broke off a few branches from the shrubs growing nearby and shook the rain from them. He laid them to one side to dry as he concentrated on lighting a fire. Using a fire stick, bow and thong, which he kept in his quiver, and a small, cottony bit of shredded bark, he worked to create heat. Smoke appeared and he blew carefully on the smoldering bark, laying it tenderly in a bed of wood chips and, when it ignited, feeding it with a few of the twigs. He could soon feel the warmth of a small fire spreading. His body relaxed and he lay curled on the bare earth around the flames like a cat. The shivering stopped and his skin began to dry.

The thunder, lightning and rain continued unabated. Mwene Nyaga, the God of the Earth, was obviously now very busy, and with His hands full He would not notice Kimani lying here in this small dry place. The thought made him more relaxed and he looked out at the falling rain. This year the rains had been late. Everyone went to sleep at night remembering the drought three years ago. This was the first rainstorm of the year and he knew his village would be rejoicing. The children would be rushing about rolling in the puddles; the witch doctors would be reveling in their wisdom, their work rewarded. The animals and plants of the forest would accept this gift of another cycle of life, and the women would begin inspecting the pots of seed grain, picking out insect-damaged seeds and bad kernels. Their plots had been ready for planting weeks ago.

The elders would caution everyone to wait a few days before planting. Hopefully the sky would be cloudy each afternoon from now on; rain would fall late in the day or at night, and in the morning and evening the life-nourishing dew would be found on the grass. He had seen some seasons when the dew alone would carry a crop and allow it to grow, but some rain had to fall, otherwise the grain would not mature. For now, though, Kimani had no regrets. He would stay here until morning, with the warmth of the flickering fire against his belly. He used the cap of his tinderbox to dip and drink water from the small pools in the rock in front of the ledge. The rain continued strong, wetting the soil deeply, filling the rivers and streams. His eyelids fluttered and his mind drifted as he stared into the small bright fire. He dreamed he saw a party of Kikuyu warriors, jogging on a grassy plain, feather headdresses waving, leather strips with bells and shells jangling and the fur of their monkey skin leggings fluttering in the breeze, their bodies smeared with white clay, in stark relief against their black skin. Why are they traveling in the open, he wondered. A wild and foolish thing to do. It will only attract the attention of the Masai in whose territory they were trespassing.

He saw the warriors clearly, friends of his from his own age group, and he was surprised to see Muthuri there. For the others it was the sort of wild thing they would do, but Muthuri? This was not his way. He was always cautious. And where were they going? Now they had stopped jogging; they were jumping and spinning in a dance, making their own music, chanting a deep guttural rhythm. He sympathized with them whatever their goal, and he felt strong because they seemed so confident, until they abruptly stopped dancing. Then a ball of light flared up and a voice called to him, "Kimani."

"Kimani!" it called again, insistently. He tried hard to look but could not raise his eyes to the blinding light.

"Yes, I am here, Father," he said. He felt he should reply in a respectful tone, as to an elder. His eyes were still cast down when he saw his friends had moved on and now his feet were resting on warm sand, ominously streaked with red.

"Kimani." The voice was firm. "Come closer to me, my son. Do not be afraid."

He hesitated. When his feet finally moved, he could not feel any substance under them.

"Look here in this water."

He had not seen it before, but now, how obvious, there was a pool at his feet. It was quiet and still, not a ripple on its surface. At the bottom of the pool he saw cloudy plumes waving and streaming this way and that, like waterweeds.

"I see some thin reeds, Father, with shapes moving in all directions. And Father...."

"Yes, my son?"

"I cannot see my image in this water."

"Look closer. Do not give up."

He stared into the pool and focused his eyes the way he did when he looked for game on a hillside. He concentrated his mind and eye to see any detail, any small movement. As he did so, he noticed the strands had stopped waving back and forth. Now they shimmered like the light above the dry flat salt beds in the North Country. The strands parted and he saw the head of a large black snake push through. This was no ordinary snake. As it moved across the pool bottom, the weeds changed to sand and the water disappeared.

The snake's head, strong and large with a single large eye, was held aloof, and when it opened its mouth he saw a brilliant red lining, scarlet against the white fangs, with smoke coming from its nostrils. The men from his age group dressed in their warrior regalia stood in its path.

He called out, warning them to give way. "*Haya! Kwenda sasa, upesi.* Hey! Move away now, fast."

But nothing diverted them; they stood their ground and raised their big colorful shields and aimed their spears. All threw their spears at the same time, striking home in the single eye of the snake, but it had no effect; the snake went forward even more rapidly. Now Kimani saw his friends falling into the open mouth, each disappearing into the red interior with a small flash of light, like moths in a flame, leaving little puffs of smoke hanging in the air. Kimani was upset; he wanted to be with them, to help them; he lunged forward and grabbed at the snake with its flaming mouth and smoking head.

As he reached for the monster, his hand felt the stabbing pain of the heat, and he woke with a start, shaking off a small glowing coal from his arm.

It was pitch dark except for the glow of the embers. His backside was cold. He fed more wood into the fire and warmed himself as best he could. Four more hours would pass before dawn. He stared into the flames, conscious that he was only one small entity lying there beside a flickering light in the middle of Africa, in a dark universe that went far beyond his imagination.

Book One

African Destinies

1

Kent, England, 1893-95

"Aunt Mary's gone?" asked a young Alice McConnell in a querulous, suspicious voice. Even at an early age, she challenged her father's interpretation, a habit that irked him no end.

"I said *gone* and I mean it. Gone. Left home."

A thin, fit man with a full thatch of magnificent black hair, he looked up briefly from his morning paper at his thirteen-year-old daughter. Her light brown curls and wide brown eyes could melt his reserve in a moment. To avoid them he again sought refuge in his newspapers.

"But *where* Papa?"

"To Africa, Angola," he said, this time without looking up. He could almost hear her thinking about what he had just said, so he added, "I presume you know where *that* is," and continued reading the "Saga of the Moment," an article about the exploits of some explorer, which were invariably portrayed as the Grand Adventure.

As a surveyor he appreciated exploration to a point; that is, you set a goal and a straight course to achieve it, the line so drawn was executed at least cost to the client. But in this morning's edition he saw a "hero" gunning down native hordes, extricating chaps from the mouths of lions, fighting his way through a jungle and, in general, wreaking havoc and leaving a trail of corpses in his wake as he wandered from pillar to post.

Not George McConnell's idea of how to go about it, not at all.

"Bosh," was his summary comment, causing his daughter to turn her eyes from her porridge to the window in the south-facing breakfast room, hoping to find the answer in the view from there. Perhaps, she thought, as she gazed out onto the rolling fields below, this is not so different from the place where Aunt Mary has gone. She recalled from her atlas that starting from Kent one passed through England to Europe and the rest of the World, and since the World started with "A" for Africa, she reasoned that Angola must be at the very top of that continent and perhaps not far from where she sat this sunny morning.

"By God, I hope you don't take after her," McConnell muttered.

Which comment gave Alice more food for thought. She saw herself as just that, a younger version of her aunt.

"What will she do there, Papa?"

"Wants to finish her father's book on the *culture* of Africa," he scoffed, shaking his head again. "Bosh!"

Which made her wonder, was he put off by the idea of culture in Africa, or by Aunt Mary herself?

Nancy, their longstanding housekeeper and a fountain of wisdom, had informed Alice, "Your 'Aunt' Mary's no aunt, being as how your father's no relation by blood. Old friends is what we call 'em."

"Very old friends," said Sylvia the cook. "Mary Kingsley knew your Mum since she were your age."

They were referring to the Kingsleys of Islington, of whom Charles, author of note and uncle to Mary, was the most well known; even Alice had read *Westward Ho!* And he would have remained the most renowned, had not Mary Kingsley returned from Africa in 1895 after navigating the Ogooue River, scaling Mt. Cameroon and befriending the cannibal tribes of the region.

At that point, she had achieved the same status as those adventurers brought to the brink of a new disaster each day in George McConnell's newspaper—left hanging on a branch above a crocodile-infested papyrus swamp, or on the edge of a cliff with nothing between them and oblivion save the mist rising from a spectacular tropical waterfall.

The next morning's issue would see them again in peril.

For Alice the sagas were as good as the penny thrillers, if not better. The fact that her "aunt" was among this heroic band of explorers would further convince her at the age of fifteen and beyond that she was destined for the same life. After the death of Alice's mother, her father would find less and less opportunity to dissuade her because he had to rent out their farmland and orchards and travel as a surveyor to supplement their modest income. This would take him more and more often away from home.

"Sold the house and furniture," he announced to Alice and Nancy and shook his head in wonderment. He was at a complete loss to divine the reasons for "Aunt" Mary's actions, yet Alice and Nancy knew exactly why she had left.

Aunt Mary had been minding the Kingsley house in London for years, and had obviously grown tired of it. When her parents had become invalids, she had taken over running the household, and had taught herself to carry out repairs from reading practical manuals and magazines. Dangerously steep ladders, dilapidated gutters, treacherous slate shingles loose on a high-pitched roof and leaky pipes throughout the ramshackle house had steeled her. In desperate need of a challenge, she had decided she could equally deal with trees in the rainforest, cutting them down to provide canoes, and if necessary catching onto the vines and hanging creepers, handholds when those same canoes overturned in the rain-swollen, raging rivers of West Africa.

Still in her thirties when her parents died, Mary had set off better prepared than most men to explore tropical Africa.

Emulating her aunt, Alice subscribed to the same magazines and tried to develop the same skills, though she had limited opportunities until her sixteenth year when Aunt Mary again intervened.

"Package for you, Miss," said Sylvia.

"For me?" asked Alice.

"More tools from Aunt Mary," presumed Nancy, as she shook her head and helped Alice unwrap the heavy canvas-wrapped parcel, in which they were surprised to find a double-barrelled gun, a Purdy, and a bag of shells.

Well oiled and shining in the sunlight on the dining room table, it was frightening.

"My Lord," said Nancy. "What can she mean by this?"

"*My Dear Alice*," the daughter of the house read in the accompanying note. "*On his last trip through London, George mentioned your farm being overrun by rabbits. He said the tenant farmers had little time to waste trapping them, and I thought, here's an opportunity for you. Don't for your own sake sit at home with romance novels, as I hear girls of your generation have a tendency to do. I remember you as an active, lively creature. Keep up with life, make yourself useful and provide for the table. The piece enclosed is an old model but still reliable, and proved its value as a true friend many times in the Congo. Your neighbour, Henry Wardlaw, I am sure will show you how to use it. I was impressed to read about his exploits as a skeet shooter....*"

2

Liverpool, England, 1895

At seventeen Roger Newcome reminded some Englishmen of an American savage—a Red Indian, they would say—which, he was quick to point out, was far from reality. His nose was too small, he didn't wear feathers in his hat or hair, and he never used war paint or leather leggings. The only basis they had for this wild assumption was that he was a tall, red-haired, distinctly American male, though a prickly one at that.

He had arrived in Liverpool from Hull with little money and no prospects; luckily, he landed a position as a clerk, a job offered to him by a former colleague of his father. Though he had never been to Liverpool, everyone in the ship chandler trade had known Roger's father, Paul Newcome.

Lucky in more ways than one, Roger thought, he also had found a small room in a hotel for commercial travelers, a cheap, convenient and timely piece of luck because he now had only one pound ten shillings to his name. Lying awake in bed one Sunday four weeks after his arrival in Liverpool, Roger's first feeling was a sense of accomplishment. He felt he had after all seen much of what life could offer and had taken a great step forward toward what he called "freeing his soul."

In other words, he'd had his first ever sexual coupling with a woman.

It proved to him that the Ideal Woman did exist, the woman he had envisioned after reading Rider Haggard's novel, *She*. He had until recently confused Her with his mother, Susan Newcome, an attractive widow. Another revelation was that Susan was simply that, the mother he had left behind in Hull, whereas the woman he had recently made love to was the image of the woman who had dominated his fantasies. In his dreams he called her the "Woman of Endless Days," the woman who had encouraged him to do anything to her, anything his mind could invent, and somehow she was never cheapened by being used in this manner. Amazingly in his dreams she seemed ever willing, and never hesitated to lift her lovely dress, or show her beautiful showgirl form and large, perfectly shaped breasts, tight-laced boots and enticing manner. It was a wonder, he thought, how such a woman remained sacred in her purity and continued on as a virgin, albeit a virgin with knowledge of exactly what was needed to address his needs, which seemed unending.

He was amazed to find all of this in a factory girl who lived not far from dockside.

How he had railed against this very thing, he thought. Back in Hull with his mates in school and later at work, he'd damned them in his ignorance of life.

"Factory girls, ugh. They walk out with anyone in trousers, and expect cash in return. Where's the purity of love in that?"

Yes, this had been a lesson.

He had met her and her girlfriend at a refreshment stand in a music hall. There had been a mix-up in the drinks. They were both fresh, exciting young ladies, maybe a bit too much rouge, who by coincidence found their seats next to his. He saw them again after the performance and was certain he made an impression because the dark-haired one agreed to see him several evenings in a row. His luck held and she seemed completely captivated. To his surprise, she knew the concierge at a small hotel not far from the music hall, someone who previously worked at the same factory, and who allowed them to register as "Mr. and Mrs."

Roger had never known till then that a woman, other than his mother, could be so soft and loving and caring. And not once did she ask for money. It touched him that he had to force her to take money for a hackney cab. More money, it turned out, than was needed, but he told himself that the hours they spent together had formed a bond that would never allow questions to be raised.

"My God," he murmured, now relishing the feel of her breasts and the chance to see for the first time every hair, every tiny fold of those delicate pink lips enclosed inside that lovely mound. The object of his desire achieved after so many years. His fumbling and anxiety faded as she guided him with the same firmness and pleasant manner as the woman of his fantasies, and the wondrous sensation of it all. How much better than those secretive fingerings of his penis as he lay in his school bed.

For all his fascination and amazement, he soon realized the cost of the music hall, meals, drinks, hotel room—even for a half day—the cab fare and small gifts all added up to quite a sum. Not that it wasn't worth it, but his diminished fortune wouldn't allow another such treat for a while. He'd left a note at the hotel where she said she'd keep an eye out. Although he lied as he wrote, "Off on business, back soon," he did mean it when he finished with, "All my love, Roger."

This had happened two weeks earlier. Now he stretched, and rising from his bed he felt the familiar morning pressure in his bladder. There being no chamber pot, his first thought was the need to get his trousers on and make his way down the back stairs to the outhouse in the rear. Sundays everyone slept late, so he wasn't concerned that many of his fellow lodgers would be queuing.

As he stood over the opening in the uncovered wooden box, his fly undone, blissfully waiting for the first relief, the relief he seldom thought much about other than a calm, perfect moment before breakfast, a searing pain shot through the length of his member and struck him like a hammer blow. He squeezed the head to stop the urine in mid-flow and a cry burst from his throat. Tears welled up and his vision blurred; he couldn't believe the pain. Worse yet, stopping the flow seemed to increase the burning. Finally he helplessly gritted his teeth as he let the urine flow again.

Unlike anything ever experienced by anyone, he thought, as he went, white-faced and sweating, back up the stairs to his room. Who could he blame for this but himself?

Then why at that very moment, he asked himself, did the image of his mother and Stephen Hale come to mind?

3

Hull, England, 1895

Stephen Hale had never felt such an intense attraction toward any woman; at thirty-four Susan Newcome was still one of the most beautiful women in Hull. Her beauty, so different from that of his first wife, appealed to the emotions as well as the eye, which he had discovered the first day he met her.

Her teenage son, Roger, was just the opposite—quiet, brooding, self-conscious of his beardless face and unkempt red hair. He was a skulker, thought Stephen, and a touchy one.

Before Roger had left Hull, Stephen had found him even more difficult than usual. He had met Americans in his travels and had found them to be reasonable people, as individuals and collectively; perhaps Roger was an exception.

Stephen had retired early from the Indian Civil Service. His house sat next door to the Newcomes' cottage, which, like Susan's first husband, Paul, was smaller, older and had a less forceful personality. This distinction also carried forward to their social positions in Hull. Through an aunt, Stephen's family retained part-ownership in the shipping firm where Roger had worked as a clerk until he had abruptly left.

The Newcomes would normally have moved in different circles than Stephen, but Susan, a native Virginian, was an ambitious woman. English by birth, Paul had never liked America. He jumped at the chance to come back and take up a position left vacant by the death of his father, and once returned he had no interest in the world outside Yorkshire country. Hull remained the center of his universe, and the wharves, local pubs, bookkeeping and the shipping office held his interest until his sudden death several years after his return.

Prior to that, like Roger, he seemed to have anchored himself safely in the calm protected harbor of his wife's bosom. Within that same bosom, however, lay desires untapped and dreams unfulfilled, like dark sleek racing ships tugging at their hawsers on the tide. Her introduction to Stephen provided an opportunity to launch her modest fleet, and she intended to make the most of it.

"Mrs. Newcome, you *are* a wonder," said the wife of one of the housing agents. Her ability at renting and estate planning, barely evident during her married life, came to life the day she took control of the small but debt-free estate of Paul. She had secured the cottage in which both Roger and she lived; in addition she owned and rented several small houses in a modest section of town. She had built an income from careful management, penny by penny.

That particular Sunday morning found Stephen Hale sitting at home, at a large table facing a window that looked out over the River Humber. A fire crackled and sputtered in the grate. Spring mornings in Hull were usually chilly, and typical weather prevailed as a cold rain had fallen for the last two weeks. Rain was pelting down as he finished his second cup of tea. He sat in the dry cozy atmosphere of this room still happy and confident that this day would end as the happiest one of his life. He had two things to announce to his dearest friend, Susan Newcome: one, that he was intent on going out to Africa; and second, that he wanted her to come with him.

Susan, for whom he waited, knew the well-trimmed moustache, the sandy hair which seemed to float gently above his ears, the straight, almost noble nose and the emerald-colored eyes for what they were, part of an inheritance for which he had little responsibility. She had weighed those characteristics along with his house and business interests and had concluded earlier this week that they weren't enough.

Finally, Susan entered through the back gate, passed the kitchen and walked through to the front of the house. She was dressed for church and had on a gown of watered silk taffeta, with bright blue ribbons streaming from her waist and a hat made especially to compliment her eyes. She knew the value of well-tailored and fashionable clothes.

Impatient though he was for her arrival, he was even more disappointed by what she had to tell him; in fact, it would cause him a distress he would remember for the rest of his life.

"I'm sorry, Stephen. I can only stay a few minutes. The gist of the matter is that I'm going back to Virginia."

"Susan...," he said, devastated, as he turned toward her, then stopped. He bit his lip. He had an engagement ring in the drawer of the table and that drawer lay open, waiting. He had intended to see it safely on her finger, his happiness assured, his day complete. He had even accepted in his mind the thought of her son, Roger, as his son, a decision that required a great deal of compromise on his part. He would do anything to have her as his wife, and if that included Roger, so be it.

Accordingly, he had planned this day carefully. His servants had the day off, and, until it started raining again, he had thought it would be an ideal day to propose marriage.

So sure was he of acceptance that he had set out a cold bottle of champagne on his dresser and had fresh sheets put on his bed upstairs, a bed to which she was no stranger.

While he waited, he got up and paced the room. He had been reading the same "adventures" dismissed by McConnell as "Bosh!" and was upset by what he saw as political interventions with serious implications. Whoever planted the flag in the middle of an African jungle empire or signed a treaty with a native chief became the emissary in residence of a European power. Stephen objected to the way the newspapers puffed up these adventures to the level of a national blood sport.

Several years previous, the stories of the moment had been the exploits of a German explorer, Dr. Karl Peters, ostensibly heading a relief column to locate Emin Pasha, a fellow German and former provincial governor in Sudan, then lost and wandering in Uganda. Stephen had followed carefully the progress of the expedition. It was clear Peters' mission was nothing more than an outright grab at Uganda by the Kaiser. He was signing treaties with native chiefs in an obvious attempt at interference in a country until now considered under the protection of Great Britain. He presumed that somewhere to his left outside his window, down along the rain-washed Humber, across the North Sea, someplace in Germany, someone like him was sitting over his morning *kaffee* rooting for the home team in the local *Zeitung*.

Their first meeting occurred after Sunday service at the Holy Trinity Church off Market Place when the vicar had introduced them. The same vicar had this past month introduced her to Sir Godson Woodhead, and so had begun the chain of events that unfolded that day and almost brought Stephen to his knees in his own front parlor. At that moment he was sorry he had ever brought up the point that he had begun to chafe at commercial life in England, and was thinking of returning to the Civil Service, this time to Africa.

Why, oh why, he later moaned to himself, why did I ever say that?

"I think it's an awful idea, Stephen. You'd be throwing your life away."

"But I'm stagnating here anyway, unlike yourself. You've proved to everyone you can adapt and make a go of it. Think of what you could do out there."

"Stephen, my darling, you'll never understand me. It's quite simple. I'm a realist; a place like that would do me in and I know it."

It was then he noticed she hadn't yet removed her hat. A bad sign, he thought. Here the champagne was getting warm and now he was afraid of rushing her. He had early learned that if he leaned too hard she would turn away, yet he wanted to salvage something from their day.

"Does your aunt approve?" she asked.

"I haven't told her."

"And her interest in the firm? Who would manage that once you've gone out to Africa?"

"Once *we've* gone out. Please Susan," he said, "all I'm asking is that you consider it. You know if you wouldn't go with me, I'd give it all up at the drop of a hat. Think of it as an adventure," he added, desperately, as he slipped his arm around her waist.

He had planned his next move several days ago, and reached now for the ring, but she wasn't responding today as she had in the past.

Instead of leaning forward in his arms and kissing him, she turned and looked out the window. Then she casually asked if he knew anything about Godson Woodhead. He thought she was referring to some business she had with him, not realizing that Sir Godson had the day before been in the exact same position that Stephen wanted to be, on his knees, hand shaking, as he offered Susan a different ring.

Intuition or perhaps a premonition made him look at her left hand, which rested lightly on his breast. That's when it hit him, like a bullet, striking him right between the eyes: the realization that she had on a ring of enormous proportions, a ring so large that she would have no room left on that finger for Stephen's.

His eyes opened wide in shock, his arm fell from her waist and a pain shot across his brow.

"I'm sorry, Stephen," she said.

He took a step back, as she explained. "He proposed yesterday. I had no chance to tell you until now."

"And, it's final?" he asked, his face white and stricken.

"It's better this way, Stephen dear," she said as she moved toward the door. "Now you can do what you've always wanted. You've said so yourself a hundred times. You want to travel, to get back to the tropics. It's for the best, really. I can only stay a few minutes, he's agreed to move to Virginia."

"Susan...," he said, devastated as he turned toward her, his mind gone blank. He fought back the sickness and misery that surged into his head.

"It's for the best...," he repeated in a daze. It was all he could manage.

Her hand was on the door as she reassured him that he would always remain her friend, and then, just before she left, she reminded him of his promise to be an adopted godfather to Roger. "He wrote yesterday to say he's determined on going out to Africa. I've sent him money for his passage but he'll be on his own out there," she said. "I'm sure someday your paths will cross and I think he'd appreciate your help."

Afterwards, he sat, dazed, disappointed, gazing at the open drawer and the ring, until his grief turned to anger, anger at himself for his own stupidity. Then he got up and shut that drawer. He turned and unlocked the other drawer, the one in which lay his Webley revolver from his days in India and a letter from Her Majesty's Colonial Office offering him a post in East Africa as a district commissioner.

Yes, he said to himself, as he raised the pistol to his head, it's a good thing the servants have the day off.

Then he saw something even more harmful than a bullet: four full decanters labeled "sherry," "port," "brandy" and "whiskey" sitting on a sideboard. They found him there on the floor the next morning almost dead, but, to his sorrow, still alive. "It's for the best…," he mumbled as he crawled away from a pool of his own vomit looking for another drink.

4

Hull, England

Stephen's head ached until he learned to begin his day with a stiff peg. At first he resisted early morning drinking, but before long it seemed normal. Then, as his trips to the sideboard became more and more frequent, he achieved his final goal and each day blurred into a confusion that ended only at night when he collapsed, sometimes fully clothed, on his bed, more often on the floor. It was the only way he had found to deaden his loss.

News of Susan's wedding had spread quickly in Hull, which was in many ways a small town. He cried most of the day she departed with Sir Godson en route to a honeymoon in France, and thence to Virginia. Thereafter he rose late and drank steadily with a brief respite during dinner. With nothing left to hold on to, he slowly watched his life turn upside down, and everything he had thought of as an advantage, his house, his independence and his privacy, everything he had held so dear, suddenly became barriers on the road to sobriety.

When he disappeared into the recesses of his large comfortable home, no one came around to find out why he had dropped out of circulation. The large house with its well-stocked wine cellar was no help; the supply of drink in it was endless, and he could sequester himself in the back rooms downstairs for days on end. His servants, obedient to a fault, were of little use in rescuing him. He had trained them to respect his privacy. His sole responsibility at the firm was to act on behalf of his aunt in the capacity of an advisor; he had no other formal duties or position. His views on management were felt by those in charge to be more of a hindrance than a help; in fact, the head of the company was quite relieved when Stephen failed to show up at the office.

The vicar finally stepped in when he noticed Stephen's absence from Sunday service. He called at his house and would not be put off by the servants; he persisted until he found an unshaved, mumbling drunkard who needed more than counselling and hot coffee—he needed a job, a goal and some purpose in life. Revived and encouraged, Stephen set off with good intentions on his first step toward recovery. As directed by the vicar, he paid a visit to his aunt in Maidstone where his friend from school days, Eric Watts, an amateur sportsman and cricket buff, informed of Stephen's depression by his aunt, invited him to a cricket match to try to raise his spirits.

It was here on the sports club green that Stephen's life took another turn.

Maidstone, England

"George McConnell," said Eric by way of introducing Stephen to the surveyor from Aylesford. "George played for the county years ago. Haven't seen you in a while."

"Came into a bit of money and remarried," said George. "Now I'm retired in Sevenoaks."

"Remarried? Anyone we know?"

"Rosmé Curtis."

"I remember her. The Frenchwoman with the lovely daughter."

"Exactly," said George. "That's Dorothy."

He couldn't bring himself to add the details. His new stepdaughter, Dorothy, a petulant young woman, older than his own daughter, Alice, remained the only barrier between him and a peaceful life.

"Your wife's French?" asked Stephen, interested.

"From Provence."

"Her first husband was Jamie Curtis, a local," explained Eric. He turned back to the surveyor and confessed that, "Stephen's at odds' ends, George. I'm trying to occupy his time while he's here. He's staying with his aunt."

"Sad day," said George, "when two young fellows like yourselves can't find something more lively to do than take a seat at a village cricket match."

A bitter memory of a sobbing stepdaughter reminded him forcefully of the reason he himself was at the match, to escape a doleful household. Someone named John Allen, a captain in the Indian Army, had shown interest in Dorothy, but there had been a disappointment, something that caused Allen to board a train early one morning leaving a note. It was delivered to Dorothy at home and explained that he had been called back to London on urgent business.

Since then they had hardly seen her; she had confined herself to her room. Rosmé, normally a playful and diverting partner in bed, was now distracted to the fullest extent. She lay awake each night wondering what could be done. In desperation she had taken to instructing him before he left the house, "For your sake, as well as my own peace of mind, find her a man."

"Too bad Bobby isn't here," said Eric.

"My wife's brother, Capt. Curtis," explained George to Stephen. "He's stationed in Bombay, stays with us when he's on leave."

"Stephen served out there," said Eric.

"Well," said George, "you've just missed him. But it's of no importance." He signalled the boy who fetched orders from the local pub. "At least let me treat you to a round of our local bitter."

"And well you might offer, George, but our friend Stephen will have none of it."

"A Hull man who doesn't drink!" said George, impressed. "By God, that is a rarity."

And the thought crossed his mind that Stephen might be the answer to his prayers.

5

The Mediterranean, 1895

The memory of his short stay in Liverpool never left him. It came flooding back to Roger every evening as he lay on the deck of a coastal steamer approaching Port Said and the Suez Canal. Those thoughts and the warm, stagnant night air in the crowded stateroom had forced him to join the steerage passengers on the open deck. After three days at sea, unable to sleep, he rose from the thin, sweat-stained mattress and walked barefoot to the railing where the salt air cleared his head and he leaned against a stanchion as he gazed up. A universe of stars had appeared and a crescent moon had risen over North Africa.

His shame at having to appear before a doctor with an unmentionable disease—"Clapped," said the doctor—followed by a revulsion and disgust with humanity, and then the news of his mother's marriage to a man more than forty years older than she, convinced him that he would be better off putting as much distance as he could between himself and England. By now he thought he had left the anger and disappointment behind, but apparently not. The mere thought of his mother's marriage still brought resentment to his heart, a feeling matched only by the real cause of his anger—Stephen Hale. By stepping between Roger and his mother, Hale had disrupted a world of trust and sacred love, a world in which her friendship had been the mainstay of Roger's life. He had been happy, he thought, until that day, that Sunday at Trinity Church, when Stephen had appeared in their life.

Now, it's finished, he said to himself, there's no going back.

He stared down at the wake rising from the bow, churning up a phosphorescence so bright against the black ocean depth that it lit up the surrounding water as it streamed away from the boat and joined the ship's wake, which left a trail of brilliant white across the southern Mediterranean, marking the ship's progress, and his, as it made its way hour by hour, minute by minute toward the Dark Continent and a new life.

6

London, 1896

If Dr. Karl Peters wanted to be philosophical, no one could argue with his right to do so—after all, he had won his doctorate in metaphysics.

Today, however, he would not stand on his rights. Having left Germany and settled in England, he felt he had no rights left. An unabashed anglophile and once famous explorer, he had left the Colonial Service and emigrated, not willingly. He never did anything willingly. The principle cause of his moving had been the German judge who had found him guilty of mistreating Africans. An unusual judgment, he thought, in light of the fact that so many of his colleagues still held the life of an African so cheaply.

He had decided, so be it, henceforth I shall be an English gentleman. Just plain Mr. Carl Peters. He intended to disappear into the world of British finance and business. To start the process, he had begun a new firm, The C. Peters Estates and Exploration Company. His few London city friends predicted he would do well.

A slim, wiry type with cropped moustache, his pince-nez and slight smile belied the rumours. People said that he was a tenacious, cruel and vindictive person, a man who would never forget nor forgive the Kaiser for concluding a treaty with the British. That treaty negated much of what he had done during his time in Africa.

Still, as Albert Shimmer pointed out to him on his recent visit to London, "South West Africa, Cameroon, Togoland and Tanganyika are all within the German Empire, and the Transvaal and Orange Free State in South Africa are still in the hands of our allies, the Boers."

Albert had brought his adopted son Franz with him to visit "The Master." The Shimmer family was on their way back to Africa, and it was with good reason they came here first. The conversion of Karl Peters' Society for German Colonization to the German East Africa Company had aided the transition of Tanganyika into a German colony. Recent reports from there indicated that Tanganyika was now on the road to becoming a well-established German estate. Albert's friend, Fritz Kohl, the new commissioner for the Kilimanjaro District, could already point to tobacco, sisal and sugar plantations along with steam-driven sugar factories, and a growing respect among the coastal tribes who spoke of Kaiser Wilhelm as "Our Ruler," the "Great German Bwana" and "Our German Sultan."

"And what do you expect of me?" asked Dr. Peters.

Albert and Franz sat with him in the well-appointed lobby of a hotel off Trafalgar Square. To the impartial observer, these three men, exact and formal in their manner, were carrying out the ritual typical of so many thousands of Londoners that same day, afternoon tea. The Limoges cups and saucers were carefully balanced and the tea and buttered scones were quietly disappearing as the three of them sat in front of a cheerful fire.

"Our consortium in Germany believes the treaties you signed with African leaders are still valid," said Albert, "and they may some day provide us with a useful mandate if we ever achieve our present goal."

"Which is?"

"To win over the residents of the Kenya Colony."

"An ambitious undertaking," said Dr. Peters.

"But not impossible. Kohl tells me that many of the settlers there are white South Africans, Afrikaners. If they could be assured of private support even while the British Colonial Service and the Railway Administration ignore their needs, there might be a chance."

Albert and his wife, Elise, had a plan for the greater good of mankind. Bolstered by God's will and their interpretation of business interests in Berlin, they believed there was a coalescence of

German influence beginning in Africa. Albert was certain that the Kaiser would eventually come around, as would every right-minded person.

"Until that day, we must go forward on our own initiative," he explained.

"What 'consortium' or 'private support' are you speaking of?" asked Peters. He brushed a crumb from his mustache with a quick flick of his napkin.

"We have enormous support among the business community," said Albert as he accepted another expertly buttered scone from Franz. "We feel it would not be farfetched to see you return to Africa in the near future, and at a higher level. So at this point, we need your endorsement. In truth, neither Kohl nor I will move until we have your blessing."

"Shimmer," said Peters, "I believe you. Not when you say I will be triumphant in my return to Africa, but when you talk that way of the Kaiser. As much as I hate the man, he does have Napoleonic ambitions. He's simply too weak to take what is rightfully ours."

"Our place in the sun," said Franz.

Both men looked at him.

"I think we will all three of us live to see a Germany that is extended over the entire continent of Europe, as well as Africa and Asia," said Peters with a smile.

"Then you agree with our plan?"

"Hear me out." Peters reached for the teapot. "I support an effort in that direction. I think such a move would eventually be viewed as a historical mission, a mission to civilize the continent of Africa. But, for the present, I beg of you, do *not* mention my name while you are about your task."

"As you wish," said Albert.

"On that understanding, you have my blessing. Now, may I pour you another cup of tea?"

Albert and his wife would travel directly to Africa. Franz would follow shortly, which would mean that they would be separated for the first time in several years. A sad instance in any family at any time, but for Franz it would amount to a minor frustration, insignificant compared to what he had been through already. His life could never be worse than it had been one day five years previous on a farm north of Durban, where a Zulu gang had beaten him ferociously, leaving him close to death while they raped and stabbed his mother, then slit his father's throat with his own straight razor, and made off with his family's cattle and possessions.

Albert adopted him and took him back to Germany where he recovered and went to school. The Shimmers hardly noticed that their adopted son bullied the lower form students mercilessly; when so informed, they defended his actions and counselled Franz, not on the value of mercy or forgiveness, as there was little of that to spare in their own makeup, but in the channelling of resentment. Therefore, it was not surprising that soon after that he enrolled in a course of engineering he gained a reputation as the youngest and most ruthless student ever.

Once in possession of a diploma, the Shimmers convinced him to come back to Africa to help them in Nairobi. That was where they were now headed.

"You said he was told to leave Africa because he was found guilty of mistreating them?" asked an incredulous Franz, as they walked away from Peters' hotel.

"Yes," said Mr. Shimmer. "He used to be known as a man with a strong whip hand."

"But how is it possible to mistreat niggers," asked Franz, "if all they ever understand is brute force?"

His adopted father looked at him and smiled, "Perhaps in his case, he may have been *too* strong." He looked into his son's eyes to see if he understood that.

"How so?"

"He was known out there as the '*Mikono wa Damu*,' the 'Man with Blood on his Hands.'"

Franz shrugged. More important to him was the twinge of a nerve as he touched a scar at the base of his neck, a scar that represented a grim souvenir from a place to which he had sworn he would never to go back, but to which he seemed now drawn by destiny.

Tanga, a port in German East Africa, 1897

Tuesday morning it was steamy and hot, not an unusual condition in Tanga where the only relief, slight at that, came when the sun sank below the horizon.

In a small building near the harbor, the district commissioner, Fritz Kohl, sat with Albert Shimmer. In front of them on the desk were several stacks of currency and gold rupees. They were finishing up their business as Shimmer signed a receipt. They stood up and shook hands. Shimmer then placed the money into a canvas valise.

Through the open window they could see the Indian Ocean.

Tanga lay on the coast seventy miles south of Mombasa. On the wall behind Kohl was a map of eastern Africa with Tanganyika colored dark gray. Uganda and southern Sudan were still British and therefore still pink on his map, but the pink was a dirty pink. It was shaded with gray to indicate German interest and influence. The only area that stood out pure and bright was Kenya, but even there he had already penciled in some gray shading along the coast.

Shimmer picked up a pair of binoculars from a table in front of the window and turned to focus on the face of one of the passengers who had just landed. A young man in whites was remarkable for what he lacked: he had no eyeglasses, no mustache nor any beard to speak of, and no hat.

"English," said Shimmer. "Recently posted. He's on his way to the High Commission in Mombasa."

Moments later Kohl walked out onto the dock while Shimmer watched from inside the office. Kohl was dressed as usual in his starched white commissioner's uniform, which seemed a size too big, an effect heightened by his habit of wearing an enormous sun helmet.

"Mr. McCann, I believe?" said Kohl.

"Yes, I'm David McCann. How did you know?"

"I was told by the consul's office to meet you. I'm one of the few here who speak English."

"And you are?"

"Fritz Kohl, at your service, sir," he said as he indicated a waiting rickshaw. "I thought you might like a lift to the guesthouse. I believe you're on your way to Kenya?"

"Yes."

"So, it's your first time here?"

"I've been to Cape Town previously," said McCann as he nervously watched a porter strap his suitcase to the back of the rickshaw. His unprotected brow had begun to sweat as he stepped carefully into the shaky vehicle, and was about to sit down, but hesitated; he had decided then to brush off the seat as the rickshaw started with a jerk and he fell against the commissioner. Eventually he found his seat and they trundled on.

"Is that the famous Tanga rail line?" asked McCann, recovering his poise as they passed the rail station adjacent to the wharf.

"More like 'infamous,'" said Kohl. "It's not even forty kilometers long and not very efficient. But this year we hope to begin extending it."

"To?"

"Moshi."

"Which is only ten miles from the Kenya border."

"Exactly. And once there, it will help my district greatly. We need transport to the coast in order to encourage the development of farm exports."

"Farm exports," said McCann, his mind grappling with what he was seeing. To the untrained eye it appeared to be a squad of African soldiers. They were standing at attention in the station yard, armed with repeating rifles and neatly dressed in the uniform of the German East Africa Army.

Though native troops were used routinely in India, Sudan and Egypt by the British Army, McCann knew from the political reports that the settlers in Kenya didn't trust Africans. The use of these local recruits interested him on two points—one, they were a cheap source of local military, and two, they seemed well trained and ready to fight.

7

Kikuyuland, Kenya, 1897

Roger had landed in Kenya two years earlier. Arriving in Mombasa, he had found a job on his second day ashore: a caravan company had literally snapped him up. Always on the lookout, the contractors sought out healthy males fresh off the boat and arranged for them to go out with experienced hands. He had impressed everyone as a quick learner, and on his first trip he taught himself a great deal about transporting provisions, caring for pack animals, selecting Swahili porters and fitting out for the long haul.

Once on the road he discovered for himself that the herds of game animals in Kenya were real and spectacular. Nothing could have prepared him for what he saw. "Overwhelming" and "teeming" could hardly describe the situation. An ocean of game spread out before him. It made man and his settlements appear as small dots, islands of little or no significance; the human paled in comparison to the wild habitat.

Learning each day from his mistakes, he made one firm promise to himself after that first trip: he would never work for a contractor again. From then on, he was his own man. This thought made him stop. He had been traveling through this countryside for several days with only brief glimpses of the slim black people who lived there. Leaving the plains below and then the forest of the uplands, they had trekked higher and higher, and each day brought a new view, new vegetation, each more exotic than the last. Today they passed through tall bamboo thickets, tomorrow would be the grass above, and what weather, thought Roger, almost saying it out loud, but the porter next to him understood only Swahili, the language of the coast, so he kept his thoughts to himself as he stopped and breathed deeply.

The clean cool air was a great relief from the humid atmosphere of Mombasa. The dry season had settled over the brown plains below, but here in the highlands, everywhere he looked he saw green and moist vegetation, almost as if they were walking through an English countryside.

Higher up on the rocky crest of the hill above the bamboo, he suspected it would be cold at night because of the altitude, but he had no other cause for complaint. His health was perfect and it was amazing the way each breath reached down deep into his lungs like an invigorating tonic, a new jolt of clean air with each step. The pure, cool air and the sun shining straight down close to the zenith made him giddy as he enjoyed this flawless African day; but he would not dare to remove his hat until they reached a shady resting spot. He thought this should be soon as it was almost time for their midday tea, and they had now entered the bamboo where he had expected to stop the caravan in the shade. To his surprise, once they entered the thicket there was little shade. The upper portions of the shoots were not thick enough for that, and now humid stagnant air closed over them, becoming warmer with each step.

The porters and the caravan guards, the *askaris*, were unusually quiet.

Too bloody hot, he thought. We can't go on roasting like this; we'll have to stop soon.

His temper began to rise as forward progress slowed. He had been in thickets before; getting through thorn bush was difficult enough, but hacking through this bamboo was more exhausting than he had ever imagined, and now they were deep into the area inhabited by Kikuyus, a tribe notorious for its treatment of strangers.

Few Europeans had ever lived in this region without coming under pressure to leave. The displeasure of the Kikuyus was always expressed in clear and certain terms; knowing this, caravans were reluctant to travel through here.

Kikuyus seldom showed themselves, and they never ran the risk of a fight in the open. They would wait in dense grass or behind some bush, watching for gaps in the line of porters or for stragglers. Then with only the slightest sound there would be the twang of a small bow or the hiss of a slim, sharp-pointed poisoned arrow, from which even a glancing cut was lethal. Roger had also heard that whenever a Swahili porter strayed from a caravan, he could expect a spear in the back. Neither did the Kikuyu take kindly to incursions by other tribes; they were constantly at war with the Masai. The uneasy feeling in his stomach had been growing every minute since they entered the thicket, and it was small recompense to know they might be more interested in his trade goods than in him.

But who knows, he thought, trying to put the best light on it, it may be possible to bargain with them.

There were other concerns that plagued his mind. During the dry season the bush country in the dry lowlands became hostile to all life. Men and wildlife naturally migrated to the uplands, attracted by the forest foliage, the grass sward and the cool, moist environment. The larger animals, elephants, rhinos and buffalos, had no choice—they had to migrate because of their considerable appetites for fresh vegetation each day. Thus, in the dry season, elephant herds meandered inside the forests on the hill ridges, which were also their breeding grounds. Towards the very end of the dry season they wandered even higher into the giant bamboo groves through which Roger's caravan was now moving; here they opened wide tracks and clearings as they went from one watering point to the next. Later in the year, as the rainy season took hold, they would reverse their tracks. Leaving the highlands, they would go back down to the plains where verdant pastures awaited.

This natural cycle of dry and wet governed all life in this part of the world, but nothing came between the elephant herd and their migration. While the animals were on the move, no caravan dared use the old elephant tracks, because the matriarchs, the ferocious old cows, would never retreat, and it would take more than a rifle to turn them inside a thicket. Roger knew their migration would not start for another month or two, so he had no worry in this regard. He was more concerned about the progress of the caravan.

Once he realized the tall poles offered little shade, he thought they should just push on and get through, but he soon found it was more complicated. Each bamboo shoot presented a barrier. Some could be pushed aside, but, unlike the brute force of an elephant herd, which could break off large poles with a crack echoing through the hills like a rifle shot, his donkey caravan would make slow headway against the poles, some of which were six inches in diameter. The bamboo swayed and creaked when pushed, but sprang back to its original position, so each animal had to work against each pole anew. Aside from the old woody shoots, new growth had sprung up since the last elephant passage; this at least could be cut with their sharp bush knives, *pangas*. They cut through the smaller stems with one stroke, but larger, thicker stems required more work. Looking back over the trail he could see many stumps left behind; dangerously sharp, they could impale or slit open a bare foot.

Danger seemed to be all around him as the relentless sun burned down into this noisy wallow of animals, porters and askaris. The fully loaded donkeys pushed forward with their gunny-wrapped side packs leaving no room on the sides of the trail. Everyone was sweating.

Roger's clothes clung to him like hot, wet blankets.

"Bloody hell!" he said to Musa, one of his Mkamba gun bearers, not that Musa understood, but it helped Roger to let off some steam. He was concerned about the second gun bearer, Mutua.

"*Kurudi pale*, go back down," he said. "Tell Mutua and the cook to catch up. We'll stop soon. Tell everyone to look for one of the old elephant watering holes."

To himself he noted it would be best to find some place quickly, even if they hadn't gotten as far today as he wanted. He was worried—Mutua might be in some sort of trouble and he couldn't afford losing him. Even if he were successful in getting the local tribes to give up staple food for trade goods, he would still need his porters to get the food back down to the trading posts and the small towns.

Places were springing up all over the plains below, as British and European immigrants settled in the Rift Valley. The presence of the British Army gave them the protection they needed against marauding natives, but everyone—settlers, military, colonial government, civil servants and missionaries—depended heavily on caravans from the Coast for their daily needs. Maize, wheat, rice, salt, tea and everything else had to be carried to them. Roger was hoping to find local food supplies, which would circumvent this long chain.

He had started this trip with his own pack animals and provisions. On reaching Naivasha, a small town that lay directly on the caravan route below in the Rift Valley, he had broached the idea of going north into Kikuyuland but had been refused permission.

"For your own protection," said the district commissioner, Mr. Cole.

So, Roger, being Roger, had made a long detour east as if going back to Nairobi, and then, surreptitiously, started up into the hills.

The sweat continued to roll down his face as he swore and slashed at the bamboo in front of him. The panga had to be handled with a firm arm and concentration, else it would glance off the shiny outer surface of the stems. Even then, the sharp vibration in the knife handle was satisfying; at least, he thought, we're making some progress.

"Now what!"

Musa had dropped behind to find Mutua and the cook, leaving Roger at the head of the column with the porters and the donkeys spread out behind him. The noise coming from the rear of the column sounded like an attack.

"*Hi. Hi. Hi. Haya!*"

There were sharp cries and a loud crashing in the bush.

They've scared up a buffalo, he thought. Probably a solitary male left behind by the herd.

"Now we're in for it," he muttered, as he moved quickly toward the first pack donkey where he kept two of his rifles, the Henry repeating carbine and his Webley large bore, both recently purchased from white hunters retiring in Mombasa.

He pulled the heavy double-barreled rifle out of its old leather scabbard and opened the breech. "*Ngoja hapa*, stay here," he said to Mareta, the tracker closest to him. "*Angalia kitu yote*, watch everything."

He was already reaching for two of the formidable cartridges in the pocket of his safari jacket as he stumbled down the trail through the trampled and sharp-edged cut bamboo, sweat building all over his body.

Squeezing past the pack animals, rifle held with one hand, its breach open, he had no time to stop and think.

"*Haya. Haya. Pale.* Over here!"

It sounded like Ali, the cook, on the right.

Straight down along a small path off the main trail, he heard running feet. He stumbled along as best he could while jamming the two cartridges into the chambers and racking the breach closed. He clicked the safety button on the stock to the off position.

Ali must be close by, he thought. He could see a small clearing ahead; then Mutua dashed by from right to left followed by an enormous gray-black Cape buffalo.

It moved crashing into the bamboo downhill to his left, foam and saliva streaming from its nostrils and hairy mouth edge.

He ran after them, following toward the clearing, but he slowed the minute he heard Ali and Musa yelling from inside the bamboo. He would never have a clear shot inside the thicket, but, as both he and Ali knew, anyone could hide there forever because the animal would not be able to maneuver fast enough to catch any one person, and there was no wind to carry their scent to the animal.

He stepped into the clearing and thought, best to wait until it tires and gives up. No sense in bashing about.

"*Bwana. Bwana. Pale*, over there. *Nyati*!" He heard Ali yelling from inside the thicket, at almost exactly the same moment Mutua suddenly came out of the bamboo running back across the clearing.

"Over here, you idiots. *Hapa. Hapa*," Roger yelled, and within a minute both Musa and Ali piled into the bush on top of him. Mutua, who was a hunter in his own right, continued unhearing across to the other side of the clearing and back into the bush.

In a frantic whisper Roger urged Musa and Ali to go back

up the trail. He could still hear the buffalo crashing about below them. Mutua was somewhere out there.

"Lying doggo, I hope," he whispered to himself.

Mutua, however, was working his way back through the bamboo toward the trail, listening for the buffalo, moving only when the animal did. The breeze coming uphill saved him. It was in his direction so the animal had nothing to go on, but that could change. Any air movement, however slight, could go any which way. He sensed he was going further away from the animal with each step and so turned back looking for the fastest way to the side of Bwana Roger. He did this unthinkingly, the way an impala searches out a grazing zebra, knowing the zebra with its large ears would always hear a lion. When grazing with its ears laid back, it was an indicator of the "all clear."

Mutua thought of Bwana Roger the same way, more as a sign of safe passage than anything else. He had little trust in any *mzungu* as a protector, even though he had followed him on two safaris. He had heard too many stories at night around the caravan fires about men like himself impaled by the very same Kikuyu spears that the white men always seemed to escape.

He had faith in nothing but God, his Wakamba brother, Mareta, who was now minding the pack animals on the trail above, and his own nimble wits.

He could hear Roger calling softly, so he answered back.

"Bwana, *yuko pale*, he's over there."

Roger sighed in relief. "He's safe."

The two of them now started back up the trail to join the others, both grateful at having avoided a confrontation with an angry buffalo. Roger had by now some experience killing game while on safari. Killing elephants and buffalo in open country was in many respects easy for him, but one had to think twice before shooting at large animals inside this wild growth. If he killed it outright, well and good, but if he only wounded it the animal would be a problem, because Roger could not stay behind. He would have to abandon an enraged and dangerous beast. Cape buffalos with their strong, sharp horns and fast reactions were more feared than any other animal, including the lion. He did not want to be remembered by local people for creating a menace, but, on the other hand, as a white foreigner, he was at the mercy of the country.

And, there were the Kikuyus....

They caught up with Mareta and the donkeys and, though Roger was tired and wet through with sweat, he again urged everyone on. They set off trudging along the track, now more nervous and closer together.

"Stop. Wait!" Roger said.

He could hear something on the trail downhill behind them.

"Oh, God. He's coming up the trail after us!" He turned to shout, but the Swahilis, Wakamba and the donkeys needed no further instruction, just the tone in his voice was enough. They scattered in every direction, forcing their way into the thicket on all sides. He was left standing there, thinking and trying to concentrate on how to position himself for the best shot. Holding his rifle at the ready in front of him, he slowly retreated, backing into a new growth of bamboo at the head of the trail.

He had not been paying much attention to his surroundings, and who could blame him, with this animal close at hand. Not watching too carefully as he pushed backward further into the bamboo, but in haste, glancing nervously over his shoulder, he saw the open sky. Then he heard a strange humming noise rising above the sounds of the bush and the buffalo moving along the rough trail.

Obviously the animal had been sidetracked by something, probably by one of his valuable pack animals. Without thinking he stepped backward again, but this time the bamboo gave way so quickly he could not stop his fall from the edge of a small rise, and felt himself falling out of the thicket into a clearing.

"What the hell. Uh-oh!"

Now he was on his back. His hat had fallen off and his loaded rifle had fallen by his side. He raised his bare white head and lifted an elbow and saw against the strong sunlight what looked like thousands of black people.

The humming noise had stopped, replaced by dead quiet as the white-rimmed, hard black eyes of five hundred Kikuyu warriors focused on him to a man.

8

Kikuyuland

Roger looked around. A lone white man, he appeared to have dropped from the sky.

No one moved.

Roger took this as a sign that they were as amazed as he was.

As nonchalantly as possible, he raised himself to full height; holding onto his rifle, he brushed off his trousers, disregarding the fact that they were caked with a week's worth of grime, sweat and dirt; he strolled over to retrieve his hat. In his mind was the question, Where is Mutua and bloody company?

At this point he could do nothing but bluff. He turned and walked directly back toward the assembled crowd grabbing and holding up a handful of grass, which he understood was a sign of peace. He guessed many had never seen a white man before and curiosity might be an advantage. He decided to be as normal as possible.

"*Hamjambo*! Greetings everyone!" he said.

All quiet still.

"*Habari gani*? How are you?" he said, his voice rising, assuming someone could speak Swahili. He continued in a loud voice, "*Jina langu ni* Roger," but was interrupted by a young man with an especially ornate monkey skin headdress. He held up one hand and walked toward him. "My name is Roger."

The young man also held up one hand and said, "Greetings to you, Mr. Roger."

It was not difficult to imagine Roger's surprise when he heard this from the mouth of what he presumed was a savage, bent only on murder and pillage.

"Greetings, I say again, I am Kimani. I am chief here. What do you want?"

Roger's mouth hung open.

"You seem surprised that I speak your language."

"But...how...where did you learn it?" He looked at him, helpless to divine where this Kimani had come from.

Had he also dropped from the sky?

"I have been to the Mission School. But I want to know what you are doing here?"

At which moment, Mutua, the ten donkeys, the Swahilis and Mareta appeared. A quick glance told him that none of the porters had gone missing. As Mutua explained to Roger later, they had all watched from the thicket. When they saw Bwana Roger on speaking terms with the headman, they decided to throw in their lot with him rather than risk a trip back through Kikuyuland.

"Who are these?"

"They are my helpers," said Roger. "They have come in peace like myself. We are here to trade and buy what we can."

With the arrival of Mutua and the remaining porters, Roger felt a bit more confident. But their arrival also seemed to be a signal for the other five hundred Kikuyus to come over to see what was happening.

As long as the conversation was between a chief and one white man, there was no movement, but now it was different. "I can prove I come in peace," said Roger as the crowd approached. "As you can see I have left all my guns and the remainder of my army in the thicket to avoid trouble. But if there is trouble, my army and those from Naivasha will come here to destroy many Kikuyu."

"I believe you," said Kimani, smiling at this *mzungu*, this brazen white man. "At least I believe what you say about trade. But you have come at the wrong time."

"Wrong time?" Roger was puzzled.

"This is the wrong season for ivory."

"I'm not here for ivory. I want to trade for food, food to take back to Naivasha, and I'm willing to pay well for this."

"Food?" said Kimani, wondering if he understood correctly. "What do you mean, *chakula*? Food to eat?"

"Yes, any food that I can carry. I will pay for quantities of peas and beans or any grain."

"We are not used to this," he looked into Roger's eyes. "We do our trading in Ngongo Bargas and Fort Smith, and also now some in Nairobi. Why do you want to trade here?" He spread his arms and hands out to indicate the village and *shambas* that could be seen all around them on the hillside.

Roger looked uneasily around. It was indeed a strange landscape compared to the Coast and the plains. He also noticed his porters were trying to guard and protect the donkey loads; some of the warriors were already poking and prying into the cases. This added more reason to come to terms.

"We've already seen the trading in Ngongo Bargas," he said. "But that's nothing, a small business. I want to build some centers here and trade for many more things. I want to deal with the chiefs. There's much to be gained by working with me. Will you let us stay here to talk some more about this?"

Kimani did not have to think long. He could already see in this man a solution to his problems of late. Many of his people no longer liked to go down to Ngongo Bargas. It had always been difficult to travel there, but now it was more so. It was true that the Masai were at peace in these trading centers, but anyone going or coming from there could be attacked at any time. It was dangerous to travel about, and now the Kikuyu clans were becoming more aggressive among themselves, demanding tribute from one another when any of their own trading parties crossed the others' territory.

Better to deal with this man and let him run the risk between the stations, he thought. In his mind also was the idea that somehow he could use this mzungu to forestall the day when the Kikuyu would have to deal with the Iron Snake.

"Yes, you can stay with us, and we will see how well you do." He had no real fear of this small party; they could be turned out with little or no effort. Look at the way their eyes show concern for their safety when the warriors move near them, he thought, as he held up his hand and said something to the crowd. Then he turned back to Roger.

"Come with me. I'll show you where you can stay. There is one man here of my age, Muthuri. He also went to Mission School and speaks English and Swahili."

It was as simple as that.

Kimani said something to an elder who turned and spoke further to the crowd.

They began to disperse, and their place along the route was taken by village children and women who wanted to know what was happening. Kimani led the party back down toward some thatched huts on one side of the village.

Roger stole a glance at Mutua, who smiled and shook his head; he was thinking, that Bwana Roger, he is like a baboon; there is no keeping him from the honey pot.

In Muthuri's Hut

You will find a different world here and a hard life from which you may draw some ideas, but I'm afraid that's all you will find. After all, you are not an African. But I think if you will sit here with me and listen, and watch, you will see what I mean.

But, if you do sit, don't fidget; there's nothing to be afraid of here.

What did you say your name was?

Roger.

Good, I am Muthuri, the village storyteller. Here, take some food. Yes, I know, it does not look like your food, but remember, the smell and the taste are more important than appearances. Kimani's father used to say that God gave you those facilities in order to use them, so do not turn away. You will never understand unless you face these things, and without understanding there is no basis for feeling. It is what you wazungu call sympathy.

I can tell from your face you think it is disgusting, and I understand that, because Kimani and I used to eat wazungu food at the Mission. He liked it, but I thought it was pretty weak stuff. How can anyone develop into a strong person if they eat that all their life?

Now see this food? The thing you have in your hand? It is not, properly speaking, a "sausage," even I know that. I know what your sausages look like, and I know why you make that face. But remember, this is a special dish, a treat; it is the intestine of a sheep stuffed with congealed blood and chopped meat.

Don't worry, it is safe to eat. It has been roasted. Nyama choma, as they say, roast meat.

In that gourd you'll find pombe, the beer made of fermented millet. It flows slowly into your open mouth like weak porridge. Sour and strong, it smells like some ancient form of life.

"It must be an acquired taste," you say. Ha, that is funny, because in this place, it is not a question of "acquiring," nor is it a matter of "taste." It is a question of life.

You eat and drink to survive. As in the plains, the weak or young animal that falls behind is eaten alive by the pack of wild dogs that follows every herd.

So, eat well my friend and keep running. Never look back to see if the dogs are behind you. They will always be there. They never sleep.

9

Machakos, Kenya, 1897

The Honorable Geoffrey Brian Scofield Stanford, "Brian" to his friends, eldest son of the Fourth Baron of Manchester, had never given the impression that he was a "nester." Tall and thin, with a receding hairline from age twelve, with unlimited funds at twenty-one, he threw himself at life and in the process broke his left leg in three different places on three separate occasions. A wild horseman, hunter and master of Manchester whoredom, he knew he was destined to settle in Africa. No other place would accommodate such an obstreperous, rowdy person. And how often when growing up had he heard his father's decision, "Send him to Africa." His wild, spendthrift friends stood by helplessly as they watched his obsession with that place take root and grow. They knew he read the same papers as George McConnell and Stephen Hale and loved to play the role of the adventurer-explorer-hero, but his tribal fiefdom, Manchester and environs, was too circumscribed, and he sensed from the beginning that the exotic setting of the Saharan desert and the misty green jungle kingdoms of the Old World tropics were the ideal testing grounds for him. He was right.

Others came to Africa as a last resort, but with Brian there was no choice; like his idol, Cecil Rhodes, it was his destiny. His first attempt to gain a foothold on the continent provoked anger and disbelief. Perhaps it was the nature of this man, no longer a young whippersnapper; he had grown old in his early middle age but he still had the ability to outrage. He had offered to buy from the Sultan of Zanzibar a sixty-six year lease on a tract that he had the gall to qualify as "only that land from the Coast to the inland lakes," neglecting to mention that he was referring to an area in excess of two hundred thousand square miles. Refused in this, on his thirty-first birthday he decided to leave England to fulfill at least one burning desire, to lead a camel-mounted hunting expedition into Africa from the north, a decision that coincided with the plans made that same year by Queen Victoria and her government and subjects to celebrate her Diamond Jubilee in 1897.

The adventure got off to a slow start, beginning as it did in the Red Sea port of Berberra, a quiet, stiflingly hot town on the Somali coast, the sort of outpost where little happened save the arrival and departure of coastal steamers. While waiting for the supplies needed by his expedition to be assembled, Stanford won a land deed in a game of American poker. Offered in lieu of £175 as security against an inside straight, Brian knew from the moment the ship's captain put it on the table it was his. A deed signed "x" by a Meru chief and witnessed by a white father, it entitled him to the right, in perpetuity, to farm 100,000 acres on the slopes of Ol Donyo Sabuk, a small mountain northeast of Nairobi.

On a whim, he re-routed his expedition to follow a track across Ethiopia to Wajir in Kenya; from there he continued south until he arrived one day on the verandah of a missionary in Machakos.

Mr. Harris, an Anglo-Indian civil servant, at that time acting for the district commissioner, remembered the day well because the missionary's houseboy had come to him in a fright.

"A vagabond, sir, possibly a thief, wrapped in a bundle of rags, has arrived at my master's door. He says come quick!"

Mr. Harris, accompanied by two Indian sepoys from the Machakos fort, went with the boy to the house where, on all sides, stretching down the slope and behind, into the alleyways and yards, rested a caravan of 250 camels loaded with provisions, rifles, tents and trading goods. Under the supervision of an army of Somali guards and a host of Abyssinian camp followers with their livestock, it was one of the largest caravans ever seen in Machakos.

They found Brian sitting on the verandah pouring himself a cup of tea. Mr. Harris stepped forward from the crowd that had gathered and in a loud voice asked, "What is your business here, sir?"

"Need I have business?" asked Brian as he helped himself to another piece of pound cake. The missionary hovered helplessly nearby. "May I not pay a social call without bringing suspicion on all and sundry?"

Since he said that in impeccable English, Mr. Harris threw up his hands and shrugged at the involuntary host, a small bearded priest from Surrey. "I'm sorry, Father. But he does appear to be one of yours," the implication being that under the universal "rule of reciprocity," one Englishman had to provide for another in the wild. His cook and houseboy, now apprised of the situation, appeared with biscuits to supplement the cake. Beyond that their master made no further move to welcome the stranger, possibly because he was put off by his appearance. Brian's leather shooting jacket, badly torn and crudely patched, hung in shreds across his unwashed, suntanned shoulders. His hands, covered in filthy bandages, were so bruised, blistered and scratched they could hardly hold the teacup. His encounters with angry animals and fierce plants had left him in a terrible state. Unshaven and smelling strongly of camel dung he turned to his host and asked, "Father Glascock?"

"Yes," said the priest, bowled over by the idea that anyone outside his immediate order would know him by name, or would even know that he was posted to this remote corner of the world. Brian removed a tattered leather wallet from an inside pocket and placed it on the table by the teapot.

"And this is your signature?" he asked, as he unfolded a grimy piece of paper from inside the wallet.

"Yes," said the priest after examining the land deed.

"Thank you very much for the tea and cake," said Brian. He stood and made his way back to his camel train. "Come and visit sometime, Father."

"But…," stammered the priest, "who are you?"

"Your new neighbor. I understand Ol Donyo Sabuk is only about thirty miles from here."

The enormous caravan suddenly came to life as it wheeled about and with a great amount of jostling and groaning from the camels, and jingling and jangling of the camp followers with their multitude of pots and pans, followed their leader out of Machakos to his new home.

He also bought a plot in Nairobi and built a house for his wife, Lady Stanford, who could not suffer the young Somali girls who ran Brian's household and provided for his needs. Brian used to say to all his settler friends, "It just happens, there is life beyond Manchester."

In Muthuri's Hut

Roger said to himself, I'm lucky to be alive, as he lay back on a pallet of skins on the floor in Kimani's village and drifted off to sleep. Yes, this is just right, I've always been lucky, and this is the way it is, here and now, he thought. This is all I'll ever need....

...He felt the early afternoon sun through his thin shirt as the sounds of the steamer traffic at Victoria Dock in Hull faded behind them. The cacophony on the wharf was replaced by the pleasant sound of water rippling against the wooden hull and the creaking of the rigging as the mainsail of the small cutter caught the wind and moved them away from shore.

Every time they sailed out like this, the boat would heel over the minute they left the shelter of the docks, almost to the moment when thoughts of work and everyday care slid from his shoulders and the sea air rushed to his head, clearing his brain. Now they were in a world unto themselves. With the tide going out and a mild offshore wind following, they would quickly pass Marfleet and continue running down the open estuary. Later, tacking across and back up along the western shore, with the ebbing tide and a change in the wind to help them, they would be back in the harbor in time for an early evening meal at their favorite quayside restaurant.

"That's all I ever need, you know," he said, looking into his mother's face, "just the two of us and a nice quiet day on the river." Yet he knew in his heart that his nemesis could not be far away.

"A nice outing, dear," Susan agreed with her son as she trailed her hand in the cool water that bubbled and gurgled past the transom on the lee side. A bottle of cider lay cooling in the straw hamper in the

shade of the small shelter, the cuddy, just aft of the mast. The mainsail was taut and full with the steady breeze. Roger set the sheet and lashed the tiller as he always did, leaving him free to move around.

"Thank you, Roger," she said as he poured a mug for her. She sat shaded by her parasol, her day dress tucked under her. That was her spot, the place where he had rigged a baffle to shelter her from any strong breeze and a light rug to provide a snug, cozy seat. Her blonde hair was held in place by a comb.

"Greetings," said Stephen, as he emerged from the cuddy.

How the hell does he fit himself in there? Roger pondered. He'd have to bend into an "S" to do that. Bloody fool, sticking his nose in where he's not wanted.

"Oh, so you're still here," he said, knowing that Stephen would completely ignore him. "Who invited you to join us?"

"Susan, beautiful and illusive," said Stephen as he kissed her full on the mouth and slipped down beside her on the deck. She smiled in return as he plucked out the comb. Her hair streamed down over her shoulders as they embraced, ignoring Roger who, helpless, bottled up his anger and resentment. He went about the deck tidying up the lines, checking the rigging, embarrassed to see his carefree day dissolve into silent rage. He knew what they were up to without even looking. He could hear their sighs and kisses, and imagined them running their hands over one another. Finally, he could no longer contain himself. Under the hamper among the life jackets he kept a signal flare pistol, loaded and in perfect working condition.

"You never bloody well know when you're going to need it," he murmured, as he reached in and grabbed it. He turned, and in a few quick strides he was standing over them.

"Get off her, you bastard!" he yelled. He saw his mother's eyes widen, her eyelids no longer flickering languorously under the effect of the sea, the sun and Stephen.

She stared at him, horror-struck.

"Get off her, I say, or I'll break every bone in your body!"

"Wait, this is wrong. You don't…understand…," Stephen stammered, as he rose facing him on the deck. "You have absolutely the wrong impression…."

He never finished the sentence. The flare blasted out of the pistol and lodged in his abdomen as he careened smoking, burning and staggering along the deck clutching at the boom, which was always too far away. He fell over the side, the magnesium in the flare still on fire, continuing to burn in his body, lighting up the blue-green sea around him as he floundered and flailed in the water. His face contorted in pain, he disappeared into the wake astern.

"My God!" Susan screamed as she fell to the deck in a burst of tears....

...Roger woke from his dream.

It was pitch dark in the hut and for a moment he did not know where he was, until he heard Muthuri growl in his sleep. Though still a young man, Muthuri sounded like some grizzled old animal when he slept.

Roger stood and made his way in the dark to the door of the hut, where he quietly lifted the small beam that barred the door and stepped out into the moonlight. There he found himself standing on the edge of a misty ridge looking down at hundreds of huts below. Other than the soft chirping of the insects and frogs in the nearby forest, not a sound came back to him.

Here he was, he thought, staring into the middle of Africa, a place he had sought out to satisfy his deep craving for adventure and simplicity, and now, without realizing it, this same place had already begun exerting a special charm over him, a feeling he would never understand, now or years hence.

Another growl came from inside the hut, so he closed and barred the door and went back to bed.

10

Mombasa, Kenya, 1898

Bwana. Bwana. Wake up. It is time for breakfast."

Roger woke with a start. He sat bolt upright, staring straight ahead, chest heaving, sweat streaming down his unshaven face and neck. It had been months since he had left Kikuyuland.

Today he was back on the Coast, but still the dream persisted until he shook himself awake. Only three years had passed since he had left England to come to Africa, yet he knew he looked as if he had aged ten years. He threw aside the damp sheet from the cot, rose to his full height, stretched, and lurched from the dark stuffy closeness of his tent out into the sunlight of a bright tropical morning. He turned to one side, unbuttoned his fly and urinated against a palm tree. Looking back over his shoulder he could see Mombasa Harbor and a lone steamer maneuvering in the calm waters below.

Dorothy Hale and her stepsister, Alice McConnell, stood under the shade of the boat's awning with their fellow passengers, the remains of their breakfast behind them on cloth-covered folding tables. They had been all morning getting to their present anchorage. From here they could see the green foliage of the coconut palms and the stark white of the seafront buildings with their scalloped facades. The only outstanding feature of the harbor was the large ancient fortress at the entrance, the infamous and forbidding Fort Jesus. The town itself appeared to be a nondescript collection of white stucco buildings and coconut palms ascending several small hills, each with its peaked-domed white mosque and pencil-like minaret.

It was Sunday and in the distance they heard a lone church bell ringing. The clear tones carried across the still water as under the awning they could see and feel a slight breeze wafting over the bay. It stirred the calm water, whipping the glassy surface into ripples and for the first time in several days brought them the smell of land.

Hatches were being opened and from the deck below came the odor of cargo that had been sitting in the hold baking under a tropical sun. The crew from a lighter swarmed over the gunwales like a gang of pirates and set to work hauling out a hodge-podge of provisions—potatoes, coal, cooking oil, tarpaulins, caulking, sacks of beans, flour—literally everything on which the life of a white man depended. This would provide the basic stuff for numerous caravans that would make their way across many miles of Africa.

The two women watched from above in apprehension as the coolies on the lower deck dodged the occasional rat and the swarms of cockroaches that scurried out of the baskets and the wrappings.

"I see him," said Alice. "There, over there on the left." Her brown eyes brightened as she waved her hat. "Stephen. Over here."

"For God's sake, Alice put your hat back on!" said Dorothy as she waved away the flies now buzzing around them, and pulled down the mosquito veil on her sun helmet. With landfall in the tropics came a wealth of problems including flies and mosquitoes. "And give Mr. Shimmer back his binoculars."

"Thank you, Franz," said Alice to a slim young man in whites who stood with them.

"A pleasure," he said as he focused his binoculars on one face in the crowd on the wharf: the tallest of the Europeans, in summer whites and sun helmet, with a sandy-colored mustache. He stood head and shoulders above the rest.

"Is that your husband, Mrs. Hale?" he asked.

"I would assume," she said, but refused his offer of the binoculars. "What is that stench?" she asked.

"I believe it's the harbor, ma'am," said the first mate, who stood by with two Goan deckhands to open a gate in the railing. He smiled as he said, "You'd never need a lighthouse to find Mombasa Port on a dark night."

The Goans opened the gate and lowered a rope ladder equipped with wooden steps. Several lighters waited below to carry passengers to shore. In the process one brown foot inadvertently brushed Franz's white dress shoe.

"Back off, you filthy little idiot!" he said.

The Goan cringed. An Indian of Portuguese descent, his whole being, his fate rested in the hands of the first mate. The mate touched his cap and said to Franz, "Sorry, sir. Won't happen again," then he glared at the deckhand.

On shore Stephen could clearly see them leaving the ship. He watched as railway and military officers, settler families and well-to-do Asian businessmen clambered down the ladder. They were followed by a young woman who stepped quickly down the wooden rungs and jumped off the last step, landing in the arms of the smiling first mate. Must be Alice, he thought, as he watched her join the ship-weary group of passengers already in the lighter. Even at that distance he could see that she wore a floppy hat with no veil and what seemed to be the latest in safari outfits, a divided skirt of light cotton with dark breeches, a leather belt with pouches and half-boots with flat heels.

In contrast, Dorothy now stepped carefully onto the ladder in a full skirt. The captain himself was there to hand her down. The passengers in the lighter looked up apprehensively to see her struggling with each step. Stephen noted that her full petticoats and high-heeled boots made progress slow. Even as the first mate and several deckhands guided her, she descended with some difficulty into the lighter.

Roger, now dressed and sitting on his horse, stood far up on the hill watching this scene through field glasses.

He focused on Dorothy's sun helmet, called a *topi* by the natives. Hers was equipped with a substantial veil that she had tied securely around her throat with a pink ribbon. He shook his head at the thought of how practical that would be in this country, then he trained his glasses on the remaining passengers waiting on deck and picked out Franz Shimmer. He watched him as he stepped back from the sun and stood in the shade under the awning. In contrast to the others he was dressed in whites. No stranger to the tropics, thought Roger, as he shifted his gaze to the pile of matched luggage that rested behind him and saw a rifle case sitting on top of the heap.

The lighter cast off and the crew rowed toward shore. A second boat moved in to start loading the remaining passengers and Roger shifted his glasses to the wharf where he focused on Stephen Hale, who had moved forward ready to receive his new wife. As he watched that face that had appeared so often in his dreams, he found it hard to let go. But, he told himself, as he turned his horse's head and trotted down the road toward the train station, I've got work to do.

Stephen helped his wife out of the lighter while the others held back, almost as if they wanted no responsibility if she tripped. She stepped carefully onto the wharf and he swept her into his arms and kissed her.

"Dorothy, darling Dorothy," he said. Her sun helmet stayed firmly in place while his toppled to the ground. He kissed her again through her veil as everyone stared. A man kissing his wife in public was a strange and curious thing in Mombasa, still a very conservative outpost of the Empire, and predominantly Muslim. The entire population of the island consisted of about six thousand Indians, Goans, and Baluchis, six hundred Arabs, fifteen hundred Swahilis, two thousand freed slaves and one hundred and fifty prisoners in the jail at Fort Jesus. And despite all the business created by the railway activity, only about one hundred Europeans were in residence.

Conscious now of the stares, and possibly in spite of them, Stephen turned from his wife to his wife's stepsister and gave her a peck on the cheek.

"Alice," he said, "lovely as ever."

He escorted them away from the landing area as he explained, "I have a carriage waiting. The commissioner, Ian Burns, and his wife send their regards. They left yesterday on leave so there's no reason to stay in town. We'll start today and have a picnic luncheon on the train to Voi."

"Voi?" asked Dorothy.

"That's the last stop on the railway. We go by caravan from there to Machakos."

"Oh, look," said Alice, "there he is again." Stephen's eyes followed those of Alice and Dorothy as they stared at Franz Shimmer, who had just stepped out of the second lighter and was greeted by a tall middle-aged woman.

"It's Mr. Shimmer," said Dorothy, as the young man saw them, lifted a very stylish sun helmet and nodded to them in greeting.

"And that must be his mother," said Alice, with a glance indicating the woman at his side.

"Mbiti, Kiamba," Stephen called to his two African servants. "*Saidia*. Help us!"

They stepped into an open carriage while their luggage was loaded onto a flatbed wagon, and the two vehicles started off. They were followed by a crowd of aggressive beggars and street children that ran after them with hands outstretched for money until the first corner. Then the drivers whipped up the horses and outdistanced the crowd. Dorothy settled back and with a guarded glance looked around at her new surroundings. She was obviously pleased to be with her husband and seemed to enjoy the role she was now playing as a wife of a government official, but she was appalled by the smell, the unwashed rabble and the cloying humidity.

She pulled a handkerchief from her purse, sprinkled it with cologne and held it to her nose. Alice peered out at the crowd ready to take it all in.

"Thank God that's over," said Dorothy. "My poor Stephen, what a trial!"

"It's not all that bad, darling. In fact you'll enjoy it," he said, looking at her with an anxious look. "You only see that sort of crush when you have to meet someone at the dock, which only happens occasionally." She drew closer to him, intent on putting the disturbing image of the harbor scene out of her mind. Suddenly, as they drove along the main thoroughfare, she saw a Swahili porter being dragged through the streets in chains.

"Disgusting!" she said as she drew back from the scene. "Is he a convict?"

"Deserted a caravan most likely," said Stephen. "They're very strict here with anyone working as a porter."

"Not much different from slavery, is it?" asked Alice.

"There isn't any choice, you see. The best jobs are with the Railway and the Indians have been brought in to do that. So the Africans fish or work on the docks, both dangerous occupations with little pay, or they go to work as porters hoping to make their fortune."

The guards prodded the African as he stumbled along. At one point he glanced up at the carriage with angry eyes.

"Dreadful!"

"They're used as human machines to carry goods for hundreds of miles," said Stephen.

"And their salary?" asked Alice.

"Ten pounds sterling if they make it back here to Mombasa alive. If they get diseased or injured along the way, no one cares."

"And what's being done about it?"

"Nothing, as far as I know. I'm hoping the Railroad will make short work of this sort of thing."

They rode on in silence.

11

When they reached the train station they found it crowded with people, railway equipment and supplies. Work had already started on what would be a six hundred mile railroad from Mombasa to the interior. Hundreds of Indian workers were stacking, loading and unloading rails, lumber, firewood and metal crossties. Large piles of crushed gravel, coal, water barrels, rolls of copper telegraph wire and hand tools lay everywhere.

"Good morning, Roger. Everything in order I see," said Stephen as he looked at their neat pile of luggage in the midst of chaos. "Meet my wife, Dorothy, and sister-in-law, Alice."

He turned to his wife. "This is Roger Newcome, an old friend. He'll be in charge of the safari caravan when we reach the end of the rail line."

Roger touched his well-worn hat but left it in place as he nodded at Dorothy. His young face was friendly but weather-beaten. Stephen then turned and indicated another young man, clean-shaven and in whites, with well-groomed light brown hair that stayed perfectly in place as he doffed his sun helmet and smiled at her.

"And this is David McCann from Ian's office, who insists on escorting us to Voi. God only knows why. I'd think you'd have enough work to keep you busy elsewhere."

"A pleasure to meet you, ma'am," said David as he gently shook Dorothy's hand. "Your husband underestimates the importance of his post. But now you're all here, I'll tell the stationmaster to proceed. We've been holding the train for you." With that the local passengers scrambled onto the flatbed cars and Stephen, Dorothy and Alice stepped up into their carriage. Roger and David were left to take charge of the baggage.

"Oh, Mr. Newcome, those packages," said Alice as she turned and pointed to several leather cases, "those are my shotguns. I'll carry them inside."

"Anything you say, miss," said Roger as he and David exchanged glances. They were impressed. Young, single white women were a rarity in Kenya, let alone one who could shoot.

"Darling, who was that young man on the wharf?" asked Stephen as they sat inside the coach.

"Oh, him? Franz Shimmer. We met him on board. His parents moved to Nairobi last year. He said they know all about you."

"Shimmer? He's South African?"

"No, they're German," said Alice.

As they looked around inside the compartment, they saw only one other passenger, a sturdy-looking fellow lying on one of the open benches at the other end of the car sleeping with a blanket covering his face, his baggage on the rack above; his clothes showed him to be no stranger to the African bush.

"What an awful-looking man," whispered Dorothy, "and the other as well."

"You mean Roger?" asked Stephen, who also lowered his voice.

"He really does stand out doesn't he," said Alice, in her normal voice. She saw no reason to whisper, "even in this unholy crowd. And his accent, isn't it unusual?"

"He's American. I met him and his mother in Hull years ago. They're originally from Virginia. She remarried into a Yorkshire family." He seemed embarrassed at the direction the conversation was headed and after a pause, added, "I promised to look after him."

Then he pointed out the window and said, "The Railway has now reached Mile 100, just beyond the Voi station. If there are no stops, it should take us a little over four hours."

It was a workday and locomotives were being switched and shunted on and off the main line. The train driver already had steam up; he let out the brake, pushed in the throttle and they began a slow forward-chugging movement. Gathering speed, they passed rapidly through a tropical landscape with palm trees in abundance, interspersed with millions of pieces of paraphernalia, supplies and equipment. Crossing Macupa Creek, a breath of fresh sea air from the creek below rushed through the compartment, and for a moment it seemed they were flying through the air.

"Enchanting," said Stephen as he smiled at Dorothy, who had taken off her topi crossing the bridge. Her hair was blowing in the breeze.

Roger and David sat on either side of Alice on the seat facing Dorothy and Stephen, a fold-down table between them.

"We seem to be steaming right along," said Stephen.

"Oh, I forgot to tell you," said David, "they finally got the new F Class engines. They're built in Britain, much stronger than their counterparts in India. Now, what about some lunch?" He lifted a large hamper onto the table. "We have cold sandwiches and drinks courtesy of Railway headquarters."

He passed bottles of water to the two women. Roger elected to have a beer.

"Same for you, Stephen?" asked David, who fancied a beer himself.

"Water, please," said Stephen with a reproachful glance at Roger.

The train was chugging through the *bundu*, a forbidding landscape, dominated by thorn scrub with an occasional baobab tree sticking up above the plain. Bizarre-looking, their large, bloated trunks were topped by a maze of branches that seemed to be growing out in a tuft, resembling an expanse of bare roots reaching in confusion for the sky.

"My porters call them 'the tree God planted upside down,'" said Roger, turning to Alice. Stephen, in a more authoritative voice, said, "It's fascinating to think that all of this land now belongs to the Railway. Am I correct, David?"

"Yes, one mile on either side of the railroad or survey line. When you see it laid out on a map, it stretches across the country like a long white snake. The total area along the right-of-way encloses over seven hundred thousand acres. And now we have a real land rush on our hands. White settlers are vying for plots even in this region, though as you see, it's difficult soil for farming. They still want the land."

"And they'll never give it up," said Roger.

Everyone stared at him.

"Eventually they find there's no rain for months on end, and the streams are too brackish for drinking; then the ultimate insult, the heavens open up and it rains like you've never seen before, making them wish they'd never asked for water in the first place!"

Suddenly with a loud *thud*, a spearhead penetrated the wooden side panel, the sharp, gleaming point just inches from Dorothy's pale arm. She screamed and cringed in her husband's arms. Roger jumped up, pulled a carbine from his baggage and stood ready while McCann lunged toward the open window. Stephen drew his Webley service revolver from his large briefcase and wrapped one arm around his wife, as he watched Roger rack down the cocking lever of his carbine and take up a position by the opposite window.

The man sleeping on the bench woke briefly, raised the blanket from his face, looked around and then turned over and went back to sleep.

David leaned out of the window and shook his fist at the grinning native who stood watching the train as it rapidly disappeared.

"You bloody savage!" He pulled out the spear, threw it down and then turned back to the carriage to comfort Dorothy, who was terrified.

"It's nothing," said David. "They're like little children, with their bows and arrows and spears. They don't understand what they are doing half the time."

Roger snorted at him, cleared his carbine and sat down.

"Hogwash. Why don't you tell her the truth," he said as he turned to Alice. "Fact is they hate us, and with good cause. This Iron Snake is cutting right across their land, such as it is." He looked out the window. "Don't let the terrain fool you, miss. It may not look like much, and they can barely scratch out a living on it, but it's all they have. And regardless of what the Railway says about it being 'theirs' under a 'treaty,'" he sneered at David, then looked away, "it doesn't belong to them and they know it."

"By the way, Stephen," he said, looking across at him, "if his aim had been a bit higher, that spear would've come right through the open window and pinned you to your seat." He gave a sardonic laugh, clearly enjoying the effect of his words on the other two men.

Dorothy was still upset, and it seemed to Alice that she was on the point of crying. David reached into the food basket, took out a bottle of brandy and offered to pour a small glass for her; she ignored him, and instead settled her head against Stephen's shoulder.

David offered the bottle to Stephen who looked at David and shook his head.

No one spoke after that. Finally Dorothy closed her eyes. Her veiled sun helmet lay on the seat beside her. It rested alongside Stephen's Webley as he continued to watch the dry countryside. His face was set, determined, as Africa slipped by the open window. Within a short while a quietness settled on the party, very much like the fine African dust coming through the windows. It built up slowly and surely until they could no longer fight the heat and stagnant air.

Inside the car, hats began slipping over their eyes, heads began lolling, as the hypnotic clickety-clack of the wheels and the slow rolling and rocking of the suspension did the rest.

12

The whistle sounded loud and clear, waking them with a start.

"Watch closely, Miss McConnell," said Roger, as he pointed out the window. "See that large gray form by the acacia tree out there?"

"Oh, my. Look. Elephants, dozens of them," she said, her eyes now wide open, no sign here of sleepiness. Roger smiled as he watched her reaction.

"That small one on the edge of the herd is a young male; he won't be allowed in the inner circle until he earns the right. And see over there, the baby following its mother."

Alice squealed with delight as the family of elephants slowly made their way forward.

"And over there," said Roger. "Wildebeest, zebra and a few gazelle. We'll see more of them on our way to Machakos.

"Look," cried Alice, "wild pigs!"

"We call them warthogs here. Excellent when roasted. Also, great sport to hunt. I gather you've hunted before, miss?"

"Mostly rabbits, birds and the odd deer or two, but this is amazing."

The train began slowing as it approached the new station at Voi.

"And who are you?" Roger asked the man who had been sleeping in the corner of the compartment. He had awakened as the train slowly chugged into the station yard, and was now rubbing his face as he sat up.

"Oh," said David, who suddenly remembered, "I forgot to introduce Capt. Jeffrey Porter, recently retired. Capt. Porter's a professional hunter from Rhodesia, known to us in India as 'J.O.' Never did find out what the 'O' stood for, sir."

"Professional hunter?"

"Yes, J.O.'s here to hunt down the man-eater, aren't you, sir? I forgot to tell you, Stephen, that's why I came down with you. I have to report back to headquarters on the problem, which I hope is a minor one."

Roger and Alice both stared at him as if transfixed.

"Yes," said J.O. getting his baggage down and dusting it off. He stuffed a pipe in his mouth and put a well-used, battered old *terrai* onto his sunburnt head. "Damn good to know we have some other hunters among us," he said as he winked at Alice and Roger. "May need all the help we can get."

He stepped through the door, which was reverently held open for him by David, leaving the others still sitting in their seats. "Minyama!" he called out. And from somewhere his Matabele gun bearer materialized.

The railhead was some distance from the station yard, and beyond that lay the river and the bridge construction site. Looking over the yard, it was obvious much progress had been made; foundations had been laid out for buildings and workshops had been set up. Until a few weeks before, the return trains to Mombasa had to run in reverse and thus required more time on the return journey. Now a triangle had been completed and engines could be turned around. But, despite this progress, work had completely stopped.

"The railhead crew will not go near the bridge site," explained David, "and as you'll notice, they'll hardly venture from their stockade camps. It seems a lion recently killed several of their colleagues, so it's a total shutdown until something's done about it."

The arriving party for the first time noticed how quiet it was as they stepped down. After conferring with the British engineer in charge, Stephen decided they should not travel immediately; with a man-eater around, it would be best to wait to see how J.O. would deal with it.

"Also," said Roger, with Alice's bright eyes watching everything intently, "he may need some help."

They unloaded the caravan animals, which were led into thorn *bomas*. Then the packs and supplies were stored in fortified huts guarded by caravan askaris equipped with muskets. The porters pitched their tents in the main camp and Stephen and his party followed David up to the railway guesthouse where they intended to settle in with J.O. As they passed the railway camp, hundreds of eyes followed their progress. The workers sat in their enormous compound, an enclave that did not have enough latrines or proper drainage, and where rubbish was left standing in fetid, rat-infested heaps. In low areas sewage stagnated in slimy puddles creating a smell strong enough to make even the men wince.

"*Wait*!" cried Roger. The startled party came to a halt. "Careful. I must warn you about these things. You see that dark red moving line?" he said as he pointed to something on the ground; they all looked where he pointed. "Those are *safari* ants; they go about their business with no concern until you step on them, then they have pincers that bite and pinch like nothing you've felt before."

This was the last straw for Dorothy. Fatigued by the journey, upset by what she had been through, distracted by this talk of man-eaters and now these terrible ants and the stench, she fainted. "Help me, David," said Stephen as he caught her in his arms; luckily, the guesthouse was just a short way.

As he passed Roger, Stephen hissed, "Safari ants! My God, you're no help at all."

When they reached the house, Stephen and Alice stayed with Dorothy while she was put to bed to recover. The rest of the party retired to the verandah and David called out to the Swahili cook to bring some tea.

"He always puts the water on the fire when he hears the whistle of the passenger special at four o'clock," said David. At that moment Stephen and Alice joined them.

"Dorothy's resting. I promised her she's not going to be moved until something is done about the man-eater. Capt. Porter, I presume you'll be doing some stalking tonight?"

"I'll have a go at it, but I can't promise much until I know more about the situation."

"I'd help," said Stephen, "but I think I'll be of more use here."

"And, if you don't mind," said David, "I think I should also stay and help out at the station house."

"No problem," said J.O. "Good thing I had a little sleep on the train. I'll set up a night guard and see what else can be done. I might even be able to flush out the culprit, but we haven't much time left tonight. If we do anything it has to be done soon."

The sun was now gloriously setting across the river, of which they had a clear view. The plan was for Roger and Minyama to go with J.O. to reconnoiter. "But first," said J.O., "let's make certain you're well armed here."

"I'm carrying my revolver; surely that's enough," said Stephen.

"Yes, under ordinary circumstances. But just to be on the safe side, Roger, you'd better leave them your large bore." He loaded it and moved the safety catch to the safe position with a click. Alice watched his every move as he placed it carefully on one of the beds.

"Here's some spare ammunition," said Roger in a helpful way, wanting to make up for the scare he had caused Dorothy, "and I see Miss McConnell has her 12 bore; that should suffice."

Roger with his carbine, J.O. with his heavy double-barreled rifle and Minyama carrying a light sporting rifle started down the hill to look over the terrain. They were joined by an Indian foreman, Mr. Joshi, carrying a magazine rifle, standard issue on the railways. He had been sent by the engineer to brief them on what had transpired.

"For some time now," he explained, as they walked along, "we have been passing through the 'Fly Belt,' where we lost fifteen hundred out of our eighteen hundred transport animals to tsetse fly. We thought then we'd seen the worst of our troubles, until we came into the 'Lion Belt.'

"Unluckily, we are at present too far away from Mombasa to return each night. The only workers who leave here now are those who have been released, the ones who are scheduled to go home to India because their contracts are complete, and also, of course, those who have died."

"And you lose a fair number of men?" asked J.O.

"Well, it seems we cannot avoid it. It is very rough work here and diseases abound. If a team member comes down sick, he must be treated on the spot, which is why we have set up a small hospital. But even then, many die."

"Do you ever find traces after the lion attacks?" asked J.O.

"Yes, and the remains, if they can be found, are cremated in camp according to the Hindu tradition, then the ashes are released into the river."

"And if he was a Muslim?" asked Roger.

"In that case, the corpse, or what is left of it, is placed in one of the wooden coffins that we keep in the camp store just for that purpose, and he is sent back to Mombasa."

"Is this the first time you've been attacked like this?" asked J.O.

"No, not at all. We had attacks by man-eaters even before we reached Voi, but we thought this would pass like everything else. However, this lion now has become even bolder. We have had several attacks during the day as well as night, and all this has happened over a period of one week. It even wanders into the compound of the guesthouse," he added, as J.O. glanced at Roger.

"And the last attack?"

"The last victim was a coolie taken last night. That has decided the issue. The complete workforce gave up and returned to the main camp, the place you passed on the way here. There is another small group barricaded in the bridge construction camp where we are now going. But they are adamant, sir," said Joshi turning to face J.O.

"They believe this lion, '*Shaitan*' they call it, 'the devil,' will breed more if left unchecked and they are not going to budge until they see its carcass."

J.O. had already been made aware of the seriousness of the problem by the commissioner, Ian Burns, who after noting the horrifying toll had written to him that, "This lion also presents a problem to the government and to the Empire. It is delaying the construction of the bridge; which, in turn, as I cannot overemphasize, is important to the movement of troop trains and, ultimately, the security of Uganda. The whole East Africa colony is put in peril because it now depends on this route."

Capt. Porter had literally just gotten off the boat the previous day and, on David's direction, boarded the Voi train where he spent the afternoon dozing until he woke in time to hear Roger talking about the wildlife and hunting. J.O. was typical of the professionals arriving in Africa, following in the footsteps of Cornwallis Harris and Frederick Selous, the archetypes of the white African hunter. There were as yet few white hunters resident in Kenya; most had settled in South Africa, which even now was being hunted out. In J.O.'s case, he had spent five years hunting in Matabeleland, but had been reduced finally to raising ostriches. A market in feathers had been created by the latest fashions in England, the Continent and America, and this had kept him going. But he saw the game vanishing before his eyes. He decided to leave his wife and two married daughters there and come to the new elephant and lion territory in East Africa.

He had killed lions, but had never before stalked a man-eater. He had read up on their habits and decided on that basis that his previous experience in South Africa did not much prepare him for the work. Many of his lion-hunting clients had preferred to use light rifles, such as the 7 mm Mauser that Minyama carried. Such a rifle offered a challenge because it made you concentrate, especially if you knew accuracy would be the only thing between you and a three hundred pound vicious brute charging at you with the speed of lightning. In the present case, however, he knew he would be up against an animal that was faster, craftier and probably well over four hundred and fifty pounds in weight. "That's why we need reliable knockdown power," he said to Roger, indicating his double-barreled Holland, a heavy .577 caliber rifle. "If we were using these larger bores for elephant and rhino, I'd normally use a jacketed lead bullet, or 'solid,' because of its penetration through tough hide, but for lion with their soft skin they'd go right through their body. So I'm taking no chances—I've loaded soft core hollow bullets for both rifles. By the way, what's all this about hunting? Have you been doing that for a living?"

"No, not at all," said Roger. "I operate caravans. I'm taking this present party to Machakos, but along the way I've got to feed them."

"I see," said J.O. "Strange how everyone develops a taste for game meat once they get out into the open air. And you've shot lion before?"

"Never. Though I've bagged buffalo and several elephants."

"Well, let me give you some pointers; this drill is entirely different, and much more dangerous."

They stopped for a moment while J.O. emphasized his point. "On open ground a lion charges full out, doesn't require much space to get up to speed, and will come at you in a few seconds. Hundreds of pounds of muscle landing on you with claws extended, they'll already be slitting through your clothing and into your flesh like twenty open razors the minute they're on you.

"While that's going on," he continued, "she—and invariably, it's a she, the males are lazy and make poor hunters—will be sinking her large sharp teeth into your skull with the ease of a gourmand biting into a grape. Damn lucky for them they have some whites around now." He nodded at the workers in the construction site camp as they approached it.

Roger immediately bristled at that statement; he felt he had an obligation to speak up for the black man. "You mean to defend them?" he said in a belligerent voice, ready to argue and on the verge of branding J.O. a bigot.

"No, not at all. I mean to distract the lions. You know, of course, they prefer eating whites over Africans and Indians, if it's any consolation," he said as he smiled at Roger who looked taken aback, "because of the higher salt content in our flesh!"

13

On arrival at the camp on the bank of the river, J.O.'s party found two bomas that had literally battened down the hatches. They could see the workers looking out through the thorn fence, afraid of moving out of these fortified compounds. The night previous, a lion had made its way through a weak spot in the fence and had roamed at will among the screaming workers. It had finally been driven off by noise and firebrands being thrown at it, but not before it grabbed an unlucky man by the throat and dragged him kicking and screaming back through the fence and out into the nearby bush where, shortly after, the terrified workers could hear the crunching sounds of their companion being eaten.

After examining both compounds, J.O. asked Mr. Joshi to show him the remains. On arriving at the spot they could find nothing except one leg from the knee down, two leather sandals and a pool of dried blood.

"See there," he said as he pointed to the rough patches on the skin of the leg. "They lick the skin off to get at the blood. Their tongues are like course sandpaper."

"Wait," said Roger.

"What's wrong?" asked J.O.

"We're being watched."

They froze in their tracks as everyone carefully looked toward a nearby thorn bush.

"There!" said Minyama, and they looked where he pointed. On the ground under the bush they saw a red turbaned head and a face peering out.

"He's alive...," yelled Roger, but stopped short as J.O. pulled the severed head from the bundu and laid it on top of the remains.

It was getting dark as they walked quietly back to the compound and J.O. ordered the remaining workers transferred to the smaller stockade; that could be more easily guarded by Minyama armed with his Mauser. From the livestock left behind in the first compound, they selected several goats and tethered them inside the compound where J.O. and Roger would wait on their own through the night.

Darkness set in as Mr. Joshi settled down in the smaller boma with Minyama. J.O. positioned himself with Roger behind a small shelter inside the larger compound. They sat as motionless as they could, the Holland in J.O.'s lap, the carbine resting on Roger's knees, muzzle pointing toward the goats. Near midnight, while he was fighting to stay awake, J.O. heard a peculiar sighing just outside their barricade. It was a very distinct sound accompanied by a foul smell that permeated the compound, a smell that, J.O. knew from his reading, was associated with man-eaters.

"Lion," he whispered into Roger's ear. Although no moon was present, they could see slight shadows by starlight, and he soon saw movement near the goats, who had stopped bleating—a further sign something was about.

Incredible, J.O. thought. He had not heard a sound of any animal going through the weak spot that they had made in the fence, especially any animal the size of a lion. But, there it was. He could feel its presence. He had been sitting most of the night in a position that had been comfortable at the start, but now his joints were numb. The tension had removed the sense of pain and he was slow in raising his rifle. He leaned forward to shoot at a shadow when the lion turned and bolted. Its large padded feet sounded like drum beats thumping on the ground, and suddenly a shadow went up and over the fence—all within seconds.

They both fired out of desperation at the place where the shadow had been. The noise echoed and re-echoed through the African night, but the muzzle flares revealed nothing, except the goats, frozen in silence.

They called over to the others and told them there was nothing for it but to settle back and wait for morning. When the dawn finally came and with it the first light, they left the compound with heavy-lidded eyes. Badly bitten by mosquitoes, they examined the area outside.

Hardly expecting to find a trace left behind by this wily creature, they looked carefully at the base of the thorn bushes, where to J.O.'s amazement Minyama found a small patch of light brown fur and several drops of blood. They walked back to the smaller compound and, over a cup of tea and some biscuits, they were joined by two askaris who had been sent down by Stephen to find out about any developments; otherwise the whole area was still completely deserted.

"Well, I see there's no need to wake anyone around here," he said as he saw the many eyes staring out at him from behind the protective barricades that interlaced the compound.

"Not much to go on," said J.O. in recapping what happened. "We probably hit it with a glancing shot, but it's all we have. We'll have to try tracking it into the bush. We'll need some extra water bottles." He looked at Roger, Minyama and Mr. Joshi, hoping for some response.

Everyone looked at each other; then they all volunteered to go with him.

"Good," he said. "One of the askaris will have to stand guard here, and the other has to report back to Stephen." He nodded at Roger and Joshi. "Nothing like company when you have to go through thorn bush to beat out a lion, especially one that's been wounded." He normally used a pack of dogs to do this because it was too risky to spare men in this kind of work, but now there was no choice. Roger sent one askari back up the hill with a note to explain what had transpired, and that they would probably return before evening.

"Right," said J.O., "let's start immediately. I'll try to pick up the trail here; you two follow closely. From now on we'll use hand signals only."

He and Minyama showed them a series of signs before they went down on their haunches and began a careful investigation. They picked up another blood spot and could roughly begin making out the track. Soon he was able to lead the way, walking slowly, while the two neophytes followed.

J.O. was good at this. He had learned the art under the tutelage of bushmen in the south, looking for tracks on soil still damp with the morning dew, observing thorn branches or blades of grass to see if, once bent, they had sprung back, and, if so, were they all the way back to normal.

As they progressed, he pointed out the blood drops that were near to, but not on, a footprint. He concluded from this the lion had a long superficial wound on its rump, not healing quickly, with blood trickling down one hind leg. Painful, he supposed, but not critical to the animal. As they went deeper into the scrub, Minyama climbed a tree to have a better view; Roger gave him a lift into an acacia tree while the others continued on the spoor.

Minyama soon caught up with them and signed to J.O., "Movement in the thick brush ahead!"

J.O. signaled them to stop and listen carefully; the air was still, except for the whine of insects. There were no birdcalls or other bush sounds, a sign to J.O. that a lion was close by. The spoor led to a small natural opening directly ahead of them as all around them the maze of thorn bush closed in, the bundu at its worst. They had to go now in single file. J.O. had taken one step forward, when suddenly out of the bush a female lion charged.

There was no time to plan. J.O. operated on instinct alone. He dropped to his right knee and let go with the Holland, then fired a second barrel for good measure. As he had predicted, it was the combination of large bore and soft bullets that saved them, because the sheer force knocked the animal right off its feet. He grabbed the other rifle that Minyama handed him and sent two more bullets into the brute. Almost simultaneously, the engineer and Roger let go with several volleys, but J.O. told them to stop firing. The lion was dead.

He picked up the Holland from the ground and reloaded as he rose and walked slowly toward it. Joshi followed at a discreet distance. The animal had dropped not twenty feet from where J.O. had stood. J.O. held his rifle at the ready as he and Minyama knelt down to examine the lion's head, especially its teeth, to see if they had been deformed or scarred in such a way as to prevent their hunting normal prey, a typical reason why lions become man-eaters.

Roger, who was not far behind as they stood admiring the kill, turned to his right where something had caught his eye. It was another lion, a large male, racing towards them. Roger yelled to J.O., who stepped back to raise his rifle, but tripped over a rock. Joshi stared, mesmerized by the evil eyes of the creature. Minyama, who had left his rifle on the ground, drew his knife. Roger, following J.O.'s lead, dropped to one knee, steadied his rifle, stared down the barrel sighting the head and mane, and squeezed the trigger. He racked the lever down and quickly fired three more rounds, sighting as the rifle steadied, stepping aside only when he saw the animal tumble to his right in a large furry ball with dust and dry grass flying in all directions.

"By God, man, you've saved our lives!"

Minyama, who had known J.O. for many years, had never seen him so surprised and happy. But it was short-lived, as he realized that neither of these were man-eaters.

It was hard to admit: they had failed. "All that noise and shooting," he shook his head in disappointment. "We've probably scared off any man-eater by now."

All four had started back to camp, when suddenly a shot rang out from the direction of the hill.

They stopped in their tracks. A second shot rang out.

"Good Lord," J.O. said, his pipe almost falling from his mouth. "That's a large bore!"

They broke into a run back up to the guesthouse on the hilltop.

Breathing heavily and sweating for all they were worth, they came over the rise where they were joined by Stephen, who during the late morning had started down the hill to see what was happening.

The yelling and screaming echoing down toward them sped them on their way, and they came crashing out of the scrub at the edge of the compound to find Alice. She was standing in the doorway of the guesthouse holding a large-bore, guarding a lion carcass that lay on the step below, its blood pouring down from a gaping wound in its large swollen head.

A crowd of excited workers had gathered round, yelling, crying and thanking her and God for interceding. They were all speaking at once.

"*Ma*! *Ma*! " they called out. "Thank the heavens for this woman!"

The hunting party, still somewhat elated, was put to work dragging the carcass out into the center of the compound in front of the house so others could see it, a three hundred and fifty pound female with two large holes in her forehead. J.O. immediately bent down and examined its teeth.

"It's a man-eater alright. And see here, a recent wound on its rump."

"Could anything beat this?" asked Stephen.

Dorothy, paler than usual, waited nervously inside the house with a Swahili houseman who was looking out of one of the windows.

"What happened?" yelled Roger, trying to make himself heard above the din.

"It was getting on toward late morning," said Alice. "It was very quiet in the compound. Stephen and Mr. McCann had gone off and no one was about. Dorothy was sleeping on one of the beds. I was fascinated by the large-bore, especially the double trigger, which is similar to my shotgun, you know," she explained to the crowd who stood in silent awe at her feet.

"I heard a strange, sighing noise from outside and looked out the door. I thought it might simply be someone sleeping there," as she pointed to the rough string bed of the houseman lying in the shade. "The door had been left open to catch some fresh air. Then I saw it, the head of this creature as it slowly climbed the stairs. And without waiting, I stood in the doorway and blasted away."

She now descended the steps and walked up to the carcass, the crowd parting before her, but she stopped in mid-stride and pointed at Roger's foot.

"Oh, Mr. Newcome. Isn't that what you warned us about?"

"What?" he asked innocently, staring at her.

"Those safari ants crawling up your leg."

He looked down with amazement and saw he had trodden on

an ant trail. The fierce little beggars had already started up his leg inside his trousers and at the first stinging bite, he leaped into action, jumping around like a madman before he suddenly broke into a flat dash heading for the river. Pandemonium broke out as they cheered him on; yelling like demons as they gave vent to their feelings on the death of the "devil," and simultaneously chanted praises to Alice, their savior.

With the tremendous noise going on, it was almost impossible to speak. Stephen went in to see Dorothy, while J.O. and Joshi explained to everyone, as well as they could, that two more carcasses were waiting below. More yells of delight came from the crowd as Joshi and Minyama led them down to the other site, and J.O. stood there shaking his head.

He slowly removed his hat and bowed to Alice.

"Madam," he said. "Your humble servant. Never have I seen a braver soul or a cooler head, and I have seen many, many lion kills. You, ma'am, are quite a woman!"

14

Two days later they set off for Machakos. Now the work of the porters began; each carried several days' rations in addition to a normal head load, a total of seventy pounds. Under this weight and in the purgatory of the thorn bush and the African sun, it was a heroic task for anyone. The presence of wild animals and the uncertainties of life on the road made progress even more difficult. The marching order was always the same: Roger and Stephen in the lead on horseback, followed by the two women also on horseback. The porters and donkeys followed with the headman, Allidina, and several askaris took up the rear. The road surface had been worn down and widened by hundreds of caravans, wagons and carts. Now it was comparatively well traveled, but still there were days on end when they met no one. Dorothy from the first day expressed fear of attack, but as the journey progressed, with Stephen by her side, those fears began to diminish along with the memories of Voi and Mombasa. It was hot and dry during the day and cool at night, with no rain on a clear road, and the porters did all the work. Alice found it wasn't an arduous trip at all; indeed, she was enjoying herself immensely.

"What more could you want?" said Roger as they sat around their campfire on the third night out. "Game overrunning the place, exotic birds, extraordinary plant life, and at the end of the day dinner by candlelight."

"And it's so quiet and peaceful," said Alice.

"You've gotten quite skilled at this," said Stephen to Roger, "but it must still be hard to provide a selection of meat every day."

"It's not too difficult when you've been doing it for a few years," Roger said, then turned to Dorothy and asked in a still recognizable Virginia accent, "Do you hunt, ma'am?"

"I've no interest in that direction, nor do I have any need. Alice more than makes up for my deficiencies," she said as she gave her stepsister a hard look. "I will never forget that dreadful beast lying at your feet. It's beyond me how you could face such a monster."

"I doubt it will ever happen again," said Alice. "Am I correct in that man-eaters are rare once we leave the railway camps?"

"They occasionally show up in villages," said Roger. "But I wouldn't expect to see them in open country. On the other hand, there are lots of game birds here, if you're interested. The hunting party goes out every morning at four." He turned to Stephen and asked, "Why don't you come along?"

"Love to, but I still have work to do, which reminds me, we should turn in."

He and Dorothy got up and walked toward their tent.

"Coming, Alice? You've got another long hot day tomorrow."

"I'll turn in in a minute," she said as she poured another cup of coffee. To Roger she said, in a low voice, "You're right, it's everything I ever heard or read about, but I'm afraid Dorothy's finding it hard going."

"I see that. My men and I are trying to make sure she's troubled as little as possible."

"I don't think Stephen realizes how difficult it is for her. She's led a very protected life. As for myself," she said, her smile reflecting the light of the fire, "I couldn't ask for anything else, especially sleeping under a night sky with every star in the heavens blinking down at you. I have a feeling that in years to come, people will pay a fortune for this kind of experience."

"Since you enjoy it so much, why not come out with us tomorrow?"

"Thank you, I'd like that. Give me a call when you get up. Now I'd better say good night, otherwise Stephen will be worrying me about getting to bed early."

"Look there," Roger said the next morning, "near your foot!

There's a scorpion. Be careful." She moved to one side. They were circling back to the caravan after unsuccessfully stalking a herd of gazelle. "By the way," he continued, "if you're stung by one, remember it leaves the poison sac attached to the stinger, just like a bee. So, if you carefully scrape it with a knife edge you can remove the bulk of it and you won't feel a thing."

"Can you imagine what it must be like to be a small animal at that level," she said, as they crouched together watching the large insect.

"The stinger must come at you from above and down, sort of like a matador placing the *banderilla*!"

"Oh, dear. Now I've done it. Oh my," said Alice jumping up, as she squirmed and hopped about. "*Siafu*, safari ants," she cried as she went racing behind a thorn bush to pick off the ants from her boots. A few had already gotten inside her cotton breeches. Observing the proprieties of the situation, Roger and the Africans stood to one side, smiling and shaking their heads, but respectful of their fellow hunter. Shooting a man-eater was a formidable effort in their eyes.

"Oh, God. Roger," she yelled. "There's something in the bushes!"

Motioning to the gun bearer and trackers to stay where they were, he raced to her side, rifle at the ready. He could not help but observe her disheveled appearance, boots and stockings lying about and her breeches drawn up exposing one lovely white leg. The grass and bushes on one side were suddenly pushed apart, as Stephen and his gun bearer appeared.

"Roger. Good. Just wanted you to know…," he said as he stopped and stared. Roger lowered his rifle.

"I...I don't understand...," said Stephen somewhat taken aback. "What's...?"

"Oh, Stephen, it's you," said Alice. "You gave us a fright. We thought it was a rhino or some such," as she continued putting her clothing back in order.

"Yes," said Roger, turning red as a beet. "Bit of a problem with siafu. Miss McConnell's turn to suffer."

"Well," said Stephen. "Sorry to disturb you, just wanted to save you a bit of trouble. I thought I could bag a gazelle closer to camp." He was obviously chagrined at what he had seen.

On their way back to the caravan, his uneasiness was not calmed by the fact that he had just been at the working end of a large-bore. He was not used to people pointing loaded rifles at him. That evening before tea he stopped by Roger's tent. "I wonder, Roger, if you realize what you are doing," he said, staring at the young man who sat there pulling off his boots.

"Doing?" Roger asked, as he looked first at Stephen and then at the boot that he had just pulled off. "I don't understand."

"I'm referring to my sister-in-law. She's still quite young and impressionable and I don't like the idea of the two of you going off into the bush like this."

"Well, what's to be done?" said Roger, turning red in the face and staring back hard at Stephen. "It's her choice. She likes to hunt and she's as capable as any man at defending herself."

"I realize she likes to hunt, and I also realize you have to provide for the table, but from now on I think I'll go with you rather than her. It'll make my mind easier anyway."

Roger continued to stare at Stephen, dumbfounded.

"Well," Stephen paused, not knowing what else to say. "See you at dinner." He turned and walked back to his tent.

"Absolute balls!" muttered Roger under his breath.

Roger settled into his bed after dinner. He had a splitting headache but had suffered in silence during the meal. The cicadas began their evening symphony and his eyes closed as he drifted into an uneasy sleep....

...Stephen again came out of the cuddy, walked past him and slipped down beside her on the deck, as she smiled in return and they cuddled together, completely unaware of him. Roger's anger and resentment came bubbling over as before, but this time he realized he had a ready arsenal. He no longer had to depend on the same old signal pistol; now there was a revolver with a handle that fit his hand perfectly.

He drew it from its hiding place and was soon standing over them again.

"Get off her, you bastard!" he yelled. As he stood there, he was even more shocked to see it wasn't Susan; it was Alice underneath him.

And she was smiling up at him.

Horrorstruck, he yelled again, "Get off her, I say, or I'll break every bone in your body!"

"Wait, this is wrong.... You don't...understand...," said Stephen as he rose facing him on the deck. "You have absolutely the wrong impression...."

...The explosion and muzzle flare woke him instantly, and when the flash subsided, he realized it was pitch dark and deathly quiet. What the hell am I doing? he asked himself. The sparks of cordite powder from the muzzle were sparkling in a pattern on the canvas surrounding a hole directly in front of him.

Suddenly, all hell broke loose. Lanterns were being lit; people were stumbling around outside throwing lighted patterns and shadows on the tent wall. The fly of the tent was thrown open.

"Roger. For God's sake, man!" yelled Stephen. "Are you all right?"

"I don't know. What happened?"

"You don't know?" said Stephen, his face contorted in angry surprise. "You almost shot us!"

"I...I must have had a nightmare," said Roger, who was kneeling on his bed, revolver hanging loosely in his hand.

"A dangerous practice, keeping loaded weapons around," said Stephen as he stared at the revolver. "You must be mad to keep that thing in bed with you!"

"Sorry," he said, still dazed. He carefully placed the gun on the camp table. "Bad habit that."

"And a damned poor show," muttered Stephen as he walked back through the crowd of porters.

"*Hapana fakiri*," he said to everyone, trying to calm down the porters. "Not to worry, *ina salaama sasa*, it's fine; it's all right; go back to bed; it's nothing."

"His pistol went off by accident," he explained to Alice, who had rushed to his tent to sit with Dorothy.

"Alice, be a good girl, will you, and stay with her for a bit."

He went back around the camp with Allidina and quieted everyone before turning back to his tent. The next morning over tea, he questioned Roger again.

"Are you aware of what might have happened?"

"I swear it was an accident."

"We'll be in Machakos in a few days," said Stephen, "and that's the end of *this* safari. I'm definitely going to report this to Mombasa. You had better take another look at how you handle weapons, and how you relate to clients, or you're not going to be in this business for long."

Roger had no reply other than to focus his blazing blue eyes on Stephen's back, watching him as he carried tea back to the tent for Dorothy.

After Susan had left him, Stephen had thought on several occasions that it would have been better had he just shot himself. That would have ended his pain over a loss he could never recover from, and he'd never be saddled with her son again. At least that would have been that, he thought. He was still thinking about that as he stopped briefly outside his tent, bent down and looked at the entry hole made by Roger's bullet.

It was just inches from where his head would have been.

Book Two

At Home in Africa

1

The land surrounding Machakos town is dominated by a series of low mountain chains that stretch throughout the Ukambani region. Interrupted now and then by large steep-sided ravines, the terrain forms a natural barrier that isolates the Wakamba from the Masai who roam the plains below. The Wakamba, the predominate tribe in Stephen's district, were well adapted to the drier conditions that prevail there and it was evident that agriculture ruled their life—so much so that their year was divided into growing seasons, starting with the short rains in late October, which lasted into early December, a season called *Nthwa*, followed by the long rains of March through May called *Uua*. The cool foggy season, *Nundu*, came in June and July, and the year ended with the long dry season, *Thano*, during August and September.

For Stephen, the basic simplicity of Wakamba life and their preoccupation with survival brought a sense of disappointment when he first arrived; he could not help but contrast Africa to India, where the princes lavished fortunes on frivolities. Survival in India was a concern only of the huddled masses; in Africa it seemed to be a concern of everyone, every day. He looked in vain for some exotic expression of their life, some graceful dance, unique dress, food, speech or architecture that would set Africa apart. Where was the sophistication derived from thousands of years of history? he wondered. He saw nothing here of the learned arts, theology, painting, calligraphy and poetry that characterized India.

He could even see the Indian caste system as a form of sophistication, especially by those at the top of the heap, but such a thing was nowhere in evidence in Ukambaa, where even the social system defied explanation. He could barely believe what he had been told, that it was basically a community founded on the premise that every person was born equal, with elders and strangers given privileges. Otherwise, it was an open society with few complications. He hid his feelings, but he never cast off the suspicion that maybe Susan Newcome had been right to stay away.

Maybe that applies to myself as well, he thought; maybe I'm just completely out of my element.

He had not been long away from his post, but it was impossible for him not to be distracted as he looked out at the sprawling settlement from a distance and realized how shabby the place was. It required no practiced eye to see that Machakos had a long way to go to catch up even to Mombasa, which was itself no paradise. In fact, the new town of Nairobi being built west of here was already more developed. Worse yet, he thought, as he glanced at Dorothy who rode beside him, it had been decided that, to save time, the railroad would bypass Machakos and go directly into Nairobi. At some future date a spur line would be built, but for now the emphasis would be on the main line; his district would have to wait.

Before he left, he had told his Anglo-Indian assistant, Mr. Harris, to organize a welcome, something he could be proud of on his return, something that would impress his wife. He looked forward to that as the caravan swung down the road.

Dorothy had little knowledge of Africa; perhaps that's why she was so easily impressed by Stephen's mastery of the rudiments of the local language, and his title, District Commissioner. It did seem grand to her the way it evoked a sense of respect and authority, especially when trains were delayed for their arrival. But as they rode forward and she saw the settlement looming, her sense of pride quickly wore off. She and her husband were at the head of the caravan; Alice and Roger rode behind as they came down the hot dusty road. It was midday when they reached the outskirts of Machakos, and suddenly drums appeared out of the caravan baggage and at that point they were joined by hundreds of children.

In Mombasa and the rail stations, and also in the railway camp at Voi, the mixture of Arab, European, Asian and mulatto faces had diluted the reality of the country. Here in the hinterland away from all that, Africans stood out. Many were naked and black, their blackness thrown into deep contrast by the sun-bleached environment. This was their country; here on this dusty soil they stood in their own right, Africans in Africa, thousands of them watching her as she rode by. And they weren't bashful, they didn't avert their eyes, they stared back, and for Dorothy that was a frightening experience. Their constant companions were also there, cattle, goats and dogs, thin to the point of emaciation; they stood with them as if in support, and they also stared. At first, Dorothy stared back until she realized that the caravan itself, the porters that made it up, and her protector, even though he was a district commissioner, were all very small in comparison to what appeared to be an enormous crowd. With that thought came a feeling of inadequacy, especially when the drumming stopped and she noticed it was so quiet she could hear her horse's footsteps.

"They seem wasted beyond recovery," she said to Stephen in order to break the silence, which was overpowering.

A second thought came to her—why do they even bother to tend this scarecrow collection of livestock? Suddenly, a cry went up from an older woman standing at the edge of the crowd, a cry that startled Dorothy and made her wonder, had she read my thoughts? Another cry formed deep in that wrinkled old throat, and like the high-pitched call of some wild animal, came gurgling up and out. Then hundreds of women took it up.

"Ululating," said Stephen as he watched her face.

The cry swept from one side of the valley to the other and echoed out across the hills, becoming louder as they went. Then the porters again began drumming and singing. Now the noise rose to a terrific level as more and more black, naked bodies appeared from somewhere and followed the caravan as it moved in slow procession toward a low wooden building.

On the verandah, a group of missionaries and a small collection of army men, government staff, settler families and a contingent of local chiefs gathered to receive them, as instructed by Mr. Harris.

Roger noticeably hung back, and as soon as the caravan stopped he helped the porters unload the animals. After his safari experiences with Stephen, he was anxious to leave and planned to go directly on to Nairobi that same day without stopping.

A week later he would be back in Kikuyuland and rid of all this.

Stephen helped Dorothy off her horse and escorted her forward. She paused on the top step to brush the dust from her gown. Then she untied the ribbon releasing her veil and carefully folded it back over her topi. Only then did she step forward and begin shaking hands and nodding at individuals as Stephen introduced them.

Behind her came Alice.

At this point Dorothy still had some perspective. From the verandah she could still see the countryside, until the crowd followed her up the stairs and gathered around. Now they parted only as she walked forward.

And the dust, she thought. It had followed them from the beginning. It had been there on the train, on safari, and it was still there billowing out above the crowd and up onto the verandah.

They had never left it.

Dust.

She stopped and waited for something to happen. People, mostly black, swirled around her as she waited, she wasn't sure for what. Maybe, she thought, a door would open, a wall would slide away and beyond that would be a country house, or at least the green of an English hillside, a lawn still moist with morning dew....

But no, there was nothing like that. There was dust and bright sunlight, and a dry hot vista of black bodies and scrawny animals all casting their mournful eyes in her direction. And the ululation, a sound she somehow associated with death.

She turned to Stephen who stood at her side. "Let's go home," she said.

"Of course, darling."

They reached an open door. "And here's our cook, Syani." The cook motioned with his hand and she looked into a large, dark room with shuttered windows, a room stifling in the noonday heat. Syani smiled at her and bowed low in greeting.

She looked beyond him. Dust motes floated in the thin slivers of sunlight coming through the crudely built wooden shutters.

"Stephen, this is all very well," she said in a resigned voice, "but, really. I'm tired. Let's go home."

"But darling," he said, "this *is* our home."

From where she stood, she could see the hard-packed mud floors, the rough unfinished furniture from Mombasa and the motley collection of chipped dishes and saucers; and on every surface was a fine layer of dust, at the sight of which she fainted, landing in a heap at the feet of the cook.

In Muthuri's Hut

So you have come back, Bwana Roger.

You must tell me about these places you go to when you leave here. I've heard much about Mombasa. The Europeans at the Mission School were always saying they were dying to go there. Is it the same as the Heaven they are also dying for?

No? I had begun to think it was a spiritland from which I would be barred, as I do not follow your Christian God.

Oh? You say anyone can go there.

Well, the next time you go to Mombasa, you must take me with you.

Now, you wanted to know why we spared you on that first occasion when you dropped from the sky?

Ha, that's an easy one. It was Kimani's wish. And let me tell you, you're a lucky man. We knew you did not "drop from the sky," because we had watched you. We had followed your caravan for several days. You see, other caravans used to come along that same trail, but they were not so lucky—the elders will tell you. As young men they used to wait in the bushes. They thought it was great fun to pounce on them.

Can't you see how exciting it would be to go after an Arab caravan? The slavers, ivory hunters, traders, whatever. It made no difference, we drove them all out. And they were not saved by their muskets. Those weapons and many of their trade goods became part of clan property.

Here, look at this. Yes, a musket, an old one, but it still works. My father took it from an Arab.

The slavers? What happened to them? Ha. Some were left where they fell, food for the hyenas. Others were carried down to the main trail and left there as an example.

That's the way we are. We fight and hide rather than submit.

Some would say the Kikuyu are lucky, others that we are a privileged race, because we have always occupied the forest and the best sections of the uplands, but I feel our success is due to our nature: we never give in.

If you watch us you will see that we fight, individually or together as a clan. Sometimes we fight at a distance with poisoned arrows, sometimes at close range when forced into hand-to-hand combat. But always, if we take an Arab prisoner, we make them suffer before they die. That is the reason you wazungu and the Arabs have such respect for us today. Is it any wonder Kikuyus are seldom taken as slaves?

The Masai?

The Masai are also a tribe to be avoided. If the Swahilis and Arabs meet a Masai war party, an impi, they know it is best to pay them off in trade goods. They barter for the right of free passage and then move quickly along the trail, because if slighted in any way, they will overrun a caravan on the plains, like the onslaught of a demon. I have heard you wazungu compare it to opening a sack inside your tent to find a large angry animal inside.

In appearance the warriors of both our tribes are similar; we differ in that we carry arrows and a bow. We both wear animal skins and headdresses made of feathers and carry long spears, sharp knives and have large shields made of hide tough enough to stop a musket ball. But there is one more thing we have in common. We are both watching you. We are both studying the differences between you and the Arabs.

Why? Because the Arab caravans took slaves and ivory, then they left and the country returned to normal. Like walking in high grass, the path closed behind.

But you wazungu, you are different.

It is not obvious to us what you want. In the beginning you were all treated as curiosities; now it's unsettling. We have seen your caravans increasing in size and number. The grass hardly has time to spring back before another arrives. And more and more of you have stayed behind. You don't leave.

What to do? At present we wait. We eat our meat and drink our beer and are grateful to Mwene Nyaga that we are still alive, but I am sure some day something will happen and it will not be pleasant.

By the way, I'm curious. You say you are an American, and you have red hair. Is that like being one of the devils?

Devils.

Yes, that is what I said.

That is what the White Fathers called them in the Mission. The wazungu who live in the south, in Tanganyika. The Children of the Kaiser.

2

Hundreds of thousands of game animals were now on the move across Kenya. Alice rode out in the early mornings to watch them as they thundered across the arid land south of Machakos. Normally, the migration did not begin until the dry weather of the beginning of the year, but this year the short rains had failed; in place of rain came soot and smoke from grass fires. In the face of that, the animals moved relentlessly toward the old floodplains in Masailand, riverbeds and lake edges in the far south, places where water and green grass might still be available. They left behind a parched, brown landscape and they would not return to the plains until rain fell.

She had watched through field glasses as the dust rose from the heels of the leading wildebeests, those eerily mad-looking, bearded antelopes, sometimes bounding and jumping and twisting as they ran.

The same dust floated high in the still air and lingered for a while before coming down, settling hours later on the shaggy backs of the same herd as it still raced blindly across the horizon. The massive herds attracted populations of vultures, hawks, hyenas, wild dogs, jackals and lions, which lived off them for months. They feasted each evening on the animals that fell by the wayside. There was hardly need for them to hunt, since their prey would just fall in their tracks from sheer exhaustion. The scavengers and predators, like sleek shoppers in a European meat market, could afford to wait until the best cuts were presented, as they leisurely made their way across the plains following this fantastic array of animal life.

Alice and the Hales had settled into their new life in Machakos, a process helped greatly by Jimmy Harris. A thin, middle-aged man with a dark complexion, he lived in a small building separate from the residence but close to the district commissioner's office. His wife, a short, fat Bengali woman, cooked delicious Indian sweets, wrote poetry and raised seven children. Jimmy's main task was to deal with official correspondence, daily reports and accounts. He also looked after the store of arms, paid the sepoys who manned the low stone fort, and reported back on anything of importance happening within the local population.

Because he was a Christian, he liked living in Machakos. During the early days, this place had been an important center for missionary families, several of whom had stayed on, prospered and multiplied. They were responsible for the school, the health center and the church.

There was even an orchard, a farm that had been started five years ago by a missionary family from Australia who had planted the apricot, quince, lemon, apple and plum trees that provided the expatriates with a small but precious supply of fruit. In the dry season the orchard was like an oasis in the middle of a desert. The same family introduced eucalyptus and wattle trees to the region, and helped create the settlement, which further attracted both Europeans and Asians, who, in turn, brought the Somali traders from the north to keep the trading posts and supply the stores.

From a settlement, it was now evolving into a town, a slow process that to Stephen's chagrin could not be hurried. Not that he had worried much about development since returning from Mombasa. The burden of work had fallen on Jimmy's shoulders well before that, and now Stephen was taken up entirely with looking after Dorothy. He left Jimmy to worry about local problems, of which there were many because the rains had failed. Animals without water were dying more frequently of rinderpest, a plague that never seemed to vanish; the cattle could not fight the disease in their weakened condition. Stephen now remembered even the poorest areas in India as being lavish in comparison to this place.

To add to the misery, villagers were being ravaged by smallpox, something that could be prevented if immediate steps were taken—it was possible to apply cow lymph using a scratch inoculation—but little could be done without initiative. To compound the problem, food was becoming scarce. Since no solution to these problems was in sight, Jimmy did not bother Stephen with the details.

"While bellies are full, it is a very quiet and peaceful life here," said Mutu, the Mkamba chief of the region directly surrounding the settlement. "Let us see what happens now that we have reached the bottom of the grain baskets."

Pressed further by the deepening drought, Jimmy suggested to Stephen that possibly he should hold his first *baraza*, or informal court. Everyone in town attended these, so it was important to make a good impression. They were considered great entertainment; people came from miles around to sit and listen to the recitations by the plaintiffs and their supporters, and they also provided a forum for ideas or mobilizing the community in efforts such as food distribution or animal and health care.

"If you think it would help," said Stephen, but he didn't seem enthusiastic.

"Where do they hold them?" he asked later after he had given it some thought.

"Under the old fig tree in the middle of the town square."

"Good Lord," said Stephen and he was about to launch into another homily on the need for a proper community building, a place where public meetings could be held, when he checked himself. He recalled he had earlier made that same point to no effect.

Mr. Harris seemed unaware of the need for such development.

"Oh, sir, before I forget," said Jimmy, "this morning a runner arrived with this note."

He handed Stephen a crumpled piece of paper.

Stephen looked in vain for an envelope or some semblance of modern business correspondence. He had set down a rule that Mr. Harris should emulate the high commissioner's office in Mombasa; in that place a proper file was kept for every item coming into the office. Even the envelopes were to be fastened to the back of the file folder for reference, if needed.

"There was no envelope," said Jimmy, reading Stephen's thoughts, "and we have already gone through our annual supply of file folders."

For Stephen that was the last straw. He gave up any further attempt to make things right and correct, and walked back to the residence where Dorothy and Alice were waiting luncheon.

"It's from the Shimmers," he said as he sat down to a four-course meal that required five people to prepare. Syani cooked, Kiamba served, Mbiti gathered the wood for the cooking fire, a Somali shopkeeper delivered the ingredients each morning to the cookhouse in the rear of the residence, and the clerk in Mr. Harris' office hand-printed the menu daily.

On instruction from Mrs. Hale, a complete dusting was carried out in the residence every day prior to serving this luncheon. This was done by Dorothy's own maid, Karegi, assisted by Sarah and Mary, two young women from the local Mission. Since Dorothy did not yet know the local language, or Kiswahili, the lingua franca, all messages and instructions from her were passed on through Stephen when he met briefly with the household staff each morning. At these meetings the staff noticed it was always, "Memsab wants this, and Memsab wants that." Alice helped as far as she could with the use of an English-Swahili phrasebook and supervised some of the housework. Even then, as Stephen looked across the table at Dorothy, he could see that for some reason she looked worn out, and he was at a loss to say why.

"The Shimmers?" asked Alice, looking up from the chicken broth, in which Syani had sprinkled a few tinned peas to create what was called on the menu card "Vegetible soup." With fine-chopped potatoes, the same soup was converted on Day Two into "Vichisois"; thickened with flour, it later appeared as "Creme chicken soup."

Syani seemed to be limited to seven recipes for the same thin stock.

"Seems they're on their way to Nairobi from the Coast," he read from the note, "and they've decided to break their journey here."

Dorothy sighed. "You've never met them, Stephen. Their son Franz is boring."

"No, I haven't met them, but I understand from Mr. Harris that they've bought the Palace Hotel in Nairobi."

"Makes a pleasant change," murmured Alice, who occupied her mornings hunting. Tired of chicken, and finding that Syani knew all about roasting yellownecks, the local version of pheasant, she had begun a serious effort to provide, as advised by Aunt Mary. Perhaps later, she thought, she'd be able to put wild pig on their table, but only if the warthogs became less elusive than they were at present.

"Always nice to have company," Stephen said, looking earnestly at his wife. "Especially now that you've gotten the household so well organized, dear."

Dorothy showed little interest. Her days were taken up with reading and writing long letters home. She poured her heart out to her mother, so much so that she seemed to have little else to say to Stephen or Alice. They both looked elsewhere after their brief encounters during meals. That constituted all the conversation that Dorothy felt up to, and it was no secret to everyone that she hated the place. The one thing she held fast to was the fact that Stephen's contract called for a full month's leave next year; once back in England it was almost certain from her attitude that she would never again leave home.

The Shimmers arrived within two days to find Alice desperate for a change in the routine, Stephen starved for contact with the outside world, and Dorothy ready to retreat to her bedroom at a moment's notice. The fact that their guests were German was of little importance to Stephen. In his haste to make them feel at home, he encouraged them to stay on a few extra days, despite several cold stares from Dorothy. Indeed, Albert and Elise were the perfect guests. They brought with them dried fish from the coast and fresh coconuts, with which Jimmy's wife made an excellent fish curry, enjoyed by Alice, the Hales and the Shimmers; the Harrises were not invited on orders from Dorothy. She did not approve of junior staff at her dinner table or any other social occasion.

The Shimmers also helped make up a foursome at bridge. A welcome change, thought Stephen, since Dorothy did not play cards.

The first few days of the Shimmer visit passed quickly. Franz went hunting with Alice but desisted after the first occasion. Alice felt he shot as if he were in a competition to kill as many animals as possible, while he expressed no interest in her expertise with the new bow and arrow she had been given by Mbiti. Stephen had more luck with Albert who listened politely to his idea of developing a market in Nairobi for produce from Machakos.

One day at dinner, a meal for which everyone dressed, Stephen in his dinner jacket had just taken his place at the head of the table and had started carving the bustard, a bird shot that day by Alice, when Franz mentioned that during his stay in Mombasa he had met the new railway superintendent for Nairobi.

"Oh?" said Stephen. "Who is it? Anyone we know?"

Kiamba had begun pouring champagne from a bottle the Shimmers had brought with them from Mombasa. He purposefully filled Stephen's champagne glass with water, since Stephen made a point of not drinking alcohol.

"Possibly," said Albert. "John Allen."

At the mention of Allen's name, Dorothy, suddenly pale, stood up and excused herself as she left the table.

The Shimmers looked at Stephen who shrugged his shoulders; he had not a clue as to why she had done that. Alice was of no help because she also got up and excused herself, murmuring that she had to look after her sister. The Shimmers and Stephen were left to finish their meal in silence, although Alice returned briefly in time for dessert. "Dorothy's resting," she said, but within a short while, she also went to bed, leaving the Shimmers and Stephen to their coffee while they watched Kiamba clear the table.

Finally, when it seemed he could put it off no longer, Stephen got up and retired for the evening, leaving the company to their own resources. His guests retreated to the privacy of a sitting room in the guest wing.

"It looks like a real opportunity," said Albert, pouring himself a cup of coffee from the tray set there by Kiamba.

"It is obvious, isn't it," said Elise.

"I don't follow," said Franz as he reached for the brandy decanter and poured himself a small drink. "What opportunity?"

"Elise has been talking to the local people," said his father. "They're disgruntled with their new DC. They say he has no initiative, no spunk. He leaves everything in the hands of Mr. Harris, who is ineffective. They are beginning to starve in the outlying areas and still he does nothing."

"Why is this important?"

"You're new to the country, Franz," said his mother. "Machakos is an important post, politically."

"It's also the largest garden community between Mombasa and Lake Victoria," said Albert. "The railroad will need supplies from here, but I detect some disappointment on the part of Mr. Hale. He's already been told they are going to bypass this place, so when the rains come he'll have the devil of a time getting produce into Nairobi to fill their needs."

"The only other area of production is that controlled by the Kikuyus, who are impossible to deal with, let alone approach," said Elise.

"So there is already some tension," said Franz.

"Yes, and it's not likely to diminish, unless Hale shows some initiative."

"That's why Kohl thinks we should start here."

"What would be our first move?"

"Two things," said Albert. "We must keep Hale off balance so the local people continue to be disgruntled, then we must make their situation worse."

"How?"

"A raid on the villages, perhaps."

"Slavers?" asked Franz.

"A good start," said his father looking approvingly at his son. "My Arab friends on the Coast would jump at the chance, especially if we pay their caravan costs. We might even be able to make a profit on it."

"And for now?"

"For now, we must play our cards carefully. That young man, McCann, said that Stephen most likely will be appointed provincial commissioner, in which case his authority will extend to Nairobi as well as here. Apparently he's an old friend of the high commissioner's; they served together in India."

"So, he'll go forward even if he doesn't do well in this post."

"That's the way they operate," said Elise. "Old school ties are more important than performance."

"And how do we start?" asked Franz.

"First, Elise and I have to continue on to Nairobi. I'll be in contact with my friends at the Coast from there. Meanwhile Franz, you must make friends with Hale."

"What about the wife? She's not going to survive in this place. She doesn't even speak the language."

"That's where Jakoby can help," said Elise, in reference to a Zulu servant that Kohl had sent to them in Nairobi. "She speaks English and Kiswahili. If she was working for her, we'd have a constant source of information about the Hale family."

Albert finished his coffee and got up. "Well, we have a busy day tomorrow; I'm going to bed."

Elise followed, and stopped at the door. "One last thing, Franz," she said as she glanced at the decanter.

Franz swirled his brandy before he drained his glass.

"Mr. McCann mentioned that Hale once had a problem with that."

At breakfast the next day, the Shimmers were inquisitive, especially as Dorothy had not appeared.

"She's not well," said Stephen. "I'm positive she's come down with something."

"Perhaps my wife should have a look," said Albert. "She used to be a nurse."

Stephen admitted Elise to the bedroom and she agreed Dorothy seemed to be suffering from some sort of infection. "It looks suspiciously like the early stages of blackwater fever," she said.

"And that's serious?" asked Stephen.

"Quite," said Elise. "If allowed to progress, it is lethal in the advanced stages."

"We heard a great deal about it in Mombasa," said Albert. "It's nothing to trifle with. If I were you, Stephen, I would get her into Nairobi just in case. We were told that the Railway has set up a hospital there and they have doctors who are experienced in such things."

"We could take her in our wagon today," said Elise. "It's only thirty-five miles. If we could borrow a mattress we could make a bed for her under the awning."

"And, if you'd like, Stephen," said Alice, "I could go with her."

She was anxious to see Nairobi.

"Well," said Stephen, resigned to the inevitable, "I suppose it would be for the best."

He felt guilty about shipping off his wife, but he had to admit it would ease the pressure he was feeling, though he was surprised at the alacrity with which Dorothy accepted the invitation. Her only concern seemed to be the fact that she had to leave behind her maid, Karegi. That was done with the understanding that Alice would be there to help, and that the Shimmers would provide her with a place in Nairobi while she recovered. Once those arrangements were resolved, she allowed them to help her into the wagon, a formidable vehicle brought to Kenya by South Africans; it required eighteen oxen to pull and several held in reserve as spares for the team.

From her vantage point under the awning, Dorothy looked back. She could not know it then, but that would be her last view of Machakos, spoilt only by the dust rising up from the oxen as they plodded forward. Then she fell back on the makeshift bed and slept while the wagon lurched this way and that. Unlike her arrival, witnessed by thousands, her departure was a quiet affair watched only by Stephen and Franz.

"I'll stay on for a few more days, if you don't mind, Stephen," said Franz. "They won't need me at the hotel immediately."

Stephen put his hand on Franz's shoulder and said, "You and your family are a godsend. I don't know how I'd get on without you."

That evening over coffee, Stephen had his first drink in over a year. After all, he told himself, he really enjoyed Franz's company and it's only a small drink.

"Excellent French brandy," he said.

"God knows, you deserve it," said his new friend.

Three hours later, he could hardly walk toward his empty bedroom. Along the way, he tripped over Franz's foot, which somehow found itself in his path. Franz laughed at his friend's clumsiness, but offered no assistance as Stephen crawled the remainder of the way into his room where he curled up on a zebra skin rug. He slept the rest of the night on the floor.

3

"What's all this about John Allen?" asked Jenny.

"You've seen him," Alice replied, "what do you think?"

Jenny was a large, dark-haired Irish woman, married to an army officer, Captain Dan Lloyd. She passed her time with Alice while she waited for her husband's orders to come through. He had recently been given command of the Naivasha garrison and within a month or two they would move out there.

"You're right, we did meet him in Mombasa, and he's quite handsome. But Dan thinks he's a martinet. Very full of himself, he says, and he also thinks he's too short for an army man."

"Dorothy was engaged to him."

"No!"

"Exactly. And it was more than an engagement—she was ready to throw herself at his feet, but that apparently is nothing new to Allen. I've been told that lots of women are attracted to him like that."

"But what happened?"

"He walked off. Left a note saying he had business elsewhere and that was that. She was devastated. Never said another word about it until we heard he had arrived in Kenya. Now she writes to him in Mombasa, daily."

"And?"

"He replies at length."

"What about her?"

"No change, but it's obvious she enjoys the role of the invalid. I can't complain because it's no problem for me, as long as we have the Zulu woman here."

"You mean Jakoby. What a stroke of luck. I'm surprised the

Shimmers could spare her." Jenny sat across from her with a cup of tea.

"She does everything," said Alice, "and I suppose looking after a sick room is child's play compared to what she would face at the hotel."

"I told you it would work out," said Jenny. She was the one who suggested Alice should rent a house rather than stay at the hotel. "And Roger?"

"Off with the Kikuyus again. He thinks there's a fortune to be made out there."

"And good luck to him," said Jenny. "I've yet to hear of anyone making a fortune in this God-forsaken place. And there seems precious little money to be made here anyway, outside of the ivory trade."

"I think he just enjoys the excitement." Alice got up and stood by the window. "Would someone like Roger ever settle down, Jenny, do you think?"

"Of course he will," she said, laughing at her young friend. "Dan was the same way. A few years in the army changed him completely. Roger's a very confident lad, and he has a goal; that's exactly what you want. Maybe it's Roger who should be giving advice to Stephen."

"I hardly think he'd ever do that. He hates him so."

"And it's Stephen who'll never change, especially at his age," said Jenny. "I see he's still out in Machakos."

"Can you blame him?"

"No, Dorothy being the way she is. I had the impression anyway that Stephen's the weak one. I can see why she'd marry him, just to have someone to walk all over."

Alice said nothing. From where she stood, she could see across the room through an open door to Dorothy's room. It had been months since they had arrived; the railway doctor had yet to determine Dorothy's exact illness and she seldom left her bed. Today she was reading to Jakoby. A strange sight, the Zulu woman at her knee was older than she was.

Alice turned and looked out the window at some children playing in the courtyard not far from the schoolhouse, the place where she thought she might teach. Here in Nairobi every open spot of ground, every back alley, the road behind the school and every space between the huts within the town were used by the children for their games, most of which appeared to be chase—chase the raffia ball, chase the donkeys, chase the crows, and failing that, chase each other.

Maybe it's true what they say, she thought, as she watched them, there is no real happiness in this dark world, only moments of contentment. And, if that's the case, these children are among the happiest people I'll ever know.

She turned back to Jenny. "When my Aunt Mary arrived in West Africa, she began immediately collecting specimens of birds and insects for the British Museum. She explored the country, traveled all over, wrote two wonderful books, and what have I done? Nothing."

"Oh, I wouldn't say that. Remember, you haven't been here very long, and as you yourself said, your aunt was older and more experienced than you. We've all heard of your exploits from Mr. Jeffrey. He swears there's not another who can hunt like you, darling."

Alice laughed. J.O. was very supportive, but he thought she should come away from Nairobi. It was his impression that the place was going to become a meaner, wilder town once the railroad arrived, and Dan, Jenny's husband, agreed. "Damn it, Alice, you belong in the open air," he said. "Get married and move out to the countryside with us."

The constant influx of people and absence of drainage had turned the center of Nairobi into a miasma surrounded by dry land. Often newly arriving settlers, after tramping for weeks uphill along dry, dusty roads, were taken by surprise to finally reach this mile-high town with its cool night air, and suddenly lose a boot in a mire of black mud, mud that smelled suspiciously of raw sewage.

From her house, it was a decent walk to the post office, a temporary facility housed in a tent on a plot beside the railway station, which was still in the early stages of construction. She went every day for the exercise and to hear the news or see the developments. Buildings seemed to appear overnight. She hoped that the roads and walkways now being laid down would survive the rains, when they finally did come, as surely they must. The long rains had never appeared; now the short rains were overdue and by common consent the drought had lasted long enough.

The cloudless sky in the morning simply meant to Alice that the day would be another scorcher, which made her think of going out to Naivasha where the lake had a cooling effect, and the large fever trees cast their pleasant shade from dawn to dusk.

At least, she thought, with a sense of thanksgiving, she wasn't bedridden, or like many before her, broken by the life here. As she walked toward the mail tent, she reflected on such things and, with a sense of rue, recognized that she was getting on in years.

She'd be almost nineteen at year's end; it was time to forge her own destiny.

Little did she realize as she walked to town that within an hour of that thought her feeling of security and confidence would be shattered, as surely as if she had been bludgeoned by a Kikuyu battle club. A small envelope edged in black would be the instrument, as just after collecting the mail she had to be helped back up the hill.

My Dear Alice,

With heavy heart I report the demise of your father, George McConnell. Beloved husband and a man of stalwart and steady character, he is now dead of heart failure. I cannot tell you in so few words my feelings toward him. Truly we were in love and perfectly matched. How else can I convey my feeling and great sympathy for you and my loss?

He died peacefully in the early part of the day just prior to his lunch, to which he looked forward with anticipation, as I had prepared his favorite soup, potage de petit pois.

Realizing that it would be impossible for you to reach Maidstone in time for the burial, I have proceeded with the formalities. He will be buried as he wished, in the local church with his grave and headstone aligned in confluence with the Survey of England benchmark.

What a man your father was. He will be sorely missed by ev-

eryone, especially myself. Autumn is now upon us here; I presume you have by now forgotten such things, and I hope it remains for you a bright and sunny world. I naturally send my heartfelt thanks for the help you have provided Dorothy in her need.

I will never forget that.

In your own way you are so much like him; in truth you are your father's daughter.

I will write later with details of a financial nature and beg you, when convenient, pass my regards to your sister,
Mme. Rosmé McConnell (née Curtis)

Not often in her young life had she been so thwarted by fate; she had assumed her father would live forever. David McCann, who was often now in Nairobi, was on his way to her house when he spotted her slumped on a crate near the mail tent. He rushed to her aid.

"Alice, what's wrong?"

She was sobbing and distraught. He escorted her home and she lay in bed the rest of the day. The letter, stained with tears, rested by her side as her sorrow gradually became clouded with guilt and depression and remained that way for weeks.

Later that month she recovered enough to ride out to visit with the Lloyds in Naivasha.

They had settled in their army quarters on the banks of the freshwater lake, and often they'd go on a hunting safari south of there. They'd sit in front of the campfire embers in the mornings having safari breakfasts, strong tea with tinned milk and extra sugar, along with camp bread from the previous night's dinner.

From their tent on a slight rise in open country they could see the horizon in all directions. It was after five o'clock one morning when they set out. A streak of yellow light appeared in the east and widened quickly to light the scene. They were miles from any habitation, on an enormous plain with large herds of wild animals snorting and wheeling in all directions. Mornings like this in Africa, Alice knew, would always affect her.

The dawn softened the harsh, sometimes bizarre African landscape and created a velvet world of dreamy images, the kind of landscape you could only see in the "view" paintings that the wealthy flocked to buy in Europe. Within an hour, the scene would sharpen and everything would come into brilliant focus. In the cool morning air the animals would be there, puffs of their breath visible miles away. Further south, you could almost touch the snowy peak of Kilimanjaro. It seemed that close.

Later in the day, the same view would be lit by the sun overhead—a hot, full light like a stage illuminated by arc lamps that would bring pain to your eyes and face, so that by late afternoon you'd be squinting and staggering as the glare and heat overpowered your senses. This was followed by the cool early evening when the sun dropped in the sky, silhouetting the trees and animals on the ridges before it disappeared with a spectacular burst of glory.

That day she had been slow in starting and the animals had dispersed as the late morning heat built up on the plains. The impala already were seeking out the shade of isolated thorn bushes. These deer-like animals preferred the trees that grew on top of small termite mounds. Here the male could stand enjoying the shade and commanding a large field of view. For Alice it was one of the few good things about impala behavior. It made them easy to spot from a distance, but she and her party had to work harder to get into shooting position downwind without being spotted.

Out of the hundreds of animals they could see standing on the scattered mounds, they selected one male with a cluster of five females resting in the shade, flicking flies from their rumps with their tails. It was a perfect setting, but they now had to scramble across a thorn-covered ravine and move silently up the other end until they were just above the animals in order to get a clear shot.

On these safaris, everyone deferred to Alice because she enjoyed getting in the first shot. She now had a rifle, a 7mm Mauser, one of a pair that she and Dan had bought from J.O. Alice in spite of her hunting experience was never as confident of her shooting abilities as she would like to be. Closeness was as imperative as concentration. She was in the lead and carefully tracking the impala when a rustling in the bushes broke her concentration. She turned, ready to glare at Jenny, Dan or the trackers, but her eyes widened as she saw the dark, slithering mass of two very long, thin snakes, coiled around one another tangled into a large wriggling ball.

"A ball of death," Dan muttered behind her. Her first thought, her first instinct, was to run, to retreat up the ravine behind her and forget the impala. She hated snakes, and it was almost impossible to hit one with a rifle bullet. She needed her aunt's shotgun, which she had left with Jenny further back on the trail. Particularly frightening was the thought of what this meant out here in the bush in this climate. Here you could be certain the result of a single bite would be a festering, swollen limb, followed by a painful death. Frustrated, she admitted that she had insisted everyone follow behind her. She was trapped by her own reputation and she knew she had to stay and face whatever animal, big or small. She couldn't turn around or she would be damned.

From what she could see, these were no ordinary snakes. They looked like *mambas*, a deadly species, very aggressive on any occasion, but even more so if their retreat was blocked. They would without hesitation chase after a man or an animal, their cobra-type venom capable of stopping anything but an elephant dead in its tracks. She saw she had no choice. One of the coiled snakes had reared its head, having spotted her. She raised the rifle to her shoulder and shot as straight as she could. As the ringing of the report diminished in her ears she could see the snake's head fall back to one side.

"My God," she murmured as she bit her lip and racked the bolt forward, hoping the shaking in her knees would calm so she could aim as the second snake uncoiled. She'd been told by J.O. that two drops of venom was a fatal dose, and that each fang had a capacity of twenty drops. "If they bit you directly on a vein you'd mercifully never wake up again," he had said.

Then one of the Wakamba trackers rushed past her yelling. "*Nimashika sasa*. I'll catch him now."

As Alice watched in amazement, he simply brushed aside the dead snake, reached into the bush and grabbed the second one, which was wriggling free and had bared its fangs; it was angry and very much alive. Then the other tracker was there in a flash with a panga to slice off the head. She felt like a fool standing, waiting with a loaded rifle, while the two of them held up the still wriggling, headless trophies. They laid them out on the ground and measured them. As she suspected, each was over nine feet long, and there was no mistaking the dark olive color and fangs at the front of the snakes' mouth.

"Mambas. I'd never have believed it!" Dan exclaimed, as they were sitting at their camp table eating dinner that evening. Dan motioned with his fork to the snakeskins sewn onto light frames, stretched and drying by their tent. "Look at them. How the hell could they take one with their bare hands?"

Their safari cook explained, "These people are well trained in the old medicine." He was referring to the Wakamba. He said, "They know what can be done with the special *dawa*, the juices of plants and animals. Some are powerful medicines, but some are poisons, what we call *sumu*."

"I'll bet when you hunt with only a bow and arrow, the way they do," said Dan, "you need help from every source."

"Ah," said the cook, "a good sumu for the arrow tip is worth everything to them. This will bring down the animal, but you must be careful. The Wakamba, of all people, not only know how to kill with sumu, but they also know how to protect themselves against it with dawa. Today you saw that man pick up a snake without fear. How can he do this? I think he was cured of a snakebite when still a child. A witch doctor in his village may have used a poultice of some strong herbs. Now he takes these same dried plants with him whenever he goes. I carry some myself."

Not long after this, they arrived back on the shores of the lake that was fringed by papyrus, with thousands of ducks and wildfowl nesting on its shores. Leaving their safari equipment and pack animals in the army compound near the Lloyd's house, they changed into swimming costumes and went for a swim in the clear cool water. Finally, Alice thought, she was free of the drought. Then she realized that she had also laid to rest the anguish of her father's death.

Lugard, the diminutive explorer who followed the larger-than-life explorers such as Livingstone and Stanley, is perhaps best described as the architect of the British Empire in Africa. After he passed through Naivasha, the British Army had followed in his path, and with unerring judgment had picked the ideal position from which to exert control over the region between Kikuyuland and Masailand. From that vantage point they could strengthen colonial law across the country and prove that once more the concept of divide and conquer still worked. The force needed to maintain such order never exceeded more than a few hundred men at any one time; however, this forward position on the main caravan route left them with a problem. They were solely dependent on shipments from either the Coast or Lake Victoria. Although situated on the shores of Lake Naivasha, a large freshwater lake, where water and game were plentiful, and, strangely, fish were absent, no staples were grown locally and only a limited number of green vegetables were to be had.

Sergeant Ross, who had been all morning drilling a platoon on the dusty parade ground in front of the garrison, stopped what he was doing and wearily eyed the corporal of the guard who kept pointing toward the road above the camp.

A small caravan was coming down from the hills above. The two soldiers stood staring at it. It was different from any caravan they had ever seen. Roger Newcome rode out in front of a column of ten donkeys and some Swahili porters, accompanied by twenty Kikuyus dressed in full warrior regalia with their spears and shields. Following behind was a platoon of battle-scarred Africans in ancient uniforms with muskets, marching to the beat of a drummer boy who kept up a steady "tharump, tharump, tharump," and just behind Roger came Mutua with a homemade Union Jack and an American flag snapping in the breeze.

4

Alice's Diary (Stanhope, Cheshire, 1945):

As I look back all those years to that Saturday I was standing on the veranda of the officers' mess, I remember that it was, and still is, a marvelous lake, with all those tropical birds flying around and crying out in the still of the early morning. And late in the afternoon, the enormous volcanic hill in the background above the lake, Mt. Longonot, used to turn purplish blue-red in the afternoon and would stay that way until the sun set.

We'd just settled in for our first sundowner. Jenny and I had pink gins; some officer friends were sipping brandy and water. A sergeant came rushing up to us to report an armed party approaching, and we all jumped up and looked out across the parade field and saw Roger's "army." We couldn't help but laugh, I mean, he was so serious, leading this band of Africans, porters and donkeys....

Two officers were standing near the railing. One, Capt. Bobby Curtis, a short, chubby, red-faced man, was examining the caravan through field glasses; he scowled at the two women behind him, and said, "It's quite funny all right, but Dan, notice they keep in step!"

"You're right. Damned if he hasn't trained them up. Bloody hell, who is he?"

"He's an old friend of Stephen's," said Alice. "He's a trader, caravan master and hunter of some repute, and an American," she added for Jenny's benefit and winked at her.

Roger dismounted and saluted Sgt. Ross. "Hope I'm not too late to catch your quartermaster. I've some supplies for him; is he here?"

"He's around back, I'll show you. When you're finished, the captain wants to see you."

That evening several officers, their wives and guests were having drinks in the officer's lounge when Roger walked in, clean-shaven, tanned and in a freshly laundered safari jacket.

"Mr. Newcome, I'm Capt. Lloyd and this is my wife, Jenny. I presume you'll join us for dinner?"

"A pleasure," said Roger, as he spotted Alice, "and do I see a familiar face?"

"Roger, what a surprise. How are you?"

"Very well, and you? Aren't you a long way from Machakos?"

"I live in Nairobi now. Dorothy has become quite sick. I had to move there to take care of her. I'm just down here for a week. Meet Dorothy's uncle, Capt. Bobby Curtis. He's on temporary duty from India. He's got himself posted to Mombasa and I'm showing him the sights."

"Well sir," said Bobby, "you'll have to tell us about these Kikuyu. I gather they're as fierce a tribe as you'll ever meet. Rather like the Pathans in my old neck of the woods, eh?" They walked to a table where a buffet dinner was waiting. Bobby carried a glass of neat brandy, obviously no stranger to the bottle.

"You know, around here we see an awful lot of the Masai," said Dan. "They've spread out all over the central area, and I've often wondered why they never annexed the land between themselves and the Somalis. I mean, how have the Kikuyu survived all this time faced with these two powerful groups?"

Roger thought for a minute before responding. "They've developed a real ability with spears and bow and arrows, so I guess that equalizes their fighting skills with the Masai and Wakamba in open terrain. And I suppose it's possible to make war against Kikuyus in open grassland if you watch your flanks and move quickly. They don't keep their livestock in the open; it's mostly kept beyond the forest fringe, but still the Masai know it's dangerous."

"Why?" asked Dan.

"Because they've developed an extraordinary weapon," he looked around and saw he had the attention of everyone at the table as he continued. "Mantraps. They use them inside the forest and any bushy terrain along the major trails. They're deep, unmarked and well disguised, so once you've entered the forest you're in a different world, a ghost world, a place where every step could be your last, and it scares the hell out of people."

"Good Lord," said Jenny.

"And the awful thing is," continued Roger, "if you fall into one, a swift death is not guaranteed. It's often painful and drawn out. It depends a great deal on the number of organs pierced and the strength of the poison they smear on the sharpened stakes."

"I can see where that would put anyone off," said Alice.

"Well," said Roger, "I know for certain the Masai won't go beyond the fringe. The minute the Kikuyu slide into the forest, they back off. They hate the idea of warfare based on uncertainty, especially with such gruesome side effects. You only have to hear the cries of someone caught in one of them to understand what I mean."

"And yet, you get on with these fierce savages," said Capt. Bobby. "You definitely seem to have befriended them."

"I've struck a bargain with them. I train their militia and they provide trade goods. So far it's worked out quite well. And how's the shooting here, Alice?" He turned and smiled at her. "Bag any more man-eaters?"

That brought a barrage of questions from the assembled guests, and after dinner the district commissioner, Mr. Cole, said he was quite impressed.

"Haven't we met before?" he asked.

"Yes, sir," replied Roger. "Don't you recall? You kindly gave me permission to trade with the Kikuyus the last time I passed through here."

"Oh, yes, now I remember," said Mr. Cole, a quizzical expression on his face.

After dinner they sat on the verandah.

"So, what happened after I left?"

"Nothing much," said Alice. "Some bad news from England. My father died suddenly."

"I'm sorry to hear about that. What are you going to do now?"

"Nothing yet. I'm enjoying life out here. I've thought about teaching in Nairobi, but I'm not certain about that or anything, really."

"And what's happening in Nairobi?" asked Roger.

"It's become quite a boom town. The railroad is going forward and the place has gone from a swampy patch to a sprawling shantytown overnight. And the social life has really improved," she said. "We now have a second hotel, a racecourse and a lending library besides two clubs and the health depot that serves as a hospital."

"I'm impressed," said Roger. "I have to go back up to the hills for about a month, but I'll be coming down to Nairobi after that. Perhaps we can meet there?"

At that point, Capt. Bobby Curtis strolled up.

"Time for our round of whist, Alice. Do you play, Mr. Newcome?"

"Not well, but I try."

In Muthuri's Hut

So you're back from Naivasha? Kimani says you did well, and now you want to expand.

Good.

You want to trade for more food.

He says you also want to meet what you call the "chiefs."

Why do I shake my head? Because the word is foreign to us.

At first we had no chiefs, until the British began calling any headman or any important Kikuyu by this title. Why do they do that?

Ah, you say it's because they were taken by the idea of chiefs. It is a throwback to the days in West Africa where the term had some meaning. I see. That accounts for it. But here you must refer to them as mutha-

maki. They act as leaders, although the real power is still in the councils, the assemblies of elders who represent us.

Us? Yes, the family, village, district or ridge, like the one we live on here. In the early morning, as you look out across our land you will see what I mean. You see the hilltops, the ridges. They stick up above the mist and the morning fog, like islands.

Yes, like "kingdoms with castles on the hills," the ones they showed us in the storybooks in the Mission. Only here we have no kings and no castles. We have ridge councils and tribal councils, the kiama that allow each elder to represent the views of a friend, relative or villager, and the Court of Nine, headed by the ndundu. This Court of Nine tries the most serious criminal cases and also hears appeals from the lower councils.

How do we enforce the law and the rulings of the ndundu?

Mostly by oath-taking. This is the real reason why we can control crime here.

Hah! You find that hard to believe?

Here oaths are taken voluntarily by individuals, by males, but they reflect on the whole family, or group of families, so it's a serious business. It's never undertaken lightly. The level or form of the oath depends on the nature of the crime, from simple lies through theft and murder.

This last is the most serious. It might require the ultimate oath, the blood oath.

Why is that so fearful? Because the wrath of the supernatural is called upon. God will strike down anyone telling a lie during the taking of a blood oath.

Ah, now you understand.

You have seen our respect and fear of magic, so you realize it must be a very strong person, and a courageous one, to step forward and put himself and his family group under the sword.

The first family to suffer a death after taking this oath is believed to have perjured itself.

On that basis the council can reverse a previous decision.

So, Bwana Roger, no matter what they tell you about us, please remember, we already have a government.

I will also say that in the old days we had less crime, less drunkenness, no prostitutes and everyone was cared for in some way. The young and old were treated with respect. You can't say that today. I have seen no improvement because of what you call "colonial law."

While you were away I have been thinking more about this, especially oathing. I think such things will remain, even as the strength of our people is wasted. I watch the settlers and the Railway putting our young people to work, and I see some are forced even to become house servants, to live under your roof.

But you must let your fellow wazungu know that their rules do not apply here. Here oathing remains the unwritten law of the land.

Why is that important?

Someday it will have you begging for mercy.

Like the lowly insect that can eat away at the inside of a wooden beam and with time bring the building down upon your head, yes, Roger, you smile, but someday I will have a good laugh, when they call on me to help pull you out from under your own home.

Mark my words, that is what the White Fathers used to say.

Mark my words.

5

Rain of shit," mumbled Jock Saylor as his head lolled back and a loud snore issued briefly from his enormous nose, signifying that he had finally succumbed for the rest of the afternoon. Jock's bosom companion and fellow cattle farmer, Ben Fletcher, was already lying comatose on the couch. Roger sat with them in the largest of the cane chairs, a mug of tea at his elbow, watching Jock's face—a study in havoc wrought by excess drink, diseased liver and chronic malaria. In what was one of the newest buildings in Nairobi, there was precious little else to look at other than Jock's face.

The dismal room was equipped with a wooden bar that at midday had to be lit by candles now that the windows had been shuttered. Year-old newspapers and a few magazines lay on a table along with a sad collection of tattered novels. The inevitable animal heads decorated the rough plaster walls, but these were in pathetic condition; the hair had begun falling out and insects had begun eating away at the exposed hide. It was altogether a grim reminder of what the local environment could do over a short period of time to the living and the dead.

Roger and J.O. were both members of this, the newest private "club," a rough-planked building. They called it the Settlers' Club and it had few amenities—a bunkhouse and kitchen—but it had been built on a small hill above the swampy town center and was dry.

They were having tea in their common room, which also served the seven other members as a dining room, library and bar. It provided a meeting place for traders, settlers and hunters during their brief sojourns in Nairobi, a haven in which they found refuge from the missionaries, civil servants, railway workers and Africans, all of whom had become as numerous and pestilential as the swarms of locusts that had recently descended on Nairobi making everyone temporary prisoners in their own homes.

He and J.O. passed the time reading and drinking strong tea, anything to keep away from the daytime gin and whiskey that was consumed by the others in excess. It was bad enough the swarms had choked off the sunlight, but now it was impossible to walk around outside without slipping and sliding on the masses of crushed, oily, insect bodies. They crawled and hopped about on the walkways and roads, as thick on the ground as in the air. Worse yet was the sound on the tin roof. For the past two days they had been subjected to a steady patter of locust feces, millions of tiny hard brown pellets that they voided as they flew overhead. There was nothing to do but wait it out. Even as smaller swarms peeled off to briefly ravage nearby cornfields, the swarms were kept at full complement; others would rejoin the main body as it circled the town. Eventually they would leave on their journey north to their breeding grounds. Their next stop would be Ukambaa where they would have lean pickings.

"Roger, me lad, this town suffers from its own production," Jock had pointed out earlier before passing into his present state, "everything a man could want in the way of food. Milk, chickens, eggs, flour, it can all be grown here. I never ate so well in me life, so ya can't blame the little bastards. They want a good meal too, don't they? Ye may think I'm daft, but I heard them last night eatin' the patch of grass behind the club, not a blade left this mornin'. Roger, did ya hear me, man, I heard them actual eatin'. Thousands of tiny mouths goin' at it."

Roger had to agree; he had never seen anything like it. Just a few days earlier the air had turned black on his way down from the hills. He had seen the Kikuyus out in their fields, lighting fires, beating drums and waving rags.

As if to make amends for all of these impositions, this morning his cook, Ali, who had come with him to town along with Mutua, brought him a plateful of them, fried up as a savory!

"Lightly fried with a bit of salt and pepper, will do it," according to Jock. "They've a nutty flavor, not bad with a large gin and tonic."

Roger recalled that on an earlier trip to Lake Victoria he had suffered through an infestation of lake flies, millions of midge-like creatures that emerged at night, clouds so thick you could choke on them, followed by termites in profusion on the wing. It never stops, he thought, and the only escape, according to Jock, was marriage or death. Which reminded him of another sign of progress—a proper cemetery, newly laid out, where several of Jock's friends had already found a home in the ultimate Nairobi "club."

"I have my eye on a piece of land that'd make a great hunting reserve," said J.O., ignoring Jock's snuffles and snores. "But I want some other opinions before I get involved. I'm going out there on safari next week with some friends."

"Who's going with you?"

"Tom and Edna Webb. They're from the Thika area."

"I know them. They've talked with me about setting up a trading center out there. Where's the land?"

"Near their farm, the other side of Ol Donyo Sabuk. It belongs to Lord Stanford, but he's willing to sell. We'll be camping in some very nice places out there and Tom knows the area. I'd like you to come along."

"Certainly, count me in, anything to get away from this," he motioned with his hand. "Also, what about asking our old hunting partner, Alice?"

"Ah, now there's an idea," said J.O. "Haven't seen her in a while. Why don't you pop over and ask her. Tell her I'll lay on a bottle of champagne and provide a warm camp bath if she comes along."

The highlight of the trip was Alice's hunting bow. She had developed the eye and timing to do it well and whenever she brought down an animal for the pot, Minyama and all the trackers had to laugh and shake their heads.

"Here is a mzungu who can hunt like us."

"Where would these others be without their rifles and cartridges?" was a question they often asked themselves, because it pointed to an important distinction between the white hunter and the African.

"You see too, she is turning darker with the sun," said Minyama.

"I think she's an African underneath," said Ali.

They gathered each evening around the campfire after supper, where on the second night Brian paid them a surprise visit. Thinner than ever, his face, even when relaxed, betrayed the constant mischief in his mind. His glinting eyes and lithe frame now resembled some of his personal guards, the dozen Somali warriors who sat with the trackers and gun bearers just outside the circle of light.

"*Habari yako*," he said, greeting everyone as he sauntered into their camp. He looked, smelled and moved like some sort of wild animal, Alice thought, as he accepted a seat by her side and introduced himself to the group. He sat there on the edge of his camp chair sipping a drink like a leopard at some strange waterhole.

She looked across at Roger. His red hair glowed in the light of the fire. Intently watching every move of Brian, Roger reminded her of a hedgehog suspiciously peering out from its burrow, ever defensive, ever watchful and prickly.

Brian carried with him a western-style bow and a quiver full of English arrows. "I heard some of you like to hunt this way," he said. "Thought you might be able to use them. Carried them all the way out here and never touched them."

They all pointed to Alice. "She's the only one crazy enough to do a thing like that," said Tom. "The rest of us prefer rifles."

"Where did you learn to hunt?" he asked, as he placed the bow and arrows at her feet.

"Mostly I'm self-taught, like my aunt, Mary Kingsley."

Brian looked at her with interest. "I met her once. She gave a lecture in Manchester. Had nothing good to say about our policies toward Africans. I had to agree, that attitude will get us nowhere."

"You mean the concept of treating them as snot-nosed children," said Roger in a louder than usual voice from across the fire.

"Up to no good every time you turn your back."

Brian laughed. "From your accent I take it you're American."

Tom, sitting next to Roger, disagreed. "There's nothing wrong with the way they're treated. You have to exert control and use a firm hand. You can't work the land out here and be gentle-hearted at the same time. It doesn't work."

"Like slaves on American cotton plantations," said Edna with a trace of malice in her voice as she stared at Roger. "Aren't they still treated that way even though they're free?"

"Whatever," said Brian as he looked at Edna, "I hate politics." He unfolded his lean, tanned body as he got up. "I only came over to extend an invitation to you all. Anytime you're in the area just pop in to my lodge. Edna and Tom know the drill: first principle is don't stand on formality." He turned to Alice and smiled at her. "I have a feeling you'd be interested in what I'm doing out here. I know your aunt would."

"And that is?"

"I'm raising improved breeds of cattle. I'm convinced I can do it using natural methods and still make a decent living off it. The idea is to provide a method for Africans to improve their lot." He stared at her. Their eyes locked for a moment until he turned away, and with a wave of his hand he sauntered off into the night followed by his Somali escort.

After he left, J.O. said, "Now there's a type you don't often see. Very independent and able to survive on his own wits if need be."

"But still, he craves the company of his own, eh?" Tom pointed out.

"We're all like that," said Roger. "Aren't we?"

Everyone stared at him. His reputation as a loner was well known.

"Well," said Alice in support, "aren't we?" She looked at them. "We all want other whites around. Friends we can turn to, or at least people we know who will sympathize in case we ever do need them."

In the silence that followed, they could hear the crackling of the wood burning in the campfire. Then suddenly there was an immense shower of sparks as Minyama appeared out of the darkness and threw an armload of wood on the fire.

"It helps to be married," said Edna as she smiled at her husband, Tom.

Alice's Diary (Stanhope, Cheshire, 1945)

...For all of us that was the best part of living in Africa, really, the safaris. Otherwise, making a living out there was not easy. But, no matter who you were in those days, you soon learned how dependent you were on your African staff. The night came down fast and dark and the solitude was complete. It's still like that just a short drive outside of Nairobi. On your own, a white person in a sea of black people and wild animals, you become very lonely, as quickly now as you did back then.

In such situations, loneliness becomes a dangerous school in which to find out who you are and where your life is going. Back home in the crowded pub or family parlor you wouldn't think of that. But out there, if you let the thought of Home feed on you, it was easy to turn to the bottle to relieve yourself of depression. The next morning in camp, or remote farmhouse, or outback station, you'd be taking it out on your cook or houseboy. But men like Roger and Brian, two people as different as fire and ice, showed everyone it didn't have to be that way, because they were both willing to work at the level of the man in the field.

Did they deserve the Kikuyus and Somalis? Did the Kikuyus and Somalis deserve them? I would say they all got what they wanted.

Roger helped the Kikuyus get into a wider field of business, and they never looked back. Brian showed his herders how to cope with old problems, applying new solutions, and they both showed everyone in the Colony that there was a new order, that you had to deal with the black man as an entrepreneur, as someone you were going to need sooner or later. They were in the minority then, but they had already learned their lesson. I'm afraid even now, almost fifty years later, many will still have to learn it the hard way, but learn it they will....

The slopes of Ol Donyo Sabuk rose up behind Alice as she and Roger sat under a large, yellow-barked fever tree watching the light change and the shadows lengthen. Before them stretched the wide panorama of the plains, broken only by the trees on the slopes of the hills beyond. Roger had just shown her the small ant holes made in the galls on branches of a whistling thorn acacia nearby.

"They're not as fierce as the safari ants, and they have a different way of life," he explained, as they watched the ants going in and out of the galls. "They're very protective of the plant. They defend it against grazing animals and they sting anything that tries to eat the leaves or branches."

"I've read about them someplace," said Alice. "The galls are hollow and make a whistling sound as the air moves across the ant holes."

"Yes," said Roger. "Listen. Be quiet, and listen carefully. Can you hear it?" They sat as quietly as they could. Her senses concentrating and heightening with every moment, a peaceful feeling came over her. She could not resist his arm around her waist, as he leaned toward her and kissed her. "I love you, Alice," he said. "I love you as I've never loved anyone in my whole life. Marry me."

The huge, low, bright red sun dazzled briefly under the cloud line as dusk descended.

"I can't marry yet, Roger," she said as she moved aside his arm and lay back on the grass under the tree. "I'm not ready for that. I'm sorry."

He turned away disappointed as he searched his mind for the cause. "Are you upset that I don't get along with Stephen and Dorothy?"

"It's not that," she smiled. "It's not you. It's me. I'm just not ready to settle down."

"But would it help if I made friends with him?"

She didn't answer. Instead she looked at the galls and the ants going about their business, every one of them intent and non-swerving in their purpose. She thought of Dorothy in her sick bed. She thought of leopards, hedgehogs and more ants. She thought of just about everything and anything but marriage.

Then she said, "I've got something to do, something my Aunt would approve of."

He watched her.

"Dorothy recently had a letter from Stephen about what's going on in Ukambaa. People are dying like flies out there. I'm going back to see if I can help."

6

It was a grim but certain reality. Whenever drought and famine took hold, the railroad thrived. Wet weather brought soft soil, mind-boggling mud, swollen rivers, insects and disease, all anathema to laying track; only in dry weather did the rail-laying crews make their best progress. They had already advanced to the station named in memory of the man-eaters that had now hopefully passed into history, Simba station at mile 226; it meant "lion" in Swahili.

Progress to date had come at a high cost; thousands of transport animals and hundreds of men were dead from tsetse fly. The work animals had been so depleted that headquarters was forced to order four steam tractors to help, and they proved to be wonderful machines. Each weighed eight tons. Fired by wood and equipped with large-diameter traction wheels made of iron, they could force their own path through the bundu ahead of the rail line and they were immune to tsetse fly. The soil because of the drought was now rock hard, almost a perfect pavement on which these tractors could move easily back and forth, as they shunted everything from the supply trains to railhead. Rails, tools, crossties, gravel and water moved quickly to the site along with food, of which the crews at railhead now required twenty-one tons daily.

Well-fed, protected from lions and free of wet season insects, the crews were capable of putting down track at a rate of a half-mile a day with a full mile often possible. They also had a new supervisor, John Allen, who had traveled up from Mombasa on his way to his post. He was scheduled to take over once they reached Nairobi. The station there, a formidable stone and corrugated iron building, was under construction, supervised by Col. Patterson, the same man who had built the bridge at Tsavo after clearing the area of man-eaters, following the early attempts by J.O. and his helpers at Voi.

John Allen, a captain in the Indian Army, had been brought on because of his background in engineering and his proven ability in managing men under difficult circumstances. He was told by George Whitehouse, the chief engineer and general manager of the Railway in Mombasa, to spend some time at railhead in Simba to get to know the operation. For this reason he had been camping out at that station with his assistant, Bill Bagley.

To the male eye, Allen, a small man in his thirties, was at best an unimposing figure, made more so by his habit of wearing linen suits, the jackets of which looked stretched, baggy and wrinkled all at once. His trousers had double creases, the curse of a houseboy who could not or would not iron them correctly. Allen seemingly could care less. His topi appeared too large for his small frame. According to the new stationmaster, an Anglo-Indian who knew a great deal about pith or solar helmets, "He stuffs the inside band with paper to keep it from falling over his eyes." Allen's attitude was born of confidence, which in turn came from his place in the world; he was the fourth son of a Marquess, and a poor one at that, which was why he worked hard at his job. Like Brian, he declined titles; instead of "Lord" he liked to be known as "John." His reputation as a lady-killer preceded him and puzzled those same men who shook their heads at his clothes and general appearance. "Why?" "How?" they would ask themselves, as they stared at him, trying to ferret out the secret of his success.

"It's all in his eyes," confessed one smitten woman in Mombasa. Too late, she had realized those clear blue eyes were not only sympathetic, but also hypnotic in their intensity.

"Or is it his soft blonde hair?"

"Or his face?" from another, who had personally touched those smooth, handsome cheeks, cheeks that had been shaved close and pampered with a faintly scented soap, for a purpose. "Close to heaven, like a baby's skin."

"And his hands, Sophie. For God's sake, don't let him get within a foot of you or you're a lost woman."

During Allen's fourth week at Simba, the stationmaster passed him a telegram alerting him to a courtesy visit from the governor of German East Africa. The governor duly arrived on the chief engineer's special train with Mr. Whitehouse. It seemed that since the German line to Moshi was keeping pace with the present railway in Kenya, some display was needed of how proficient their crew had become, and thus how hopeless competition would be.

Allen, forewarned that he was to put on a "show," was more than ready.

"Mr. McCann said they would be fast," the governor said, "but this…this is absolutely amazing."

He had been dazzled by the speed and precision of the Indian plate-laying gang as they set the metal crossties into the ballast, fastened rails to the ties, bolted the rail ends together using fishplates, then aligned them, as the next rails were carried forward from a supply drawn by the efficient and very impressive steam tractors.

That day they laid more than a mile, close to their one-day record of one and a half miles, still far from the ten miles a day achieved in the American West, but impressive in Africa.

Arriving back in Tanganyika, His Excellency stopped in Tanga to see Fritz Kohl and to describe the terrific pace at which the British line was going forward. "It's not possible for us to come close to them, even if we were to go all the way to Lake Victoria."

"I agree," said Kohl. "Until now our line has just been able to keep up. But remember, Your Excellence, as our sources informed us, they were setting out to impress you. I mean, there's no question that their plate-laying crews are fast, and they can put on a special show, but will they be as capable when they face the extraordinary challenge of the escarpment? I can assure you that at that point they will move much more slowly, especially coming down the steep slope to Naivasha."

"But still, Kohl," said the governor, "If they are persistent…."

"Yes, *if*. But, I also wonder, while you were there, you must have seen the dead cattle and the starving natives, eh?"

"Yes, but that will change once the weather breaks."

"Which may be some time yet. Meanwhile, they may soon be

fighting off raids by the local Wakamba who want food. If that happens, their pace will slow and may even stop."

He paused to take a pull on his beer. "Also, Your Excellence, we hear further that the British administration will face more and more resistance from the white population. There are many there who do *not* agree with the way they are going about things."

"Oh?" said the governor. "That is a development I wasn't aware of."

"It comes from their reliance on Afrikaners you see. In their haste for settlement, they are always using human resources from other parts of their empire. It's something they are proud of; in fact, their politicians often use that as an argument for empire-building."

"I did see many examples of that," said the governor as he finished his drink, "the Indian coolies on the railway, Anglo-Indian stationmasters and the sepoys in their army."

"And cattle farmers along with their oxen from the south. They're Boers."

"True."

"And still the British refuse to acknowledge the potential of the native blacks."

"Interesting. You may have something there, Kohl. You know the Kaiser is under pressure back home to show more tolerance in the case of the South Africans; they say that war is just around the corner."

"And is he still aligned with the British cause?" asked Kohl, shaking his head in disbelief.

"It's the influence of his English mother and his grandmother, Queen Victoria," said the governor as he stood up. "It dies hard. In any event, I hope you keep me informed if there are any more changes in the situation that you describe."

"It goes without saying, Your Excellence."

"And thank you for your hospitality. Now I must not keep the steamer waiting."

Kohl walked with him to the gangplank.

"Your moustache, Kohl. It appears to be taking on the Imperial form."

"It's the fashion, sir. One doesn't have to be in Berlin to be patriotic."

"Of course, of course. And I can tell you, your work here has already received favorable mention in my reports. *Wiedersehen*."

Later that month Allen faced his first major crisis when the water supply at the River Maji Chumvi dried up. Until then, this had been one of the railway's most reliable sources of fresh water, essential for locomotive and tractor operation, as well as a vital commodity for the survival of the rail crews. The unrelenting drought made him depend more and more on other water points, which also had begun showing signs of drying. He had sounded out Mombasa in the matter of water supply, something headquarters was not happy about. And they told him so.

"Allen," said Whitehouse at their last meeting, "one reason we've put you in charge is that we expect you to start developing some self-sufficiency. It's imperative. Every drop of water, every grain of rice or bag of flour sent out from Mombasa costs money. If you can live off the local countryside, well and good, but if you can't, then push on fast, man. Get to an area where local supplies and water are available, and get there at all cost."

Allen looked around him and repeated that sentiment. "He's right, Bill. In order to become independent of Mombasa we have to get the hell out of this place." He pointed to the village outposts where so many gaunt people came out early in the day and stood in clusters watching as they rode out to the railhead. "Look at them. It's a disaster area."

"We're going forward as fast as we can."

"I understand that, but in Nairobi there's water in excess. And we can tap into food from the highland areas," said Allen.

"You mean the area under control of the Kikuyus?" asked Bill. "As far as I know, they never seemed keen on sharing their foodstuff."

"Not anymore. I've just had a telegram from Capt. Lloyd in Naivasha. He says there's an American who's made inroads there, so the future may not be as grim as we thought."

"And for now?"

"Press on, at all costs."

Riding out to measure progress and deal with problems, they passed scenes that were impossible to ignore. As they watched, animals from herds of emaciated cattle wandering aimlessly in the parched landscape often toppled over. And the young people, every bone in their body visible, came each day to the railhead to watch the crews and wait for scraps. They would fall on any bits as soon as the dishes were cleared from the platelayers' breakfast, luncheon or tea breaks.

It was worrisome that these walking skeletons increased in number daily. Their large sad eyes served as a grim reminder to the workers to move faster, or they might find themselves in the same position.

Alice's Diary (Stanhope, Cheshire, 1945)

> *...The day I returned to Nairobi, I went directly over to the Palace Hotel and borrowed the Shimmers' wagon and their driver. Then I took Jenny and Jakoby and drove out to Machakos, where I found Stephen in a bad way. He looked much older and his dependence on the bottle had become quite obvious. His life was wasting away, and there was little anyone could do about it. We went through the town buying every vegetable, loaf of bread and piece of fruit we could.*
>
> *We also gathered many tins of beans and meat from the shops and loaded everything along with water cans and left. Stephen saw what we were doing and said we were mad, it was just a drop in the bucket. I pointed out to him that I had heard the Railway was willing to give up food in an emergency. I convinced him that once we reached railhead, or any convenient place along the line, we could load the wagon with railway food for a return trip. And if we didn't get what we wanted, we'd go all the way to Mombasa and raise hell with the high commissioner.*
>
> *He seemed quite abashed that we would go to such lengths.*

But, as he thought about it, I think he realized we were right, so he put aside his feelings that the situation was hopeless and followed us to Simba, a ride of about sixty miles, made longer by our frequent stops to give out food and water to the children. We had to refuse the adults because our supplies were so meagre. We felt the children were more in need….

"Incredible," said John, as he and Bagley rode along the track in front of a steam tractor. It was early evening, the end of the workday, and the majority of workers should have been settling in their camp at railhead. A few could be expected to be returning to Simba, but this was absurd. On all sides were hundreds of Indian workers and African villagers streaming along the tracks oblivious of the tractor.

"They seem to be running for their lives."

"What the hell's going on?"

"Man-eaters," suggested Bagley.

"Can't be," said John. "Colonel Patterson killed the last two at Tsavo months ago."

"Must be an accident."

"Then why are they running away?"

The crowd had not thinned and the tractor could hardly go forward into the mass of people. "You're right," said Bagley. "They should be running toward an accident."

Then as they rounded a bend they heard shooting. The railhead came into view, a motley collection of tents, animal bomas and piles of rail supplies. It was obviously deserted, except for the foreman, Ronald Preston, and three of his railway askari guards who were under siege by a Wakamba raiding party.

They spurred their horses on and fired off their revolvers as they galloped forward to the side of the defenders. Then suddenly, as quickly as they had appeared, the raiding party turned and ran off. In the distance Bagley saw a cloud of dust and very soon made out a wagon heading towards them.

"Thank God," said Bagley. As he said that, he turned and saw

John fall from his horse.

"Quick," said the foreman to his askaris, "get him into the mess tent."

Bagley ran forward to meet the wagon. He was disconcerted to see that three of the rescuers were women, and he was not reassured when he saw Stephen come up on horseback as the party rolled to a stop. He knew Stephen from earlier meetings at Railway headquarters and had a low opinion of him.

"Anyone injured?" Stephen asked.

"The new supervisor just caught an arrow. Might be a poisoned one," said Bagley. "If so, he's not going to make it."

"Boil some water," said Alice as she grabbed her safari pack and raced toward the tent, "and get me a cup or a pot and some clean cloth."

Inside the tent someone had lit a kerosene lantern as John lay on a blanket, eyes half closed, sweat pouring from his brow, the poison already taking effect even though one of the askaris had applied a leather belt as a tourniquet. Alice ripped the sleeve away from the wound as Jenny came in with a large kettle and several cups and said, "Thank the Lord, the cook was about to start supper when they attacked."

"Good," said Alice. She steeped a wad of dried plant material she had taken from her pack. "Clean cloths?"

"Here," said Jakoby, who came in with some linen from her own pack.

"It's not too deep," said Alice.

"Lucky the arrowhead came out," said Bagley. "It usually breaks off inside."

John watched with wide eyes; he could barely speak as he saw her take a bottle of gin from the mess supply cabinet and pour some on the wound. "This'll hurt a bit," she said as she cleaned the wound, then scooped out the dawa from a cup of hot water and placed it onto another cloth. "Release the belt," she said to Jakoby. "Let it bleed a bit."

Once the blood began to flow she laid the dawa compress on the wound and tied it tightly with a strip of cloth. John raised himself on his right arm and looked at her.

"I know you!" he exclaimed, as he stared at her with feverish eyes. "You're Alice, the angel from Maidstone."

Alice blushed as she looked at Jenny.

"Perhaps I'd better take over," said Jenny.

7

"Ah, now, Mr. Allen, rest easy while Alice has a bit of supper," said Jenny. She sat by him and took the opportunity to lay his beautiful head on her lap. "I'm an army wife," she smiled as she held a cup of water to his lips, "and I've had many other lads in my arms, son, but none like you. Here, have a drink and get your mind off the angel for a bit."

Outside the tent the askaris stood guard in front of a large fire. Some of the workers had already drifted back. The thought of supper was enough to conquer their fear of another raid.

"Our telegraph operator tells us they're sending army sepoys from Nairobi," said Bagley as he sat with Alice and Stephen while they ate by the campfire. "They should be arriving shortly. Your oxen team made such a cloud of dust the raiders probably thought you were them."

"What's your plan for tonight?"

"Once you finish eating, I thought we'd use your wagon to move him back to the station house. If he doesn't improve, then we'll take him on to Mombasa by train in the morning."

That night in the safety of the station house, Stephen found a bed in the stationmaster's office and settled in with a bottle of brandy. Jakoby sought out the servant quarters, while Jenny and Alice set up cots in the waiting room near Allen.

The bandage had been in place for at least four hours before they looked again at the wound. The patient offered little resistance as they took it off and were amazed at its appearance. It was clean and white around the general area where the skin had been pierced. Bagley had told Alice that necrosis would set in, but there was no sign of that. The blood had coagulated and the redness along the edges was minimal.

"It looks as if some kind of astringent had been applied," said Jenny.

"Anyway, it seems to be working," said Alice. "The swelling's still there, but the arm looks better." They replaced the dressing with a fresh dawa compress and John slept under the watchful eye of Jenny.

"I take it you knew him in England?" Bagley asked Alice as they waited for the station cook to brew up some coffee.

"I met him when he came to see my sister, Dorothy, but he went off one day and never came back."

"And Mr. Hale?"

"I don't believe he's ever met Mr. Allen."

"Well, I expect they'll see a lot more of one another after this, *if* they both survive." Bagley had been upset at the way Stephen had helped himself to the station brandy supply.

"You've been out here for a while, Mr. Bagley?" asked Alice.

"Came out with George Whitehouse, never thought we'd get this far."

"But you must be proud of what's been accomplished. Hasn't the caravan traffic diminished? That in itself must be a relief."

"At what cost to my men?" he said as the cook poured them some coffee.

Suddenly the door opened and an officer walked in, his patent leather boots, brass buttons and Sam Brown belt shined to a high gloss. In the lantern light they saw he wore a light silk scarf in place of a cravat. He looked like he had just been snatched from his St. James club.

"Allen here?" he asked in a clipped accent as he glanced around.

"You must be Woodham-Stayne," said Bradley.

"Spot on. Heard you chaps needed help," he smiled at Alice.

"Miss McConnell," said Bradley introducing her, "also from Nairobi. Captain Woodham-Stayne, our new security man."

"Are you an army man?" asked Alice.

She was used to Jenny's crowd, all regular garrison types; she couldn't remember anyone with a flare like this.

"Matthew's the name," he said, accepting her hand and brushing it with a kiss. "Just brought my own sepoys up from Mombasa. Not regular."

"He means," said Bill, "he's like Allen and I. We all hold commissions but we're seconded to the Railway."

"I see," said Alice smiling as she looked at her hand, which still tingled from Matthew's mustache. "And you're a friend of Allen's?"

"Right," he said. "Steady on..." He had spotted John lying on his cot.

"That's him," said Bill.

Alice said, "He's sleeping. Arrow wound. We hope it's not serious."

"Why don't you pitch up over there beside him and I'll tell the cook to provide," said Bagley. "We'll talk in the morning."

The next morning at breakfast, Bagley announced that work had once again started at railhead. "Any improvement?" he asked Alice.

"He'll survive," she said, looking at Jenny, who was spoon-feeding John. "He was walking around earlier. We might even be able to go back to Nairobi today, if I can get the nurse to part with her patient."

"Thank God you all arrived when you did."

"It was Alice's idea," said Stephen, as he sat down at the table. He seemed alert and ready for a return trip to Machakos despite a heavy night. Bagley had earlier that morning glanced at Alice as they both watched him furtively pour a large slug of brandy into his breakfast coffee. "I agreed it was a good thing," he continued, "once we recalled that the Railway had offered to release food supplies."

Alice turned to Bagley and asked, "Do you think there will be more raids?"

"The person you should be asking is Mr. Hale," said Bagley, who from the tone of his voice, seemed to have reached the limit of his patience.

"By the way, Mr. Hale," said Matthew, who carefully spread a large serviette over his uniform shirt before he helped himself to a dish of scrambled eggs, "Ian Burns in Mombasa said you'd be keeping us informed about security matters, yet we haven't heard a peep from you, till now."

"Good morning," said John Allen, who joined them at the table where he stood with his left arm in a sling, looking at Stephen. He knew from the recent letters from Nairobi that he was Dorothy's husband. "I take it you're Stephen Hale?"

The pushiness of these people, thought Stephen. Of the lot, only Alice seemed friendly. Stephen's administration was supposed to be in charge, but it was difficult when the Railway insisted on providing their own medical people, police officers, askaris, schoolteachers, and builders.

"And this is Bill Bradley, my assistant," said Allen.

"And here's Musa our cook with a second round of eggs and bacon," said Matthew.

"All well deserved," said Allen as he sat with bandaged arm between Alice and Jenny. "Difficult to imagine food like this when just outside the door there's a famine raging."

"It seems I'm the only one worried about the Wakamba," said Bill, glancing around the table, then at Stephen. "I mean, what the hell's come over them? Why are they giving us such a hard time?"

"The basic cause is rinderpest," said Stephen. "It's more severe in time of drought. The grazing areas are littered with carcasses."

"But there's been rain earlier," said Woodham-Stayne, who like Bagley and Allen was suspicious of civil administration. "I was told it was raining yesterday in Nairobi."

"Yes, but that falls only in Nairobi and Kikuyuland," said Stephen. "We've had no rain in Ukambaa or Masailand for many months. In past years when crops failed because of drought, the people turned to livestock for food, especially their sheep and goats. But this year, rinderpest is depleting their herds as they watch. Also there's a second blow—while the livestock suffered, many people in the villages who would normally forage for food are suffering from smallpox."

"Which everyone says has been getting steadily worse over the past few years," said Alice.

"So," said Stephen, "now we have young warriors, depressed at seeing their families and the elders starving to death, turning to cattle raiding in the neighboring areas, as they have done in the past. But this time they're being turned back at the edges of Kikuyuland by a more organized force. The Kikuyu seem better equipped now."

"It's that chap, Roger Newcome," said Woodham-Stayne.

"Newcome," said Allen. "Yes, we're all well aware of him." He nodded at Stephen to continue. "You were saying, Hale?"

"Well, then they turned to the plains, but there they found conditions just as bad. It seems the wildlife have also been affected by rinderpest. The game animals, zebra, wildebeest, elan and buffalo are dying as fast as the cattle. Then their raids into Masailand looking for healthy cattle prove to be useless because the Masai have disappeared!"

"And where have *they* gone?" asked Bagley.

"They've moved their cattle south to the floodplains and swamps along the Mara River. And they've taken the added precaution of posting war parties, impi, between their herds and the Wakamba. That way they prevent raids and the spread of the disease to their own animals."

"So where would the Wakamba go to obtain food?" Stephen concluded, taking a large drink from his coffee mug. "The easiest path, I'm afraid, gentlemen, is to raid your stores."

He said that in such a matter-of-fact way that everyone around the table had the impression that he felt the Wakamba were justified. The slight smile on his face did nothing to calm the tension.

Allen abruptly got up and brusquely shook his head as he walked over to stare out the window, where he looked onto the rail tracks in front of the station. Outside, workers were again loading rails and equipment into the tractor wagons. The place was busy with commerce, people coming and going; the small town was developing from scratch before their very eyes because of the railway. Yes, he thought, because of *us*, not this sorry excuse of a civil servant sitting here smelling of brandy. He turned and stared at Stephen, thinking of the enormous success they were having and that they had impressed everyone with their super-efficient Indian platelayers.

Thank God, the German governor and George Whitehouse weren't here during the raid. It would have been a shambles.

"Why the hell haven't you been telling us about all of this, Hale?" asked Bagley. "You've been sending back reports to Mombasa about weekly crop yields, numbers of traders and sizes of caravans and all sorts of trivia."

"And until now," said Woodham-Stayne, who also stood up, "you've not provided us with any inkling of this large and potentially dangerous problem."

"As to your request for food," said Bagley, "we have an immediate problem. There's very little left because your damned Wakamba have made off with our weekly supply."

It was Stephen's turn to react. Red-faced and bristling, he looked at Bill and Matthew. Then Allen opened his mouth to speak, but Bagley continued, "I mean, *really*! Here we've been taken up with building a railroad, while you've been preoccupied with raising apples, breeding cattle and all sorts of social rubbish."

"Now Bill, calm down," said John Allen, realizing that they were going too far. "I'm sorry Mr. Hale. I've heard about Dorothy, very distracting all that."

Suddenly the door opened and the stationmaster came in to announce the arrival of a relief train from Mombasa.

"Well that solves several problems," said John. "Mr. Hale, if you'll have the driver bring your wagon alongside the loading dock, we'll provide you with a load of flour and rice." He turned to Bagley. "Bill could you see to that? And Matthew, I presume you'll deploy your men and sort out the new arrivals?"

Alice and Jenny gathered up their belongings.

"And you're staying on?" Jenny asked her former patient.

"No," said Allen. "Matthew has commandeered a railway wagon. He's taking me and Bagley into Nairobi where we have much to do, and I can get medical attention. Can we give you two lovely ladies a lift?"

Stephen's wagon was quickly loaded and the driver had pointed the team toward Machakos when Alice went over to talk to him.

"Sorry about that scene over breakfast," she said.

"It's not your fault, Alice. The Railway believes they're beyond reproach," he said. "They think everyone in the country should bend to their needs. Well, some of us have our own thoughts about development. There are many here looking forward to the day when this damned railroad is finished and those people are out of here."

"It sounds like you'll have your hands full for a while."

"Alice, I never had a chance to thank you. Your visit made me realize that I've got to get a better grip. I've let too much slip since Dorothy left. Now everything's going to change, everything's going to be different." He held out his hand and patted her on the shoulder as he said, "Trust me."

She watched him and the driver pull out of the station yard. A half-full bottle of brandy fell from the wagon seat and shattered on the roadside. She hoped that was symbolic.

The railway wagon was more comfortable than the ox wagon. It was a springboard provided with a better awning and padded benches that gave Jenny a chance to sit next to John, while Matthew shared a seat with Alice, Bagley sat up front with the driver, and Jakoby sat on several bags of mail in the back. They soon caught up with Stephen who followed the same track as they to Konza, where he branched off and with a wave went north to Machakos. Since they still had thirty-five miles to go to Nairobi and were in no hurry, they decided to stop there for the night. Tents were pitched on a rise above a small river and while the team was watered and supper was being prepared, John had a chance to talk to Alice about her sister.

"I've written often this past month."

"I know," said Alice. "But still, I think she was surprised to hear from you after such a long absence."

"Did you ever know the real reason I left Maidstone so abruptly?"

"No, she never confided in me. I thought you had a change of heart."

"It was more complicated than that. I was concerned about her family. In fact, I should have said something to your father, but Dorothy wouldn't have it. I had to leave everyone in the dark; that's the way she wanted it."

"Why did you go?"

"When Dorothy was a child, her uncle Bobby was always, as she said, 'Too much interested in her.' He never actually molested her outright, but he frightened her so with his attention and pawing, she never quite got over it. She felt that's why she's always been afraid of life."

"Uncle Bobby!"

"Yes. You see, I didn't love her, but we were engaged and I felt sorry for her. Then I realized I was becoming very attracted to you, and because at that time you were still quite young, I wanted to remove my own influence. I didn't want even a suspicion to linger in your mind, and I suppose I wanted to make certain that I wasn't tarred with the same brush as Bobby, so I left."

"And now?"

"Well I got the shock of my life when I opened my eyes yesterday and saw you hovering over me, especially now that you've...," he hesitated for a few seconds, "matured."

As he said that word, he looked at her with a half smile and an expression of interest that startled her.

"I had no idea you felt that way," she said.

Later, as they sat in their camp chairs eating supper, Jenny said, "What is wrong with you, Alice?"

"What do you mean?"

"You look nervous and flushed. I can tell you're upset, even by campfire light. I hope you're not coming down with something."

In the morning as they settled into their seats and the team moved forward to ford the small river, Alice overheard a conversation between Bagley and Matthew. "Mr. Preston told me that a few days previous, one of the construction trains was derailed. He thinks intentionally."

"That's unusual," said Matthew.

"Damn right," said Bagley. "Until now the Wakamba have only been interested in food and rifles, not that kind of destruction. It's all very suspicious."

"It was my understanding that most natives would have no idea how to carry out a derailment," said Matthew.

"Apparently they learn quickly," said Bagley.

From where she sat, Alice could plainly see that Jakoby was smiling to herself.

In Muthuri's Hut

What's this, Bwana Roger? Leaving again?

This time to Machakos.

I remember you said you had friends there.

What? Not friends? Who? The guardian of the woman who you will marry. Ah-hah, now I see. Then take my advice and remember to bring along at least a hundred head of cattle. Also it is wise to keep some goats in reserve in case he drives a hard bargain.

What? You don't need animals to seal the bargain? You say you will talk him into giving her up!

Well, well. I wish you success. If you can accomplish that without turning over a bride price, you will be a hero! And of one thing you can be certain, every man here will respect you and will want to know the secret.

8

Machakos

The sign on the door read, "Stephen Hale, District Commissioner, Machakos." Roger walked in to find an office sparsely furnished, and, typical of the colonial civil service, he thought, papers and reports were lying everywhere. But the DC was nowhere to be seen. In Roger's mind was some vague idea about a new start with Stephen, a new approach that would win him over. He had thought about this on the long ride from Nairobi along a wagon track that swung south from Nairobi across a sea of grass known as the Athi Plains. Starting at five in the morning when the air was still cold and wet, he had watched the sun rise, a glorious bright yellow globe that quickly burnt away the early morning moisture.

By eight, when he started up the dusty road into Machakos, the air was hot and dry and he was already sweating profusely as the blazing heat took hold. He brought with him, as a peace offering, an idea that could resolve what he felt was Stephen's largest problem, the famine. Alice's determination to help feed the hungry had prompted him into thinking about how the Kikuyu bounty could be used for a relief effort in the Ukambani region.

Nestled further inside that idea, of course, was another hopeful thought, almost in some ways a dream, a dream in which Stephen would thank him for his help. He would put his arm around Roger's shoulder, as his father, Paul, used to do whenever he had done his sums correctly. He would ask him to forgive him, and yes, Roger thought, he'd let Stephen make the first move. Once that new feeling of fellowship was in place, he'd let him compliment him more on his success with the Kikuyu. Then the notion would pop into Stephen's mind that Roger and Alice had much in common, and, perhaps, thought Roger, just perhaps, he would be allowed to pursue a closer relationship with her. Once married, he thought, his first move would be away from that damned Settlers' Club.

He looked into Jimmy Harris' office next door. Again more papers and no one present. He left his horse tied to the railing outside and walked up the road to where he saw a crowd gathered in front of the DC's residence. One young man drenched in sweat was kneeling in the dust, chest still heaving from exertion.

Mr. Harris came out of the residence as Roger walked up the stairs.

"What's wrong?" Roger asked.

"This young man is from Lema, a village on the banks of the Athi River. He has run all night and early morning to tell us."

"What?" asked Roger.

"He says '*watu wingi kuuana*,' almost one hundred people have been slaughtered at his village by foreigners with guns, '*farenghi*'!"

"Good God. And what are you doing about it?" He looked behind Jimmy, assuming Stephen would be coming out at any minute. "And where's Mr. Hale?"

"I've been trying to rouse him, but I'm afraid he is not responding."

Roger brushed past him and strode into the residence. He found the master bedroom. A quick look around, the bedclothes in disarray, the glasses, bottles and smell of stale drink told the story. Stephen lay fully clothed on the bed snoring. Even if he could wake him, Roger knew he'd be in no condition to help.

He turned and went out to where Jimmy was trying to reason with the crowd.

"My God, what can we do?" Jimmy whispered to Roger. The crowd looked angry.

"This is awful," said Roger, feeling somewhat helpless himself. All dreams of married bliss and a benevolent new relation had fled from his mind.

"And Mr. Hale will not get up," whispered Jimmy, keeping one eye on the crowd. "We must do something."

"I agree."

“But what can I do?” pleaded Jimmy. “If I leave my post, Mr. Hale will be very upset. We have askaris and sepoys from the fort, but I cannot let them go off on their own!”

“If you want,” said Roger, “I’ll go with them and find out what happened. It’s only twenty miles. I can be there and back before Mr. Hale wakes up.”

“Oh, my God, thank you, Mr. Roger.”

Within minutes, Roger was in his saddle riding out of Machakos, grateful to be eating an early lunch packed by Jimmy’s wife. He was followed closely by a guide, Mulembe, and a small troop of sepoys and askaris on donkeys. They were accompanied by a dozen men on foot. Mulembe said it would take them about six hours to get there.

Of all the thorn trees and bushes in Kenya, the most attractive are the young saplings of *Acacia albida*, the apple-peel acacia, so called because of its thin, red-brown, curly pods. A fine specimen, with its delicate creamy white flowers in lovely scented spikes on one small branch, had now collapsed under the weight of Roger’s lunch, which he had spewed all over it.

He retched again. His stomach contracted with such force that his body shivered. He had never seen such a horrible, nerve-wracking sight; even in the worst sections of Mombasa there was nothing to compare to what he had found in Lema. What further agonized his brain was the quiet, the stillness of the place, broken only by the buzzing of flies, thousands of them, swarming over the carcasses in bold disregard of the human nature of the substrate. They crawled in and out of every body opening, intent on sucking up the oozing fluid before it became crusted and dried, at which point their only recourse would be to buzz about and wait until a scavenger ripped open another part of a body, exposing a moist surface. Rigor mortis had set in, leaving the corpses with arms, legs and heads pointing in different directions, the horror still frozen on their faces, as if, in this earthly paradise, in Africa, they had met with the same fate as the dead found in the ashes of Pompeii.

He remembered seeing sketches of the casts made of those people, the forms left after they had been incinerated in place.

Would to God they had gone to such a fast, merciful death, rather than this! he thought, as he stumbled away from the sight. The scavengers continued their work; vultures strutted about, moving only at the last moment as the party approached, unable to fly because they had gorged themselves. The bodies were a day old and beginning to bloat as Roger staggered about in the compound, eyes streaming, handkerchief to his mouth and nose. At the edge of the murder scene the vultures hopped in front of him, thoroughly annoyed that they were being bothered in their pursuit of this grisly meal. The dark, leathery, featherless heads and sharp hooked beaks, ideal for insertion into and operation within the body openings of any unlucky cadaver, were covered with gore that in turn drew more flies, flies that massed about the upper parts of the vultures' heads as they watched the interlopers with goggle-eyed irritation. The heat and stench in the humid, dank compound was too much for him.

"Mulembe, what happened here?"

"Arab slavers, Bwana." His eyes stared into Roger's face, who looked back red-eyed, disbelieving, unable to divine anything, or to find any emotion on Mulembe's face. Had he known how many times this man had seen such horrors, he would not have searched for feeling on that blank countenance.

"But slavery's banned, dead, it's not allowed, for God's sake!"

"Yes, Bwana, it is not allowed, but there are men from the Coast who still roam the outlying areas, still taking young men and women. They kill the elders, the sick and the infants."

"Where are the village men, the warriors?"

"They were caught outside; shot on the trail."

They walked back and saw many had obviously been ambushed from a rocky outcrop that looked down on a slope. In open country along the riverbank, it was a perfect field of fire from which there was no escape.

"They fought. See, their spears were cast. Here is one Swahili from the slavers' caravan that was speared." The spear had caught him in the chest and came out the back. Others were lying with him, but not many. "From the signs, they were returning from a hunting foray," said Mulembe. "And Bwana, look here, shell casings." He placed several in Roger's hands. "They must be from a repeating rifle."

"But, slavers?" he stammered in disbelief. "How is this still allowed?"

"It is not," Mulembe offered. "They will avoid the eye of the government in Mombasa by going north along the coast. This is the main track. It follows the Athi River all the way to Malindi." With a stick he drew a map on the ground.

"Thence, they go by *dhow* past Lamu and the old German colony at Witu and finally north to Somaliland where there is still a market. They move at night along the riverbank and will pass unobserved through the countryside."

"And where are they now?"

"Probably a day or two's march from us along this track."

"Mulembe, take some of the men and see what can be done here to bury the dead, then...."

"Ah, Bwana, the people here are afraid of touching dead bodies. Only the elders can do that."

"Very well, they must send for elders from nearby villages to move them. Also send a man back to Machakos for more men and shovels."

"Now," he said as he knelt beside the dirt map, "there is still time to cut them off."

"How can that be done?"

"You must select two young men from our group and tell them to race south to this place," he pointed to a spot on the ground.

"The village there is Kikumini," said Mulembe.

"They will take a message from me; I'll write it now." He had torn a page from a notebook and was scribbling away as he spoke. "Who is the chief there?"

"Machoka, but he will not be able to read what you write."

"Then tell the messengers what the note says, and tell them to say it is from Mr. Hale, the district commissioner. They must tell Machoka to send a runner to the next village further up the river."

"Mutembuku."

"Right, and there they must alert that village to be on the look-out and be prepared as they will be in the path of the slavers. Also tell Machoka to have some men ready to help us. We will follow the river track and will pass his village two days from now."

A woman carrying a small child was brought to them. She had been hiding in the bush.

"Who is that?"

"She is one of the few women left. She says there are several others who escaped with her and they are still hiding."

"Ask her how many were in the raiding party."

"She says four farenghi with guns, Arabs. They had twelve donkeys with provisions and about twenty Swahilis. When they left, they took away twenty-five people from here in chains."

The woman said something further in an undertone.

"Also, she says there was Memsab's maid from the DC's residence, Karegi, a young woman visiting with her father when it happened; she was also taken."

"With one or two day's start, what chance do we have of catching up with them?"

"A good chance, Bwana, since they move only at night and will be slowed down by their captives. They may also be planning to attack other villages, which will cause them some delay. And what are we to do?"

"We are going to travel as fast as we can today and into the night along this track. We will share the askaris' provisions, so we'll have enough food and water for about three days. Then we will replenish our supplies at Kikumini. Check everyone to ensure they have enough water, and go with this woman and see if there is any food that we can carry. We leave in fifteen minutes."

They left the village at a trot, Mulembe and a tracker in front, followed by the sepoys and askaris, then Roger on his horse, scanning the bush. Several of the men on foot took up the rear. The sun soon disappeared, but the moon shed enough light to allow them to continue along the track. They had to dismount often for fear of tree branches, but along certain stretches they made good time. Within two days' march they saw the first evidence, a young lad lying dead by the trail with chain marks and deep cuts in his neck and wrists. He had been hacked to death, either because he had resisted, or because he just couldn't keep up the pace.

"They will not fire a rifle for fear of raising the alarm, but see, Bwana, the boy is not long dead. We are very close."

And indeed, a scout came back shortly to report he could see something in the wooded slope of a forest rising from the river, several thin ribbons of wood smoke; they were probably taking their meal before the march began again that evening. Leaving the river, the rescue party went inland to Kikumini, where they found a small band of warriors waiting with their chief, Machoka, who greeted Mulembe and was introduced to Roger. They had already sent a messenger to Mutembuku, and found that the slaver caravan had been driven off. It had retreated to the woods to regroup and, as they surmised, to rest during the day. But they would certainly be leaving soon. This meant that Roger's party had only a few hours to act and it was a good half hour to the top of the hill from Kikumini.

Roger split up the sepoys and askaris, reinforced them with some of Machoka's men and sent them off on both flanks, as he, Mulembe and the remaining men went up the top of the rise. They dismounted there and walked carefully over the summit. Waiting until they knew the others were in position, they looked down on the slavers' camp and saw them packing up. Three Arabs were directing operations, while the Swahili porters were forming the caravan line. The fourth Arab, the leader, was lingering on a blanket in the shade of a tree, a female captive tied shivering to a nearby stump. It was obvious that she had been the object of his attention during the early course of the day.

"Bastard," Roger swore under his breath.

Before the slavers knew what had happened, Roger had sent his horse and the donkeys crashing down ahead of them as he and the askaris shot down one of the Arabs from above. Two others quickly raised their hands, while the Swahilis scattered into the bush where they were caught and slaughtered on the spot by the askaris. The leader rose from his blanket with his hands up.

"Mulembe, take his keys. Unlock the survivors then chain these men in their place."

Mulembe picked up the keys and began unlocking the collars and undoing the chains, but then he stopped and pointed to the bush. Roger turned to see a young white man carrying a hunting rifle walk into the camp clearing.

"Thank God you came along," the man said shaking his head.

Roger was surprised by his English, perfect but with a trace of German, or was it a South African twang, he thought. He looked familiar. It suddenly came to Roger. It was the man he had seen on the boat.

"Who *are* you?"

"Franz Shimmer."

"But where the hell did you come from?"

"I've been prospecting along the river. I left my boat tied up about a mile from here. Some of the villagers said there was trouble so I walked over."

"Could I see your rifle?" asked Roger.

Franz handed him his rifle and said, "By the way, I'm a very good friend of Mr. Hale."

Roger looked at the rifle, a Mannlicher repeating carbine. He fired one round into the air, retrieved the spent casing from the breech and compared it to several taken from the scene of the ambush. "It's identical to the other .256 caliber casings," he said. "There can't be another rifle like this for hundreds of miles around."

"You don't believe me? You bloody bastard!" yelled Franz, eyes narrowed to slits like those of a cobra. "I'm Franz Shimmer, don't you understand! I'm a friend of Stephen's."

"I don't believe a word you say," said Roger, remembering the bodies festering in the sun. "You may have stayed away from the village while the massacre was in progress, but you were certainly involved in the ambush. Mulembe, tie him up. Better yet, use some of those chains."

"You imbecile. This is a mistake you will sorely regret."

Roger turned on his heel and was about to walk away, when he was startled at the sight of Stephen Hale on horseback, at the edge of the camp clearing. Unshaven and fatigued, he had just arrived.

"He's right, Mr. Newcome. Mulembe, release Mr. Shimmer and tie up those Arabs instead."

Roger was flabbergasted, "But...Jesus, man, didn't you see what these bastards did at Lema?"

"Yes, I saw. I missed you by just a few hours." He dismounted and walked over to where Shimmer was standing, and said resignedly, "This isn't the first time this sort of thing has happened, and it won't be the last. And I assure you the Arabs will pay for it."

Roger pointed to Shimmer. "But what about him?"

"Didn't you hear me? Franz was obviously trying to help."

"If you'd believe that, you'd believe anything."

"Mr. Newcome, calm down, you're not in charge here. Now, Mulembe, we'll camp here tonight. Franz, you're free to go or stay as you please. Your family in Nairobi is probably anxious."

"Shit. I can't believe this!"

Stephen turned to Franz. "Don't mind Mr. Newcome, he's easily upset." He ignored Roger and handed back Shimmer's rifle. Then he paused and addressed Roger with enforced courtesy. "Mr. Newcome, thanks for your trouble. I think I can handle this from now on. By the way, what did you want to see me about?"

"Nothing that can't wait." Roger was seething.

"Did you want to come back to Machakos with us?"

"No, thanks," he said, mounting his horse as he silently and viciously cursed Alice's guardian. Then he abruptly turned his horse's head and rode off into the bush.

9

The house Alice had rented in Nairobi was a spacious, one-story affair with a galvanized tin roof. Acting on Jenny's advice, she had sought out Mr. Jevanjee, an Asian contractor involved in the early development of the town, and with his help was able to avoid the rough wooden hovels that were springing up all over. She had seen the outside of Roger and J.O.'s "club" on one occasion and that was enough to decide her on Mr. Jevanjee. His houses and shops were built out of stone, so they were cool in hot weather and watertight in the rainy season. He also had a small flower garden laid out in front and a vegetable plot in the rear, both watered by the wastewater that ran from the kitchen and bath drains.

Alice's life had changed considerably with the death of her father. The largest question she now faced regarding her future was whether to stay on. Initially Rosmé had begged her to stay because of Dorothy, but Jakoby had taken charge.

Relieved of further obligations, Alice presumed she would have to find a job teaching or nursing, or else leave, but one month after her father's death she was notified that he had bought her a substantial life annuity, which made her an independent person. Not without strings. Up until his death her father had worried that she would overnight become another Mary Kingsley, so, on hearing from Rosmé and Dorothy about her earlier exploits, he decided to include in the annuity a clause specifying Stephen in a discretionary role—he was signatory to all transactions, thus insuring that she would demonstrate moderation in her daily life. In effect, Stephen would now act as her guardian until age twenty-one. She had heard that, true to his word, he had started a food distribution program. A good start, she thought, but it discouraged her from doing anything more in that direction.

Why stay on then? For one thing, she was developing quite a string of admirers. John Allen stopped by during most afternoons to see Dorothy, then lingered to talk to Alice; David McCann, recently appointed as acting DC in Nairobi, was so taken with her that he had bought a house nearby so he could more easily stop by in the evenings; Matthew Woodham-Stayne escorted her to the railway and army clubs on weekends where she found herself in demand at dances; and virtually every day when Roger was in Nairobi he would stop by. Then a racing season had been organized; the dry weather allowed pony racing on the flat. Every race day J.O. would come around to take her to the races. He took no umbrage at being mistaken for her father, since he looked and acted just like George McConnell. They both enjoyed the arrangement. Undoubtedly he missed his two daughters and five grandchildren in Matabeleland; at least she assumed so, as he talked so often about them.

Despite all this attention, she was restless. Perhaps, she thought, it was time to seek out adventure rather than wait for it to come to her. She looked again at a brief message hand-delivered that morning from Brian. He said he would be in town for some settler meetings and wondered if he could stop in. He mentioned the fact that Christmas was just around the corner, and it surprised her to think of him celebrating Christian holy days. So be it, she said to herself, when, startled from her reverie, she heard a knock on the door, reminding her that Roger was back in Nairobi.

She had found that he was still bitter about what had happened at Lema, but at least seemed more willing now to listen to her advice on how to get along with people. She met him at the door and sat down with him on the verandah, where Jakoby usually served tea at that hour, an arrangement that pleased him enormously.

"I never had a chance to talk to him that day," he said.

"What would you have said, if he had listened?"

"I thought I could arrange something. After hearing about your idea on famine relief I talked to Dan Lloyd. He liked my suggestion that food from the Kikuyu area might be sent over to Machakos. But first, he said I had better talk to Stephen. So when I got there I was excited and ready to discuss my ideas; in the end I just couldn't do it."

"Don't let it get you down," she said as she lightly touched his clenched fist. "Stephen has to return the Shimmers' wagon sometime. I'll talk to him then. Meanwhile, I understand he's mobilized his own program."

"You know, you really are incredible," he said as he grasped her hand.

"How so?"

"Because you can cope with anything. That's why people look to you for advice." His eyes began misting over, and she suddenly thought he was about to propose again, which drove her to pull her hand free and say, "Oh, I almost forgot, Dorothy wants to see you."

"Dorothy? Now there's a surprise." He stood up and went in the house where he gently knocked on the open door.

"Come in."

"Yes?" said Roger, entering the room. "You wanted to see me?"

"The famous Mr. Newcome," said Dorothy. She was propped up in bed on a mound of pillows. Mr. Jevanjee had built shelves near the bed that held books, writing paper, magazines and a phonograph with a stack of records. It looked as if she had settled in for the long term. "I understand you know my young friend, Karegi."

"No," said Roger. "I don't think so."

"She came to me from Machakos. Her father was killed in a village called Lema. She said you rescued her."

"That may be. There were many people involved."

Karegi came in dressed in a simple shift and he recognized her immediately. She was the woman on the blanket that day. She looked at him quickly, left a tea tray and went out.

"She says the German, Shimmer's son, planned to take the captives on his boat; that's why he was waiting there," said Dorothy. "He is evil through and through and I'm afraid Stephen's badly influenced by that man."

She indicated a chair and he sat; she smoothed the blankets by her side.

"Have you ever stopped to think about people like Franz and the others, expatriate males?" she asked.

"In what way?"

"The expatriates out here all seem to be very independent. They'd like to think of themselves as 'romantics' because they have some story to tell about a mysterious or shady past. But I believe many are here only because they have trouble getting along with other humans."

"You've obviously thought about them a great deal."

"Yes," she said. "It's really all I can do now. I know that many people think I'm too weak and frail to survive on my own. I admit that. I've never said otherwise. I also admit it was a mistake to think I could make a life out here; I can't. I'm not strong enough and I know it. But I'm beginning to think it's really these others who are more in need of help than myself. The expatriates have grand ideas about driving the Africans to 'help themselves,' as they say, when in reality they are causing a great deal of damage. And strangely, they never speak about their largest weakness, their dependence on one another."

"Why is that a 'weakness'?" he asked.

"It isn't, but they make it seem like one because they won't admit it, like a child unwilling to admit he loves his mother. The fact is they are as incapable of relating to one another as they are to people in general. If anyone is like a child, I'm beginning to think it's my fellow Englishmen here in Kenya. They've been let loose from school, only to find their playground is now a place called East Africa."

Roger wondered how Muthuri would respond to that idea.

"And is that how you see me, Mrs. Hale?"

"I've thought long and hard about what you said on the train trip to Voi." She had been smoothing the blanket almost continuously since Roger had come in, as if she were smoothing over rough patches in her life. Now she stopped and looked at him directly. "When I first arrived I was perhaps in a stronger position to be more sympathetic to the needs of Africa. But I'm no longer in any position to help, because I've made myself known.

I've admitted to being a loser and now I'm nothing more than an innocent bystander."

"Innocent?" asked Roger.

"You're right. Maybe I shouldn't say 'innocent.' Just not very effective. You know, other than my friend John, you and Alice are the only two white people I trust here. All the others are like naughty children who refuse to obey their nanny. Look at how the settlers sneer at the civil government, and John tells me that they, along with everyone in Nairobi, drink entirely too much now, another sign of immaturity. He says he can hardly keep his staff sober."

"I know," said Roger, "and the Shimmers don't make it easier."

"What do you mean?"

"I learned yesterday that they have brought in massive quantities of cheap brandy from Germany. They're selling it all along the Coast and in every trading center upcountry at a price cheaper than that of soda water."

"And Stephen? I gather from Alice, he drinks more than he should."

"Yes, that's obvious, but what I find maddening is the way he defends Franz."

"That's the way he is. He says the Germans are grossly misunderstood."

"He has a point," said Roger. "I'm sure they are, but not in the way he thinks. If I were in his shoes I'd be much more suspicious."

"But all this is hardly why I asked to see you."

"Yes?" asked Roger.

"It's about Karegi. I'm certain she'll become pregnant. She's a strongly religious Mission girl, and a Catholic. There's virtually no way she can support a child on her own. Especially if anything ever happens to me. She'd have to go back to the village. Yet I know, and Alice agrees, she has the makings of a capable nurse. I've already talked to Dr. Sharpe, the railway physician; he's agreed to take her on as a trainee, providing Alice helps. She's already coaching her."

"What do you want of me?"

"Simply to watch out for her and help her if she gets into difficulties. In a way, I'm asking for what your mother asked Stephen, to watch over you, if he could."

"You know about my mother and him?"

"Of course. It was common knowledge. I've never told him I knew. He still thinks I married him blindly. He's never had any real understanding of my mother, Rosmé Curtis. She's a formidable woman; she's French, you see, and she was right to agree to my marriage. If it had worked out as she planned, I would have made a better man out of Stephen. That would have happened if we were at home. As it is, Africa and Stephen together were too much for me, and now I'm afraid I've lost him to drink. And Africa too has almost slipped away; that's why I'm trying now to make amends."

"Rest easy regarding Karegi," said Roger. "I'll keep an eye out for her. By the way, I'm sorry you're still not feeling well."

"Thank you, but I'm doing much better, now that I've stopped feeling sorry for myself."

"I guess we got off on the wrong foot from the beginning."

"That was entirely my fault," said Dorothy. "I've realized since then that you're a very sincere young man."

She smiled at him and lay back on her bed; the interview was over. "And don't give up with Alice. It may still work out for the best."

Mombasa, Kenya

The small troop of Indian sepoys marched in front of Stephen as they trudged up to the gate of Fort Jesus, pushing three dusty, ragged-looking men in front of them. A platoon of Swahili prison guards was standing by to receive them. The sun overhead scorched the open yard and baked the cobblestones so that it was impossible to stand still, the heat searing even the most calloused feet. The guard detachment had no boots, only white puttees. They waited in the shade under an arch until summoned by Capt. Bobby Curtis, who came strolling out of the officers' club. The guard fell in, forming a square around the prisoners.

"Stephen, old man," Bobby said, and reached up to shake hands. "Just in time for luncheon. And how are the ladies?" Stephen made no move to dismount.

"Alice is well, but Dorothy's quite sick," Stephen said as he sat on his horse. "She's in Nairobi. I can't stay, Bobby. I've got to get over to the commissioner's office. I'll come around later before I head back. I just wanted to make sure they delivered these three."

Bobby's nose went up as he suddenly smelt something bad. He looked with distaste at the slavers. "God, what a pong. Caught with their hands in the cookie jar, what?"

"Here's the charge sheet; as you can see, it's all very serious."

Bobby motioned to Stephen to lean down closer as he whispered up at him. "Hate to grouse about such things, old man, but it would save us a great deal of trouble if you simply take them around back. There's an outside ledge there. Unchain them and just yell 'Stop'; give our sentry chaps some practice, what?"

Stephen recoiled and his horse reacted as if it had stepped on a venomous snake. "Are you *mad*?"

Embarrassed, Bobby shot back, "But they're only wogs."

"Put them in a proper jail cell," said Stephen sternly, as he wheeled his horse. Bobby watched Stephen ride off, his sepoys trotting behind with muskets held at port arms.

"Damned queer fellow," he muttered, as he walked back to the club over the hot pavement. In his mind he thought of him as "poor Stephen," a sorry figure, really. And to think he had traveled all the way back to Maidstone from Calcutta just for his niece's marriage to this man. On second thought, he said to himself, he would never have missed that. He reached the shade of the fort wall and walked on. Lovely little Dot in her wedding gown. It made his eyes bright with emotion as he recalled the early days when he would ride that little blonde angel on his knee. Life was not kind to others, he knew. He had heard from his sister-in law, Rosmé, about Dot's disappointment with life in Africa. Maybe Nairobi would be better for her, he thought, and his mouth watered as he recalled the curry buffet waiting for him. He himself got along very well as a bachelor overseas, but for someone like Stephen, well, the poor chap looked decimated, he thought. Could be he was off his feed. Looked just like Don Quixote on that horse. Tall, thin, droopy mustache, bit foolish out there in the bundu arresting Arabs. Waste of time, there's so many of 'em.

Damn, he suddenly remembered, there was something he should have told him. The thought "waste of time" did it. His face lit up as he remembered. That's it, waste of time looking for the commissioner. He's off in Zanzibar again. Ah well, he'll find out for himself.

10

Isabelle, wife of the high commissioner of the Kenya colony, greeted Stephen in the loge. A slim woman, her hair was piled into a delicate coiffure resembling an intricate nest. That and the silk material of her day dress gave her the Japanese look recently made popular by Whistler in England.

"Lovely to see you again, Stephen," she said as she gave him a brief kiss on the cheek and rested her cool hand on his warm arm.

They knew one another from India where Ian and Stephen had been posted together. It was late Friday afternoon and many of the house servants were off observing their day of rest. The Muslim prayer services for the afternoon had just ended and the *muezzins'* calls still echoed down the warm alleyways and out against the hot plastered walls of the houses.

She had a sultry, disheveled look, which told him she had just risen from her siesta couch.

"Michael," she called to her Christian servant, "put Bwana's bag in the guest wing and make us some tea. Now tell me all about your exciting life in Machakos."

She had already read his telegram to Ian about tracking down slavers. "Weren't you afraid they might turn on you? So brave," she said, in a wonderfully purring voice.

She reminded him of a slim cat rubbing its back against his leg. Next, he thought, she'll jump into my lap and rub her soft face against mine.

"Quite an adventure," he replied, blushing. "But I can't see that kind of thing happening again. I think the only excitement after this will be the occasional murder trial among the natives, or an elephant or two going on the rampage."

"Which, as I remember, was cause for some alarm in India," she said. "Weren't they driven wild with rage when they were in heat? What did they call that?"

"I believe it was *musth*, and it was only the males who went berserk; the females were always very sedate."

"Isn't that always the way," she smiled, her hand now touching her hair, smoothing it along the side of her neck.

Like a cat licking its fur, he thought.

"I see you will very easily fall into the life at Machakos. You'll become a typical up-country district officer. But do you think that's so very good for your mind?"

He could not help thinking of a photograph of Susan that he kept under his pillow now that Dorothy had gone from his bed. Why did that make him think of her? A realization flashed through his mind. It was the scent. Isabelle wore a deep floral perfume similar to Susan's, while Dorothy preferred a light cologne, one that dissipated easily in the dust and heat of Africa.

"I don't have much choice. A few of the army lads play a rough form of polo on weekends, but I'm not much for that sort of thing."

He noticed for the first time her smile.

"And I don't have the talent to while away the hours on the violin or piano," he said. "I'm afraid reading and long walks are the thing for me."

"Well, if that's the case," she said, "you must help yourself." She pointed an exquisite finger to the shelves in the library next door. "We have an extraordinary collection, passed on from the liaison officers and the Sultan's staff years gone by. Quite exotic and very entertaining."

They chatted on for a bit before he went along to the guest wing, which was in a separate section reached by a connecting hallway. It consisted of several bedrooms and sitting rooms, only one of which was occupied; an older couple was staying there, a retired military man and his wife, intent on starting a farm north of Mombasa. They planned on leaving the following morning and were busy shopping for farm tools and packing up provisions. He washed up and laid out his dinner clothes on the bed.

Dinner that evening consisted of a clear soup, some local green leafy vegetable, a small bush pig roasted with an orange in its mouth and flambéed bananas for dessert. The Bengali cook had been assisted by Michael, the houseman, because whenever pork was on the menu, the Muslim servants refused to go near the kitchen for one full day.

Isabelle was in a cheerful mood, despite her admitted dissatisfaction with life in Mombasa. She had told Stephen that her marriage to Ian had survived the past six years only because she could draw on some inner strength. Stephen took that for what it was worth. He had heard she had been notorious for flirting before her marriage and he knew that was the sort of character trait that was accentuated in the tropics where the warm, exotic atmosphere fed the imagination. Here in Mombasa Stephen knew Isabelle would be an endangered species, a beautiful woman in what was predominantly a bachelor colony. He also knew Ian traveled a great deal and that she had virtually a free hand. Furthermore, behavior that was looked upon as scandalous in London was perfectly acceptable out here. He knew she could only be seen with certain men, of which the supply was extremely limited. None of the young single officers would do. Other young men in the army, railway and foreign service, possibly all willing, were not to be trusted; they lacked the discretion that came with maturity, or from a private life away from the barracks. Of the mature males, most were married; a few had their wives with them in Mombasa. Those who were alone kept African mistresses or Arab boys. He also suspected that there were probably several white businessmen in Mombasa who would be very much interested in her, but the better business connections they needed to maintain with Ian would keep them in check. He felt a tug of sympathy for her, despite his respect for Ian. It was madness, he thought, to leave her alone like this.

After dinner he begged off further socializing. Conversation with the settler and his wife was heavy going and Isabelle seemed too distracted. He wandered back to his room to finish a report on irrigated farming using water from the Athi River. The breeze of early evening had died, the heat radiating from the walls and the still air closed in around him. Lying down he tried to sleep, but it was difficult. The continuous whine of mosquitoes just outside the net made them seem perilously close to his face. Following the incident at Lema, he had again sworn off alcohol, although many reasons came to mind as he lay there as to why he should drink. His experience with malaria in India had taught him to take extra care; unlike others who accepted fever and a short life as inescapable, he religiously took quinine followed by one peg of neat gin each evening from a flask. Tonight he felt particularly vulnerable and had several doses before settling again into his bed intent on sleeping. The guest wing faced the older, crowded section of town away from the sea, a disadvantage because of the street noise and lack of air. It made the room uncomfortable. He rolled over on his back and thought about Isabelle and the stories that had been passed around in India, indiscretions on her first trip out, undying friendships with former beaux and her obvious desire to be close to men. It was easy for him to imagine himself lying there in place of others, her body beside him. Hot, restless, he threw off the sheets and lay there naked. He lit a candle and reached for the book he had been reading. His mind, unable to concentrate on the printed word, was on edge, as if it were expecting something. Then the door, which had no lock, slowly opened and he was surprised to see her standing there in her nightdress.

"I saw the light," she whispered, "and guessed you were awake. I've brought you some books."

She seems to think it is the most natural thing in the world to be here, Stephen reflected. He had grabbed for the sheet to cover himself, but stopped. Something told him not to bother. "Thanks," he whispered back, as he raised the netting. She sat lightly on the edge of the bed.

"Couldn't sleep anyway. I wonder if I have a fever? Could you feel my forehead?"

He reached up and gently felt, convinced his own hand was probably now sending out enough warm energy to create a fever if a fever were not there. "Yes," he lied. "A slight fever, but it could be caused by anything, just walking about at night."

"Ah. Your hand feels so good against me, would you mind if

I just rested a bit?" She leaned back against his bare shoulder, a movement that encouraged his arms to slip around her as she turned her face up to his and her mouth formed a pout. Their lips came together.

"Stephen," she whispered in his ear. "My brave exotic warrior. I want you so much," she said suggestively.

"Yes," he whispered, as he lifted her nightdress and kissed her body, unable to control himself, moving downward. "Yes, my pussycat, purring, soft ball of fur, yes," and he pushed his face between her legs, his tongue working its way into her. "Yes."

Later, she lay quietly on the bed, her eyes half closed, a sheen of perspiration on her brow. He got up and rinsed out a wet cloth in the basin, then gently moved the damp cloth over her forehead and down across her naked body onto her legs. Passing it across her stomach and downward between her thighs, he watched her pale legs twitch in the candlelight as he gently patted the cloth close to the source of all heat, or so it seemed to him, as his hand brushed against the warm pleasant radiation that rose from there and heated his body and imagination.

He rolled her over and entered her from behind.

"Yes," he whispered, "my little tiger cub."

"Fantastic to be back," said Ian as he sipped a gin and tonic, looking bright-eyed and cheery after his latest sojourn in Zanzibar. A short, paunchy, red-faced Scot, with a gray bristly mustache and tufted thatches on his head, he dominated the room. "You must come over there with me sometime, Stephen. Isabelle hates the place; can't see why. The sultan's the soul of respectability, first-class food and drink, absolutely exotic life, and it's all there within the palace."

"I must say, though," continued Ian, "you look the better for your stay in Machakos, old man. Thinner. In fact, looks fit as a fiddle, doesn't he, Isabelle?"

Ian did not ask one word about the drought, the famine, or the countless people dying even as he sipped his drink. He was confident that Stephen was dealing with the problem. Later he confided in Stephen that the foreign office was on the verge of appointing him provincial commissioner; they wanted Stephen to take charge of the whole region from Ukambaa to the escarpment, a region that included Nairobi. "I thought it would help to post David temporarily in Nairobi, until the appointment comes through. That way we'd have some presence there." To forestall the damned railway, he might have added, thought Stephen.

That evening he found sleep even more difficult than usual. He wandered into the large dining room and looked down from the window, his favorite view, the Old Harbor and lights twinkling along the shore. The small boats in the moonlight reminded him of Hull. He went back to his bed, lay down and stared at the ceiling. Why am I so restless? he wondered, tears welling in his eyes as a fit of despair seized him, and without any provocation, tears streamed down his face. He couldn't believe that his little romp with Isabelle was the reason for his despondency—the expatriates did that sort of thing every day in Kenya. Yet he couldn't very well go to a brothel, not a man in his position.

What's wrong with me? he wondered. Then the remembrance came to him, the images, the horrors of Lema and the faces of those villagers, and somewhere in the back of his mind was the idea that maybe he shouldn't go back to Machakos. Regardless of what Ian thought and said, he knew many of the problems were of his own making. He also knew that by now no matter what he did, those problems had become insurmountable. Depressed and lonely, he reached for a bottle of brandy on his night table, blew out the candle and lay back as the word "Susan" escaped him, just before he placed the bottle to his lips and upended it in the dark.

11

Roger was surprised to see Capt. Bobby at the gate to Alice's house. He had been about to call on her, mindful of the season; after all, despite the terrific heat of the day and the tropical sun beating down on the two of them, it was Christmas Eve. Proof of that was the appearance of Christmas decorations and a gaily painted banner that was now being put up by Jakoby. It proclaimed to all a "Merry Christmas."

"Capt. Curtis," he said, opening the gate for him, "I'm Roger Newcome. We met in Naivasha."

"I remember. You're the young man who stays out there with the Kikuyus, what?"

"Yes. And are you visiting?" Roger asked as he followed him along the path.

"Invited, sir," said Bobby, who was looking forward to the holiday festivities. "Came to see my favorite niece, Dot. And you?"

"Likewise," said Roger as he spotted Jakoby on the verandah. "Greetings, Jakoby. How are you?"

"Fine, Bwana Roger. As you see, I am making progress. And how are your Kikuyus?"

"This is Jakoby," said Roger by way of introducing her to Bobby, who was not used to being introduced to servants. He stopped on the top step and stared at her as if he had never seen an African before.

"Like us, she's an expatriate," said Roger. "She's from South Africa."

"I thought she wasn't your typical black, eh?" said Bobby, who was astonished by Jakoby's "cheeky" ways as she moved about the verandah. She gave the impression that she owned the place, he thought. "Zulu is she?"

She giggled at this chubby, red-faced man in uniform. For some reason she found him enormously funny. "Memsab Dorothy says you must wait out here," she said. "She has a guest."

They sat down on some wicker chairs.

"Rather like a vacation for you," said Roger to Jakoby.

"The work at the hotel would make me old before my time, Bwana," she said, "and I am still looking for a new husband."

Mary, the house girl, appeared and asked if they wanted some refreshment.

"Some tea, Bobby?" asked Roger, who was quite at home here.

"Not the right climate for tea, old boy. Too hot and dry. Doctor tells me I have to keep the body fluids topped up, eh? Prefer a brandy and soda."

Mary went inside to get his drink.

"And how's the railway progressing?" asked Roger.

"Splendid!" said Bobby. "They'd just finished the station at Kima before I got there."

"That's about 260 miles from the Coast."

"And not a bad go," said Bobby. "Only takes twelve hours from Mombasa. You stay overnight at the station then come on to Nairobi the next day. It was the last fifty miles on bloody horseback that required most of the effort."

"And traffic is picking up?" asked Roger.

"I had plenty of fellow passengers."

Suddenly the front door opened and John Allen came out, followed by Alice. He stood there in his wrinkled clothes and smiled at them as they shook hands and exchanged greetings.

"John's head of the Railway here in Nairobi," said Alice. "His family's from Sevenoaks, Bobby."

"Not far from where Dot grew up."

"Mr. Newcome," said Allen. "I've seen you here on several occasions. We should sit down some day and have a talk, perhaps at the club."

"Not likely," said Roger. "I haven't joined."

He knew why Allen was so friendly. He wasn't the first. Quite a few people now showed an interest in his connections with the

Kikuyu and their legendary abilities in terms of food production.

"I've invited Roger to tonight's dinner," said Alice.

"And your uncle?"

"Bobby," she said, "we've all been invited to Christmas dinner tonight at the railway club. Can we tempt you?"

"Sorry, old girl. Promised everyone at the army club I'd spend some time with them. I might pop in, if I can break away. But I'll definitely be over early tomorrow for tea, if you don't mind."

Mary reappeared with Bobby's drink as Allen put on his topi and left.

"Memsab says she is ready now," said Mary. Bobby took a large gulp from his drink and shook his chubby face as he caught Jakoby staring at him.

He followed Roger and Alice inside.

"Poor little Dot," said Bobby as he reached for Dorothy's hand. "How are you?"

To Roger it seemed she hadn't changed much since her arrival at the Mombasa dock, except that she was a little thinner and at that moment her cheeks were flushed; probably because of Allen's visit, he thought.

To Bobby she looked quite ill and despite a hurried, whispered warning from Alice before they entered the room, he had difficulty hiding his tears. He searched his niece's eyes for some response, and then tried to kiss her warm cheek as he continued to hold her hand. She turned her head to avoid him and said, "Ah, yes, Uncle Bobby, you're here. I'm afraid we can't offer you much hospitality."

He stood there sniffling and looking very sad.

"It's only a rented house," she explained. "Where are you staying?"

"Not to worry, little one," he said. "Plenty of room at the army club. Not much time here; did they tell you of my plan, eh?"

She shook her head.

"Well, never mind, little angel," the tears were flowing down his cheeks. "We'll soon have you back on your sea legs."

He turned to Alice, "The effect of sea air, marvelous tonic. She'll be right as rain before we clear Durban."

Dorothy turned her eyes toward Alice and Roger, appealing to them to rid her of her uncle.

"That's enough for now, Bobby," said Alice. "Dr. Sharpe has sent word he wants to see her later today, so we must let her rest."

To Dorothy's obvious relief, Alice and Roger escorted Bobby from the room.

Mary served them tea in an alcove off Alice's room on the other side of the house. "Well, Uncle Bobby," she asked, "what do you think of your niece?"

"Made my heart sink when I saw her face," he said as he disregarded the teacup and helped himself to some fruitcake and a large glass of sherry. "She definitely needs to be up and about, you know. I always say without exercise and a good appetite, we're nothing."

"I know she's thin," said Alice, "but she still has enormous spirit. She can easily manage short walks during the morning. Don't you agree, Roger? She always seems on the verge of some dramatic recovery."

"I agree it's hopeful."

"What I'm proposing," said Bobby, still snuffling, "is that since I'm being transferred back to India, I would come back in a few weeks and take her to Mombasa. Then we'd go with her by steamer to Durban then on to the hospital in Cape Town."

He helped himself to the decanter of sherry. "Well, Alice, what say you? You have until the day after New Year's to decide."

"So you would prefer she goes on to Cape Town?" said Alice.

"We're not going to see another opportunity like this for a while."

"And it'll be another few months before the railroad arrives in Nairobi," said Roger.

"What does Stephen think?"

"I saw him in Mombasa," said Bobby. "He agrees with me. He's afraid she may not make the recovery we've been waiting for, and we'll miss a chance to get her out while we can."

Alice said nothing.

"Well then," said Bobby, "I presume you'll be coming with Dorothy to Cape Town. Good." His cheeks reddened further with the prospect of a sea cruise with Alice as a companion. "I'll reserve a stateroom for each of you and I'll stop by tomorrow before I head back to Mombasa."

At the railway club, John Allen put on a waltz record. He had commandeered the dining room and the club phonograph for this occasion, a special night, and he brought all his social skills to bear as he took Alice in his arms and whirled with her around the room. She laughed at his boldness, and almost from the minute she arrived at the club she understood from his attitude and determination that "something was in the wind."

Everyone else stood around the drinks table and watched the happy couple as the waiters poured champagne.

David McCann arrived late and tried to attract Alice's attention. He had gotten used to people reacting when he came into a room—after all, he was now acting DC of Nairobi—but no one tonight was responding as they should.

"She can't hear you," said Roger, shaking his head in dismay. He had no idea himself of how to make any headway in this kind of social situation. On safari it was different; there he felt confident; but here it was useless, and he could only appear at his worst. He wasn't helped by the fact the dinner jacket he had borrowed from J.O. was obviously too large; also his black tie was crooked and his shoes needed polishing.

"She has eyes for Allen and that's that, I'm afraid," he said to Jenny, the only other woman there. Jenny hated dancing.

"But where do I put this?" asked David, as he held up a slim box wrapped in colorful paper and tied with an expensive silk bow. He, like Roger and the others, had on a dinner jacket, but in his case it had been tailored and fit beautifully. He also felt he had an inner advantage, in that he had recently rediscovered religion. He rather hoped that it showed in his young face, and he thought it might, because he knew from the mirror just before leaving his house that he was glowing.

In order to ensure he made the right impression, he had read several verses of Genesis to focus his mind before setting off. That was the reason he was late arriving, and he was determined to speak to Alice alone, but from where he stood the field already looked crowded.

"Just sling it on the pile," said Bagley, indicating a growing stack of presents by the side of a small acacia tree decorated with Christmas ornaments.

"Those are *all* hers?" asked Matthew in amazement. He stood with the others watching Alice and John. He and Dan Lloyd were in dress uniform, while Jenny and Alice had on their best gowns.

"Impressive, what?" said Dan. Matthew could not tell if he was referring to the pile of presents, or the couple, the *only* couple, dancing.

"How about a glass of champagne?" Alice called to them, as she stopped dancing for a moment. Five male hands reached for glasses for her from the tray of drinks.

"No, please. I meant for yourselves," she said, laughing at them.

Perhaps, thought Jenny, Alice simply couldn't see the longing in their eyes. Or else she's purposely ignoring the pain they were going through to present the best sides of their character. Otherwise, Jenny felt it would be cruel for anyone to laugh at them like that. The poor dears were falling over one another. "And Alice," asked Jenny, indicating the parcels alongside the tree, "may we open our presents?"

"Of course," said she. "Everyone, please start." But they waited and watched in trepidation until she came over and reached for the first gift. Then they wondered who would be the lucky one.

"It's from David," she announced, and read the card before she unwrapped the gift, a black lace shawl.

She was ecstatic. Previous to this dinner, she had never had such attention, and somehow she felt it was proof she had made the right decision to stay, because now everything seemed to be coming together. It also helped that John Allen had made certain that everything would be perfect. On his side, he intended to ask Alice to go for a walk later that would take them by his place. Despite the fact that he was the shortest person in the room, he felt confident and in charge. After all, he thought, I've planned the whole evening around her.

Suddenly another person entered the room. Brian.

Dressed in a dinner jacket and looking extraordinarily handsome because of his height, he strode in just as the phonograph stopped. Everyone was surprised. He was notorious for staying away from Nairobi as much as he could. Though he was recently appointed by the settlers to head up their organization, they seldom saw him in town. The other surprising thing was that he was carrying a bundle, a soft blanket wrapped around something.

He had the attention of everyone as he walked over to Alice, bowed and said, "Merry Christmas, Alice. And thanks for the invitation to dinner. I've brought you something from Ol Donyo Sabuk."

As he spoke, the bundle moved.

Whatever was in it was alive.

David stepped away, but Alice was entranced. She reached forward and folded back the edges of the blanket. Inside, the small furry head of a baby cheetah poked itself out. Blonde-furred with black spots, it mewed.

"Oh my!" said she, as she plucked the little animal out and held it to her breast. Suddenly the blanket moved again, and another head popped up. A second baby mewed, and Alice gave a small scream of delight as she took the second one and cuddled both. She looked at Brian with bright, moist eyes and kissed him on his bronzed cheek.

"Oh, Brian! What treasures! Everybody, look at them. The little darlings!"

In the background a waiter had started the music again; the waltz played and the champagne sat untasted as it fizzed on the trays. Every male in the room looked at Brian and wondered how he could do such a thing. Their presents sat ignored, because at that moment DeCosta, the club steward, announced dinner, and everyone went to the table that had been set for a banquet.

Brian sat next to Alice because she demanded that the cheetahs' blanket be brought close to her chair so she could watch over them.

"Where did you get them?"

"Tom and Edna found them. Their mother was trapped and killed by some poachers," he said. "They couldn't leave them or they'd certainly die." Then he motioned to a Somali man standing in the doorway. "Kona," he said, and the man came forward carrying two bottles of milk.

Roger watched with a sour expression on his face as Alice reluctantly gave up the two cubs to Kona, who placed them back on their blanket and then squatted there on the floor between Brian and Alice as he fed them.

"I'm afraid Kona comes with them," said Brian.

"Of course," said Alice, then as her mind raced forward, she said, "I'll have to have Jevanjee expand our servants' quarters."

Jenny had also moved her chair close, so she could watch the cubs being nursed. "And you'll have to make a cage in the compound," she said, as she glanced up at Dan with a look that said, Why don't you bring me presents like that? And John, Matthew, David and Roger stared hard at Brian, the recluse from the north who had stolen the attention of the only two women present, and they found that hard to forgive.

The next day, Bobby arrived to say good-bye to Alice and Dorothy. He came in for a cup of morning tea that he took with Alice in the garden behind the house.

"Not much like a proper English garden, is it?" he asked. Then he noticed the cheetah cubs in a box that temporarily served as their cage. "I say, where'd they come from?"

"A Christmas present," said Alice. "Brian gave them to me last night. How was your club?"

"Fine. Great fun. Terrific what the chaps get up to," he said, and slowly shook his head. He looked and felt the worse for wear, so he thought this morning that the chaps must have gotten up to an awful lot.

"Did you say 'Brian'?" he said, as it only now registered. "You mean Lord Brian Stanford?"

"Yes. You know him?"

"No, but I've met his wife, Lady Stanford. She was at the army club last night with Sutherland; extraordinary, what? He and his wife at completely different parties. Quite good-looking, a bit wild though. Not my type, I'm afraid."

He let Alice pour him another cup, and then said, "Which reminds me, Alice, old girl; you know I may be able to take some leave for a quick trip back home once I leave Mombasa. Old Sutherland said he would certainly give me permission for a special cause."

Alice looked at him, uncomprehending.

"I mean, I don't have to go out to India immediately, you see. And I suppose I should confess something to you. Something I had not dared mention before."

He took her hands in his and looked into her eyes. His own were bloodshot from the evening previous, but, he hoped, expressive of what he was about to say.

"I love you, Alice. I have from the moment we met. I want to marry you."

He stopped, because she had pulled her hands sharply from his grasp. The shocked expression on her face and furrowed brow carried their own message.

"No! Bobby," she said shaking her head. "Stop. You don't understand. I don't know how you leap to these assumptions. I have no intention of even going to Cape Town with you. I've decided to stay here." She quickly recovered from her shock, but he looked devastated.

"I like the life here, and as for what you say about loving me, I'm as shocked as everyone else would be to hear you proposing marriage to your niece!"

"But I assumed since you're only my step-niece...."

"It's time you came to your senses," she said. "I suggest you stop thinking about this, go on a long walking tour in the hills, anything, anything, but get that ridiculous idea out of your head!"

Suddenly Kona, the keeper of the cheetah cubs, came in. "Memsab?" he said as he set down a fresh pot of tea.

"Yes?" said Alice.

"Brian is here," he indicated the verandah with his eyes. "He says you and the hunter, J.O., are going on a safari today."

In Muthuri's Hut

Ah, Bwana Roger, you are back, and without a bride.

What? You are still worried about Kimani. Where has he gone? What is he up to?

My friend, you should know that he is not like you or I. We have our daily tasks, our duty to life, but he has larger responsibilities.

I knew him from childhood when we were growing up and learning from the White Fathers in Ngongo Bargas. He was the first to see that these missionaries did not take well to the Masai and the Kikuyu. They professed many reasons why they distrusted us, compared to other tribes in Africa. He tried to counter these feelings, but he found it difficult to defend the ways of his people, until he learned to reason the way you wazungu do.

From what he could gather, the Masai and Kikuyu were singled out because we are aggressive and fiercely protective of our land, people and cattle. But, was this not also the view held by the Bible? he said. The sacred book which is the basis of your traditions in your own land? And which admonishes those who are Christians to look after their own families? Also when you talk about the might and power of the Queen, where does that come from? Was it not derived from the strength of her army, her castles, wealth, jewels and her crown?

Is this any different from a village headman?

Kimani argued that it was not.

He also knew that all white people were not like the missionaries. His father had told him all about Bwana Lugard, who held views similar to Kimani's father. He had made blood treaties to guarantee trade and the use of land, but he respected the rights of the tribes and showed them how to live together. For this quality he was known as "Duma," the cheetah—a good-natured, long-legged member of the cat family, a good hunter with lightning-fast reflexes; but most importantly, an animal that knows its place in the pecking order.

It walks away from a kill as soon as the scavengers or lions become too aggressive. It knows there are many more animals on the plains, easy pickings for an able hunter.

This much was clear in the way in which Duma went about his work; he sought out the tribes and chiefs with influence, but he did this in a natural way, leaving behind few enemies. Among the series of trading posts that he founded, one lay just between the Masai and Kikuyu regions, Ngongo Bargas. It is a natural meeting place. People came there often, but it was different from the usual gatherings organized by the missionaries. The missionaries want people to come to their places, to attend their schools, churches and hospitals, and who can blame them? If you were told to do this by God, Queen and Pope, who could refuse? But Duma did not need any special reason, other than that he wanted people to trade and meet on their own terms. That was the difference.

And soon, Ngongo Bargas, because of its good climate, clear water and location, became a popular place to stop.

Traders, missionaries and the first railroad survey parties were all impressed by what they saw. Later they located the new center for the railroad lower in the valley, at the swampy place the Masai call "Engore Nyarobe," the place of cold water, but they agree Ngongo is still a more attractive place. Kimani always preferred it to Nairobi, which as you see is developing into a noisy, muddy town. Some say Nairobi reflects the hate you people feel for the land and people less fortunate than you, even among your own kind. But in Ngongo, still, members of several tribes meet among themselves while the women do the trading.

Kimani was a second son, so his father wanted him to attend school there. That way he could better serve everyone by learning the ways of people like you. In our clan we have an expression "Guthii ni kuona," to go is to see. It means he who travels about is the one who knows what's happening.

So, where is Kimani? Where else. He has gone to Ngongo. He wants to become a White Father.

12

Bobby arrived at Kima station after a long, hard ride. The heat and saddle had taken their toll and he was still somewhat shocked by Alice's refusal. Damn good thing I didn't buy that ring, he thought. An Asian shopkeeper had tried to interest him in an enormous ruby, a gem he swore was genuine. Bobby had put him off and now was thankful, though he was still bewildered by what had happened. He continued to search his mind for whatever it was she thought was so wrong.

Still mystified, he stepped down from his horse and was glad to see that the railhead crew had moved on. This meant he'd have the waiting room to himself. It had been very crowded previously; but as he entered he saw immediately that there were no beds left.

Damn them, they've taken everything with them.

"*Apki salah kya hey*? What do you suggest?" he asked in Hindustani, guessing the stationmaster, Sri Nanda Rao, was from Bombay.

"Not to worry, Sahib, there is an inspection coach on the siding here. It has an upper and lower berth and is equipped with a small kitchen and latrine. And I can provide a cook," he added, "along with some food, water and linen at a small cost. The Sahib will be as snug as can be, at little expense."

"And when does the return train start from here?"

"Again, no problem. This inspection coach must be returned to Mombasa. We will simply connect it to the return train early in the morning, and you will have the advantage of it all the way to Mombasa. I will supervise this myself."

"I say, damn good," said Bobby. "And you'll see the horse gets back to Nairobi?"

"Also no problem, and I will tell everyone not to wake you. But remember, close the door *kabesa*, tight. The lions are always roaming here after dark."

Bobby slid the door of the compartment closed and sat down to a plate of curry and a bottle of beer. Then he climbed into his bed with a flask of brandy and extinguished the candle. It soon became deathly hot in the car with the door closed. The windows were open, but they were shuttered to prevent petty theft, and so provided little relief.

Quiet descended on the steamy coach, except for the heavy breathing of Bobby, until about two o'clock, at which time every evening he had the unbreakable habit of relieving himself. His bladder was used to this, and responded so strongly to the routine that it could no more give up that nightly function than its master could give up drink itself.

He stumbled forward in the dark but found the latrine, located in the compartment beyond the kitchen, had been locked by the stationmaster.

"No matter," he muttered as he slid the main door open and stepped out onto the platform of the coach. There the pasty white color of his naked body and his bulky outline created an amazing sight in the light of the full moon. His bladder relaxed completely as he leaned against the railing. A pleasant experience, similar to leaning against the lee rail on a boat at night in the Indian Ocean. A pungent odor came back to him as the urine splattered on the warm tracks below, and he shook his member a few times before he turned to go back into his hot, stuffy bed. At least now, he thought, I can sleep soundly until late morning.

Suddenly, he was startled to see an African clergyman standing at the foot of the platform, smiling up at him. An African, bold as brass, dressed in the immaculate white cassock of a missionary, brandishing a large revolver.

"Now, Mr. Bobby," he said, no longer smiling, "come down those stairs slowly with your hands up, or I will shoot you dead without remorse."

Bobby did that, but not without one observation. As he descended, naked, to the ground, he muttered, "Hell of a way for a

White Father to act, if you ask me."

The following morning the cook slid a breakfast tray inside the open door before quietly closing it. He then went to work cooking the morning meal for the crew. The stationmaster, as promised, supervised the coupling of the inspection coach to the down train, and on reaching the Mombasa rail yard, it was shunted to the side. One week later the police askaris found all of Bobby's clothing, including his uniform, neatly laid out on top of his baggage. His underwear, boots, flask, socks and cap were all there, untouched, but their owner was nowhere in sight.

Outside on the platform there was nothing but a small pool of dried blood.

In Nairobi, the Shimmers had bought the Palace Hotel, where they had taken over the second floor for their own use. The ground floor was divided into five small rooms with a few amenities for paying guests and no bar, only a tearoom. The other hotel, Lowe's, was preferred by most travelers because it had a dance floor and a large bar, though neither place was considered anything but third class accommodation. They both were so rough, guests moved out as soon as possible. Many preferred to pitch a tent in the suburbs rather than stay in either place. It was a mystery how the Shimmers made a living at it. The residents were convinced that the Shimmers were into smuggling, but for the life of them they couldn't figure out what they were smuggling, or where they were smuggling it to. All that was known was that the two men traveled a great deal while Elise stayed put, managing the business and showing little favoritism; all guests were equally ignored once they had registered.

In contrast, the rooms inhabited by the Shimmers were kept immaculate, and they had an excellent cook who served them food and drink of the highest standard, all of which was paid for promptly, in cash, from a large safe in Elise's office.

Shortly after New Years, Albert returned from an extended trip. He had spent Christmas in Pretoria, and then stopped in Tanga and Mombasa on his return. After dumping his baggage in the hallway, he retired to his large bathroom where a hot bath was drawn and he proceeded to wash the grime of Africa from his body. Then he sat and discussed with Elise and Franz what he had heard during his trip.

"Milner's still at it, trying to whip up a war. The man's a maniac; everyone says the British public is not interested, but still he persists. He wants war, and there's no question about that. He wants British control over the Orange Free State, and he'll go to great lengths to get it."

"But if there is a war, do the British have any hope of winning?" asked Franz. "If it's anything like their first effort, they'd be slaughtered."

"Majuba and Jameson's Raid all over again," said Albert, as he sipped a whiskey and soda. "They never learn."

"Perhaps if they suffer badly enough," said Elise, "it will make them more likely to give up in Kenya as well."

"What's been happening here?"

"There have been several derailments," said Franz, smiling, "and more raids. And I've kept on with the brandy business. Their junior staff is rambunctious as hell."

"Also," said Elise, "I've encouraged Jakoby to get to know some of the key blacks in the area."

"But she doesn't have enough time to develop any contacts," said Franz. "She's still taken up with the Hale household."

"She's wasted there," said Albert. "I thought she'd be a great asset when and if Hale moved in to join his wife, but now the word's out in Mombasa. Hale may never move."

"Why not?" asked Elise.

"It's his drinking. They're worried. They've had second thoughts about making him provincial commissioner."

"So McCann may just stay on in place?" asked Franz.

"Yes, and Hale will stay in Machakos. One of the standard jokes in government circles is that he is burying himself out there."

"Then we need to make better use of Jakoby," Elise said. "What about getting her into McCann's household?"

"Too late," said Franz. "He's a very religious man, hires only local Mission types."

"What to do?"

"I have an idea...," said Albert.

A sturdy woman with a round black face, Jakoby had marvelous white teeth and small sharp eyes that missed nothing. Her kinky hair stood out in tufts and she seldom wore any head covering. Whites often had no idea she was not a local woman since, to many of them, all blacks were the same. But, among East Africans, she was so different as to be an oddity. It was obvious that she did not stretch her ear lobes, and instead of leather aprons and beaded necklaces she wore the loose full skirt and long-sleeved blouses of the missionary women, but no cross. Moreover, she was bold, forward-looking and a fast learner. She had not been in Kenya long before she could speak Kiswahili and some of the local languages. She and Karegi had become fast friends and shared a room in the servants' quarters in Alice's house where they presented quite a contrast. Karegi, slim, with fine facial features and high cheekbones, was considered a local beauty queen. Men, black, brown and white, stared at her as she walked to work at the railway hospital. She was untiring in the care of her person, combing and trimming her hair and applying light, fragrant oils after her evening bath. She wasn't unusually vain, but she did sometimes worry that perhaps her nose was a bit too small for her face, unlike Jakoby, who was quite proud of her flat nose and flared nostrils.

Jakoby had told Karegi that it was the fashion in some cities in South Africa for blacks to pinch the babies' noses at birth to make them look more like the white men.

"That is wrong," said Jakoby.

"Why?"

"Because the white man's face is of no use whatsoever, especially in Africa. Take their mouth. The mzungu mouth is very weak, like a baby's," she said. "Their lips are too thin-skinned and red, like berries that are going to burst and bleed at any moment."

"But they often call one another thick-skinned," said Karegi, laughing. "And they don't bleed easily."

"Good," said Jakoby, "because if they did, they would blame the Africans."

Another of Jakoby's complaints held that the whites were always worried about their food. "They are suspicious of Africans who offer them good hard seeds and fruits as part of the local fare. Instead they eat soft food that every African knows is not good for their teeth. And they won't listen if we tell them otherwise, eh? Somehow it is the African who is always wrong."

"You are too hard on them," said Karegi. "Remember, they come from a different world."

Jakoby was not assuaged. She was convinced there was something wrong with a race of people who could not even hear ordinary sounds like animals moving softly in the bundu, or see beyond a few yards without putting on their spectacles.

"It is the same with their noses," she said. She knew their prominent beaks were constricted and very tender inside. The proof of that observation was demonstrated whenever they wrinkled them up when confronted with rich or strong odors. In the process, their faces looked like those of the jungle creatures, the apes and gorillas.

"Yet no one dares tell them about these things."

She felt sorry for them, because, in their ignorance, they continued to become more and more grotesque. Even their forehead was a hindrance, as they could not go out in the sunlight without a hat, otherwise it turned red and inflamed, then blistered as if they had nodded off too close to a cooking fire.

"Like Mr. Shimmer, at the hotel," she once told Karegi. The Africans called him "*kiboko*," meaning "hippo." Like many whites, he didn't like the sun. A plump man, he always wore long sleeves, safari boots and trousers, and, because he was completely bald, he added a big slouch hat, a terrai. "He has stayed pink underneath even after a year in Africa."

She puzzled over his local name, until one day someone showed her a hippo along the banks of the Nairobi River. They only left the water at night when the sun had gone down, then they could graze undisturbed along the riverbank. At night when the moon was full, she saw what they meant: they had delicate pink underbellies like Albert Shimmer after his bath. Kiboko, she said to herself, as on her last visit to the hotel she had taken her turn with the others peering through the keyhole. It fitted him to a T.

"As far as whites are concerned," she concluded, "there is nothing there for us. Leave us with our flat noses, strong teeth, keen eyes, sharp ears and black skins. We will survive."

13

The day after the Christmas dinner, David folded back the beautiful lace shawl he had given Alice as a present, and gently kissed her nipple, which had risen in expectation.

"Alice," he murmured.

It was happening exactly as he knew it would happen, he said to himself, and he began to explore further. His hands and mind were completely taken over by this erotic dream.

Suddenly, another hand reached forward and placed itself on top of his.

"What do you think you're doing?" David said, angrily. He hated being interrupted when he was lying dreaming in his bed, "and who do you think you are?"

"I am Jesus of Nazareth," said a gentle-voiced creature, a young man with a shining face who had walked into his bedroom and stood over him as he lay there. He firmly took hold of David's hand and withdrew it from Alice's breast and placed it instead on His own bare chest, a chest which David noted was remarkably soft, as soft as Alice's, he thought.

It also lacked any growth of hair, and he could now feel the heart of Christ beating. That shocked him into waking.

As he roused himself from sleep, he heard again those words, "David, you must be strong and faithful to me until you are married to a Christian woman. Promise me you'll never again waver from your devotion."

"Yes," whispered David. "Yes...."

He got up and in a fit of anxiety paced back and forth in front of his bedroom window, then stopped and looked out over Racecourse Hill, where he could see the disorganized assemblage of shanties, tents and houses that made up Nairobi. Not far from where he stood was Alice's house, dark, unlike the others where he saw flickering lights, candles and lanterns still burning at this late hour.

That reminded him—Jesus had previously warned him that there would be a great conflagration. "All the sinners in this town will be burned alive. Only those who abide in me will be saved. My Father's revenge will be complete and merciless, except for a few, like yourself, David, a chosen few, those who have repented their earlier ways."

David's father was a high church bishop. He had left David's rearing to his mother, a wealthy woman who indulged him so that he had been spoiled as he grew up. Now the advice he received weekly from her had begun to make sense, and he realized that there were all sorts of things that he'd have to deal with and soon. Marriage was one of them.

He had to make certain that Alice was aware of how important it was for her to marry him.

If she did so, she would be saved in body and spirit. Thus he vowed again to do his best to encourage her during the little time remaining to them.

"What was it like where you came from?" asked Karegi, intrigued by her friend Jakoby. They often sat out on the top step of their room, which faced the small servants' compound behind Alice's house, watching the kettle boil on the communal stove. It reminded her of the Mission school in Machakos where Father Glascock had told her that she was destined to become "a handmaiden to the Lord." Instead, she had stayed on as a house servant after she had been raped. He persisted and assured her that her mistreatment in the hands of the Arab slavers was simply a test on the part of the Almighty.

"God wanted to see if you were strong enough to bear a life of serving Him," he said, and because she had survived, and appeared unaffected by that experience, he thought she would make a fine nun.

"The man is a crackpot," said Dorothy who presumed Karegi

was already pregnant. She sent Alice to bring her to Nairobi where she intended to train her to be something other than a house servant. In this one case, Jakoby agreed with the Memsab; more often she thought Dorothy was a silly woman in need of a good whipping.

In contrast to Father Glascock, Jakoby knew that her friend had been deeply hurt. The wounds were not easily seen by some Mission priest who knew nothing of life. She knew Karegi hid things well, but Jakoby could hear her crying softly in the night, and she could interpret the stifled screams and frightening whimpers during Karegi's nightmares. She knew what these signified. Inner fabric ripped to shreds. She cursed the Arab slavers for what they did.

The other servants would gather around when Jakoby sat on that top step. They loved to hear her stories and dreamed of seeing the places she described as she sipped her tea.

"Like many of you," she said, looking around at their faces, "I was a village girl. But I lived in a hut unlike anything you've seen here. It was a Zulu hut. The white men called them 'beehives,' because they looked just like that. We built them in a round compound called a '*kraal*.' But then, everything about the Zulus is round, even the headdress worn by my mother. It was perfectly round, a disk like the sun, and the baskets; we kept everything in the round hut in round baskets. Some were woven so fine they could hold beer.

"The first time I saw a white man," she continued, as Karegi handed her another cup of tea, "I was so frightened I screamed, and the village women and children came running. They thought I was being carried off. But when they came out of their huts and saw him, they also turned and ran off. We were all convinced he was a walking dead person, a corpse that had lost all color; later we were told it was all right, but even today whenever I see Mr. Shimmer at the hotel, I still think of that first time.

"When I was quite young I was married to a man from the mines, and went with him to Johannesburg. I had several children, but each time before giving birth I was sent back to the village, where I left them to be raised by my sisters. There was no life for them in the city. My husband became a member of a secret gang they call the '*Izigebengu.*' The whites called them 'Ninevites,' the people from the old city in the Bible; why, I don't know. I had to learn English because of his work, and I used to help him recover wages due to Zulu men in that city. At that time it was common for the white man to fire a servant just one day before payday. And then they could turn him out without any severance. Ha! We kept a list of those who were selected and we would wait for our chance. My husband and others would grab him in the street at night and beat and rob him, and then divide the money with the servant.

"Finally my husband was caught. He died in jail and I was hired by Mr. Shimmer, who brought me here."

"And you have been here for some time," said Mary, the young house girl.

"Yes, too long. I want to go back to my home."

"Will you take us with you?" asked another.

Jakoby laughed. "What would your family say, that I am stealing young girls, eh?"

"No," said Mary, "they all have much respect for you."

"And Memsab says you are precious," said her friend, Sarah.

What could she mean by that? Jakoby asked herself. She had watched Dorothy gradually change this past month, from a healthy woman into a living corpse, a bed-ridden ghost, whose only faults seemed to be that she was both white and foolish. Worse yet was the way Dorothy curled up in bed so that she had come to look more and more like an unborn child. This proved a point to Jakoby, who saw the wazungu as undeveloped fetuses taken too early from the womb. "That is why they never develop a true black color," she said.

"How do you know these things?" asked Karegi.

"Look here." Jakoby opened a large book and showed her a detailed medical drawing.

"Where did you get this?"

"It is one of the Memsab's books. See, 'Foetus,' that is their name."

"Yes, I know. I have seen them in the hospital."

"And they have started the same epidemic here in Kenya," said

Jakoby as she turned the pages entranced. Karegi had heard that before; it was another of Jakoby's expressions. In Jakoby's view the black people of her Zulu ancestry, descendants of real kings, had been plagued by whites for hundreds of years in Cape Town like a disease. From the day gold was discovered in Johannesburg until now, they continued to interfere with Zulu life in South Africa. Here in Kenya, she was sickened to see them infecting this country as well.

"Who can tell where it will end. This sickness will take over the world. Do you know where their power comes from?" she quizzed the servants gathered below the step as she accepted yet another cup of tea. "I will tell you. They were first conceived as a pair, a boy and girl inside a black body, but their ancestor mother died before this first pair was born. They were cut from the womb, and now they preserve themselves as albino mutants. We see how the parasitic worm becomes king of your body. And what color is it, heh?"

"White!" they responded.

"The wazungu thrive in the same way as the parasite. Their seed comes from another world, maybe from under the ground where such things dwell. Just notice any seedling of any plant, while it grows underground, before it comes to the surface. What color is it?"

"White!" they responded again.

"Yes, that's it. Also, notice they do not get power and strength from their work like we do. Their power is in the money they pay us. They give us back a small amount and take more by selling everything they put their hands on. The doctors tell us a leech can draw off a small amount of badness from your body, but only at the cost of a great deal of blood, heh?" Again her audience nodded in concert.

"And that is what the wazungu tell us. By taking a great deal of money for their trouble they are helping us to survive. Now you know even though they give us back some of the money, they are reluctant to do even that. How many do you know who are not given their fair wage?"

"Quite a few," they said and nodded at how wise this woman

was. She had answers to many of the questions they had been afraid to ask their mistress or the missionary fathers. And, if what she said about her activities in Johannesburg was true, she was the first African they had ever met among the house servants who had stood up against the white man.

As she got ready to go to bed that night, Karegi asked, "You seem more and more taken by these things tonight. What has all that to do with us?"

"I want to make the British pay," said Jakoby. "And I have the encouragement of the kiboko, Mr. Shimmer." She showed Karegi a large stack of rupee notes in a basket under her bed. "These wazungu assume they are all born to be kings. I have been told to leave here tomorrow night. I have no choice. I am not in as good a situation as you; you can return to Machakos when Memsab dies. You have good ties with the *bwana mkubwa*, the big man, Bwana Stephen. But me, what about me?" she paused.

"Won't the owner of the hotel take you back?" asked Karegi.

"Yes, he would take me back," she said. "But recall that I would be forced to work there like a slave."

"But what else can be done?"

"I am going into business here starting tomorrow."

"What do you mean?" asked Karegi.

"I have many Wakamba friends and one very good Kikuyu friend, the man they call Kimani. It is said that he has gathered together a select group of warriors in Ngongo Bargas. All of these have seen how the wazungu draw blood from the cow, even though the cow is hardly able to stand because of the drought. They want me to join with them to make them pay. I want you to know why I will not be here tomorrow. You will also hear from me as I begin my new work. For now, I want you to swear secrecy with me."

She spat on her hand and reached out. Karegi in turn spat on hers and shook hands to seal the bargain.

She left the house early the next morning and met Ngali wa Mutua, an older Mkamba woman who had worked in an Asian shop in town. This woman had lost all her children and husband to smallpox. Along with her came a band of men who were equally disenchanted with life as house servants. They all looked up to

Jakoby as their prophetess and leader. Her background in the large cities of Africa and knowledge of the world complemented that of Ngali, who could read and write. It seemed to them, with all this, they could not fail.

14

It had been quite a while since Stephen had come to town. Like Brian, he simply found it more convenient to stay away. He was here today to return the Shimmer's wagon. Alice had sent him several reminders, so he decided he had to act; after all, he wanted to keep in their good graces, and he wanted anyway to pay a social call. He hadn't seen them since his return from Mombasa and he wanted to encourage Franz. In some vague way, he thought he might be a possible suitor for Alice.

Anyone would be better for her than Roger Newcome.

He also planned to confer with David McCann, another young man for whom he had respect. For some reason, David had not been in touch; more and more Stephen had to rely on Ian Burns passing him information from Mombasa. It almost seemed as if David was ignoring him.

Lastly, he was obligated to visit Dorothy and he wanted to get that out of the way first. He had some bad news, something that he wanted to pass on in person.

"Where's Alice?"

"On safari, Bwana," said Karegi, as he entered the house.

"And Jakoby?"

"Also gone."

That's strange, he thought. He'd better bring that up with the Shimmers. Presumably, they knew she was gone. "They probably needed her back at the hotel," he said.

"No, Bwana," said Karegi. "She is gone away."

"And you?"

"I spend much of my time at the hospital. Memsab says I must."

"But who looks after Memsab?"

"Sarah and Mary are always here, along with Kona."

"Kona?"

She pointed to a lean Somali squatting in the courtyard intently watching Stephen.

"He also stays here now. He helps Miss Alice."

Dorothy's room was dark as he came quietly through the doorway. Karegi had told him that she kept the windows shuttered day and night.

"Dorothy."

She turned her head towards him, obviously disappointed, and said in a low voice, "Oh, it's you."

"I stopped by to tell you some bad news." he paused. "Bobby's dead."

Her eyes flickered, but otherwise she showed no emotion.

"Did you hear me, Dorothy? He's dead. The army's confirmed he was taken by a man-eater on his way back to Mombasa."

"Yes, I understand, Stephen. It is dreadful news, and I'm really sorry for him," she replied wearily, "but now I want nothing but to be left in peace. I'm quite ill."

"I thought you'd want to know immediately. They found blood on the platform of the train. They believe his body was dragged into the bush at Kima. I'm arranging for his belongings to be brought back here for you."

"Don't bring them here. Give them to Alice. I never want anything more to do with him. And, Stephen, before you start, don't lecture me. I never really had any feelings for him, other than loathing, and as for you, if you really loved me, you'd leave me alone!"

He said nothing for a while, then turned away. "I can't believe you've grown to hate me like this."

She slowly shook her head as she stared at him. "I don't hate you, Stephen. I simply think you could be a much better person than you are. Literally, you're throwing yourself away. Why can't you be like John Allen? He's always so positive."

"Allen?" he said in a bitter voice, almost spitting the name out.

"Or," she said, "Roger."

"Roger!"

"It turns out he's actually a very intelligent young man," she said. "I've talked to him at length. He's very informative, although he does seem very suspicious of the Germans."

"For God's sake," said Stephen. "Don't listen to him. He's a troublemaker."

"Nonsense. Anyway, is that all you came to see me about?"

"No, of course not, Dorothy. You're my wife. I'm here to see if I can help."

"Then why do you lecture me every time?"

"I don't mean to," he said, beginning to regret he ever came. "It's just that I want to see you get well. I miss you a great deal." He held one of her delicate, warm hands.

"Oh, I imagine you get by quite well without me," she said with little feeling.

"Dorothy, I've bought a new house in Nairobi. It's a surprise just for you," he pleaded, squeezing her hand for emphasis. "Jevanjee tells me we can move in March, once my appointment comes through."

"Are you mad," she said, pulling her hand from his as she had a fit of coughing. "Leave me alone. I'm not moving anywhere. Can't you see, I'm not well!"

The vehemence in her voice surprised him, especially for a person with a debilitating disease.

"Anyway," she said, "what difference would a new house make? You loathe me, you and your friends in Mombasa."

"That's not true, Dorothy. And we are still man and wife. I've asked Ian and Isabelle for help."

"Oh, *that* trollop!" she said, as her cheeks flushed red. "I've heard of *her* escapades from John."

She stared at him. "You've been involved with her, haven't you? Ah-ha. You can't even look at me. No wonder you're always sticking up for her." She now lay silently resigned, as if waiting for something to happen.

"I've had all your belongings brought down from Machakos," he said, gently. "Syani has set everything up in the new house, and he's keeping it spick-and-span just for you."

"Oh, *now* I see," she turned to him. "You're anxious to get rid of any evidence in Machakos of your being married. You've taken up with some black trollop, eh? I suppose next you'll want Karegi to come back and help you keep house? Well you can't have her; she stays here with me. Now get out, I'm tired."

"You're disturbed by the fever," he said in desperation. "Good bye, Dorothy."

He could not bring himself to kiss her.

"Dr. Sharpe," said Stephen as he opened the door and motioned him to come in.

Dr. Sharpe had asked to meet him at Stephen's new house that evening. Otherwise, it had been an unproductive day for Stephen. He had looked up David, only to find he had gone off to Mombasa. The Shimmers had invited him to an early dinner at the hotel, but they didn't encourage him to linger and he soon found himself back here, alone with his only recourse; it sat on the table in front of him, a new bottle of brandy and several bottles of soda water. Syani was nowhere in sight.

"Sorry I can't offer you much else. I'm just here tonight," he said as he poured them both a drink. "What did you want to see me about?"

"I wanted to talk to you about Dorothy," said Dr. Sharpe, accepting his drink. A small man with a sallow complexion, he sipped his drink, but only after adding a large dollop of soda water. He carefully noted that Stephen hardly diluted his.

"Yes?" said Stephen, expectantly.

"I've come to the conclusion after several months that your wife does not have blackwater fever or anything like that."

"Oh? Then what does she have?"

"Nothing," said the doctor. "As far as I can see, there is nothing organically wrong with her."

"But that's hard to believe, she's so pale-looking."

"Yes, I know," said Dr. Sharpe, adding more water to his drink. "When I first saw her, there seemed no question about blackwater fever. It's so prevalent and clear in its symptoms; but I've tried every test I know, and now I believe her condition is due to some sort of eating disorder."

"What do you mean?"

"I've seen similar cases among the Europeans in India. It happens when someone simply decides not to eat, or they cannot eat because of some religious principle or mental block. It's a matter of the mind." He paused as he took a sip of his drink. "Oh, there *is* something else I should tell you, as I told her today. She's pregnant."

"*What*!" Stephen exclaimed as he slammed his glass down on a table. "How do you know?"

"It's obvious. She's several months gone," said the Doctor. "She said she realized something was different and thought it due to other causes. This afternoon when I saw her, she gave me the impression that she wants to have the child, but in her condition I wouldn't advise it."

Stephen woke in a daze. He knew something momentous had happened the night before, but couldn't remember what. As he sat up, he felt very sick and stumbled quickly out of bed into the washroom, where he saw clear evidence that he had thrown up during the night. Now he had the dry heaves and retched noisily into the washbasin.

What was that noise? he wondered, a knocking going on inside his head. Dreadful, he thought, something's finally snapped.

He stumbled out of the washroom and saw the man they called Kona, framed by the early morning sunlight that almost blinded Stephen. It made the Somali look like he was on fire as he stood in the doorway of Stephen's bedroom. The door for some reason was wide open, and beyond that, over Kona's shoulder, he could see the front door was also open.

Then it came to him: in his drunken stupor he had left all the doors open last night, and he realized that the knocking was this strange man rapping on the door jamb with his stick. He was staring at Stephen, watching the mzungu wrap a towel around his pale body.

"Yes, yes?" Stephen said as he shook his head. He wanted him to stop rapping; he also wanted him to stop staring at him like that.

Hasn't he ever seen a white man before? he asked himself.

"*Kwa weh-weh*, for you," said Kona, as he placed a note on Stephen's dresser before he turned and walked out, leaving the doors open as he went.

Very strange man, thought Stephen. Didn't address people as he was supposed to, using "Bwana," and the way he carried on! Somalis, he thought, very independent people.

Why would Alice have someone like that around?

He opened the note. It was from Dorothy, asking him to stop in before he went back to Machakos. In a flash he remembered what Dr. Sharpe had said the previous night. He felt faint, and then a wave of nausea again swept over him, leaving a chill. Still he was able to recover enough to wash and dress.

When he came into her room, he saw everything had changed. The shutters had been thrown open. Sunlight streamed in and Dorothy was sitting up in bed with a breakfast tray by her side. She seemed like a new person, healthier-looking; her hair was brushed and she had developed a rosy complexion overnight.

He in contrast felt as if he was at Death's door.

"You know?" she said, almost as soon as he came through the doorway.

"Dr. Sharpe told me," he said. "He seemed very sympathetic. I'm sure he'd give you something to take care of it."

"It?"

Stephen found this conversation difficult, distasteful even, but he had no recourse. "I'm sorry," he said. "I have to be candid. I can't believe you'd want the child. Anyway, according to him, you'd never survive childbirth in your present state. It would be disastrous."

Dorothy, bright and happy when he arrived, was now crestfallen. "Why?" she said. "Why do you say such things, Stephen? What even gives you the *right* to say such things?"

"Admit it, you've never been strong," he said.

"You mean like Alice?"

"Yes, if you want. Like Alice."

"I'm sorry you feel that way."

"Why?"

"Because I want to have the child."

Stephen turned away in disgust. "You're mad. It'll kill you."

"At this stage, I don't care," she said. "Anyway, it might be better for everyone if I did die."

"I'll never understand you," he said as he moved toward the door.

"I agree," she said, suddenly relieved. She seemed to have put aside all his concerns and now ignored him as she turned instead to her breakfast tray, where she continued eating a large helping of scrambled eggs, sausage and toast.

Outside the house, Stephen had one foot in a stirrup when he saw Alice riding up. She was followed by two of J.O.'s trackers with several pack donkeys. Beside her on two other horses rode Brian and J.O. They tipped their hats to Stephen, waved good-bye to Alice and went on their way.

He watched as the trackers unloaded her safari equipment and a small antelope carcass.

Kona came out and without a word carted everything inside.

"Alice," said Stephen.

"Well, this is a surprise, Stephen," she said. "We missed you at Christmas."

"Yes, I got your message and returned the wagon yesterday," he said, somewhat abashed. "I've just been with Dorothy. I wonder if we could talk?"

"Certainly, why not. Come in, we'll have some tea or coffee. You look like you could use it."

He had not yet shaved that morning and his hands would not stop shaking.

"I'd prefer to talk out here, if you don't mind."

"Well?" she said as they stood on the path.

"Extraordinary," he said. "I hardly know where to begin. She's pregnant."

Alice's face lit up. "Why, that's wonderful, Stephen," and she reached forward to hug him, but he backed away. "But," she said, still excited by the news, "you must be very happy."

"Not entirely," he said.

Then to break an awkward silence, he added, "I see you're still going on safaris. That man with J.O. looked familiar."

"Oh, yes, Brian," she said, amazed at his reaction to the news about his wife. How could he take all this so calmly? He looked as if he could care less. "He should be familiar; he lives not far from where you are."

"Ah, now I recall," he said. "Mad as a hatter." He mounted his horse and looked down at her. "Why don't you go around with a better crowd, Alice? There are so many young people around here with good Christian backgrounds. David McCann for one. Mark my words, he'll go far in the civil service."

As she watched him ride off, she thought, for a new father he seems to be a sad case. It must be the drink, she concluded; it's finally deadened his feelings.

Then she turned and dashed into the house into Dorothy's bright, sunny room, and without another word pushed aside the breakfast tray as she climbed onto the bed and hugged her.

"You've heard," said Dorothy as her tears of joy mingled with those of her sister. "And Alice, what a mess you've made," she said laughing, as she looked at the food all over the bed.

"Who cares," said Alice, as she again hugged her and they both laughed and sobbed as they now shared their joy in Dorothy's child, and for the first time in their lives felt like sisters.

Book Three

The Iron Snake Arrives - Nairobi

1

Nairobi, May 31, 1899

"Pity we couldn't have gone a bit faster," said Ian Burns to his wife Isabelle.

"We're only a week late," she said, referring to Queen Victoria's eightieth birthday.

They were sitting on a wooden stand in front of the spanking new Nairobi train station. The stand had been specially built for the occasion and was decorated with flags, banners and bunting. To one side the high commissioner's personal band was playing and a crowd had gathered to watch the arrival of the first train from Mombasa.

And what a gathering, thought Isabelle, looking down on the settler families with their children running in and around the legs of fiercely impassive Masai warriors in full regalia; Asian businessmen with wives in bejeweled finery; African chiefs, standing alongside villagers and house servants; army staff officers and sergeants rubbing shoulders with sepoys and askaris; and white hunters in their safari jackets. A few dour-looking missionaries stood away from the crowd, while the band struck up "Rule Britannia" for the third time.

Regular twice-weekly service was expected to begin soon. At present the passenger trains stopped for tea and dinner the first day out of Mombasa and breakfast and luncheon the next day before arriving in Nairobi. From the start it was one of the most exciting train rides in the world, with clear views of enormous herds of game roaming the plains, in numbers never before seen by Europeans. And Nairobi itself was a hive of activity. Once a sawmill had been set up, barracks, storage sheds, workshops, clubs and other rambling structures quickly appeared. Bungalows with verandahs in the Indian colonial tradition were in demand because of the weekly arrival of traders, settlers, missionaries, ivory hunters and adventurers all looking for housing. Everyone had great expectations. The station acted as an anchor for the town; around it sprang up at first a few dozen, then several hundred small wooden shops and huts. Two main streets ran north from the station through the center of town, Station Road and Victoria Street, parallel thoroughfares, and the space between them was hotly sought after by Asian businessmen from Mombasa.

After the station, the second most prominent buildings were the hotels; Lowe's was the largest, just east of the station. Its dance floor doubled as a courtroom, its bar served also as a council meeting room, and a windowless shed in the rear, a storeroom, was used as the town jail. The rough nature of the place was balanced somewhat by new shops featuring the latest goods from England, and by race weekends, which were conducted in a very proper manner, and afterwards the rousing parties at Lowe's, which often left some still under the tables when the sun came up.

A robust and cheerful master of ceremonies turned to the official delegation and said, "It is my proud duty to introduce Ian Burns, High Commissioner of the Kenya Colony," to scattered but strong applause. "His wife, Isabelle," he continued, as some men applauded and several children laughed at her hat; "Lord John Allen, Superintendent of the Railway here in Nairobi," which was greeted by hearty applause from many of the Railway and army officers; "Bill Bagley, his deputy," which likewise received much applause; "the Honorable Brian Stanford, Chairman of the Settlers Association," after which he had to pause because of the loud cheering, hearty applause, and several revolver shots; "and his attractive wife, Lady Stanford," which produced some applause, and some murmurs; "and, finally, Mr. David McCann, District Commissioner," a finale that elicited only scattered applause, and quite a few boos.

Ian stepped forward and gave a short but stirring speech about everyone in the colony pulling together, and then Isabelle cut the ribbon that had been strung between two planks as a symbolic gesture. "I pronounce this railway station officially open!" A cheer went up from the crowd as the first train from Mombasa came chugging into the station, and the band again struck up "Rule Britannia," one of only three tunes in their repertoire, the other being "Hielan' Laddie," Ian's favorite, and "The Blue Danube" waltz.

"And now the moment you've all been waiting for!" said Ian, as the crowd quieted down. "I hereby declare the station bar officially open!" A much louder cheer went up, "and Her Majesty's Government proclaims that, for the next half hour, through the courtesy of Mr. Albert Shimmer, all drinks are on the house!"

"Yeaahh!" Most of the men in the audience turned and headed for the bar. Isabelle led the official delegation into the waiting room for a glass of champagne while they paused before luncheon.

"One thing I couldn't help notice," said Ian as he cornered Allen, "is the town center. It's an absolute pigsty. Your colleagues promised me on many occasions they'd clean up the place and drain it. I suppose it now comes down to you."

"I know what you mean. Previously we had no time for town planning—'haste makes waste,' and so forth. But now it's different. I'm making the town my number one priority."

"Your headquarters even suggested on one occasion burning the place down and starting over again," said Ian. "I hope you've got something more rational in mind?"

Allen laughed. "Mr. Burns, you can count on me. When I say I'll look after something, I mean it."

Ian and Isabelle were staying at David's house, and they were about to head in that direction when Allen walked over to Stephen, who had come into town for the occasion. He was standing with a brandy and soda in hand watching the crowd at the bar. The noise from there was deafening.

"How's Dorothy?" asked Allen.

"Why do you ask?" said Stephen, ignoring him as he continued to watch the crowd. His voice was slurred though it was early afternoon.

"What do you mean, 'Why do you ask?' I'm her friend," said Allen.

"Friend?" said Stephen as he turned and glared at him.

"I don't know what you're getting at," said Allen who hesitated because Stephen was taller than he, and looked down at him now as if he was some repellant insect.

"Like everyone else in town, Allen, I'm on to you." He leaned forward and pointed a finger at Allen's chest. Some of his drink slopped forward, wetting his shirtfront. "You're a blackguard, an opportunist and a little sneak. Any female in Nairobi is fair game for your line."

Allen didn't look away. It was hard for him to be heard above the noise, but he flushed and replied indignantly, "I'll be damned, if it isn't the kettle speaking."

"What do you mean?"

Allen nodded in the direction of Isabelle. "Everyone in town knows about you and our favorite 'hostess' carrying on in Mombasa."

Stephen blushed and reached for Allen, "You...."

Suddenly Ian came up to the two men, and said in a voice that could not be ignored, "Stephen, are you coming? Isabelle and David are waiting."

Stephen glared again at Allen, then unsteadily turned on his heel and stalked away.

Alice was present briefly at the station for the celebrations, but left as soon as the ribbon was cut. Life had changed completely for her and Dorothy. The coincidence of Karegi and Dorothy now expecting and the presence of Alice's six-month-old cheetah cubs gave the house a new perspective, almost like that of a nursery, and in such a state, men were not encouraged.

Roger visited less often, and when he did show up, he was more standoffish than he had ever been. J.O. was taken up with work; his services were much in demand clearing animals from agricultural land. Matthew was given the task of mobilizing security in advance of the railway's next leg, west to Lake Victoria; to get there they had to traverse parts of Kikuyuland, and further west where another fierce tribe waited for the Iron Snake with blood in their eyes. The Nandi were still carrying many grudges against the early explorers and survey teams. He had his work cut out for him. Of the usual crowd, only David came by on a regular basis, and he always seemed on the verge of saying something important, but would stop short on the least excuse.

John Allen had ceased coming to the house altogether and when Alice did see him in town, or at one of the Clubs, he avoided her. "Any word from John?" Dorothy would call out when Alice came back with the mail, which was now sorted and held at the station while a proper post office was being built. She asked that question less and less frequently as the weeks went by.

With the coming of the railway, order, efficiency and change seemed to be in the air, and overnight they had begun talking of the mobilization needed for the "Big Push" to get to Lake Victoria. Their enthusiasm was reflected in a new spirit of development within the town, and it seemed to Alice that everyone would be expected to become more responsible as life became more sophisticated. If that happened, she felt the wildness and lawlessness abhorred by Dan and J.O. would lessen. The one person she originally thought would rise to the occasion and help in this development was Stephen, but he had gone in the opposite direction, and she had almost decided that the only path left to her would be for her to go out to Machakos and physically rescue him from his boozing.

One day J.O. arrived back from a trip and as usual presented himself to Dorothy, wished her good health, and then begged her leave to take Alice off to the races. That's the way he was, Alice realized, always a gentleman, and so, always welcomed in their house. As she walked with him among the crowd at the racecourse, now a proper oval, he asked if she had seen Allen recently.

"Not at all," she said. "I assume he has more important things to do."

"The reason I ask is that you once seemed very taken by him," said J.O.

"No more," said Alice. They stopped at a tea kiosk and sat in the shade. "What's he doing?"

"Well," said J.O., "he's changed, almost overnight." He ordered a pot of tea; they had a few minutes before the next race.

"Changed?"

"He's become rather obnoxious. I seldom have a decent word from him nowadays," said J.O. "And, I hate to say it, but he's taken up womanizing in a big way."

"In some ways I'm sad about that," said Alice, "but Jenny would say he's only reverting to type. He was like that before we knew him."

"There's a further complication," said J.O., obviously somewhat embarrassed.

"In what way?"

"He seems to have attached himself to Brian's wife."

"Lady Stanford?" asked Alice, as she also became embarrassed. Both she and J.O. had become fast friends with Brian. It was his independent spirit that made them both respect him, though they often made excuses because of his exotic nature. Every time Alice looked at the two cheetahs and Kona she thought of him, and she didn't appreciate the rude remarks made by Roger or Stephen, which often smacked of jealousy.

"That answers one question I had," she said.

"What's that?" asked J.O.

"Why Allen's been cutting me. But what I can't understand is why he's stopped coming around to see Dorothy." J.O. couldn't answer that.

The cheetahs were growing fast. To accommodate them, Alice leased a long strip of land from Jevanjee that extended from her house down to a tributary of the Nairobi River. On this land Kona built several huts and fashioned a long run closely fenced in with thorn bush. Every morning Alice worked with him training them to hunt small animals, as they tried to wean them off a diet of chopped goat meat. She planned eventually to release them, but for now they demanded her full attention. Late in the afternoon about a month after the railway had arrived, Kona called her from the house. It was a short walk to the enclosure. Inside the rough gate, Kona pointed to the doorway of the second hut, and smiled broadly.

She looked into the dim interior and there sat Brian.

"Good God, Brian. What are you doing here?"

He sat back on a string bed that had been covered with soft animal skins. The cheetahs kept him company. "Sorry to intrude," he said, "and I can't get up without disturbing them."

"I'm just surprised," said Alice.

"Kona's hut is the only place left in Nairobi where I can get some peace and quiet," he said.

"Stay there," she said smiling at him, as he looked like he might get up. "Don't move. You look quite at home."

"It's surprisingly comfortable," he said.

She sat on a small carved wooden stool where she could watch him. "Did I hear correctly? You're the new chairman of the settlers' organization?" asked Alice.

He nodded yes.

"You're the last person in the world I would imagine in that sort of post."

"They see me as some sort of God on earth," he said. One of the cubs chewed lustily on the fringe of his new leather shooting jacket. "Though I don't encourage them, and I certainly try to avoid them, they search me out. They tell me I'm extremely popular and they elected me by unanimous vote. Not one dissension."

"Why?"

"I think it's because there are too many cliques. Even among the South Africans, some are Boers, some are British, and neither trusts the other. Then there are absentee landowners from Mombasa who are suspicious of the white managers who rent their land around here. And of course, there are the cattle and plantation farmers with small and large investments who are always at one another's throats. I seem to be the only one not driven by vested interests." He smiled at her and pried the fringe from the jaws of the cub. "Also it may be because I bought everyone a drink after the last meeting."

"What about your wife? Don't you ever go around to see her?"

"I always stop there," he said.

Her eyes had now adapted to the dark and she could see the slight smile on his face. On a child it would be considered the smile of a mischief-maker. "But not before sending a messenger to announce my arrival." He looked her in the eye as he said, "That sort of arrangement must seem strange to you."

"No stranger perhaps than that between Stephen and his wife," she said.

"That's not the same," said Brian. "In his case she's in need of medical attention, and he has to stay at his post."

"And in your case?"

"I married Beryl because my family owed her father a great favor, and she's never been one to restrain herself." He shook his head as he said, "I hate to shock you, Alice, but I'm certain she had previous love affairs with just about every male in our wedding party." He was correct, Alice was shocked, and it showed in her cheeks, which flushed as he said that.

"You see," he said, "I knew you'd be upset. You have to realize that Beryl and I were both very wild people when we married. I think from the first day we assumed we'd lead separate lives, and we did."

"So it's strictly a marriage of convenience?" said Alice.

"We never saw it otherwise, and we're very honest about it."

"But don't either of you want something else?"

"Like what?" he laughed at her. "You mean like a proper home life, children, a fire in the fireplace and 'a bun in the oven,' as they say?"

She flushed again. "What's wrong with that?"

"Nothing, and I wish it were so for everyone, but it's really not for the likes of me."

"What is for the likes of you?"

"I'm quite taken by the life here. The Africans have an uncomplicated way about them that suits me. They have few social problems and set no rigid distinctions between classes."

"Ah, but they seem very set in their ways when it comes to tribal differences," said Alice. "I've heard that even the Somalis have strong clan traditions. I'll bet they must find those difficult to set aside."

"True, but that doesn't affect me. Their idea of an extended family is such that it takes in virtually everyone from the outside. Kona tells me that they even exchange wives between clans; that way it makes it even more difficult to pick a fight. I mean, there can't be as much animosity when in-laws are present on both sides of a confrontation. Anyway, I don't belong to any clan, therefore I'm immune."

"Which could be to their detriment, in some cases," Alice said. "They'll never improve their lot by just taking in anyone who shows up out here."

"Ah," he said laughing at her, "then you *have* been listening to the stories about the Mad Fifth Baron."

"It's not just you, Brian. It's like Dorothy says, there are many people out here that Africa would be better off without."

"So, hedonists beware, is it?"

"That's the strange part of this—you may think of yourself as a hedonist," said Alice, "but you're not."

"I was taught that whatever is pleasant or has pleasant consequences is intrinsically good, and I should strive for that."

"Who would teach you such nonsense?"

"The Manchester 'scholars.'" He smiled, as he thought of how they would get along with what John Allen called the 'Angel of Maidstone.' She was known by that in many places now, and not just in Nairobi.

"Jimmy Harris told me when you first arrived in Kenya, you were in rags and so damaged physically you could hardly hold a teacup. He said he had no idea there were still men on earth willing to subject themselves to such pain and suffering, just to reach a cattle ranch."

"I don't call that suffering; I call it 'splendid torment.' I enjoyed every minute of it."

"Ah, but now your secret is out. We know you're head and shoulders above many of the other settlers. People I respect say that what you're doing on your farm is exactly what is needed out here. So it's probably not luck that the settlers chose you—it's divine intervention. The Africans are lucky you're on their side. It's just too bad that…."

She looked wistfully at him.

"What?" he asked. "You think I should be more conventional?"

"Less visionary perhaps."

"Never," said Brian. "I am and always will be a dreamer. I'm convinced my quest for the 'happy valley' has ended successfully because of that."

"Happy valley?" she asked.

"Something I recalled when I was walking in the desert, 'Wanderers in that happy valley, through two luminous windows, saw Spirits moving musically....'" He let the cubs go as he heard Kona calling them from outside.

The cubs scampered out as he asked her, "What do you call them?"

"Lizzie and Jane."

"Oh?"

"After two young ladies in *Pride and Prejudice*," she said.

"Why?"

"Because both were set along the path of expectations by Jane Austen. I'm afraid it's bound to be the same with the cubs. Once released into this world, they'll have to search out masters, and I hope they find two with moral value and substance, above and beyond worldly fortunes."

"I see. You mean somewhere out there is a Mister Darcy waiting for Lizzie, or at least a Mister Collins."

"I would advise her to accept either."

"That surprises me," he said laughing. "I would have thought you would be for Darcy or nothing."

"The world is moving too fast even for me," she said. "We no longer have the luxury of thoughtfulness."

"That must have been hard to accept."

"Why would you think that?" she asked.

"Because you're perfect. You're an attractive, bright young woman, who holds everyone to a high standard. A standard to which you measure up to yourself. If I'd had a sister, or if I ever have a daughter, I'd wish her to be exactly like you."

When he said that something jarred inside Alice, and she realized that she had a physical and emotional feeling for Brian, a feeling that went beyond the usual warm feeling she had for J.O. or the fascination she had for Roger and the others.

"Perfect?" she asked, wondering if she really wanted to be known as such. It was bad enough being referred to as an angel.

"As you put it to me earlier," he said, "it would be strange if you thought otherwise of yourself. I was surprised to see how much like Dorothy you are."

"My sister?"

"Yes. What little I know of her. I gather she also expects everyone to measure up. And if she were stronger physically, I'd say the two of you would make a formidable team."

Kona again called and Brian followed her out as they watched Kona train the cubs.

"By the way, if she ever did get well enough to travel, the Webbs and myself would be grateful for some company. We'd want all of you and J.O. to come out on a visit."

"We'll see how it goes here first," said Alice.

Kona had trained the cubs to sit while he went down to the far end of the run. With a sharp cry he released three rabbits and two chickens. As soon as they heard him say, "*Nenda*! Go!" they sprang forward. Lean, hungry and fast they gracefully ran down their first meal of the day.

"Like a pair of high-born young ladies at a coming out party," said Brian as they watched. "I pity their Mr. Darcy when they find him."

2

Alice arrived back one morning from her trip to town to find Dr. Sharpe's rickshaw waiting outside the house and the front door wide open. She ran forward from the gate and found chaos. For a moment, a surge of pleasant surprise passed through her mind. She's having her baby, she thought, it's come early. She saw Dr. Sharpe in attendance and Mary, Sarah and Karegi carrying basins of water and bundles of sheets from Dorothy's room, exactly the way she had expected it to happen. The only thing lacking were smiles, she thought. Why is everyone so serious? Then, one look from Karegi who shook her head, no, told her something was wrong.

"Alice," said Dr. Sharpe as she came into the room. He was holding Dorothy's wrist. Dorothy looked very quiet, almost as if she were asleep. He lowered her wrist and said, "Come outside."

"What's wrong?" she whispered, as she followed him into the living room. She suddenly broke out in a cold sweat. Her breath came in gasps as she looked at him.

"She must have taken something," he said, and looked at Alice to see if she was registering what he was saying. She seemed in a daze and he reached for smelling salts in his pocket, just in case.

"Taken something?" asked Alice.

"She's dying," said Dr. Sharpe. He waited for that to sink in, then he said, "I've stopped the bleeding and Karegi is looking after her, but she won't survive. She's lost too much blood."

"But what happened?" cried Alice, who felt weak yet her instincts told her she had to respond, to help if possible. "Doctor, you said she took something?"

"I'm not sure. She had a miscarriage. I suspect it was self-induced, but we'll probably never know because she lost consciousness before I arrived and never woke. I'm sorry." He looked beyond her at Kona, who stood at the front door, and beyond him a crowd that had gathered. "Someone should ride out and tell her husband."

"Yes," said Alice, turning toward the door. "Kona!" she said. "Find Mr. McCann. I just left him on the road. Tell him he has to ride to Machakos, immediately." Then she turned back to Dr. Sharpe. "Isn't there any hope?"

"Very little. I'm going back to the station. I have another urgent case, a worker mangled in the railway workshop, but Karegi knows exactly what to do. If anything changes, send Kona for me immediately."

As he left, Alice walked softly back into the bedroom, still bright and airy with the shutters open; she saw one sheet lying in a bloody heap on the floor and Karegi wiping Dorothy's forehead with a wet cloth. Mary returned to take up the sheet and clean up some splatters and smears of blood still on the floor near the bed. Alice, now weeping openly, sat and looked at her sister. She placed a hand gently on her shoulder but there was no movement, and hardly a breath from the still figure whom earlier that morning Alice had left chattering away with Mary about toys. How to make a raffia toy seemed her only concern. To Alice the thought of suicide brought to mind someone depressed, sad beyond all measure, and that was not the Dorothy she remembered. She couldn't believe it. And yet the proof was all around her, especially her blonde-haired sister lying there with deathly white cheeks, and colorless, expressionless lips. Almost dead, thought Alice, shocked by the realization.

Suddenly Dorothy's head tilted toward her, her eyes flickered and she seemed briefly to recognize Alice, as she murmured, "He still loves me, I know it…," then her eyelids closed and the slight motion of her chest ceased. Startled, Alice looked up at Karegi, who placed her fingers on Dorothy's throat, then looked at Alice as she slowly shook her head. Dorothy was dead.

"I've decide to sell this place back to Jevanjee," said an impassive Stephen, sitting with Alice in his new house. "In many ways I'm glad Dorothy never saw it, because we couldn't have lived here anyway."

She said nothing. She stared at her hands.

"Did I tell you, my promotion didn't come through?" said Stephen bitterly. "I found out last week. Anyway, she'd never have agreed to stay here. We should have just gone home to England."

Alice sighed. She tried to be understanding. It was the day after her sister's death, and she was afraid this cold attitude of Stephen's toward everything associated with Dorothy would affect her as well.

It was too much for her and she almost said something but decided to hold her tongue. Didn't he have any feeling at all for what his wife cared about? What she had wanted for others? Alice had told Stephen of Dorothy's last words, but in her heart she could not think of how the love of this man could ever have been of any significance to her sister. She herself had come that far in their relationship that she almost hated him.

"What shall I do with her things?" she asked, as they waited for Dr. Sharpe; he had promised to come over to discuss the funeral arrangements and the details of Dorothy's death.

"I have no use for anything in this town," said Stephen. "Give them away, or keep them, as you wish, Alice. I could care less." He got up and went to the sideboard.

She heard the clinking of his glass and could hardly control herself. It was a mixture of intense sorrow at her loss and anger at this man that had made her eyes dry. Previously they had been bleary with crying. Now because of him she could no longer cry. He was about to drown himself in drink, yet she had nothing to turn to but a life without a sister. The rest of her family, what little remained, were thousands of miles away. She'd have to make do with whatever resources she could muster in herself.

Dr. Sharpe arrived and came into the living room where she sat; Stephen remained standing and indicated the bottle to the doctor, offering him a drink, which he declined. The doctor placed a piece of paper on the table and said, "Here's a copy of the signed certificate. I've said on it that the primary cause was hemorrhage following a miscarriage, but I felt you both should know the details."

Alice waited without emotion, while Stephen took a stiff drink and said, "Details?"

"Yes. In cases like this it's not possible to be delicate, so I won't go on unless you feel it's needed."

"Tell us," said Alice.

"They had just brought a bad case into the hospital, but I left because Karegi said it was an emergency. I was reluctant to go, but I trust her judgment, and of course she was right. When I saw Dorothy, she was in extreme pain; the membranes had broken and she was passing blood. She also had diarrhea...." He paused because Stephen had turned white.

"Go on," said Alice, ignoring Stephen.

"There had been no earlier indication of labor. She was still in the early stages of the third trimester and I could see she wasn't ready for anything like this. My immediate diagnosis was that the birth had to be aborted or she would die. I therefore did my best to work and pull the fetus forward, and in the process I had to collapse its skull. During all of this she was comatose, she never woke."

Stephen suddenly dropped his glass. It shattered on the stone floor as he raced to the washroom.

"Please, Dr. Sharpe," she said. "I still have to ask. I have to know. Did she take anything?"

"Everything I saw pointed to the effect of a strong abortifactant. She must have taken something, but it didn't make any sense. Previously she gave me the impression that she wanted the child and the pregnancy seemed to be developing well."

"She *did* want it," said Alice. "She was looking forward to it. Could she have taken anything in error?"

"Impossible. I quizzed Karegi and the two servants closely. There was nothing available to her that would cause that, unless...."

"Unless?"

"Unless she sent someone, a lad off the street, maybe, for one of the quack medicines available in any of the shops here. One of the curses of this kind of rapid growth, especially when there's such a lack of civil government, is that there's very little oversight. You can buy anything you want. I'm sorry I can't be more helpful, but I will ask around to see if any of the shopkeepers sold anything recently."

After he left, Alice walked home. She didn't bother to say good-bye to Stephen, who had disappeared into his bedroom. David waited for her; she earlier had asked him to help her draft a telegram to Rosmé explaining what had happened and that they planned on burying Dorothy immediately. They couldn't wait for Rosmé since the trip out would take several weeks. As she read through the draft, she realized it was the exactly like what had happened to her and her father.

Poor Rosmé, she thought, first her husband, then Bobby, now this.

Then she waited with Jenny and David until a wagon arrived to take Dorothy's body to the church. It had been placed in a wooden coffin, one that Dr. Sharpe had sent over from the railway supply. They had a carpenter working full time building coffins, one of the items in constant demand in Nairobi.

Stephen sequestered himself in his new house until the day of the funeral. By the time of the funeral service he could hardly stand. David McCann had to go with J.O. to bring him to the church. Afterwards, at the cemetery, the coffin was carried from the wagon by J.O., David, Dan, Jimmy, Roger and Dr. Sharpe—an easy task someone said, because it was so light. Not many people were there, other than the household servants from Nairobi and Machakos.

One absence noted by the servants was Jakoby. Another absence conspicous to the wazungu was that of John Allen.

Stephen had let it be known he wouldn't be welcome.

Brian arrived and came up to Alice at the gravesite. She was dressed in black and veiled, and he comforted her as the service went forward. Once the first clod of soil was thrown on the coffin, the group dispersed. The last people to leave were Karegi and Roger, which was appropriate because they each had some special debt to her. Otherwise it was a quiet good-bye for Dorothy, typical of the way her life had gone in Africa. "A passing hardly noticed," it said on her headstone, which at that moment was being chiseled in the railway workshop.

Stephen had a carriage waiting, and after saying good-bye to Alice, who refused a lift from him back into town, he went on to Machakos.

3

Sarah now collected the post, as Alice had given up her daily walk to town. Today she came in with a handful of letters; one was from Aunt Mary.

Dearest Alice,

I heard from Rosmé that you have decided to stay on in Kenya, and was delighted to receive shortly thereafter your letter from that place which confirms my good opinion of you.

Yes, losing a sister under those conditions must be devastating. Especially as there can never be a recovery to normalcy as you two knew it. In that sense, such an experience is heart wrenching. However, in deference to her and her Uncle Bobby, and your father and dear mother before that, you must, after a proper period of grief, seize the opportunity to do something of value to commemorate their memory, and fill the enormous gap left in your life after such a loss. In England one sees every day memorials and endowments, all I'm sure worthy causes, but in your case, you are in that part of the world where the simplest good deed will be remembered by God's children for years to come. It is impossible in Africa to sit by and watch, while our white, well-meaning colleagues wreak as much havoc as the Conquistadores of the New World. I am certain, if you look, many worthwhile tasks will come to mind.

I myself turned to recording historical and scientific descriptions of culture and geography, and I believe I found solace there because it carried forward my father's goals. You too will find your place. Pray God, the activities you involve yourself in will at the least be something that will commemorate their memory and His.

"Alice, you can't just mope around here day in and day out," said J.O., who came to visit every weekend after Dorothy died. "You've got to get out."

She had stopped going to the races; instead she spent many hours sitting in a chair in Dorothy's bedroom reading and staring at her sister's bed.

Roger enlisted her help briefly in buying some furnishings for a new house he had bought in Nairobi, and Jenny and Dan had stopped by on their way back to England for home leave; they had hoped to coax her to come with them. All to no avail. The house was so empty and quiet it rang with the least noise. In place of the footsteps and manly conversation of Alice's beaux now came the twittering of the Kenya starlings.

They previously enjoyed the complete freedom of the small garden in front of the house and the verandah, but these superb varieties, as bold as their drab European cousins, would not be satisfied until the shutters were opened so they could flit in and out of Dorothy's bedroom.

Dorothy had encouraged them with crumbs from her teacakes and lavish breakfasts. It seemed to Alice that her sister had wanted to share her approaching motherhood with all of nature. They looked at her with their jewel-like, sparkling eyes, as she watched them pluming their brightly colored iridescent feathers, and she sighed and longed so hard for Dorothy that her heart ached.

She wished she could push back time, because there were now so many things she wanted to share with her sister. Why hadn't she thought of this earlier? she asked herself. And now time was again fleeting while she sat there.

Karegi had been confined to bed and was expecting at any moment, and the cheetahs were growing by inches every day. Kona had taken complete charge. In the early morning he created a sensation as he walked them through town on leads. He took them to a grassy plain in the south where he let them hunt for smaller prey. Without fail they turned and came running to his side when he called, "*Njoo*, come." Chopped goat meat was still irresistible. But he knew some day the two of them would vanish.

"Like the two sisters," he said to Karegi. "One has already gone."

"J.O.," she said, as she sat watching the starlings on the windowsill, "do you know what it's like for me now?"

"Oh, I've been through it all, Alice," he said as he stood in the doorway. "Before Muzzy and I had our two daughters, we lost a son to yellow fever."

He refused to sit when he came to her house. Earlier he had indicated that he would only sit down if she came out of the bedroom. "That's why we moved to Matabeleland. Change of scenery, new life, and it helped, greatly. By the way, now that they're both out of the nest, she's thinking of coming up here."

"She'll like Nairobi," said Alice, as she reluctantly got up and moved with him to the verandah. She hated to see him standing like that.

Mary waited until they sat before she brought in their afternoon tea.

"I've gone in with Roger on his house," he said. "We're planning to expand it while land's cheap. One or two more extensions and it'll beat the Settlers' Club hands down."

"How's he doing?"

"Very well. He's set up a new trading post in Naivasha, probably making money hand over fist."

"I know. He spared nothing in ordering all that furniture," she said.

"He's the only trader the Kikuyus will trust," said J.O. as he accepted a piece of fruitcake, formerly Capt. Bobby's favorite.

"Where do you go now on safari?"

"Many places; the railroad makes it much easier to get around. I'm even taking parties out to *photograph* animals, would you believe? But I think the most relaxing thing is to go 'round and visit Brian," he said, buoyed up by the prospect. "He's invited several of us for next week, that's his birthday. The Webbs agree with me, it's like a spa. They love it. The lodge itself is absolutely spectacular."

He watched her eyes glint when he said that, and believed now he had made some progress. Like Kona and the cats, he had gradually coaxed Alice out of her den of misery. Sitting there on the verandah, he now saw her rising to the next level of training; soon he'd be letting her off her lead.

As they came over a rise and looked down, they saw a small river that had cut its way through the dry plain, leaving a dark line, as if God had drawn a thick, shiny blue crayon across a sea of light brown grass. Brian's hunting lodge stood on the upper bank of the river. It was an enormous collection of low brown buildings surrounded by a wall and built in the fashion of the Masai *manyattas*, adobe-like structures. Rounded and arched, they were fashioned with soft-rolled surfaces everywhere; there wasn't a sharp corner or straight edge to be seen.

One main building, a tall grass-thatched, three-storied, castle-like building, stood above the rest. Obviously of modern construction, it incorporated local materials, such as mud and wattle. The whole complex spread out over several acres of dry countryside like a small town, and, except for the central building, fit well with the landscape.

The sun was going down as J.O. and Alice arrived. A Somali herder took their horses at the main gateway and others followed with their baggage, leaving them to make their way toward the central building. It was now dark enough as they walked that many huts along the interior alleyways were lit by oil lamps and braziers. A haze had settled over everything and the smell of incense from the braziers aroused and excited their nostrils. It reminded Alice of high mass and benediction in the Catholic churches back home. Throughout they heard a refrain, a low cacophony, voices singing, the tinkling of small bells, and the abrasive clacking and thonking of the carved wooden camel and goat bells. Those animals settled down in their guarded pens close to the high mud walls surrounding the town. Somali guard patrols passed them on their way to set in place the heavy bars on the main gate. They then mounted to the platforms above the walls where they watched out for Wakamba raiders.

Intruders would have a difficult time getting in.

A few minutes later they arrived at Brian's 'castle,' where they were greeted and shown to their rooms. Alice found a young Somali girl waiting to help in the room assigned her. It was decorated in the Eastern style, low divans strewn with Persian silk carpets, lovely woven cloth hangings on the walls, and from somewhere came the strains of Turkish music and the sound of running water.

She washed up and stretched out on one of the divans. The maid had left her a flagon of cold water and some fruit on a platter. She had eaten half a small delicious peach before her eyes closed and she fell asleep.

Two hours later the maid woke her and reminded her that dinner would start soon. She washed her face and was about to step back into her safari clothes, when the Somali girl pointed to the dresser. She opened it and found a simple white *guntiino*, a full-length Somali cotton dress. Close by were a pair of gold lamé sandals and a dozen amber necklaces of all sizes and shapes. As she dressed, the girl explained that traditionally, unmarried Somali women braided their hair, an option not available to Alice because she preferred her hair short. A final glance in the mirror convinced her she looked more like a young Greek woman of antiquity than an African beauty.

As she came out of her room, she realized that every nook and cranny was lit by small lanterns, yet the interior of the "castle" was open to the evening sky. The moon and stars shone down into the central court and reflected off a shallow pool, through which came a flood of water from an underground spring. Two Somali women tending the lamps quietly passed her on her way to the dining room. Wandering along the same path she could see a maze of arches and corridors at ground level that led back into the complex itself. She turned off the main path to look closer and found herself in a small room to one side of a pavilion. Brian sat there, cross-legged at a low table, looking more dreamy-eyed than ever.

"Alice," he said, as he slowly and carefully rose to greet her. "And you've been transformed."

She looked lovely in her Somali dress.

"What's that?" she asked, pointing to a small snuffbox.

"Angel dust," he said matter-of-factly. "I'm afraid you caught me in the act. I take it occasionally, like snuff."

"You mean, it's cocaine?" She was shocked.

"I prefer 'angel dust,'" said Brian as he slipped the box into a drawer.

"From the tone of your voice," he said, offering her his arm as they went on, "I take it you disapprove. That's your prerogative. For me it's an occasional relief."

"Why?" she asked. It seemed to her he was playing with fire.

"The lodge and all of this involvement in Somali life and tradition is fine," he said, "but every now and then I need a short vacation."

They had arrived in the main hall, where they found J.O. and the Webbs waiting.

"Anyway," he said smiling at her, "it's not for the likes of you."

Several waiters were on hand to serve them drinks.

"Who are all these people? The ones who live here?" asked J.O.

"It's a mixture, mostly Somalis, some Abyssinians and a few Samburu people," said Brian. "They have two things in common—dry country cattle raising and their nomadic way of life. They get on together here surprisingly well."

They walked on into the dining room and sat on carpets around a wide table, supporting themselves with pillows as dinner was served.

"Tonight we have Persian cooking," said Brian as he clapped his hands and large platters appeared of *zereshk polo*, rice with barberries, *koresht-e-fesenjan*, chicken in pomegranate juice, and *koresht-e-ghormeh sabzi*, lamb with black-eyed peas and fenugreek. "I'm afraid you'll have to indulge me."

"And here's to the birthday boy," said J.O., raising a glass.

"By the way," said Tom, looking at the wine, "what *are* we drinking?"

"Persian wine," said Brian, "from Shiraz."

"Very much like sherry."

They followed Brian's example and ate with their hands, pulling the tender meat apart and savoring the Eastern spices. The rice and meat dishes were followed by vegetarian casseroles, soupy lentil dishes, several types of yogurt, baked fruit, figs and honey and *bamieh*, a pastry rich in eggs and honey.

A small band of Turkish musicians played while they ate, and then a belly dancer appeared as the company lay back and enjoyed the performance. Alice could clearly see why Brian thought of himself as a hedonist. His reputation for hard work among the herders meant that he technically didn't fit the definition, but he's made a very good start, she thought, as she watched him nodding his head at the dancer, keeping time with the music.

They had all brought small birthday gifts, and watched while Brian opened them. Among the presents were a large packet of rose-scented soap, as a reminder of England, from Edna and Tom; a pearl-handled Colt Dragoon revolver from J.O. with a card, "Always handy in close quarters"; and an autographed copy of *Travels in West Africa*, by her aunt, from Alice.

After coffee and liqueurs, they said goodnight and Alice went to her room.

She sat there on a divan in her Somali dress and thought about how different Brian's life was from most people she knew. He obviously had adapted well and had brought much of his own life into conformity with local traditions.

She opened a book she had been reading, a romantic novel about a heroine, cautious to the point of being a prude, who had resisted the advances of an Italian count, only to throw herself into the arms of an English suitor masquerading as a gentleman. He turned out to be a complete scoundrel who jilted her. At that point, the heroine had seen it all, and had lived through some amazing experiences, but she became an abandoned, broken woman, until toward the end of the story, when the count reappeared and carried her off from the London slum where she was working as a seamstress. And they lived happily ever after on his Tuscan estate.

Which made Alice wonder.

Of the many suitors in her life, how would she ever really know who among them was trustworthy and romantically truly considerate. And were any of them scoundrels-in-waiting?

It could be that she might even now be committing errors of omission because, like the heroine, she was being too cautious.

"But I'm perfect. That's what he said," she murmured.

Am I really? she thought. And it was that challenge, a dare posed within herself, that made her close her book and walk back to the small room where she previously had seen Brian and his white powder.

She opened the drawer and looked in. Yes, it was still there. She took the box out and opened it. It made her think of the light-colored fine dust of Machakos, the dust that brought back a memory of Dorothy, and how she used to complain about it. The dust that drifted and slipped into everything she owned.

What would Dorothy have thought of this? Alice mused, as she stared at what must be something very expensive, else why keep it in this precious silver and jade snuff box. Very attractive container, she thought. Then she said to herself, *angel dust*. She wondered as she sat there why it had been, and was still, so damned by everyone.

She had read someplace that it could be addictive, but not in single doses. She felt something in the air, and as she looked up she saw a glimmering reflection on the ceiling, the moon shining full on the water outside the door.

Yes, she said to herself, there was something in the air. And she realized it was not dust that she was thinking of, but a sense of danger that hung there even as she sat. It drifted and swirled all around her. It got into her hair and onto her skin, and without much more thought, she took a small quantity of the powder between her thumb and forefinger and placed it tentatively into one nostril. Isn't that the way people take snuff? she reasoned. Then she snuffled and it seemed to infuse itself directly from her nose into her brain.

To be certain, she sniffed another pinch, then she sneezed and the dust rose up in a cloud in front of her face. She tried to collect it and restore it to the box, but it dissipated in front of her eyes, as she felt herself being overtaken by an extraordinary feeling.

Now wide awake, she suddenly had become very alert. She got up and wandered out of the room along the path, listening to the sounds from the courtyard that had become amplified. Fascinated, she knelt close to the water to hear the peeping and croaking of frogs that were prolonged into echoes. She lowered herself finally into the shallow water, where she watched her cotton dress float up. Underneath it, she felt every part of her naked body tingling, aroused, as she laid further back in the cool water and stared up at the moon and stars. There above her in the night sky, she saw a vision of Brian like a golden cloud.

He floated down and covered her body, which she could see outlined inside her wet cotton dress.

Wonder of wonders, she thought, it glowed. Her body glowed! It cast off a golden light that flowed from every pore, and her mind was pleasantly overtaken by sexual desires, desires in forms and functions that she could not deny, as she experienced an orgasm, her first.

Afterward, still very excited, she fell asleep listening to the water running by her ear…

…In a vivid dream she saw herself as a young girl walking in a green field following a white rabbit, who smelled strongly of brandy.

She followed him to a large hole in the ground, but no sooner did they enter than the ground gave way and they fell through a deep, dark tunnel. Still tumbling, they popped out into the sunlight and found themselves on a croquet lawn. A game was in progress, and she was told by the rabbit to hurry and take a mallet.

"Quick, quick! Do as I say!"

"Why?" she asked, and it seemed to her she was again talking to her father, and once more questioning him about the simplest things as they sat at the breakfast table in their old cottage in Kent. "Don't argue with me, Alice," said the rabbit. "Just *do* it! And hurry, hurry, for God's sake, girl, here she comes."

She heard "Hail Britannia" played once more by the high commissioner's band, and went forward, mallet in hand, to greet the

Queen, only to trip on a wire hoop. She fell just as the Queen stopped and looked down at Alice lying on the lawn. The Queen reminded her of Isabelle Burns, with her hair piled high in an elaborate fashion. "My scissors," demanded the Queen. And a fat little man at her side, who spoke with a Scot's accent, said, "Aye, milady." He bowed and passed her a large pair of shears. Then he held out a ribbon for her to cut. She took the ribbon and flung it to the ground, and pointed her shears at Alice and shouted, "Off with her head!"

Alice turned to the white rabbit, who was very agitated. She could tell that because his nose started twitching rapidly as he grabbed a cup of brandy from a tray.

"Why?" she asked.

"For God's sake, Alice! Hit the ball, can't you? Hit it. Hit it, or she'll kill you. I know her. She's capable of anything."

"Damn me, Alice," said a toy soldier who came rushing up. He had on a tall red hat and a sword that wouldn't stop rattling. "He's right. I say, old girl, he's right as rain. Hit the ball or you'll buy it, just like Dot." He grabbed at the cup from the rabbit's paw and they fought over the brandy, splashing it all over themselves.

"Don't listen to them," said a well-dressed man, in all respects a gentleman, and exceptional only in that he was but two feet tall and had a card in his hatband with the single word "Mad" written on it.

"Take this instead," he said as he opened a snuffbox, inside of which was a small sign that said "Sniff Me!"

Suddenly the box lid was snapped closed by the extended claws of a cat's paw. She looked up and saw an enormous cat, who, even as it smiled, cried, "Come to me, Alice, and abide in me, I will save thee." He smiled so broadly and opened his mouth so wide that it stretched far and wide and she could see his many glittering teeth. She was about to step forward into this enormous maw; anything, she said to herself, anything, to escape the Queen, who hovered over her screaming, when another voice said, "Too sharp, Alice. Too sharp. Don't trust the bastard." This came from a round, roly-poly hedgehog.

"Here," he said, "I'll save you. Jump into my pouch, it's as simple as that." And he conveniently held open a large pouch that sat across his belly. "Mind the ants," he said as she tried to get in, which wasn't easy. Everywhere she placed her hands, sharp quills made her wince.

Then she looked beyond the Queen and saw the dead face of Dorothy staring out from a hedge, at which point she became frightened. "Not to worry, you foolish little girl," said the Queen, "the scorpion will take over."

She suddenly vanished into thin air.

What did she mean by that? Alice asked herself as she saw that everyone had gone. And with them the safety of the hedgehog's pouch, the protection of the cat's mouth, the escape provided by the little box, and even the mug of brandy. Gone.

"All gone," said a voice behind her. She spun around and listened. It was coming from the hole she had entered by.

"Yes," said the voice, as a large brownish-red scorpion scurried out of the hole. It had a steel medallion strapped across its breast, so placed that it covered its heart. On the medallion was written "Poison! Do Not Touch!" Then she felt a shadow passing over her head and looked up to see a huge stinger quivering above her face.

"Oh, you'll be a fine addition to my collection," said the scorpion. "You, along with Dorothy."

Then from somewhere came the voice of the rabbit who said, "I told you. I warned you." His voice lingered as an echo reverberating faintly in her mind, "Off with her head...."

"Alice," said a familiar voice.

"Did you hear me?" asked J.O. "I said pass the sugar."

She was sitting at the breakfast table with J.O.

"By the way," he said. "Pardon me for saying so, but you look awful this morning."

"I know," she said, as a flurry of fears and thoughts came swirling into her mind. This morning she was dressed sensibly in her safari outfit. At some point in the night, her Somali dress had disappeared and in its place was her nightgown, something she could not for the life of her remember putting on.

"Perhaps this is all just too much for me, J.O.," she said as she passed the bowl. It slipped from her hand and the sugar spilled onto the table.

"Alice," he said, "I have to say that this morning you remind me of my oldest daughter. I never thought I'd see the day when I'd say a thing like that about you."

"Why?" asked Alice, as she watched him spooning the sugar back into the bowl.

"She's so flighty, never knows where she leaves things. Would forget her head, if it wasn't fastened to her body," he said as he laughed and shook his head at the very idea.

Alice felt that if she had lost her head she couldn't blame anyone; if anyone was guilty, she knew it was herself. What in the name of God was I doing last night? she wondered.

In her bath this morning she had, with some misgiving, and much trepidation, examined her private parts. As guilty as sin, she thought. The White Hare was right, the Queen's going to be very angry with me, and the scorpion's going to kill me, just like he killed Dorothy.

She dropped her head into her hands on the table and sighed a great sigh.

"What in God's name have I done?" she mumbled through her fingers.

J.O. sitting across from her said, "It's only the sugar, Alice. I'll call the server."

He leaned back to see if he could catch the eye of the Somali houseman, something he had tried earlier with little success.

Suddenly Brian came through the curtained door, startling in his dress. Barefooted, he had on a Somali head cloth, and had wrapped himself in a Somali red- and white-checked sarong. He also had a cloth draped around his neck and shoulders. As he swept in, he stopped behind Alice's chair and reached forward and placed his hands on her shoulders, which were still hunched over, her head still between her hands.

"You were absolutely marvelous last night," he said, and then laughed and turned to seat himself.

Her head came up quickly. Her reddened eyes sought him out. He calmly settled into a large flat chair at the head of the table, one with many cushions, obviously his favorite. He perched there with one leg cocked underneath him as three Somali housemen rushed up with trays piled high with food and coffee.

Something like jealousy passed through J.O.'s mind as he thought, why should he get all the service, and the food? I was here first. He had a second thought, one that he gave immediate voice to. "Marvelous was she?" He stared at Brian. "What do you mean by that?"

Alice also stared at Brian, but maintained a stony silence.

I should have obeyed and hit the ball, she thought. Further distracted, she said to some mythical figure inside her head, "I'm sorry."

"What?" asked J.O. staring at her, "*You're* sorry. Are you well, Alice? It's not for you to say anything, damn it."

He turned to Brian. "I said, what did you mean, sir." J.O.'s eyes were flashing.

No one could ever ignore him when that happened. It was indeed a scary and impressive sight, and demanded an immediate answer.

"I heard her wandering around last night," said Brian, who shook his head and smiled at Alice, "but I went back to sleep. Later Idina and Wallia, the house matrons, called me and said they found her wading in the pool. They dried her off and put her to bed." He turned back to J.O. and in a very contrite voice said, "But you're right. I'm the one who should be sorry. It was damned careless, won't happen again."

"What won't happen again?" asked J.O. in the tone of a wounded father.

"I shouldn't have served that Persian wine for dinner," said Brian. "It's so rich tasting it's hard to know it has as much alcohol as port." He looked at a blushing Alice and said, "But I trust no harm was done. Though they both said you told them a fantastic story about someone called Alice and her looking glass. They were highly amused, and want you to come to their compound today and tell it to some of their friends."

Alice looked at him, relieved.

In her mind she resolved never to do anything like that again, even if Aunt Mary were to directly intercede.

"Now J.O.," said Brian, "what about something to eat? Your plate looks empty. And Alice, come along, have some coffee, you'll feel better for it. And here's Edna and Tom."

The Webbs came in and sat.

"Fantastic place," said Tom. "Slept like a baby."

"So restful," said Edna. "The sound of running water everywhere."

"Made me a bit uneasy," said J.O., and they all looked at him.

"Had to get up several times in the night," he said ruefully.

Everyone, even Alice, had to laugh at that.

And J.O. noted to himself that it was the first time he had seen her laugh since the funeral.

Later, Brian asked all of them for advice about a project he had started with wild game animals, oraxes and kudus. He planned to raise them in herds alongside cattle. "I got the idea from the herdsmen. They said game animals occasionally become domesticated, and they're a hell of a lot easier to take care of than cattle."

The remainder of the morning was taken up by a tour, as Brian showed them around the cattle pens and model villages where self-sufficiency was the goal.

"What's all the *shauri*, that commotion?" asked Alice indicating with a nod of her head.

Somewhat recovered, she was showing a lively interest in Brian's projects. "And that stink." Wrinkling up her pert nose, she said, "Awful, smells like something dead these last two weeks."

"It's the cattle," said Brian. "They're turning back another herd."

They watched Somali herders and dogs chase away a group of emaciated animals that had wandered too close to one of the compounds.

"They look wretched, what's wrong with them?"

"Rinderpest. Once it reaches that stage, the Kamba herdsmen separate them and let them wander till they keel over. They generally find their way here looking for food and water."

"Why don't they just shoot them?" asked Edna.

"The herders can't afford the bullets," said Brian. "And we can't let any more die around here. Have to drive or drag them into a ravine to the east. They fence them in downwind and away from the river."

"What about your cattle?"

"They keep their own herds in compounds where we feed them. But, as you can imagine, it's a difficult job getting forage nowadays. We have to use river water to grow our own. We hope to maintain a minimum herd for breeding."

"So, unlike the rest of us," said Tom, "you won't have to replace range animals once the weather breaks and the epidemic dies down."

"Meantime," asked Alice, "can't anything be done?"

"There isn't much. Quarantine seems to help."

"But this is a problem that should really be taken up by people like Hale, in Machakos," complained Tom.

"I know he's a relative of yours," said Edna looking at Alice, "but he never seems to do anything."

"I've heard the Germans have developed some vaccine, but the numbers and logistics here in Kenya are against us," said J.O.

"If he were to take it up, how could he help?" asked Alice.

Brian looked at her. He was curious as to what had happened last night. This morning he noticed his snuffbox sitting empty. "Well," he said, "for starters, he should send someone out to the villages to show them the advantages of keeping their animals healthy and separated from other herds. The older people know this already, but the younger ones ignore their advice."

"Or maybe they're just careless," said Tom.

"I doubt it," said Brian. "The young herders are just as anxious as anyone to get ahead."

"Like smallpox," said J.O. "I hear your Somalis intentionally stay away from Kamba villages where it's rampant."

"But it's easier to deal with smallpox than with rinderpest," said Edna.

"Again," said Brian, "someone should show them how to vaccinate themselves against it. It can be done locally with cow lymph."

"We've already done that with all our workers," said Tom. "They're fine."

4

Athi River Station

The small station not far from Nairobi was aglow with lights. Inside, the railway staff and askaris had gathered in the waiting room. It was Sunday evening and Mr. DeSuza, the recently arrived stationmaster, a devout Catholic, stood at the head of the table and tapped with a fork on an empty glass to get their attention.They had just finished eating their dinner, which, surprisingly, had been provided by DeSuza. He had asked the staff to join him in a special meeting, and, because of the free meal, everyone was there, including the signaler, the askari and the clerk, as well as the points man, who was responsible for the switches.

"I have called you here," DeSuza said, "to ask you to reconsider your lives."

He looked around to ensure his point had gone home. His audience stared back.

"I know from the station record book that none of you are Catholic, and I also know that none of you are even Christian." At this point everyone looked worried; they had come for the dinner, now they didn't know what to expect. "I see a spiritual gap here that can only be filled by the Catholic Church. My fellow Catholics from Mombasa will soon be starting a chapel here, a small but important place close to this station. This chapel will be different from the other Christian places already here."

Everyone knew the Protestants controlled the local church, the school and the health station. They were powerful, and this looked like a revolution of sorts, which made his audience apprehensive. DeSuza was well along in presenting his scheme to start a Catholic core group that would counteract the effect of the Protestants, when the outside door suddenly slammed closed with a *bang*.

Startled, the clerk jumped up and tried to open it. It wouldn't budge—it was barred from the outside. He turned to the door connecting the waiting room with the station office, again a formidable thick wooden slab, just in time to see it also slam shut. Everyone raced to the windows, which were properly barred to prevent any access as a precaution against sneak thieves, but now they effectively prevented any exit. The room had been quickly converted into a perfect jail.

"Wait," yelled DeSuza. "Stop! You people out there, stop!"

He turned to the clerk and the askari. "Where are the arms, the rifles?" he cried.

"They are all safely stored in the office, Bwana."

And so DeSuza had to watch as a gang of what looked like Wakamba thugs, led by a strange-looking African woman, removed substantial food supplies from the storerooms next to his station. Sacks of flour and rice went first, and in rapid succession crates of tea and sugar, then boxes of ammunition and the whole collection of rifles and several pistols. All were carefully strapped down or securely tied to the pack frames on the backs of the station donkeys. The last to go were the blankets and cooking pots from the kitchen, some still containing the remains of their supper!

"My God Almighty," cried DeSuza to the clerk, Abu. "Can't we do something?"

"*Haya*, Bwana, it is a dead loss. Let us not provoke them now since they are well armed. We can only wait until they have left. The people here, the Protestants, will come and let us out, then we can telegraph the authorities. See, there they go."

The string of loaded donkeys marched out of the compound heading for the bundu, and beyond that to the trail along the river. The station staff remained locked in the waiting room in the station, which was some distance from the village. Later that night, several of the wives discussed what was happening. They assumed from the shouting and banging noises coming from the direction of the station that their husbands were carousing. They had decided that the new stationmaster was nothing but a drunk and reprobate, disguising himself behind a pious cloak of words and pronouncements.

"*Haya*, this Indian comes to us and tells everyone he is a holy man, yet listen to that noise!" they said.

"They will soon be so drunk their legs will fail them and they will have to be carried home."

Meanwhile everyone, including the Protestant mission staff in the village, had gone to bed. They had not been invited. Early the next morning, expecting to bring her husband home after a wild night of drinking, Selina, the wife of the clerk, finally arrived at the station to find it locked. Pinned to the door was a note from someone called "The Jakoby Raiders," thanking the Railway for its generosity and promising that the food would be fairly distributed within the region.

In Muthuri's Hut

Now Bwana Roger, let me tell you something for your own good. It is about the thing that lies inside us that is more powerful than any weapon.

I recall in the Mission they once told us, "The Pen is mightier than the Sword."

Kimani and I had to write that out, many times over, and we struggled every time we wrote it, because each time we had to put aside our doubts. In real life we had always felt that the Word was mightier than anything, including the Pen and the Sword. And we thought, of all people, the White Fathers should understand that. But they did not.

I'll give you an example.

Among the Wakamba, a small group of villagers are sometimes attacked by mass hysteria, a "germ" or "seed" that spreads quickly throughout a village, thence to a region. The single "germ" may be a word which comes from one "possessed," or anyone who has been subjected to a visit by some force you cannot see, and from whom the "word" or "light" spreads very quickly.

I am told that even the elders will not intervene. In some cases, it may go no further than a village, but even then it will prove destruc-

tive. The local way of life and the inbred habits of a lifetime are cast aside; a period of chaos reigns.

Another example close to home is the oath taking among us Kikuyu.

Here the words used in the making of the oath will rule a person's life and there is no turning back. Thus, Kimani and I think mass hysteria or oath taking could be used someday to bring havoc, without a single arrow or spear being thrown.

Take the case of a headman whose clan members work on a plantation, or on the railroad. If that headman so desires, he could keep many people away from that work, and they would have to obey, kabesa, that's final, there would be no argument. So, the Word could be the ultimate weapon against the wazungu.

You've heard of the woman, Jakoby? I think she could be one of the seeds, the "spirits" among the Wakamba. And before long, with just a few words, she could be the start of a mania.

Did I tell you she is very close to the Germans? Kimani heard that from some Wakamba at the trading station in Ngongo.

As to Kimani himself, he has cast off the cloak of the White Fathers, gathered a band of young warriors, and he wants me to join them. They are sworn to follow him under oath in a sacred war. They come from many places—Ngongo Bargas, Thika, Limuru, and Kibale. They reject these new rules and regulations. They are willing to live off the land and stay together, and they intend to move into the forests in the north.

Yes, the Word. It may not stop the Iron Snake, but in the future it will make you wazungu think twice.

5

It was now July and Karegi had given birth to a son baptized Zaliwatena, which meant "new life." Father Glascock carried out the baptism. No husband was present, but he had long ago abandoned such niceties, although, right up to the day of the birth, he never gave up the hope that Karegi would become a nun.

Alice volunteered Roger and J.O. as godfathers. She had by then recovered from her experiences in Brian's lodge and felt it was a good sign that her next move was preceded by another letter from her aunt, her last from England as later that year she was to leave for South Africa. She was about to take up a nursing post there following the recent outbreak of the Boer War:

> *I can only commend you for your decision to stay on, providing you are making good use of the opportunities presented to you by God. Neither Rosmé nor you described the work you are doing out there in Kenya, but I know for a fact that much must be needed, as we often hear reports in the newspapers about the ravages of smallpox and rinderpest. I realize you are not a trained nurse, nor do you have any special knowledge of the medical profession. But still, in your situation, I assume you will be able to help somehow.*
>
> *If you do undertake any such effort, I would suggest you begin at some basic level. Go out to a village, bring some helpers and see what can be done of an immediate nature. It doesn't have to be an undertaking of a large sort; just start on a small level and see if it will grow of its own accord....*

Alice felt confident enough in her next project to buy a wagon and some mules. Food distribution from an ox wagon had taught her the advantages of reliable transportation. The ox wagon had been reliable, but it was also cumbersome. A mule team and light wagon seemed more appropriate because this time food transport was only secondary to what she had in mind.

When she was ready, she drove out to see Stephen. She planned her trip so she'd arrive at noontime when he would still be relatively sober. He agreed to what she suggested, but then as everyone knew, he had little choice. He was under considerable pressure to do something, but, being the kind of man he was, he couldn't help but remark that village-based programs, though they sounded worthy, were seldom of any use.

"Anyway, you'd better take Kiamba with you," he said. "As for a vaccine, there might be a supply in Mombasa. Albert's there this week; I'll telegraph him to see if he can locate some."

"Telegraph?" asked Alice.

"Yes, the Railway finally got around to installing it. Although it may still be a long while before the rail spur arrives," he said, reaching for a telegram form.

"If he does locate some," she said, "tell him to send it to me in Nairobi."

Alice's Diary (Stanhope, Cheshire, 1945)

> *...The moment I arrived there I knew I had come to the right place. I felt I had stepped into Aunt Mary's shoes. Kiamba and I had chosen the village of Kathambani, not far from Kaani on the main track, less than ten miles from Machakos. We intended to stay one week to make sure our effort started on the right foot. We knew we'd be welcomed because of our wagonload of food. The first thing we did was to stop at the headman's hut and ask if we could meet with the village elders. Then Kiamba explained that we wanted to use Kathambani as an example, to show other villages what could be done to improve their daily life. Once our program had started, we wanted permission to bring visitors from other places.*

They agreed, and we set to work at once. Our first action was to mobilize some villagers to build a hut for us. We could use that when we were in residence; also we could store food there between trips.

Meantime, I stayed in the hut of Kathuke, the headman, and Kiamba stayed with a friend just a few doors away. The first morning after our arrival we were told a famous medicine woman, a seer, Syonduku, was visiting the region. Kathuke had invited her to meet with us and talk about what we intended to do.

They were greeted by a slim woman with a colorful headscarf and elaborate beaded earrings in earlobes that had been stretched. She had high cheekbones and a wide face with a pleasant smile. It was hard for Alice to believe that this woman had had five children; she seemed quite young and much healthier than any of the women of the village. After greeting her with respect, Alice said through Kiamba, "We have been told you are well known here." Alice spoke only Kiswahili and presumed the woman spoke only Kikamba. But she answered Alice directly in Kiswahili.

"First, I pass to you greetings from your friend, Jakoby."

"Jakoby?" asked a surprised Alice. "You know her?"

"She is traveling with my friend Ngali wa Mutua, a woman from my home village."

"So, you aren't from the Kikuyu region?"

"Ah," said Syonduku, "you are a sharp observer." Her fingers went up to her beaded earrings. "They also say you are a hunter, eh? I admire that in a young woman. I myself have been traveling to many places looking for food for my family and village. The Kikuyu region is rich and bountiful, but I have come back to my homeland to help because everyone here is suffering."

"Kathuke tells us that you can foretell the future?"

"More than that," she said as she looked at Alice and Kiamba and then at the hut that was being built for their future use. "The people here are very impressed by what you propose, but everyone is still wondering, what brought you here? Are you a missionary?"

"No. Our goal is a simple one. I want to help the people."

"Then perhaps I can be of use," said Syonduku. "I have had much experience in the life and ways of these people. What is it you intend to do?"

Alice explained that she wanted to help stop diseases from spreading, to show people better methods for raising cattle and for raising healthy children, and to restore the life and vitality of the village.

"How will you cope with smallpox?"

"By vaccination."

"What is that?"

"We have some lymph from cows that had cowpox." She held up the vial from Mombasa. "We scratch the person's skin and put some on, and that person will be safe."

Syonduku looked carefully at Alice.

"Why are you looking at me like that?" asked Alice.

"I'm trying to see what is inside," she said. "You know there is a problem with wazungus. They give us a bottle and say 'Take this,' or 'Drink that,' because they cannot believe we are capable of understanding what is in it."

"And in this case?" asked a worried Alice. Until then she had been brimming with self-confidence and determination. Now she suddenly thought of her hunting experience when they had encountered the two mambas. She had found herself way out in front of the hunting party and in a tight spot, because she so often put herself forward.

Was this another case where she should have held back? she asked herself.

"Now that I have looked into your face," said Syonduku, "I am satisfied. You are a person to be trusted."

"Thank you for your confidence," said Alice, and at that moment she had a twinge of conscience. It was her aunt who had commented on the fact that she had no medical training, other than some experience with poisoned arrows and hunting accidents.

"What is our first step?" asked Kiamba.

"Well," said Alice, as she got up and walked out into the village compound, followed by the other two, "we must begin vaccinating everyone."

"Ah," said Syonduku, shaking her head, "you are very ambitious. But, you are new at this. I myself started organizing meetings in villages years ago. I found you have to go about it more carefully. First, deal with a few people who are interested, then show the others what can be done."

"I think she's right," said Kiamba.

"You mean we should perhaps select a small group of volunteers?"

"Yes. Once they're vaccinated, the others will follow."

"And what am I to tell them?" asked Kiamba.

"Explain that we will first scratch their skin, then we will apply this dawa." She had already set out a chair, a clean hatpin and the vial. She was ready to start.

"Oh," she added, "one other thing. You must explain that they might feel badly after the vaccination, but that is natural, it will go away."

"Ah," said Syonduku. "You have had the experience?"

"No," said Alice, although it seemed to her perfectly natural that she should have been exempt from that. She looked at Kiamba: surely he had been vaccinated? He shook his head, no.

"You mean neither of you has been treated?"

They admitted that was so.

"Well," said Syonduku, "maybe we should start first with you two."

So, that afternoon in front of a large crowd of women and children, Alice and Kiamba showed the villagers how it was done. But even after vaccinating themselves, no volunteers came forward.

"We must give them time to think it over," said Syonduku.

"Perhaps we should hand out some food," said Alice.

"No," said Syonduku, "that is not a good idea." She took Alice aside to explain. "It is better to give food only after something is accomplished. These people are used to working for what they gain in life. It drives them on, even though their life is not an easy one. I suggest you distribute food *after* they finish building your hut, then they will understand."

"I see," said Alice.

"Or, you can give out food once they can demonstrate that they are following your advice in regard to cattle or caring for their children."

So, after touring the village and further discussing Syonduku's ideas, they had supper and Alice settled into her camp cot.

During the afternoon, the skin near the site of her vaccination had become hot and inflamed, but she thought by morning it would be better.

Later that night she woke in a sweat and called out to Kiamba.

Syonduku came in with a lantern to explain that Kiamba was sick and could not respond. "His arm does not look healthy. We must see what can be done," she said.

Several of the village women gathered to help Syonduku. They held the lantern while she looked at Alice's arm. The vaccination had turned into an oozing sore; the arm below it had swollen, and she could see small red lesions under the skin.

"Boil some water, quickly," she told one woman, and to another, "put some wet cloths on her forehead and cool her. Now, go next door and look after Kiamba. He has the same problem."

Then she went to her hut and searched in one of her several baskets, one full of native medicines. She took out some turmeric and a powdered root from the tree she called the *Mrongo*, or drumstick tree, a tree with elongated dry pods that grew in the Mombasa region. From these she made poultices and an infusion with which she treated Alice and Kiamba, but it was several days until they recovered from their fevers; even then they were weak.

"What went wrong?" asked Alice when she could finally sit up.

"Your blood was poisoned by the vaccination," said Syonduku. "You are very lucky to have survived."

"It must have been your medicine that saved us," said Kiamba, pointing at the powdered plant material.

"Ah," said Syonduku, laughing, "don't be so quick to make judgments. The medicine I gave you oftentimes doesn't work. But I give it anyway, because sick people feel better when something is done. It may have little or no effect."

"But we got well."

"I think the reason you survived was because you are both young and healthy. If you had been children, or very old, it would have been a different case. Also, you see the people here, they are thin and weak; they would have died outright."

"Good God," said Alice. "If we had inoculated the whole village, everyone would have died!"

"But they didn't."

"But," said Alice, "how will anyone believe us after this? Our whole program is lost."

"No," said Syonduku, smiling at her, "all is not lost. I will show you how to do what you want."

"Why would you do that?" asked Alice, who at the moment had very little faith in her own abilities.

"Oh, my Little Sister," said Syonduku, who could see the bewildered look in Alice's eyes. "Have faith. I believe you both were sent here by God. Mwene Nyaga wants to help us, but he sent us a messenger who is new to the ways of the world. She will need a little help. Once you are truly well, I will show you how to do things."

Alice lay back on her camp cot. She remembered reading of one scene where Aunt Mary had unexpectedly come across a band of men deep in the jungle; they had decorated themselves with shells, beads and strange ornaments. Her aunt thought she had stumbled upon a secret society, which in that region would not be treated lightly: death was the usual punishment. She tried to escape, but was caught, brought back and made to sit under a tree. "Why?" she asked. "Why are you prolonging the agony?"

It turned out they were not members of a secret society, but monkey hunters. Their prey, curious to a fault, was attracted to the odd things that they carried with them, and they thought Mary would be the ideal bait for monkeys, because she was the queerest thing they had ever seen, and they were certain the monkeys would think so too.

"What do you have in mind?" Alice asked, feeling now a bit like monkey bait.

"When I ask for volunteers in these villages," said Syonduku, "many more come forward, because, unlike you, I do not mention inoculations. I ask them to step forward for a dance. I call it the *Kilumi* dance. It lasts a week and is a religious undertaking. During the dance my spirit conveys messages from God."

"Messages?"

"Yes. I show them how to cleanse their village and their own spirits, and I act in place of God to bless their crops. Now, does this give you any ideas?"

"Of course," said Alice as she sat up, bright and excited at the prospect. "During the dance we could show them how cattle quarantine would work, and how child care could benefit new mothers."

"Exactly. We would work as a team. But one thing I would say from the outset."

"What?"

"When you offer this food 'in kind,' make certain you concentrate on those men and women who will respond in a serious way. For example, you should choose the young men who will be most interested in caring for their cattle."

"How will we know them?"

"Why, we will choose those who plan to marry," said Alice's mentor, amazed at Alice's naiveté. "They have a commitment to preserve as many of their animals as they can. Also, with child care, you must speak from experience."

"But I haven't had any children," said Alice.

"No children?" said Syonduku, again astonished.

"Not married," said Alice, now a bit ashamed that she had put it off.

"How will you cope?"

"I don't know," said Alice. Then rising to the challenge, she thought of something. "I'll bring Karegi with me the next time I come here."

"And smallpox?"

"I'll ask Dr. Sharpe to show Karegi how to do proper vaccinations using local cow lymph. I'm sure it will work." In return for showing Alice how to organize a Kilumi dance to promote her program, Syonduku made Alice promise that in the future she would take marriage proposals more seriously and make some progress toward raising a family.

"Your mother and father should help," said Syonduku.

Alice explained that her parents were dead.

"Then I will help you in their place," she said. "If you achieve half of what you propose, I will help you choose a husband. Now, for our Kilumi dance, in order to attract the men, we will need some meat. Perhaps some of the impala in the clearing not far from here...."

"Ah," said Alice as she patted her rifle case, "now there is where I think I can help."

6

Kikuyuland, Kenya

Looking for advice, Kimani went to see a friend and mentor, Njuguna. He sat with him outside his hut and shared a gourd of beer. "Tell me," said Njuguna, looking intently at his young friend, "Everyone is asking, why are you going your own way?"

Kimani had come here for advice, not to have more questions thrown at him, so he said nothing.

"You should stay here and help us," said Njuguna, impatiently. "Help guide the Council of Elders. They are not as concerned as you are about the future, and that worries me."

Njuguna had a great store of visions and dreams. The subject of snakes was an obsession with him and he talked often of how the legend had come to pass. "The Great Snake has appeared as they said it would," he said. "It came out of the ocean in Mombasa, now it has worked its way across Kenya."

"And like a bad dream come true," said Kimani, "we now see that the rail line is aimed directly at us."

"I have not yet seen the Snake," said Njuguna, as he shifted on the mat and put aside his beer straw. He was worried about his friend, but even more, he was worried about what was happening to their land. "I think it will operate in the same way as any large snake. It will be greedy for bigger and bigger meals and will squeeze the breath out of anything that dares stand in its way. The wazungu don't want it to slow down."

"I agree," said Kimani. "They seem pleased at what it is doing."

"And the second part of the prophecy?" asked Njuguna. "How

is that progressing?"

"It is coming true, as we speak. Famine and pestilence have arrived as predicted, and now while we are being weakened by such things, it will eat away at our only hope, our land."

"You recall Duma, the British man who took control of many plots?" asked Njuguna.

"I heard often of him from my father. And Mikono wa Damu, the German, who did the same thing in the south. They made many of the headmen sign treaties."

"I think they were preparing meals for the young Snake," said Njuguna.

"So, without the treaties, the Snake would have starved."

"Yes, at that time we were being deceived. They said there were many reasons for us to give up those parcels of land."

"In the Mission," said Kimani, "we were told that it would help stop slavery, families would be safer and our lives would be easier. Machines would till our land and carry the heavy loads. Muthuri and I were shown pictures of this new life as proof."

"Yet the feeding was going on as they talked. The land was going to the Snake."

"And nothing has changed."

"These wazungu," said Njuguna, as he spat in the dust, "they will cause us much harm. But the story is not finished. You know the expression '*Iri kanua itiri nda*,' hey? You may have something in your mouth but it may never reach the stomach, hey?"

He looked at Kimani to see if they understood one another. Kimani's face was as much a puzzle to him as the *mwano*, the pebbles, bits of bone and odd bits of sacred and mystic things that he kept in a gourd and cast on the ground each day to foretell the future. He was hoping to see in his pupil's face the solution to the problems that faced the Kikuyu nation. But, after staring at him for a while, he averted his eyes and once again took up his beer straw.

As with the mwano, he thought, one should never look with hope in your mind. One should always look first for the truth.

Portsmouth, England

"Your Highness," said Dr. Karl Peters as he bowed low before the Kaiser. "How may I be of service?"

Count Bülow had invited him to Portsmouth because he thought it might be of interest for Kaiser Wilhelm to confirm what they had already heard from the governor and Fritz Kohl about opportunities in East Africa. The count had earlier discussed with Peters the fact that even as the Boer War had begun, Germany had agreed not to interfere. The Kaiser was keen on personally helping the British to win a peace. "But his subjects," he said, as they sat having tea in this English town by the sea, "are upset by what he is doing."

"Naturally," said Peters, who could understand their resentment. "They feel Germany should support the Boers; don't we all."

"It is futile. The British have already rejected his offer of help."

Accompanied by the Kaiserin, two of their sons and Count Bülow, the Kaiser had landed at Portsmouth, from where they were due shortly to start for London and a banquet with the Queen. Like Peters, the Kaiser was happy to meet another unqualified German anglophile.

"Do you really think we can make progress in East Africa?" he asked as he gave Peters a bone-crushing handshake.

"How do you mean, Your Highness?" asked Peters. Warned beforehand that the Kaiser compensated for his withered left hand by projecting strength in his right, he had held the handshake for as long as he dared.

"What if Kohl is correct? He predicts the British will be soured by their experiences in this Kenya Colony. Should I make her an offer to buy it?"

"All I know is that it has good potential for farming," said Dr. Peters, cautiously.

"And perhaps not much else," said the Kaiser, who was impressed by Peters' grip. "An earlier report by one of their own geologists said the region is poor in mineral wealth."

"But it may be more important in other respects," said Bülow.

"Such as?"

"It would allow us a way through to Uganda," said Bülow.

"Which has better agricultural soils and water in excess," said Peters.

"Remember, Sire, Napoleon felt that access to the Nile was one of the highlights of his career."

"And the Romans before him," said Peters.

"As for making them an offer," said Bülow, "it might be best to wait until the price is right."

"Wait?"

"The British public is daily becoming tired of supporting the Railway," said Peters.

"If and when the government changes, or gives in," said the Count, "you could then make a reasonable offer informally through your grandmother."

"And for now?"

"Continue to apply pressure in an unofficial and informal fashion," said Peters. "A strategy that is identical to what Kohl is doing."

"Thus no one could ever accuse you of anything but peaceful intentions."

"Hmm. I'm still not convinced. And I would be very displeased to hear of any overt aggression between the Germans and the British out there. Remember, gentlemen, I am about to again offer my resources to the Queen to help negotiate a peace between the Boers and Great Britain. I would not take it kindly if I were made a fool of behind my back."

"Absolutely, Your Highness," said Count Bülow. "At present our understanding is that the troubles out there are all of a normal and natural origin. They arise from friction between elements of the government and the natives. German official influence and German nationals are not involved—am I correct, Dr. Peters?"

"Absolutely," he said.

7

Where have you two been?" Stephen nonchalantly asked when Alice and Kiamba returned to Machakos after an absence of four weeks. He had settled into a comfortable chair on the verandah and was looking through a pile of reports as Syani brought him a large tea tray with sandwiches. On the same tray were a brandy and water and the afternoon post. He opened one of the letters and began reading it as he reached for his drink. "Oh, Syani, bring another cup for the Memsab." He acted as if they had just been around the corner, and expressed no interest in what they had seen or accomplished.

It was quite possible, she thought, that he had forgotten entirely her earlier conversation in which she told him of what she intended to do out there.

"We've been to Kathambani."

"Oh?" he said, looking up from the letter. "Isn't that near Kaani?"

Alice recognized the handwriting on the envelope. It was from England, Stephen's aunt in Maidstone.

"Yes. Kiamba and I have started a small program there," she said as she watched Kiamba tie the team in the shade of the verandah.

Kiamba had told her on their way back to Machakos that Bwana Stephen now seldom came to the office, and often at night and more recently during the day he would suddenly yell out, complaining of the *wadudu*, the insects. When Kiamba or Syani went to see what he was talking about, they found nothing.

She looked at Stephen as he reached with a trembling hand for a sandwich. He seemed to have aged markedly. "Aren't you even interested in what we've been doing out there?"

"I'm sure you've been very helpful, Alice." Syani appeared with another cup. Alice poured herself some tea and asked Syani to bring food and water for her mules.

"When you have a chance tomorrow, sit down with Jimmy," said Stephen. "Give him all the details. It's just that I've been overwhelmed by requests for help." He pointed at the pile of papers. "The whole district's suffering and we don't have the resources to do more than the minimum."

"What about the food program you were going to start up?"

"I've purchased quite a bit of grain and that's been distributed locally."

"Purchased?"

"Yes, from Aden." He held up a letter and reached for his drink. "My aunt contributed the funds. She has a heart of gold, Alice. You remember meeting her at the wedding."

"But," said Alice, "I thought you said you were going to make some regular arrangement with Ian Burns to have food brought in from places like Kikuyuland? I know Roger's still keen on the idea."

"Roger Newcome." Stephen sighed and set his glass down. "He's trying to make a killing off a desperate situation. Money seems to be the only thing driving him, and the sad thing is he doesn't need it. I happen to know that his mother married a very wealthy man. All Roger has to do is make peace with him and he'd have more funds than he could deal with. Instead he's taken up the life of a caravan leader and a commercial man, a *bagwallah*."

Alice could almost predict what was coming next.

"Stubborn, strong-willed...." He started on about why Roger was a useless character, when suddenly he stopped.

He looked as if something had caught solid in his throat.

For a minute Alice thought he had choked on his drink as his face crumpled and he threw his head back and sobbed, "I'm guilty.... A hell of a crime, Alice."

She was startled, then frightened as he brought his head forward, tears flowing down his face. "I killed Dorothy."

Her mind clouded with anger as she listened to him.

"It's bothered me for weeks," he said. "I'm so thankful to have finally confessed."

"*What* are you talking about? How could you have done such a thing?"

"I killed her. I killed her, as surely as if I had driven a knife into her heart."

"I don't believe it," she said. "It's the drink talking."

"No," he said. "I told her she should have an abortion. I told her I wanted it that way. It must have preyed on her mind. She did it because I told her to."

Alice shook her head as she watched him. Not only was he older and weaker than she had ever known him, now his bleary eyes and sallow face were pathetic.

"Don't you see, Alice?" he persisted, as he leaned forward and said, "She got hold of some pills and did it to satisfy me. I killed her!"

"But it doesn't make any sense," said Alice. "Why would you have wanted to kill your own child?"

Stephen's head snapped up and he looked at her as if she were insane. He raised his voice as he said, "Will you *stop* saying that!"

"What?"

"You keep saying it was *my* child." He shook his head. "Don't you realize, it *wasn't* my child, it was Allen's!"

"Allen's?" said Alice, shocked by what he was saying.

"Yes," he said, looking at her. "Listen to me. Dorothy and I stopped having intimate relations."

"I can't believe it," said Alice.

"We hadn't touched one another that way since she arrived in Africa." Stephen, now dry-eyed, continued. "It had to be him, and half Nairobi knew about it."

Then he said something that upset her further.

"And now you," he said glaring at her.

She stared back. "Me?"

"Yes," he said. "You're next."

"*What* are you talking about?"

"Everyone knows about how you're carrying on. First with Roger, then Allen, then Stanford. Good Lord, you're playing with fire."

Alice was angry. She had sat through his tearful outburst because she was sorry for him; now she saw him in a different light.

"You have no idea, do you?" she said. "You really have no idea of what you've done."

"Don't throw that in my face, Alice," said Stephen. "I did it, and I accept that. I admit I encouraged her."

"No," she said, as she looked at him in wonder at his stupidity. "I don't mean that. I can see now it wasn't your baby, it was Allen's. But who made her want to get pregnant? And who let him do it?"

He reached for his glass, wondering what she was getting at. He had already confessed to a killing. It was misadventure, he thought. That's the word came to his mind, the kind of word medical people used, misadventure.

Alice persisted. "You killed her by not being the husband that she always wanted. Do you think another man would have allowed that to happen, a person with character?"

"You mean someone like Roger," he said, contemptuously.

"Yes," said she. "You may think what you want about him, but if he were married, he would never have let Allen do that to his wife. So I have to agree, you did kill Dorothy. But not in the way you think. You killed her by neglect!"

"Will you stop playing the angel? Look at you. How can you talk about fidelity when you've encouraged advances from every male in a hundred-mile radius like some animal in heat."

She shook her head in disbelief.

"Poor Bobby," he said with a trace of venom in his voice. "It was inevitable."

"Inevitable?" she said. "What do you mean?"

"You sent him into the jaws of that man-eater. The police in Mombasa found a notebook in his luggage. I couldn't show it to anyone I was so ashamed. It described how you were spreading rumors about him, how you were flirting with him—that's why he left that night on his own. He was supposed to have waited to go back the next day with Woodham-Stayne. If he had done that, he'd be alive today."

"Flirting with him?" said Alice. "I wouldn't flirt with Bobby if he were the last man on earth! And as for starting rumors, it wasn't me who let the cat out of the bag about how he used to diddle your wife when she was a child."

She jumped up and stared down at him with anger in her eyes. Then she turned as if to walk away.

"What an awful thing to say," he said as he stared up at her. "Who would have started such a rumor? Wait," he said, as he answered his own question, "don't answer that. I'll bet it was that bastard, Allen!"

He started to rise from his chair, then fell back, almost crying again as he looked at her.

"Alice, you've changed beyond recognition. It's not like you. It's Nairobi and the poisonous nature of the place. You have to get out of there. Come back out here to live. Get to know some decent people again, people like David. Did you know he's now a very religious young man? And quite pleasant. He'd be a great husband, or Franz."

"Franz!" she said. "That man's despicable."

"Franz Shimmer?" said Stephen. "Don't say that, Alice. He has an extraordinary future and his family is well off."

"Stephen, I knew this would happen." She walked toward her mule team, which was still hitched to the verandah railing.

"What?"

"Your brain has gone soft." She stepped up to the wagon seat and turned the team so they faced the road.

"You can't leave now," said Stephen as he went to stop her. But it was too late. She trotted the team onward toward the main road.

"There are lions roaming between here and Nairobi," he yelled.

"You forget, Stephen." She loosened the rifle in the scabbard by her seat as she wheeled onto the road. "I'm not afraid of such things." And then she was gone, riding into the soft light of the afternoon with the setting African sun reflecting off her hair like some avenging spirit.

By midnight the center of Nairobi was generally quiet. Often wild animals stalked the streets, especially hyenas that rummaged in the garbage pits. Frogs, chirping and croaking in their back-street miasmas, were by that time of night loud enough to drown out the snores of the guards sleeping on the verandahs of the shops and houses in town.

Ben and Jock, tired of staring at the last of a long line of now empty beer bottles in the Settler's Club, decided to retrieve their horses from a nearby stable and go home. The owner lived above the stable.

"D'Silva," yelled Ben, "you Goan thief."

"Open up, we want our horses!"

No light appeared and no one responded in the upper story. From their tone and general demeanor, it was almost guaranteed now that D'Silva would rather die in his bed than come down to help them. "Bastard. We'll never get 'em out of there. Bloody coward. He's probably hidin' under the bed. Just shoot the lock off, man, and we'll be on our way."

"Can't do that. Bloody town askaris'll be here in a flash. Look around for a plank; we'll pry the door loose." They staggered back up the side alley looking for a likely piece of heavy wood, when suddenly two Kikuyu men and one middle-aged black woman dressed in a long missionary dress entered the alley.

"*Haya. Ngoja hapa*," yelled Ben. "You three, stop right there. Where the hell do you think you're goin'?"

They stopped, and the leader of the three said in perfect English, "We're on our way home. Let us by."

"My God, Jock. Did you hear that, a nigger with an Oxford accent. Get out of here. Yes, *you*—you bloody savage. I'm talking to you, turn around and get off this street. It's reserved for white men. Go on," he said as he drew his pistol.

"I mean it," he threatened. No one moved.

"You think I'm too drunk to shoot, eh? Just watch me." He raised the gun to eye level.

"Jock. Watch me shave off one of those precious ear lobes, eh. I'll plunk the left one, bet you a pound."

"You're on," said his friend, who was now relieving himself against the stable wall.

The gun exploded and true to his word, he nicked the left ear of one of the men; but surprisingly, he didn't flinch. Instead he stared at the drunken shooter and slowly shook his head, as if saying, "You shouldn't have done that."

Quick as a flash he let go with his throwing club, knocking Ben cold, while his mate, Muthuri, jumped the other and quickly beat him to submission while Jakoby held him down.

All three then disappeared out of the alley before the town askaris came racing around the corner of the stable.

The sergeant in charge of the night watch was startled to see a woman driving a wagon down the main street into the lights of the railway station. It was Alice returning from Machakos.

"Sergeant, what was that shooting about?"

"Nothing, ma'am. Two settlers playing vigilante, drunk as lords. But what are you doing up? This is a dangerous place at night."

"Just taking a moonlight ride," she said as she rode on.

8

"It's hard to believe, isn't it?"

Bill Bagley and Matthew Woodham-Stayne stood with John Allen on a grassy knoll outside of Nairobi looking down over the edge of the escarpment.

"Look at the drop-off. I've never seen anything like it."

"And where's the new route?" asked Matthew.

"Show him on the map."

Bagley laid out a large map on the ground and pointed to the new route. "Here," he said. "As it stands now, it saves us 114 miles."

"But," said Allen, "the 1,500-foot descent is so steep we'll need a special tramway to lower equipment and cars."

"Sounds like an enormous job."

"It's only temporary," said Bagley. "Eventually we'll put in a permanent rail down the side of the valley."

"And we'll be on the valley floor faster than schedule," said Allen. "From there we'll move quickly to the lake."

"Now," he added, "I'll leave you both here. I have an urgent meeting in Nairobi."

"Meeting, my foot," said Bagley as they watched Allen walk briskly toward his carriage.

"Bagley," yelled Allen the following day. They were well settled in their new offices in the Nairobi Station, which was still the largest and most important building in the town. "Come in here!"

Bagley's office was next to his. "Yes?"

"Now listen to me." Allen's thin, sharp nose quivered when he was angry. Bagley saw it going now, a mile a minute. Like a stinger, he thought, wondering where and when it would strike. No wonder he was known to his houseboy as "*Nge*," the scorpion.

"What the hell are we doing paying out sums of money like this?" He held up a tally sheet, familiar to Bagley because he had drawn it up.

"Yes, I know what you mean. I sent that to you to draw your attention to it. It's the cost for food under our local contractor, Mr. Newcome. Prices are going up steeply as the drought continues."

"And what's this?" he held up another tally sheet, also familiar to Bagley.

"That's the cost for the new askaris. You remember we agreed with Matthew at our last staff meeting. We'll need more protection as we go further into Kikuyu territory."

"And presumably with more askaris, we'll need more food, and with the cost of that going up we'll need another budget. Is that your reasoning?" The stinger looked poised to strike Bagley in the throat. "Well, we're not going to ask for a new budget. We're going to make do with what we have. Cancel the askari contracts and telegraph Bombay to hold off on any shipments of contract Indians."

"But we'll need guards for the new sections of the line," pleaded Bagley.

"Wait, Bagley. Think. How did we operate in India when we went through hostile territory? I'll tell you." He pounded the desk. "We deployed troops along the right of way, laid temporary track through it as fast as we could, and then moved the troops further on."

"But we did keep a skeleton force in place."

"Yes, but only while we replaced temporary track with permanent rails; that way we kept the numbers down."

"And transferred some of the cost out of the immediate budget into future costs for repairs and maintenance," said Bagley.

"Exactly," said Allen. "By the way, don't you think it's strange there's been no resistance in the area? Matthew thinks the Kikuyus have caved in. They've gotten too involved with the food business."

Bagley pointed to the food tally sheet. "Because of rising prices."

"Right. They're not going to bother us right now. In fact, now is exactly the time for us to put the India method into action!"

The light came on in Bagley's eyes. "So we'll simply shift the greater part of the security force to the valley below."

"Bagley," yelled Allen one week later. "Come in here."

Bagley muttered to himself, "Now what?"

"Yes, Allen?" He had stopped calling him John.

"Just thought of something." There was a smile on Allen's face—a bad sign, thought Bagley. "I was chatting with Matthew about the food situation and our mounting costs. He mentioned that the army, on occasion, can use their powers of military confiscation for the good of the Empire."

"You mean an emergency?" asked Bagley.

"Or 'a military need,' as he phrased it," said Allen. "He reasoned that the Nandi raids in the west on our survey parties amount to just that, in which case we could confiscate food stores in exchange for food vouchers, eh? Anyway, I thought it was worth thinking about."

Bagley nodded. "But we'd still have to pay out for the vouchers, so what difference would it make?"

"I've thought about that too," said Allen. "We'd exchange the vouchers for goods, food or cash *once the emergency is over*. Then we'd have our new budget and food in excess. Of course, we'd set a fair exchange rate to base the vouchers on, eh? What do you think?"

"Well, it would resolve our immediate needs, and once the rains start, we could easily pay back what we owe using excess food. But I see one large drawback here."

"What's that?"

"The DC, McCann. He'd never give us permission without approval from Ian Burns."

"We've some leeway there. First, we could plead ignorance and just not tell him. Then the minute we start down the escarpment, we're out of McCann's jurisdiction. That's where the Naivasha district technically begins, and the DC there is our good friend Walter Cole, an old army man."

"So by the time McCann wakes up, we'll have a clear bill of health from the Naivasha side."

"And," said Allen, "we'll be free of the damned Kikuyus and the sniveling bureaucrats around here."

But once confiscation of food stores began, resentment built up and the situation quickly turned sour. The heavy hand of the army didn't help. Railhead had moved to Kijabe and the line had prepared to start down the incline, but it was heavy going. Then on the first occasion that food was taken from the New Alliance Trading Post in Naivasha, a shop owned by Roger Newcome, he let the army know about his concerns immediately, and in plain language.

"Notice, Bagley," said Allen, "the minute he puts his foot in, we see an increase in the number of incidents, derailments, raids on our storerooms, poisoned water wells, and so on."

"You're right," said Bagley. "The bastard's using the Kikuyus to get back at us."

9

Alice was sitting with Roger and J.O. on the verandah at Alice's house. They had just finished luncheon when Kona handed Alice a note.

"Incredible," said Alice. "It's from Jakoby. She says Bwana Bobby's alive and he can be ransomed for one rupee for every pound of weight. She's set the price at 350 rupees!"

"How do you know she'll give him up?" asked J.O.

"I think you can rely on her," said Roger. "She seemed like an honest person when we knew her."

"And they definitely said they would do it?" asked J.O.

"Well, we'll see how it plays out," said Alice.

Kona stood at the gate and peered carefully down the road, which appeared to be as empty as it ever was at two o'clock in the afternoon. "*Yuko pale*," he called to Alice. "Look, over there."

Alice, teacup in hand, looked where he pointed.

"What the hell is that?" exclaimed Roger.

A donkey cart rambled into the compound with a short, excessively fat, dark-skinned man sitting on its wooden floor whipping the lone animal forward. He was dressed in several wrappings of dirty cloth, greasy skins and had a wild growth of hair and beard.

They went down the stairs for a closer look.

"It's unusual to see a fat African anywhere," said J.O.

"He must be an Arab trader from the Coast, but why is he by himself?"

Then suddenly it clicked. "This must be their emissary," said Roger. "The one sent to collect the ransom."

The cart stopped and the man descended, and in a flash threw his filthy arms around the lovely Alice. He embraced her fully, as she cried out, "Good God! You filthy beast."

She squirmed free.

"Wait. Alice," said Roger. "It's your Uncle Bobby!"

"Right on, old boy," he said and there were tears streaming down his dirty face as he shook hands with J.O. and Roger, then he quickly waddled up the steps, almost sprinting to the top as he flopped onto a settee.

Firmly taking possession of that piece of furniture as if he would never leave it, he said, "In the flesh, so to speak, alive and well, and happy to see you all!" He babbled on. "Damn it, old girl, have you got a brandy and soda?" And with gusto, he began finishing off the remains of their lunch.

"Any ham?" he asked. "Dying for a piece of bacon.... Not allowed any pork."

"Kona," said Alice, "tell Mary to bring a large brandy and soda and more food. So it *is* you. What happened? We've just had a stone tablet carved for you at the church commemorating your death as, 'Taken by a lion at Kima.'"

"Not so, old girl. It was that damned Kikuyu friend of yours." He looked daggers at Roger. "And before I forget, thanks be to God for my wits.... Bloody wogs...devil take 'em!"

Mary appeared with a large glass and the fixings. Bobby gulped down half the glass, and, gasping, called for another while he finished the first, and simultaneously tried to drink the cream from the tea set. "On second thought, just leave the bottle."

"Take your time, Bobby, there's no hurry," said Alice.

"You're sure it was Kimani?" asked J.O.

"The very one. Took me from the train at Kima, poured out some cow's blood on the platform then marched me, naked, through the bundu for miles."

"I can see how others might do something like this," said Roger, unbelieving, "but Kimani?"

"Was he alone?" asked Alice. "And where does Jakoby come in?"

"First, he seems to have gone underground," said Bobby. "Disguises himself as a missionary on occasion, that's why they all call him *Kasisi*. It's obvious he's taken the law into his own hands.

Even has his own band of cutthroats. They've started some awful movement against the Railway. By the way, when's dinner?" He finished off his second drink and began eating a cold chicken that Kona had set out.

"No question, they're out to get us, old boy," he said to J.O. as he continued with his mouth full. "And that damned Zulu woman was no better."

He suddenly stopped eating, then swallowed as he exclaimed, bug-eyed, "Kimani *sold* me to her, damn it. *Sold*, I say. What animals!"

He resumed his gorging as he said, "I couldn't keep up with his crowd. Though I certainly learned to walk—must have covered a thousand miles all 'round!"

"But what could she want with you?" asked Alice, smiling at the thought.

"She said she wanted me as a white slave. Can you top that? Threatened at one point *to eat me*, but her gang said they wouldn't touch pork!"

Alice laughed at the thought.

"Not funny, old girl," said Bobby. "My life was on the line."

Alice, trying to be sympathetic, ordered Mary to draw him a bath. "And lay out some...." She hesitated. Bobby's bulk would prevent him from using any of her safari clothes. "...Sheets and towels."

"Send Kona over to our place," said Roger. "I'll loan him a razor."

"Don't bother, old man," said Bobby coldly. "If I wanted to have my throat cut I'd do it myself."

He was too excited to stop talking. "Never been so insulted in my whole life. Then she decides I'm too expensive to feed. Your precious Jakoby," he sneered at Alice, "had the gall to offer me to an Arab. But I stymied that one by letting him in on the food bill."

Kona filled his glass again, but Bobby had been away from alcohol so long it was having a fast effect; his speech was slowing. "That's the way out, you see. Here's a bloody Arab refusing to take me because of the cost of feed.... So I decide then to really start eating. Of course Jakoby had unlimited railway rations, but she gave up.... Can't give away food that's disappearing into yours truly, eh?" He winked knowingly at J.O., then his eyes closed further as he began to lean forward.

He ended as suddenly as he had started. His voice gave out, his eyes closed and he fell back onto the settee, which groaned and squeaked as he curled up on one end and fell fast asleep.

In Machakos, Stephen's aunt had sent him a letter urging him to come home. As he thought about it, he could find no reason to say no. Discouraged and very depressed, he felt he had been forced by circumstances to sit by and watch Dorothy's infidelity, and now, he felt, Alice was going in the same direction. Things could only go from bad to worse.

Yes, he thought, I'll have to leave, but somehow *he* should pay. He longed to get back at John Allen, whom he held personally responsible for all his problems. If revenge in that direction could be accomplished, it would make his resignation and trip home much easier to bear.

Why not simply walk up to him and shoot him? he asked himself, and daydreamed about that, as he nodded wisely and muttered out loud. Often that thought came to him just before he drained another glass; it was a scenario that contained the ultimate degree of satisfaction. Though in sober moments he realized full well that it was an impossible feat, chiefly because if he did that he would also have to shoot himself, something he knew from experience he couldn't do.

Perhaps I should just walk away from it all, was another thought, but his anger got the best of him, until he decided to use one of the few arrows in the quiver of a civil servant.

He'd do his damnedest to bring down Allen by bureaucratic harassment.

Intending to see his enemy crawl to him for mercy, he smiled as he fired off several letters in which he lodged major complaints about the Railway superintendent and how he had failed in his job. Ian did not rise immediately to the bait. He replied to Stephen that before taking action he intended to wait until the railway had moved further west toward the lake.

More recently Stephen had heard from McCann that Allen had broached a scheme that offered possibilities. Allen touted it as "the final solution" to the Railway's security problems—he intended to use Masai impi as local enforcers. It seemed that whenever Cole, the Naivasha district commissioner, ran into resistance from local villages collecting hut taxes, he would strike a deal with the army. They would use the Masai to carry out supervised raids and each impi in the field could keep one half the cattle captured. The other half of the herd was kept in bond by Cole until the hut taxes were paid by the party concerned. This arrangement worked so well that Matthew had suggested to the Railway that they could apply it in Kikuyuland and elsewhere. It was a case of fighting fire with fire, and would allow them to threaten anyone with retaliation from the Masai, at no cost. Allen and Woodham-Stayne had just opened preliminary discussions with the army when Stephen alerted Ian. He followed this up with a report and a personal visit to the Coast.

"Terror tactics," said Stephen, "plain and simple."

"Reminds me of what we tried in India," said Ian. "Pitted the Princely States against the Punjabis. Very attractive initially, quite useful, but it proved faulty in the long run."

"Why?"

"Too much hatred and resentment. Bitter feelings lasted a long time thereafter. But you needn't worry on that score," said Ian.

"Why not?"

"After I got your report, I telegraphed the foreign office for advice. They raised holy hell." He handed Stephen a draft copy of the telegram he intended to send to Cole. "Here, look at this."

> TO DISTRICT COMMISSIONER NAIVASHA WALTER COLE STOP FOREIGN OFFICE DESIRES YOU TERMINATE PRACTICE OF USING MASAI TO SUPPORT ARMY INTERVENTIONS STOP CONSIDER THIS MEDDLING IN INTERNAL AF-

FAIRS DEFINITELY NOT PROVENANCE OF HMG ARMY PLEASE REPLY IMMEDIATELY AND COPY SUPERINTENDENT OF RAILROAD IN NAIROBI ALSO COPY COMMISSIONER FOR THE PROTECTORATE IAN BURNS AT THE BRITISH HIGH COMMISSION MOMBASA STOP END

While Stephen pursued his vendetta, David McCann continued his duties as DC in a small office in Nairobi. Since David had no ax to grind, and was even less interested in administrative work, he was slow off the mark in criticizing the Railway. Luckily the DC's function in Nairobi was minimal because the Railway's business always took precedence; also much of what David needed to do in terms of paperwork and local action was done by his assistant, Veejay Shah, a man like Jimmy Harris in appearance as well as ability.

Veejay easily and efficiently carried the administrative weight of the office, and that allowed David to show good promise in his upward progress in the civil service. He was also supported in this by Ian, who considered David somewhat of a protégé. Proof of this came in the form of a personal request the week previous when Ian asked him to come to Mombasa to act for him while he went on back to London. Queen Victoria's death had made Ian's attendance necessary at a number of official events back home.

Now, thought David, that's exactly the sort of thing that would look good on my résumé.

Ian indicated in a separate message to Stephen that he in turn should cover for David in Nairobi. Stephen complied though he resented this; *he* had never been asked to come to Mombasa and act as high commissioner, even though he was an old friend of Ian's.

David, however, had already determined that there were reasons why Ian trusted him more than Stephen. For one thing, he showed absolutely no interest in Isabelle. David and she had loathed one another from the beginning. When David arrived in Mombasa to take up Ian's duties, he wisely decided to tread carefully; somehow he had to avoid antagonizing Ian's wife, but otherwise his future seemed assured.

Before leaving Nairobi he heard that when Allen received a copy of the telegram, the one about using Masai to reinforce Railway security, he swore bloody vengeance. And David made certain that Allen understood whom the target of his vengeance should be.

Shaking the telegram in the face of Bill Bagley, Allen had screamed, "Bastard! That bloody Hale again. This is war!"

10

Mombasa

There was a spring in Bobby's step as he walked out of the officers' club. After many months Capt. Curtis was a new man. His rejection by Alice and the sad treatment he had received at the hands of the Africans had left no scars; just the opposite—they had improved his outlook and made him a more determined person. He was certainly more physically fit because of the enforced walking and jogging during his captivity; now his largest concern was his need for a new uniform. Though he had grown fit, he had also grown significantly in girth.

While he was presumed dead, his transfer back to India had been rescinded. On his miraculous return, he was ordered to take command of a new unit to be called the 1st Uganda Rifles. It was to be assembled in Kenya from a contingent of Sikhs and Punjabis recently stationed at Fort Jesus and the 27th Bombay Infantry, which had arrived today from India. He had orders to supplement the whole with local enlistees, troopers from African tribes, an idea first broached by David McCann.

"Forge them, Bobby. Forge them," said Sutherland, who put a great deal of faith in Bobby, and provided a further incentive in the form of a commission from Indian Army headquarters raising him to a brevet major. Following a month of intensive training they would be off to Kampala to support the military effort there.

"Easily done," said Bobby, as he directed his carriage driver to the Kilindini harbor, where the 27th was disembarking. He arrived as the troops were lining up in the new yard built by the Railway. They were waiting for their equipment to be unloaded. Two young lieutenants were on hand to meet him as his carriage rolled to a halt.

Skinny fellas, he remarked to himself, noting that they both together wouldn't nearly make one of him.

Lieutenants Smythe and Bradshaw called out, "Company! Attention!" and saluted smartly as Major Bobby started to climb down. He had opened the carriage door and his booted foot had reached for the first step; his leg and buttocks almost took up the strain, when suddenly a ripping sound echoed across the yard, made louder by the fact that the several hundred sepoys stood quietly watching him. This was followed by a rush of air into his crotch. With an uneasy feeling, he stopped halfway into his dismount and delicately stepped back into the carriage where he stood up at attention and returned their salute.

"Damned awkward," he later confessed to his Indian tailor, who was given the job of reinforcing the seams and widening the waist. The immediate effect was that he continued his review standing upright, legs together, as the carriage proceeded at a solemn pace along the line of Indian soldiers. Bradshaw and Smythe, now mindful of the awesome bulk of their new leader, followed on foot. The regiment had never been reviewed by an officer in a carriage; consequently the troops were struck by the regal sight of a mighty warrior in full dress uniform passing slowly down the line. The Indian lieutenants, the *jemadars*, called forward the appropriate commands as the regimental band swung in line behind the entourage. And so, to the strains of the grenadiers' slow march, "Scipio," they celebrated their last day as the old 27th and their first day of duty in Africa with a grandeur they had never seen in India, where these things were done in style.

With considerably less pomp, but much more care, a railway crane was maneuvered alongside the ship to assist in unloading a howitzer on a wheeled carriage. This napoleon, a twelve pounder with a brass barrel, had a range of two thousand yards. Alongside the pier, several Maxim guns had already been lined up, a recent deadly invention that had proved itself in the Matabele War where four of them and fifty infantrymen were able to hold off five thousand Matabele armed with spears.

During that engagement the Africans had lost three thousand warriors before they quit.

Alice felt her life changing as the days wore on. Her village projects had shown her a new way of doing things. She now directed the energy she had earlier put into hunting into her work in Kathambani. In preparation for her next trip, she went to see Dr. Sharpe. She wanted advice about vaccination programs and how best to use Karegi; and, she realized, even before that could happen, she also had to obtain permission for Karegi to take time off from the hospital.

Dr. Sharpe had started a private practice at home. A friendly, slight man in his early middle age, he had a light mustache and a sallow complexion, which came about because he insisted on taking quinine every day. He didn't smoke, drank sparingly and sat many evenings indulging his passion, forensic medicine. They met in his library and Alice agreed to stay on for dinner. "At home with my wife and children, everyone calls me 'Charley,'" he said. "Now, what shall we talk about first, Alice?"

"Well, I presume Karegi told you about our problems with the vaccine."

"Yes, the famous 'vaccine.' She showed me the vial. But I'd prefer *not* to call it by that name. Any extract of animal lymph that has sat at room temperature for so long must change. I suspect by the time it reached you it had the efficacy of dirty dishwater."

"Even though it came from an American ship captain?"

"I'm afraid so. You see, once a ship starts on a long voyage, if smallpox breaks out, they have no recourse. They wouldn't have access to cows that have had cowpox, the usual source of fresh lymph, so they bring along vials of the sort you had. Often with the same disastrous results. But you've learned."

"Yes."

"And, as for using Karegi, I see no problem. She's well acquainted with the technique. By the way, I must tell you, I'm leaving the Railway," he said. "I don't get along with Allen. Actually, I can't stomach the man. I've held off sending in my letter of resignation but I must do something soon."

"How will you get on?"

"I thought of expanding my practice, but the natives have little money and the settlers fare no better, so I've applied for a post. The high commissioner's office advertised one for a public health officer in Nairobi and I seem to be the only candidate."

"That would be a perfect position for you," said Alice.

"If I'd been serving in that capacity before your sister died, possibly I could have helped more."

"How do you mean?"

"There's virtually no control here over medicines or drugs, of which some are extremely potent. In fact, before I left England I wrote a book about just that, compounds and extracts similar to what I think Dorothy used."

He held up a copy of a book called *The Essential Ingredient.*

"What was it she took?"

"Probably a compound known as Savin, a concoction sold in England as Bathmore's Female Pills. It's for what they call 'common female complaints.' Each pill contains .7 milligrams of juniper oil and they are extremely popular. The company claims to have sold six million boxes this past year, and I believe them."

"Are they really effective? It sounds like some quack remedy."

"There's no question about it, a combination of the pills and gin, which also contains essence of juniper, is strong enough to bring on abortion," he said. "It's common practice to take it within a week or two of the first missed menstrual cycle."

"How would she have gotten hold of it?"

"Easily available in the shops here. It's sold along with ordinary items for toothache, headache, and so on."

"And what's the effect on a woman?"

"The initial reaction is extreme. The person literally goes through hell. They claim there's little aftereffect, but I don't believe that for a minute. When I was a medical student, I took a dose as an experiment. I described it in my book and I can tell you, I suffered. As it turned out, I wasn't the first to note the symptoms. At the time I thought it was amazing what a woman would suffer through."

"And you're still interested in such things?"

"Absolutely. Forensic medicine means a great deal to me. It's a young science, but useful in so many ways."

"I admire you for that kind of dedication."

"There's no other way, you see." He picked up one of the books on his mantelpiece. "You can't very well try these things out on people, and it signifies nothing if you see an effect in an animal. It all rests with your own self."

He read,

> "...Holmes is a little too scientific for my tastes—it approaches cold-bloodedness. I could imagine his giving a friend a little pinch of the latest vegetable alkaloid, not out of malevolence, you understand, but simply out of a spirit of inquiry in order to have an accurate idea of the effects. To do him justice, I think he would take it himself with the same readiness. He appears to have a passion for definite and exact knowledge....

"That's from *A Study in Scarlet*, by A. Conan Doyle," he said. "It gave me the idea for my own book." He then picked up a second book, opened it to a marked page and read,

> "...There was an immediate, pronounced pain in my abdomen with heat and burning spreading to my stomach, bowels, rectum and anus. I experienced a wave of nausea, which spread through me as diarrhoea set in. It definitely has a strong cathartic effect. I came close to collapsing as I sat on the commode....

"That was *my* reaction to Savin."

"It sounds dangerous even as an experiment," said Alice.

"Yes, but the amazing thing is that most women return quickly to a normal life, which says something for the female constitution. I'm sure there must be other effects, but we may never know about them."

"And you survived."

"And so too would Dorothy, if she were in good health, which was not the case."

His wife, a bright woman about the same age as the doctor, looked in and announced that dinner was ready and they went in. Throughout the meal, Alice thought about what he had said, and the following day, as she made the rounds of the shops to buy supplies in preparation for her trip back to the village, she asked about Bathmore's. She found he was right; the pills were sold at several places. One Asian clerk told her that often gentlemen were their best customers.

"Especially Mr. Allen. He's bought so many boxes, we call him *Daktari*."

That set off a new round of suspicions in her mind, and here she thought she had laid all that to rest. Then she did something she should have done earlier: she made a thorough search through Dorothy's belongings, a task she had little stomach for. As if to prove the futility of this exercise, she soon found herself knee-deep in beautiful clothes, most hardly worn, with nothing to show for it. Nothing obvious, that is, until she started looking through books that she had pulled off the shelves. Dorothy had been more than a little interested in health, and had owned several medical encyclopedias. Between two of the largest volumes she found a small brown envelope labeled "Sleeping tablets. Caution. Take no more than two at any given time."

She went back to see Dr. Sharpe, who recalled that on his last visit he had advised Dorothy to get more sleep; she had been restless, too restless for an expectant mother.

"And you gave her something?"

"No, nothing. She was under no medication at all. I simply gave her advice on a better diet."

"Oh, so it wasn't you who prescribed sleeping tablets?"

"No. I was going to, but she said she already had something. Why do you ask?"

Alice showed him the packet, and he looked carefully at the pills inside. "But these are not sleeping pills, Alice." He handed her one. "They're Bathmore's pills, smell them. Juniper oil, as clear as day."

"And the packet?"

"I know the handwriting," he said. "That's from Thatcher's general store on Station Road. The clerk acts as a pharmacist. He's not trained in that, but he does it anyway. It's definitely his writing."

Alice went immediately there and confronted Thatcher. "The envelope and writing are mine, but the pills are not."

"They aren't?"

"No, we don't sell Bathmore's, ma'am."

She looked quizzically at him.

"We sell Francke's. They're blue-colored and much more effective," he said as he showed her a box. "Would you like me to wrap it?"

She went next to John Allen's office at the station. Bagley told her that he was still at home having luncheon. The telegraph clerk saw Bagley slowly shake his head as he watched her walking away from the station, and murmured those words so often asked of Allen, "What do they see in him?"

Crossing the verandah, she pounded on the door. It was opened by Allen's houseboy, Juma, who, like Bagley, was shocked. He had never seen Alice in this place. As he looked again he could tell immediately she was not like the other visitors. They were memsabs who were smiling and quite happy to be shown in. This one looked angry, and Allen's bachelor's quarters were definitely not the place for an angry woman. His rooms were furnished with velvet and silk wall hangings, mirrors and several small tables rather than a large dining table. He kept two cooks from the Coast, one of whom specialized in cozy champagne suppers.

Juma asked her to wait while he fetched the Bwana. With a worried look he went through to a sitting room in the rear of the house. Allen was there sprawled on a large sofa being fed slivers of cucumber dipped in a sweet yogurt sauce, his favorite light lunch.

Feeding him were Beryl and her friend, Anne Bagley, Bill Bagley's wife. Both were in a state of undress as they vied with one another to fill his lovely mouth.

"*Unataka nini*? What do you want?" Allen asked, almost choking. As it was, he could hardly swallow, even with the help of a glass of chilled *blanc de blanc*. Juma motioned to the door and explained he wanted to say something in private. Allen reluctantly left his luncheon companions, but once he was made aware of who wanted to see him, he brightened at the prospect. Through his mind flashed a cameo picture of Alice in that sort of *ménage a trois* of his liking and he wiped the yogurt from his mouth, buttoned his shirt and followed Juma with interest.

"Alice," he said, smiling as he approached her with open arms, "just in time to join us. We're in the middle of luncheon." He moved close to her and tried to buss her on the cheek, but she turned and stepped back.

"This isn't a social visit."

Allen waited. Alice seemed hesitant to begin. He found he had less patience for preliminaries since his arrival in Nairobi; a sign of age, he presumed. His father had complained of the same sort of thing, though the impatience of the marquess did not surface until his seventieth year. In John's case he put it down to the provincial nature of the place, and perhaps too much exposure to women who no longer presented any challenge. Another reason for a long vacation in England, he had decided, or even better, Europe. Any place, or anything, to bring back the excitement.

"Well? I don't have all day. What is it?"

She held up the small brown envelope and said, "You killed Dorothy."

If she thought he'd react to that, she was mistaken. Allen, a master at confrontation, especially with women, had only one reply, to shake his head and smile.

"You made her pregnant," she said. "Then you decided to leave her to her fate. But first you gave her an envelope with some 'sleeping pills,' knowing there was a good chance she'd take them sooner or later and that would do away with any complication, such as an illegitimate child. She put them away not intending to use them, and then Dr. Sharpe innocently suggested she needed sleep. By that time you had stopped seeing her. She took them anyway because she trusted you. You killed her, you killed my sister!"

Her face was white and her features were set. With no hesitation she slapped him. He took the slap standing without blinking an eye. Obviously it was something that had happened before.

"You're wrong," he said, his own eyes blazing with anger. "I was

Dorothy's only friend."

"Liar!"

"Before you go on," he said, "just think a bit. When she arrived here, no one really cared if she lived or died, except myself. Admit it," he said as he watched her face. "You yourself thought she was a fake. All those symptoms were leading to the obvious: she was too weak. She really should have just gone home. She should have left the tropics to the likes of us and the natives; isn't that what everyone thought?"

He walked to the window as he always did when he wanted to think. From there he looked out on the dusty streets of Nairobi with their incessant stream of exotic pedestrians and draft animals large and small. He turned now to face her and said, "What a bunch of hypocrites you all are."

He walked back toward her with a certain resolve. It was obvious he did not blame himself, not one bit. "I admired her for what she was," he said as he stood in front of Alice. "She was a sensitive woman who loved me and I never wavered in that. I knew that was all she had to live for. Well? So what? I gave her what she craved, friendship and physical love. You people gave her nothing.

"Anyway," he said, pointing to the handwriting on the packet, "it's not mine. You don't have a leg to stand on. But more than that, I resent the fact that you and Hale have the gall to go around harboring grudges. Compared to my friend Beryl, or even Dorothy, you're still a child."

"A child?"

"Exactly. The Angel from Maidstone," he said as he laughed. "You fell for that line like some schoolgirl."

Alice turned red with embarrassment and anger.

"Look at you. Another Florence Nightingale. You think men rise up from their litters when you touch their souls, when all they want is to have you touch their cocks. Basically, you're the same as hundreds of other shallow-minded, virtuous English women overseas. But then, you're a female, you can't help yourself. You're ruled more often by lunar cycles than by anything like a thinking mind. In that way you're like the blacks. And I've often thought that's why they like you so much, because you're as simple as they are. But, not to worry, someday you'll grow up and by then you'll understand what it is to be human."

"Then none of that was true," said Alice, barely controlling her temper. "What you told me on our way back from Simba station, you never had any feeling of love toward me?"

"Oh, I've had feelings toward you, but they're all of a very practical, physical nature. I bet Matthew ten pounds that you were still a virgin and I could prove it. Well, presumably, I'll never be able to do that now."

"And what you said about Bobby and Dorothy?"

"A load of rubbish. I made it up just to win your confidence. Self-centered, righteous women like you are always anxious to believe such things. Now you've wasted enough of my time. I'll have to ask you to get out. And if you have any idea of spreading rumors about me, remember, the libel laws apply out here as well as in England."

Alice felt helpless, embarrassed and empty as she walked out the front door. On her way home she decided to leave Nairobi for a while, to go back to the village and work with the people there. Perhaps she could still do some good, but for now, she thought, there's precious little in this town for me.

11

Kenya Highlands, Near Kijabe

Kijabe Town was the last terminus before the railway track started down the escarpment. The Railway had moved substantial amounts of equipment there, so at any point in the day, wagons, donkey engines and flatbed cars could be seen as they were shunted back and forth along the tracks. Large stockpiles of supplies came rolling in each day after the new rail camp had been set up. This marshaling of equipment along with the influx of Europeans and hundreds of Indian platelayers and Wakamba laborers caused much concern among the Kikuyu. They had been assured earlier by the Railway that their land would be little affected. Now it looked like an invasion.

"Bwana Roger advises us to take advantage of this," said Muthuri, as he sat hidden behind some bushes with Kimani and Jakoby. Kimani's ear was swollen and red where Ben had nicked him. He looked down on this activity from a hill above and listened with his good ear.

"He says the settlers want to grow cotton, sisal and coffee; these are plants that cannot be eaten and in which we have no interest," continued Muthuri. "If they are the only things they grow, we can still sell our beans, peas and millet."

"But these new crops will take land as well," said Jakoby.

"And there will come a season," said Kimani, "when we will return to our shambas and find nothing left. Then they will kill us off."

"No," said Jakoby. "They will not destroy you. They will keep you alive, because they need you to work these new plantations. And that could be a fate close to death."

"So the Snake is not devouring us as Njuguna thought it would," said Muthuri. "Instead, it is squeezing us. Each time we breathe our lungs fill with less and less air."

"And the wazungu will soon come and lay a mark on your land, then say all which falls inside the mark belongs to the Queen," said Jakoby. "They will convince your clan leaders and chiefs to sign more papers saying this is true. That way they avoid talking to your councils."

"She is correct," said Kimani. "The elders are not approached."

"How can we stop this?"

"With a snake it is easy, you cut off its head," said Jakoby. "With this one, where is the head? Does it lie with the Queen? If so, your arrows and spears will be useless."

"We cannot turn them unless we gather a force large enough to overpower them," said Kimani, "and we cannot do that while we are still fighting among our own clans."

"And all the time the snake is squeezing."

"What will you do?" asked Jakoby.

"We must talk to the ndundu, Ngugi," said Kimani. "He must call a meeting of the elders, the Committee of Nine."

"And you must help us," said Muthuri to Jakoby, "by gathering more rifles from the Railway stores."

The elders responded to Kimani's request. They were well aware that the villages and clans were acting independently, even though they had earlier promised to work together. The day before the meeting, Ngugi sought advice from Kimani and his rival, Kiambui. In addition, he called on a third clan leader, Njui, to provide some ideas for discussion.

"Kimani, you are never at a loss for words. Tell us what you propose."

"In my view the problem will not be easily solved. We must prepare for the long struggle. The wazungu feel their task is an easy one. I have heard them say, 'It is like taking candy from a small child.' This is an insult. And it means they are very confident. We must show them it will not be so easy. Our goal should be to see how we can sow the seeds of discontent and disarray."

Kiambui argued against the long term. "We need immediate

action...."

Ngugi interrupted. "Let Kimani finish. How would you carry this out?"

"I have already seen Kikuyus going to work on farms and ranches and I feel this is a good thing, as in the old days when we sent men with Duma, or in my case when my father sent me to observe the wazungu in the missionary schools. I wish the Council would ask the clans to support me and my men. We have already sworn allegiance to a common cause and we know our methods are effective. We would concentrate on the wazungu who have taken over isolated farms. Once they are on their own away from their own kind, they become more easily worried and frustrated. Our goal should be to demonstrate to them that taking our land or staying in our territory will not be easy. Then they will look elsewhere. We will not force them out; we will just help them to see that it is better for them to settle in other parts of Kenya."

"Now, Kiambui, your view."

"I see what Kimani is doing, and that is good. But it is not enough. We need the wazungu to stop coming here all together. We need to frighten them. We need to show them how tough we are. And we will not do that by holding back. We must strike in force."

"Njui, what can you add?"

"They will not be stopped," he said. "Look around you, they have already taken whatever land they want, and now they have machines that cannot be pushed aside. I say we should wait. When they are finished here, they will move on and that will be a problem for the Nandi, but we will be free of them."

"No," said Kiambui. "They are like the spider: one strand is first laid out, then other strands are laid down until a formidable web has been spun and the tables are turned. You wake from sleep and find yourself trapped."

"This is true," said Kimani. "I have heard them say that once they complete the main line they will send out branch lines. Some of these will go right through our villages. As Njui says, there will be no stopping them, but, as I say, we can make them regret their course of action."

"Aiee," said Ngugi who wondered how this would be resolved. While they argued, a messenger arrived with word from the old man, Njuguna.

"He has found something that may affect everything," said the messenger. "He wants the ndundu to come and see for himself."

They followed the messenger to a small stream deep in the woods. Njuguna was waiting for them with a crowd of villagers. He asked them all to sit. "Today I was approached by these villagers who are upset. The small stream near their huts has stopped flowing. I was called because is my duty as a witch doctor to solve puzzles such as this. We went back along the edge of the stream toward the source, and in the upper reaches we came upon this." He pointed to a very large, swollen python that was lying to one side. "It had expired across the small stream and had formed a natural dam. Leaves, branches and silt piled up behind it and the water spread out and is now soaking into the forest floor, diminishing the flow downstream."

Kimani had seen pythons during his forays into the forest; he could spend hours watching them feed. He often sat on a fork in a tree branch by the side of a stream where pythons lay in wait for the small antelopes that frequented a watering place. The python would slide down the bank into the water, trapping the animal in a stream with steep banks. Then it would quickly entangle the creature, tightening its coil as they floated downstream. With the air being forced from its lungs, the animal would suffocate in this deadly embrace. Then the python would loosen its own jaws by unhinging the lower section from the upper, and place its large flexible mouth over the muzzle of the animal. Gradually it would enclose the face of its prey an all-encompassing kiss that, followed by its embrace, would ensure no breath could be taken as the animal slowly disappeared into the python's maw, its horns folding back on its neck. The tail and small rear hooves would be the last trace as the python smoothly ingested an animal many times wider then itself.

"I was surprised to find a dead snake as the cause," said Njuguna, "but further still was my amazement when we discovered how this python had died." He stepped closer to the carcass. "Come here and see what happened." As they looked, they saw it had been killed by an antelope that had been eaten by the snake. On this occasion, the animal, a bush buck, larger than the usual fare, had perhaps not been completely suffocated, or perhaps had been revived by the stomach juices, and began to buck, kick and rip its way out of the belly of the snake. It had still died, and the python had gone under as well. Together they had found a common grave in the stream.

"In the history of this village, they have never seen anything like this. Njui, what do you say to this?"

"It is merely a python that has drowned," said Njui, who, though a good leader, was still young and inexperienced in these things.

"It is more than that. Kiambui, come forward and tell us what this means."

"This is completely against the nature of things," said Kiambui as he looked at the python. "It is a sign from God, and it is up to us to find out what He is telling us."

"And Kimani?"

"I agree. We must look closer to find out what message Mwene Nyaga has sent us."

They cut open the belly of the snake, carefully taking out the intestines and other organs, which they laid on the grass beside the stream. Then they looked at the contents of the python's stomach and found the remains of several smaller animals in addition to the bushbuck.

"Look at this," said Njuguna. "This snake was in the habit of taking small prey along the stream, but it also used the power of the flowing water and its own body to capture larger animals by drowning them. We know these pythons float downstream to arrive at their favorite hunting ground; later they return by land, crawling through the brush. It must have tried taking a meal here where there is less water and it did not do a good job of it."

"But the message is clear," said Kiambui to Ngugi. "You must pass this on to the Council. God tells us in this way that we must cut our way clear of the Snake while we are still alive. We must do this before we pass deeper into its belly where we will be lost."

12

Kijabe

Engine 59 was a mechanical juggernaut, a donkey engine that had quickly risen from component parts taken from old Indian Railway stock. Today it had arrived for a routine maintenance and inspection at the new railway yard in Kijabe. The first task was to test its boilers; now huge puffs of steam were coming from its stack, along with sparks, cinders and noise unlike anything Musaa had ever seen or heard.

"*Dubwana*," he yelled at it, "Monster!" as the Indian rail workers laughed. This young Mkamba had only this week appeared as a replacement worker on a bed leveling gang.

"No, no," said the foreman. "You'll get used to it. It's only a machine, a *tinga-tinga*. No problem, *hapana shauri*."

"*Labda*," muttered Musaa, "perhaps." But right now he preferred to keep his distance.

The Station at Mombasa

The assistant stationmaster in Mombasa had had an excellent lunch, brought by his houseboy in a *tiffin*, a series of brass containers that kept his food warm. It was personally packed by his wife. He had eaten every last bit of the vegetable curry dishes and rice from the small containers, carefully mopping up every crumb with *chappatis* as light as a snowflakes. He had drunk every drop of the spicy yogurt soup, the *kahdi*, which he ranked with the nectar of the gods, and finally, he had pulled a large pile of loose reports and telegrams forward on his desk to create an impromptu pillow on which his head now nestled. Wearily he looked up as he heard the telegraph key come alive.

What could induce anyone to send a message at this hour? It was just past two o'clock; the world was supposed to have come to a quiet halt. The clattering key was insistent. Adding to his concern was the fact that it was more than a line or two. It sounded as if it would never stop.

When it did, he looked up again and saw the telegraph operator busily writing down the text. Before he could lower his head, the operator came dashing by his desk with the copy:

> FROM NAIROBI STATION TO IAN BURNS COMMISSIONERS OFFICE MOMBASA STOP STATIONMASTER AT KIJABE BEFORE LINE WENT DEAD INFORMED US NATIVES IN FOREST JUST BELOW KIJABE HAVE TAKEN ONE DONKEY ENGINE AND TENDER HOSTAGE STOP ENGINE NUMBER FIFTY NINE ISOLATED BY RAILS TAKEN UP BEFORE AND AFTER TRAIN STOP ENGINE DRIVER AND CREW STILL ON TRAIN WHEN IT WAS CAPTURED STOP REMAINDER OF RAILWAY STAFF HAVE BARRICADED THEMSELVES IN STATION WAITING FOR RELIEF STOP LOCAL FORCE IN NAIROBI WILL BE NEEDED HERE IN CASE VIOLENCE SPREADS STOP REQUEST URGENT SUPPORT FROM MOMBASA TO PUT DOWN THIS NEW KIKUYU RESISTANCE STOP UNDERSTAND FIRST UGANDAN RIFLES AVAILABLE TO HELP PLEASE REPLY URGENT STOP END

Kijabe

It was early afternoon on a clear dry day and the sun was directly overhead. The sunlight glistened on the tracks, which had been laid in a cut made through an upland forest. Here the startlingly red soil interspersed with the remains of tree trunks and freshly cut brush had been hastily piled up on both sides to form an embankment for the rail line. The embankment also offered a natural wall of protection for Kimani's riflemen, who were deployed along the top, where they lay hidden on the hot surface just below the rim. Behind them, waiting in reserve in the forest, were Kiambui's men, their bodies streaked with white. Their wild-looking feather headdresses quivered with excitement as they crouched behind their large, colorful tough shields made of hide. Their long spears and short, razor-sharp swords were crying for blood.

Interspersed between them were large numbers of bowmen with freshly poisoned arrows ready to supplement the spears and rifles. Kimani had learned his lesson well, and he wished his father could have been there to see the results; he felt confident he would have approved. They were ready for battle. Further along the line toward the station, Engine 59 lay covered with a large pile of thorn bush that had been dragged into place by Ngugi's men to fence off the captured engine and its tender. Stakes had been driven and dug in to support a fence directly across the tracks and along the sides, thus enclosing the engine in what now constituted an enormous boma. Ngugi had deployed his men inside this fortress, secure in the belief that they could not fail, that no one but a fool would try to penetrate this stronghold. He ordered the train driver and the crew to light a small fire up on their cab platform and brew some tea; he was anxious to try out this new thing, the drink the farenghi were so fond of.

Not long after they had made their preparations they could hear the sound of a train approaching, the smoke and steam evident well before it rounded the bend. As it proceeded slowly into the cut, Kimani's men readied themselves on the embankment. Ngugi sipped tea from a cup as he watched the arrival of an F-Class engine, puffing and huffing. It made its way up to the point where the rails had been removed, then came to a grinding halt. He could see that this train was different. A flatcar with sandbags arranged in a protective wall on all four sides had been placed in front of the engine ahead of the cowcatcher. Behind the engine were three cars, each fortified with protective steel plates, and the engine cab likewise protected. No one was visible on the train, and as it came to a stop, an awesome silence prevailed.

Kimani's men had been told to hold their fire until clear targets were presented, yet they could see nothing. The insects began singing again in the forest behind them and the world seemed about to go on as before, except for one abrupt movement. Several sandbags were removed by unseen hands from the top of the front wall on the flatcar. As the men inside the giant boma watched in quiet fascination, a brass cannon was revealed, pointed directly at them

"Fire!" Lt. Smythe commanded from the safety of his sandbag haven. The howitzer fired one round of cannister, a scatter-load containing chain and scrap metal from the railway yard in Mombasa, along with loose gravel. It raked the left side of the thorn fence while the howitzer was quickly reloaded and turned slightly to the other side.

"Fire!"

With the second round, the boma and everything in it disappeared as if swept away by a giant hand. Suddenly Engine 59 and its tender were uncovered, unscathed, and nothing was left of Ngugi. He and many of his troops were now part of the debris scattered all over the right of way. Dead men, body parts, bits of thorn bush, and wounded, screaming and bloody warriors were trapped inside the barbed vegetation.

Later, the Railway askaris said they found bows and arrows left in place where men had been blown away. There was even a pot of tea, still warm, resting on the first step of the engine cab. The fireman and crew had wisely jumped into the woodbin in the tender the minute they heard the F-Class engine coming.

Kimani's men were astounded by the noise of the howitzer and the disappearance of the giant boma. At close range it was a terrible sound and they crouched even lower in their positions on top of the embankment. Still, they held their fire as the Punjabi and Sikh troops stayed well hidden behind steel plates.

Sandbags were now removed from the low stacks on the roofs of the first and second car, an ominous action dreaded by everyone, as they now recognized it for what it was, a sign portending death.

The openings revealed two Maxim guns. Shielded with light metal plates, they sat, well oiled and ready to go to work. They were positioned so they could fire down onto the embankment, one gun trained on the right and the other on the left side of the line. They could see every one of Kimani's men conveniently lined up in rows below them. "Like targets at a country fair," said Sgt. Pilcher, in charge of the Maxims, as he gave the command, "Fire!"

They raked both sides with a withering stream of bullets, while the howitzer was reloaded and wheeled around at right angles toward the forest.

"Fire!"

The scatter-load and gravel in the canister swept through the trees and brush with a roar and a flash, leaving behind a swath of smoking vegetation, silencing a whole section of Kiambui's spearmen. It was then wheeled to the left and opened on the opposite side, as the riflemen on board now started firing point blank into the forest. They could hardly see anything to shoot at, but the cries and screams told them that they were having some effect.

"Fire!" commanded Smythe as the howitzer continued to blast away at the vegetation.

Inside the forest the Kikuyu had been decimated. They had never seen or heard anything like a Maxim or cannon before. The few survivors tried to return fire, but the sandbags and steel plates provided a formidable protection for the trained riflemen. Within a short time there was little or no resistance.

"Cease fire," commanded Smythe.

The silence that followed was punctuated by the screams of the dying and wounded as they lay in the open sun on the hot embankment, and in the woods and thorn bush.

"They're running from the woods, Sahib," yelled the corporal of the gun crew from his post on the roof of the first car.

"Pass the word to Woodham-Stayne," said Sgt. Pilcher.

"Good job, men," said Major Bobby, who now stepped from behind a fortified section in the first car and walked carefully forward to look out a window.

"Only one request," he said as he turned back to Lt. Bradshaw, "I want that Kimani chap taken alive."

"May not be possible, sir, once old Woodie is finished with them."

Bradshaw jumped down from the car and went back to join Woodham-Stayne, while Smythe and the rest of the men went forward to relieve the station and to clear out any resistance in the area around Kijabe town. The railway staff yelled and cheered as they saw the remaining Kikuyus running toward the forest.

"Major says to send out the pursuit," said Bradshaw to Woodham-Stayne, who signaled to a man dressed in a railway officer's uniform, a man they referred to as the coordinator, to reach up and open the latch on the door of the third compartment. Suddenly a force of fifty Masai warriors poured screaming onto the track in pursuit of the Kikuyu. They paused only to spear the wounded lying on the ground.

"Can't afford to take any wounded anyway, can we?" Woodham-Stayne observed to Bradshaw.

The hot air became quieter as the screams and cries were silenced. Gradually they were replaced by the buzzing of the flies and flapping of vulture wings as the scavengers began gathering. The Masai were spurred on by their coordinator, who yelled out encouragement as they went deep into the forest in pursuit. He had instructed the Punjabi sergeant to burn anything they found in the way of huts and villages and, hopefully, to round up livestock or take women in payment for their services. This was the first time out for the Railway's new "native patrol," which Allen intended to use to restore order and security on the rail line.

"And they're self sufficient, you see, John," Woodham-Stayne explained to Allen. "We've commissioned each one as a special African trooper following David's advice. So they're no longer just tribal yobos. They're all properly enlisted."

"How are they any different from before?"

"Each one has an armband identifying them as RSF, Railway Security Force. And we've placed them under the new civilian coordinator, Franz Shimmer. So it's all proper and above board."

Kimani lay there among the dead, his eyes opened wide with fright and anger. There was blood all over one arm, which was now covered with flies taking their fill before it congealed. He commanded every nerve in his body to control the twitching, and remained immobile as a Masai warrior stepped over him, plunging his spear into anything that moved. It required all his strength to remain dead still.

He waited until the cars had disgorged the last of the troops and the Masai had moved on, then he crept over his dead comrades and slid down the embankment until he was close to the door of the first compartment. He cautiously mounted the stairs, pulling out his simi as he went. He saw Major Bobby, alone and sitting at a table sipping a brandy and soda while he filled in a telegraph form describing his victory. Kimani sprang at him so quickly Bobby was unable to respond. The scream that formed in his throat froze in place as he was slashed so deeply along the right side of his soft neck that his head lolled to one side, almost completely severed from his spine.

Kimani wiped his simi on Bobby's uniform jacket, then turned and walked calmly out of the compartment back into the woods.

13

Stephen was in the DC's office in Nairobi when news came in of the armed force going up to Kijabe. He had been asked by Ian to sit in for David while he was in Mombasa. Veejay suggested that he may want to go up there to find out what was happening, but Stephen ignored him until he realized that what was about to happen in Kijabe might fuel his case against Allen. Certain that Allen would discourage him from getting involved, Stephen waited until Veejay found out that Allen had already left on his special train, then he walked over to the Station.

"Afternoon, Bagley."

"Ah, yes, Hale." He didn't offer to shake hands. "What are you doing in Nairobi?"

"I'm acting for McCann. When's the next train to Kijabe?"

"Hadn't planned on sending any. At least not until we get the all-clear from the army."

"Well, I've decided to go up and get a look firsthand."

"Sorry. I'm afraid that's not possible."

"Then you'll damn well make it possible," said Stephen as he unholstered his Webley. "Otherwise I'm going to take you in custody for obstructing justice. I've heard civilians are involved in this action and if what you do goes outside the right of way it's no longer in your hands, it's outside your jurisdiction."

"Civilians," said Bagley with a sneer. "Bloody savages, more likely."

"I'm serious, Bagley. It's within my mandate to arrest you."

"There's a spare donkey engine moving equipment in the yard," said Bagley, resigned to the situation. "I'll have that shunted onto the main line, but I warn you, as soon as you leave the yard, I'm sending a message to Kijabe station to inform the army of your action."

Roger came galloping down the main road into Kijabe town as soon as he heard the cannon. He happened to be in his upcountry trading station and headed immediately toward the fighting, riding out along the tracks until he came upon Bradshaw, who was startled to see a white civilian ride up and dismount.

Normally he would have told him to stay back, the fighting might still be going on, but he noticed Roger seemed very upset, almost gasping for breath, and wondered if he had been hit during the action.

"Are you all right, sir?" Bradshaw asked.

"Jesus, man," said Roger, finally catching his breath. He was shocked to see bodies scattered all over. "What…?"

Suddenly a scream rang out from the surrounding woods.

"What's going on?" asked Roger.

"One of the Kikuyu stragglers," said Bradshaw, "probably speared by Woodies' men."

"Woodies' men?"

"Special force he's brought up from Naivasha. Had them ready to pursue, rather like a pack of hunting dogs, what?"

"In other words, he's using Masai, isn't he?"

Bradshaw shrugged. "They're very effective."

"Jesus in heaven, are you people insane!" He ran down the tracks to where Woodham-Stayne and Franz Shimmer stood on the embankment watching the action through field glasses.

They looked like spectators at Ascot, tracking their favorite hunters.

"Oh, a civilian," said Matthew, in a chatty informal manner, as he heard Roger arrive, gasping, behind them. "Ah, yes. Don't I know you? Newcome, isn't it? What brings you here, sir?"

"You son of a bitch!"

"Something wrong?"

Roger turned his attention to Shimmer; he was shocked to see him standing there. "You again. You love this sort of thing don't you? Mass murder."

Shimmer looked at him and shrugged his shoulders.

"You realize of course," said Matthew, "that they slaughtered a British army man in cold blood?"

"Who?"

"Major Curtis."

"Good riddance, I'd say," said Roger.

That was enough to cause Woodham-Stayne to stare coldly at Roger and say to Shimmer, "Franz, watch him, I'm going to get Bradshaw."

He turned and walked away as another scream rang out.

Franz, turning to see what had caused the scream, ignored Roger, who pulled out his revolver and fired a warning shot at Franz. It grazed his neck and made him turn, seething as he stared at Roger.

Roger kept his weapon leveled at him. "Call them back!"

"Sorry, I have no control over them," said Franz. "It's not in my hands, and I'd advise you to put down that weapon." He held a handkerchief to his neck. "We're here officially with the Railway police."

At that moment Stephen walked up. The train driver had dropped him before reaching the station; thus he avoided any confrontation with Allen. "Mr. Newcome's correct," he said, "what you're doing is illegal. Stop it now, Franz."

"Stephen, don't interfere. This is none of your concern. It's strictly Railway."

"Wrong. It is my concern. The foreign office made it quite clear a short while ago, you can't use one tribe against another."

"But they are *not* tribal people," said Franz. "They're special troopers assigned specifically to this kind of duty."

"Rubbish," said Stephen. "Call them back."

"Fire five rounds in quick succession," said Shimmer to Roger. "That's the recall."

Roger fired five rounds in the air. A Punjabi sergeant, who was below them at the forest edge, yelled out to the Masai. Shimmer waited until they had turned back, then he turned to Roger and calmly drew his own revolver, which he pointed at him.

He had counted the shots.

"And so, Newcome, you may now hand over that empty pistol. And, likewise, Stephen, your Webley, please."

Franz took Roger's pistol and threw it into the bushes, but Stephen hesitated. His first thought was that he badly wanted a brandy. He wasn't a brave person, and he was about to comply, the pistol in his hand ready to hand over, when Shimmer yelled down to the Punjabi sergeant, "Cancel that order, Sergeant. Send them back in and tell them I want a thorough job done this time. No prisoners, mind. None. Spear every bloody one of them."

At that, Stephen raised his pistol as a club and lunged at Shimmer. Franz fired, hitting Stephen in the head. He fell and his topi rolled to one side. His forehead was bloody.

Roger turned toward Shimmer in time to see the muzzle of Franz's pistol pointed at him.

"Stay where you are, Newcome. Put your hands up and turn around or you're a dead man."

When Roger stepped back and turned, Shimmer brought his pistol down hard on his head and smiled as he saw Roger fall to one side unconscious.

Lt. Bradshaw came up and saluted smartly.

"Woodham-Stayne said you might need help, sir."

He looked at Stephen and Roger lying there.

"Get some men to carry Mr. Hale back to the train," said Franz. "He needs immediate medical attention."

"And the other?"

"Place him under arrest."

"On what charge?"

"Attempted murder."

A Punjabi sergeant accompanying the Masai patrol was surprised to find that the first woman captured in the nearby village spoke English, and she appeared well educated. He handed her over to his assistant, a corporal who escorted her back to the armored train.

"Now, whatever you do, Shimmer," said Matthew, "don't draw any attention to the rear compartment in the third car."

"Why not?"

"Because we're holding Jakoby in there."

"You mean the head of that band of outlaws?" asked a surprised Shimmer.

"One of our patrols brought her in. Thought it best to keep it under wraps."

"There'll be hell to pay when the Wakamba find out."

"*If* they find out. Which is why I want you to keep it mum." He looked closely at Franz. He couldn't understand why Shimmer would show such concern; after all, she was only another native, and not even a Kenyan one at that.

The ominous and deadly sandbags had been removed and replaced with wooden chairs, which the engineers had lashed down on both sides of the howitzer. The flatcar had been decorated with several flags, including the regimental colors, and they had posted an Indian bugler in the cab. Behind the chairs sat a large tin bathtub covered by a white sheet already beginning to turn brown with a film of dust. The contours of the cloth revealed the last and final remains of Major (Brev.) Robert Curtis, hero of the Battle of Kijabe, who had to be curled into the fetal position in order to fit into the tub. The tub had been topped up with as much gin as could be found in the railway mess in Kijabe, supplemented with the Major's personal liquor supply, a generous hoard which accompanied him on most of his travels. The intention, as explained by Bradshaw, was to ship him back to Mombasa, where he would be handed over to the undertaker, who would complete the embalming process prior to a proper military funeral.

"Very much like Admiral Nelson's return voyage from Trafalgar," said Allen, who sat up front with the victorious entourage. "Rode home in a cask of arrack, I believe."

"At least," said Lt. Smythe, who had surreptitiously been dipping a cup into the tub, which sat directly behind his chair, "he's resting in the sort of body fluid he most appreciated."

"Hear, hear," chorused Bradshaw, who earlier broached the idea of having Bobby put on display when they finally arrived at the army club.

"A formal viewing of the hero," said Smythe, "and he could serve also as a sort of large punch bowl."

"Can't do that, fellows," said Matthew, as he turned and stared at these two. "If old Sutherland heard about that, he'd have both of you fed to his pit bull for breakfast."

Inside the first coach, Stephen lay on a blanket on a wooden bench. Barely conscious, he tried to focus on where he was; the pain in his head was terrific. A Sikh medical corpsman sat by his side. He had bandaged Stephen's head and the bleeding had stopped.

"Please, some brandy," muttered Stephen.

A teetotaler himself, the corpsman hesitated before he retrieved a small bottle from his kit and offered it to Stephen. To Kandar Singh that was a sign of defeat, a sign that the situation was hopeless, but Stephen drank the brandy as if it were water. A fiery concoction sold in every shop in Nairobi, it had an aftertaste of roses that made him think of Susan, as he murmured, "Her favorite flower." He had often pleased her by sprinkling his bed sheets in Hull with rosewater. Now as Kandar Singh held a cool wet cloth to his face, Stephen cried out, "Susan. I knew you'd be here." He cried out again as he gazed out the window, "Oh, don't mind the dust. I'll get Syani to clean everything. You'll see. You'll like it here. Maybe not at first, but it does grow on one...." Then he passed out.

"My God, Bagley, you missed the event of the year."

Allen sat with him and Matthew in the railway club. "Hunted down several myself. Still had blood on my shirt when we came back. Going to have it hung in the office as a trophy."

"And Newcome?" asked Bagley, as they were joined by Ben,

Jock and several other settlers. Brian, their most reliable source of free drinks, as usual was nowhere in sight.

"We missed Newcome when he first arrived," said Allen. "Luckily Franz caught up with him. Had his hands full, he said. Seems there was a great deal of bad feeling between Hale and Newcome; why, we'll probably never know."

"I can help you there," said Matthew. "Shimmer told me about a report Hale sent to Mombasa last year in which he said Newcome tried to kill him when they were on safari."

"Something to do with his mother," said Ben Fletcher, who had recovered from his earlier encounter with Kimani. "He's hated him for years."

"Fortuitous, don't you think?" asked Allen, winking at Bagley.

"Absolutely," said Bagley. "Sgt. Ross says there's enough food in Newcome's storehouse in Naivasha to keep us going for months."

"Make a damn good warning to the rest," said Matthew. "Sorely needed, been treating them with kid gloves so far."

"Not to us it won't," said Ben.

"What do you mean?" asked Matthew.

"How do you think we feel about what he's done?"

"We?"

"Us," said Jock, indicating the others. "Settlers."

"You railway blokes never ask," said Ben. "But with us, we think he's a bit of a hero. After all, he's done something we've all wanted to do for months."

"Oh? What's that?"

"Shoot a DC."

One week later as Allen addressed his staff, he made a point of thanking God for the extended drought. "A gift from heaven," he called it, and his colleagues were not slow in taking advantage of the situation. A whole new series of works had been launched to conquer the escarpment. Already a temporary line had been built down the incline, and in the steepest places a cable tramway had been set up to transport equipment and goods to the valley floor.

In anticipation, an advance party had also transported a small steamer to Lake Victoria. They were as pleased as anyone could be with their good fortune. Railhead was approaching Naivasha and they had already built a station there in preparation for the arrival of the rail line.

That night in the club, Bagley said, "Bradshaw's been waiting for you."

"Bradshaw?" asked Allen. "What's he doing here?"

"Over there," said Bagley, nodding at the lieutenant, who was standing near the front door.

"Could I have a word, sir," said Bradshaw and indicated that they should step outside.

As soon as they walked out onto the club verandah, in the light from the windows he saw a squad of sepoys standing at attention.

"Well?" asked Allen.

"I've been asked by the Supervisor of Railway Police in Mombasa to give you this, sir. I'm sorry," he said as he handed Allen a summons.

Inside the railway storehouse it was pitch dark. There were no windows. The walls were made of heavy, close-fitting planks. Roger strained to see through a crack in the door. The guard who came in with food handed him an empty slop bucket and then left without speaking. When he had woken the first day after what seemed like a long while, he had banged on the door to attract attention. The guard responded quickly by threatening him with the butt of his rifle.

He knew he was back in Nairobi from the street noises, and he knew it was night because he could feel the heat from the tin roof cooling down. There was no furniture; he sat on a sack of cornmeal in the dark. A bucket in the far corner acted as a chamber pot; on another sack there was a bottle of tepid water, a tin plate and the remains of his supper. They had left him a stub of a candle along with a few matches but, not knowing how long he would be there, he refrained from lighting it.

He sat staring at the door trying to picture the world outside. His head still ached where Shimmer had hit him. Suddenly he heard voices outside and a key turn in the lock. Not wanting to provoke the guard, he backed away as the door swung open and someone was pushed into the room. Then the door was quickly closed and locked.

"Who's there?" he asked.

No reply, just breathing.

He hesitated to reach out. He suspected his fellow prisoner was a man, but he had no idea of how that person would react. He waited and listened.

Then he smelt something familiar.

"*Who* are you?" he asked as he moved cautiously toward the other man. The scent was distinctive. It made him think of someone he had met before, someone in Nairobi. He reached out his hand and felt the other person pull away from his touch.

"Leave off, Newcome. Or I'll call the guard!"

He lit the candle stub and held it up to see more clearly.

It was John Allen.

Book Four

The Snake Squeezes

1

This is the bloody end," George Whitehouse announced to the seven jacanas. Sure-footed, long-toed birds, they ran quickly across the lily pads floating in the shallow water of Lake Naivasha in front of his tent. One of the seven stopped when he said that and cocked its head as it listened. Perhaps, George thought, that was a sign that they were getting used to him.

He continued to watch that one bird, which had definitely turned its back on its breakfast, the host of insects, snails and worms that lived on the underside of the lily leaves.

Was it ruminating on how peaceful this past week has been? he wondered.

Railhead had moved to within thirty-five miles of the lake, close enough that he could slip away to this campsite and enjoy a well-deserved vacation, until recalled to railroad business as he was today. The runner, a tall, quick Swahili man, had just arrived with a stack of urgent telegrams and now stood with one thin brown foot resting on the calf of his other leg as he waited for instructions.

Whitehouse could not help but compare him to some of the jacanas.

"The end, the bloody end," he repeated after reading the top three telegrams on the pile.

It was then he realized he had a revolution on his hands.

A large, walrus-mustached man, Whitehouse was chief engineer, and as such had faced every conceivable problem, every difficulty that could ever have happened in building a railroad in the tropics, save one, the one he thought the most unlikely. A strike by his junior staff, who were, after all, British.

I should have listened to Bagley, he thought, as he read a fourth and fifth telegram about the worsening disaster.

His office staff in Mombasa without his permission had ordered all expenses cut to the bone, including the salaries of the junior supervisory staff. "Orders direct from London," they claimed in telegram six. That action had tipped the scale. He had been warned earlier by Bagley that the junior staff was an unstable element, a seedy gang recruited from every hellhole in the Empire. Often stranded in exotic port cities where they had nothing to live on but their British passports and the goodwill of expatriate residents, they jumped at the advertisement offering free transport, accommodation and ready money.

"I mean, chaps, can the work be anything but light? Christ, it says 'ere in black and white, 'Soopervisor.' Ah, Jimmy, that's just me line, ain't it."

In order to assemble a workforce quickly, Whitehouse had let himself be persuaded that the job requirements and standards could be lowered, which was a mistake, he said to himself, because, according to telegrams seven and eight, they were on a drunken rampage, breaking up rolling stock and looting the railway stores in Kilindini.

He sent the runner to fetch his horse while he finished breakfast, dressed and said good-bye to the jacanas. A donkey engine was waiting at railhead to get him to the foot of the escarpment.

On arrival he looked up that enormous hill; somewhere, one thousand five hundred feet in the misty distance, stood a four-stage cable tramway, his only link with the rail line in Kijabe. To traverse the first stage, a rail car, in which he was the only passenger, was pulled up the incline by using a fully loaded car as a counterweight. A cable, wrapped around a drum and controlled by a brakeman, drew him smoothly up into the morning air, as he saw the full car pass him midway on his journey. Costly and slow, this method served the purpose. The next stage was technically more difficult, because the incline increased sharply. Over the next seven hundred feet a two-phased cable tramway had to be employed, in which his car rolled onto a special platform built to fit the incline, a gradient of over forty-five degrees, and then the platform itself was pulled up the hill by a cable on a winding engine.

He had to be transferred again to the next section and pulled by a second winding engine until he reached the last stage, where his car was hoisted the remaining four hundred feet by another counterweighted full car. At the top platform he finally boarded the train that was waiting to take him on to Nairobi, which Bagley thought would be the next target of the strikers, many of whom were arriving daily from Mombasa.

As Whitehouse sat impatiently watching this complicated operation unfold on the incline, he had plenty of time to read through a further sheaf of messages. The most interesting one was a note from Bagley informing him that the principle cause of his concern was someone named Harry DeSuza.

Nominally a British subject with an English father and Goan mother, he had been transferred from his post as stationmaster in Athi River after Jakoby's Raiders had cleaned out the storerooms. Arriving in disgrace in Mombasa to take up a lesser position, he had renounced the Catholic religion, abandoned his family and turned to drink. One of his colleagues told Bagley that DeSuza's change for the worse could be traced to a refused membership in one of the Mombasa clubs.

On that same morning that the Swahili runner had seen Bwana Whitehouse talking to the jacanas, Harry DeSuza sat with Albert and Elise in a hotel room in the Arab section of Mombasa, a room that had an aura of success and whiskey fumes about it. In the alley below, a drunken mob had gathered. Waving a large Union Jack they screamed, "Strike! Strike now!" They had been made bolder by the arrival in their ranks of a significant number of disaffected Indians.

Considering the fact that almost twenty thousand Indians were employed by the Railway, their joining the strike gave the Shimmers cause for rejoicing. They now felt they were on the verge of an important development.

"Come along boys! Come along," yelled DeSuza, who had thrown open the window and was leaning out, his bloodshot eyes blazing with revenge. He had held back that night in Athi River, and it had got him nowhere.

Now he was rewarded for his effort as several of the men saw him and cheered loudly.

Shimmer reached into a suitcase and handed him several bottles of whiskey, which he threw down to the crowd. "At sixpence a quart it can't be denied," said Albert. "This is the cheapest and most effective weapon ever invented."

Elise glanced out at the crowd and commented, "My God, they call them junior staff. Look at them. Every one looks like a criminal."

"Our goal is to have every man as drunk as a lord," said Albert, as elated as DeSuza by this turn of events.

"Look sharp, boys," yelled DeSuza from his perch on the second floor. He could see the town guard marching toward the crowd. "Here come the askaris. Run for it."

The crowd streamed away as the askaris charged and Albert pulled DeSuza back into the room and closed the shutters. "What happens now?" asked Elise.

"Sad to say, some of their best leaders are in Fort Jesus," said Albert. "Thank God, we saved DeSuza."

"Why?" asked the Anglo-Indian. Like his fellow strikers he was still reeling from the excitement and the free drink.

"You're going down the line to Nairobi, to join the others."

"The others?"

"You have work to do, don't you remember? Two carloads of your friends have already arrived in Nairobi."

"And Jakoby is waiting," said Elise. "She has a team ready to tear up track beyond Nairobi."

"And we'll derail some of their bloody cars," said DeSuza, though he still found it hard to forgive that "demon Zulu woman." He had been shocked when Albert brought her to the hotel and explained that they had taken her from a locked compartment of a special train. DeSuza thought they should have just left her there.

"Just remind her, I'm in charge," said DeSuza, defensively.

"Whatever you want," said Elise, stroking his shoulder as he sat on the bed. "You're in charge."

"It says so in the contract," said Albert. "And remember, ten thousand rupees if you finish the job in Nairobi. Then you're free to go home and retire."

"That's not much money," said DeSuza. "I'll need more than that."

"Of course you will." They escorted him down the stairs. It was time for him to catch his train. Albert motioned to a waiting rickshaw driver to help them up as he tried to keep DeSuza focused on the next phase.

"All you have to do is pass out the rifles when you get there," said Elise. "Then we'll provide more money, and a free ticket to Bombay."

"Rifles…," said DeSuza, trying to recall the details. The three of them scrunched up in the rickshaw as it rattled on toward the station.

"Jakoby will give them to you. Don't worry, she'll contact you. And don't forget, you must encourage them to take the initiative."

"Remember," said Elise, "make the Railway pay."

"The Railway has insulted you for the last time," said Albert.

"Make them pay," yelled DeSuza as the train started out of the station and he waved good-bye to his dearest friends this side of the Indian Ocean.

David McCann was flustered. It was an awkward time for the high commissioner to be traveling. Commander Kirkpatrick had sent his personal rickshaw to fetch David from the residency in the middle of the night. The driver had pounded on the door, waking Isabelle's servant, Michael, who had shaken David awake and passed him a note saying to come at once to a meeting. With Ian away the army needed his advice on an urgent matter. David was driven through the pre-dawn dimly lit streets of Mombasa to army headquarters, where "Big Billy" Kirkpatrick, a tall, beefy man nursing a mug of brandy-spiked tea, was waiting. He was known to the Africans as "*Kifaru*," "the rhino," because of the way he lowered his big head and squinted at you with his beady eyes when he got angry.

"What's wrong?" asked David.

"David, this is Mr. Charles Ryall, Supervisor of the Railway Police," said Billy, indicating a man in uniform who sat there in the early morning light. "He's on his way to Nairobi to put a stop to this nonsense."

"What nonsense?" asked David, still half asleep.

"The riots, man, the damned strike," said Billy, impatiently. "Yesterday we received word that they've collared one of the leaders in Nairobi. That's why Ryall's going up there, to make any other arrests necessary and help quiet things down. Whitehouse is coming back here shortly."

"Well," said David, "I approve of that. Anything else?"

"Yes, Ryall tells me that John Allen has been arrested."

"What!" David exclaimed, suddenly wide awake.

"Dr. Sharpe had me swear out a warrant for manslaughter," said Ryall. "I sent it earlier by messenger to Bagley. We've just heard back that he's acted on it. I thought you should know."

"Manslaughter?" asked David. "Of whom?"

"A woman, Mrs. Dorothy Hale, wife of the DC in Machakos."

"One other thing," said Billy. "Whitehouse said he wants you to set up a special magistrate's court in Nairobi to try DeSuza there, rather than bringing him back here. Presumably you could also hear the case against Allen, and possibly that fellow Newcome."

"I'm surprised the Railway isn't organizing its own trial for the strikers," said David.

"We have jurisdiction," said Ryall, "but Whitehouse wants the civil and army people with us on this, especially in Nairobi. He feels a lesson is in order, however, we already have enough on our plate."

"Any news on Hale?" asked Billy.

"Nothing. He's still unconscious," said David.

"If he dies, then Newcome should swing for it."

"Once you've held the hearing and charged DeSuza," said Ryall, "the Railway will carry out any sentence you impose."

"Team effort, backed by force," said Billy. "Only thing the nigger understands."

David thought first of rejecting the idea of setting up a court, but suddenly a frisson of power shot through his loins. The word itself, "magistrate," connoted the kind of authority that made people bow and scrape.

The power of a magistrate—he shook his head at the way the situation had developed. The notion that they had called him in to make certain things were done correctly was uppermost in his mind. And he would do what was required, he said to himself, as he now carefully examined the seat of the chair that had been offered to him. He was still standing, and he had hardly had time to catch his breath. His twenty-five-year-old body seemed not up to what was being demanded of it, but his sense of duty, and the knowledge of what was right, had driven him on. The Railway made it impressively easy for him, but right now they had little idea of what was going through David's head; if they did, they would have been shocked.

His mind still lingered on what had happened earlier in the evening; he had had a vision, by coincidence, one involving a court judgment, in which he had been told by Christ to try a young woman whom he had understood to be Mary Magdalene. But when they brought her into the courtroom and stripped her in front of him, he was surprised to find that it was Alice, naked, save for the black lace shawl he had given her for Christmas. So it was slightly confusing to him to find himself in Kirkpatrick's office.

Was he being asked to try a case for the government of Kenya? Or was it a case of God's will and the people of Jerusalem against a proven whore? After all, he reasoned, Alice had made love to him in his dreams on numerous occasions. "Wanton bitch" was the term that often came to the tip of his tongue whenever he saw her on the street in Nairobi, which was translated on those occasions as, "Good afternoon, Alice. You're looking radiant, as usual."

Part of his present confusion came from the fact that he had spent more and more time each day steeping his mind in his concordance, a large tome edited and revised by his father. That helped David draw biblical parallels between his contemporary life and that of St. Paul, after whom he now fashioned himself.

So there was no reason, he told his beating heart, why his forehead should be as worried as it was when he had earlier walked into army headquarters. Still wrinkled, it had become damp with perspiration as he thought of this new situation.

Magistrate's court.

"Mr. McCann, are you all right?" asked Ryall, previously an officer with the Punjab police in India. He had seen this kind of reaction before in civilians, but, he reminded himself, only guilty people acted like that.

"Care for some of my tea?" asked Billy, in a rare display of concern. He offered David his large, brown-stained mug, inviting him to sip from the side he never drank from because it was cracked. It wasn't often he shared, but in this case he had decided to make an exception.

"No thanks," said David and with a look of disgust waved it aside. "It's simply the enormity of the situation. Magistrate's court."

Those last two words had brought to his mind the whole rationale for his being. His father, the bishop, would probably have said that this would be the making of him, the high point in his career. Tribunals were, in his father's thinking, the ultimate outlet for one's views as a Christian leader, and his mother would have advised him on his appearance, as she had often done in his father's case. Which reminded him, what should he wear for a magistrate's court? He'd have to telegraph Veejay to look into that immediately.

District commissioners normally dealt with official occasions in a uniform not unlike that of an army officer, except for a large sun helmet with the solid silver DC's badge on the front. When sitting at impromptu courts, or barazas, he'd place his topi on the table where that silver badge acted as a sign that court was in session.

But magistrate's court, he thought. Now that's a different story entirely. It would certainly demand a judge's black gown at a minimum. After all, he reasoned, he'd be acting in that capacity. Then his face brightened as he remembered his old gown from Oxford days, different from the judicial cut, quite short, but it might do. It sat folded in one of his many trunks. He had taken the precaution of bringing a full set of winter clothing with him, all kept safe with camphor, ready for his next home leave on the off chance it should occur in December. He reminded himself that he should tell Veejay to go to his house and air out his gown.

"Now," he asked, "what about this strike leader?"

"He's called DeSuza," said Ryall, "Harry DeSuza. Whitehouse says he wants to use him as an example."

"Filthy little beggars, Hindus," said Billy. "Can't trust 'em, especially if they're guarding your back or flanks."

It was at that moment David wondered if it would be appropriate to bring along a black cap, in case he had to condemn someone to death.

"By the way," said Bagley in Nairobi. "Mr. Ryall telegraphed yesterday."

"What now?" asked Whitehouse.

"He said he delivered your message to McCann about a magistrate's court. He also said he'd be delayed by some of the natives in Kima—they asked him to kill a man-eater before he comes on to Nairobi."

"Good for him," said Whitehouse. "Tell him in a reply that I heartily approve."

"But, sir, this morning we received word he himself has been taken by the lion."

"My God, will it ever stop! What do we do now?"

"Col. Patterson has already gone home," said Bagley. "Perhaps we should send for J.O., or that woman, Alice McConnell. Either of them could deal with it."

In Muthuri's Hut

I had thought great things would follow on the day we kidnapped the train.

My hopes were pinned on Jakoby. She said the Shimmers had a good plan and she had faith in the Germans, although I thought they would be just as bad as the British.

We were happy because we thought the wazungu would have no idea of how to respond, and that success was ours, but I changed my mind when I heard the first cannon.

It was then also that Jakoby got frightened.

She was afraid of young Shimmer because his parents had been killed by Zulus, and someday, she thought, he would want revenge. She did not want to be around when that happened.

Where will you go? I asked her.

She said since she had a large cache of gold rupees hidden in Nairobi she had many options, but then the fighting started and we got separated.

Now she is gone, and everyone says Bwana Roger has been locked up in Nairobi.

Yesterday I at least had some good news: I heard Kimani is alive and is coming to see me, but, unless help comes from God, I don't see how things will ever change. And, though I hate to admit it, I think the Snake has won.

2

Alice had gotten her own hut in Kathambani that she used as a health station and storeroom. Away from Nairobi for almost a month, she was enjoying her stay. Day in and day out she followed the same routine, handing out medicines and carrying out simple procedures as established by Karegi on her last visit. That routine had a healing effect on her as well as the patients, who unfailingly lined up in the morning after breakfast to be treated by "*Dada dogo*," "little sister." The day she left Nairobi her brain had been in turmoil. She had never known such mental anguish, and she understood then why Roger slept in the hut of a storyteller, who regaled him with native philosophy and wisdom, and why Brian sought refuge in Kona's place.

After a few days, Syonduku arrived and stayed with her. Kiamba could not leave Machakos, as he was needed by Jimmy Harris during Stephen's absence, so Syonduku helped her carry forward a simple program of education and training, for which they gave out small quantities of food in exchange for progress. Syonduku had noticed immediately that Alice had changed, more serious about life and work, and more cautious. She was hesitant to try new things. At night she sighed and mumbled in her sleep. She was no longer the easygoing young mzungu woman.

"How have you been, *Mama mdogo*?" She called Syonduku "Auntie."

"Good. I have been to the plains area where everyone is still suffering."

"You went there by choice?" Alice knew of Syonduku's preference for the highland areas of the Kikuyus, still the best place to buy food and traditional medicines.

"No. I had to stay away from the Kikuyus. There has been a large battle there and they are very angry. Everyone says they are fighting the Snake. And you? You look thinner and older than when I saw you last. Have you been ill?"

"No. It is the men."

"Ah, that explains it."

"Sometimes when I listen to them, it is worse than being sick."

"At times like that," said Syonduku, "it is best not to listen. You smile and nod but let it pass through unheard."

"Is that why you always look so healthy?"

Syonduku laughed. "That is part of it. The other thing is my family, my children. They lift my spirit up when I go home."

"And me? What can I do? I have no family."

"You must take this place and the people here as your family. They already like you and trust you. Kathuke himself has said that Dada Dogo is now one of them."

"Maybe I could learn the language here."

"Yes," said Syonduku, seeing a bit of color come to Alice's face, "that's a good start."

Things had gone well for the people in Kathambani. They were better off than most and now they were making better use of the nearby river. Though the water level was very low, they had found ways to bring the water up from under the bed and use it for crops along the banks and on the drying mud. Kathuke had traveled in his youth to the Tana River area on the Coast and observed how that kind of irrigation was possible. Until this year, however, his village had never needed such things; now it was a lifesaver.

Like Syonduku, he expressed concern that Alice had not married. "You need to act soon, otherwise it will be too late."

"I'm waiting for the right man," said Alice.

"Oh?" asked Syonduku. "Who is that?"

"A man perhaps of my own making," she said. "And I'm afraid I have provided him with too many attributes."

Syonduku could not fathom what she had in mind, but Alice

had an idea that, at a minimum, the ideal man for her would have to have an adventuresome spirit. Like Roger, she thought, but without his temper. And an interest and faith in religion would be good, like David, but without David's strange notions and his lackadaisical attitude toward work. Of course, she thought further, her father's knowledge of the world would be important, and it would help if he had Stephen's inheritance, but didn't drink, and didn't smoke as she suddenly thought of J.O.'s pipe.

"When I was young and unmarried," said Syonduku, "I hoped for a man who was good at hunting and raising cattle. But my mother said to look instead for someone with a strong back and a courageous heart. When I did that, it was easy. I quickly met with success."

"Why? Because your village was overflowing with such men?"

"No, because, as my mother explained, if you yourself have a strong back and courageous heart such people will flock to you, and you will recognize the right one."

"I'm not sure that's all I'd want. A healthy heart and body are good, providing the mind is developed as well."

The next day Syonduku came over to see Alice after breakfast. She looked quite pleased with herself. "I've found him," she said.

"You have?" For a moment Alice thought Syonduku was going to present her with one of the young men from the cattle program.

"Here," said Syonduku as she showed Alice a book of lithographs, in particular, a Greek statue of Hercules that had been found in the Baths of Caracalla.

She glanced at the cover of the book: *The Art of Ancient Greece and Italy*.

"Where did you get this?"

"From Jakoby."

Alice turned to the flyleaf and read in Dorothy's hand, "To Jakoby, never weaken."

"Well?"

"Well, what?"

"What of this man?" asked Syonduku. "Is he or is he not what you call 'right'?"

Alice looked at Hercules. Terrifically muscled, wave after wave of lean, powerful tissue seemed to come from his abdomen as he leaned against a column, a column rivaled by his arms and legs. And he had a full, curly beard and a massive neck. The only fault she could find was that his head, covered with tight curly locks, looked proportionally small. Too small, she thought.

Syonduku waited for her opinion.

"No," said Alice, "this is not real."

"Why?"

"He was the son of Zeus," she said. "And if I remember correctly he had a troubled future. I'm afraid he would be too much for me."

"The son of Zeus?" said Syonduku. "Ah, I see. Another god. The Mission fathers seldom talked of them. Were they bad? Like demons?"

"No. They were gods, but of the Greeks and Romans, not the God of the Christians."

"But," said Syonduku, "if they are all as strong as this man, they are to be envied." She looked more closely at the picture and said, "One thing."

"What?"

"Why does he hide his private parts under a leaf? Is he ashamed of something?"

Alice was about to explain that, according to the text, the statue had once belonged to a Pope, when they were interrupted by two Somalis. They had traveled from Ol Donyo Sapuk with a message from Brian: "Alice! Must see you, urgently! Could you stop here before going back?"

3

Dressed as he was in a dinner jacket and black tie, as well as being white and British, David should have fitted in well at the club in Mombasa, but many found him strange and difficult to be near. God knows, we're used to eccentrics, they thought, but there is a limit. He ate on his own late in the evening and often carried on brief conversations with himself over a solitary brandy and soda. The club residents were used to Ian Burns, who filled the role of high commissioner perfectly. Gregarious and free-drinking, Ian's hand on your shoulder at the bar signified you had arrived, an important blessing in the closed circle that made up the world of the white Mombasa businessman. All sorts of important decisions were made informally here and it was thus important to have access to the ear of such people, but this cold fish was beyond them. He had given the waiters and club steward orders not to encourage anyone to visit his table uninvited. His concordance opened on the table while he ate also deflected casual or passing remarks.

The maddening part was that they couldn't ignore him because the third staff of life, that which lay beyond food and drink, gossip, was in short supply. They were waiting for the second shoe to drop. They already knew David was eating at the club and not at the residency because he did not get along with Isabelle—a sign of weakness, they thought. Any red-blooded male would be in her bedroom like a shot, given half the chance. Now they were certain that she would turf him out altogether, but when?

All of which was water off a duck's back to David, as he had his rickshaw driver drop him at the residency later that evening, late enough to ensure that the dining room was empty. He liked having a quiet drink on his own and he was especially restless tonight.

Tomorrow he planned to leave for Nairobi and the excitement of a magistrate's court. He had set aside that treat in his mind as if it were a special box of chocolates from his mother, or some rare and succulent tropical fruit provided by Michael, who was much taken with David. He stepped to the sideboard and helped himself to a brandy and coffee. Michael had kindly left a full pot on a warmer. Then he turned and stared out the window. Perhaps, he thought, he was standing on the same spot Stephen might have stood on when he was last here.

Poor Stephen, he mused, probably dead by now. That awful American renegade. If there were justice in this world, he decided, it would have to come from a swift and powerful retribution, an act that allowed no compromise, almost a cleansing ritual, like the killing of a lamb, or the sacrifice of a firstborn child as called for by the patriarchs. Everyone reveled in those blessings, he said to himself, and he waited for a sign from God that he was right. If so, he'd condemn Roger Newcome to death without even waiting for him to beg mercy.

Below on the water in the moonlight his eye caught a white form, a sudden flurry. Foam, perhaps? An aberrant wave? No, because it was rising from the sea. A bird, he wondered, as he watched it clearly outlined against the night, a white specter flying in a direct line, closer and closer to the open window. Finally, it swooped in a wide circle and landed on the windowsill. He stepped back. A glowing, radiant angel stood there; small in comparison to what he remembered from ecclesiastical statuary, this angel was only about one foot tall, but it so impressed him that he fell to his knees.

"Hail, David," the angel spoke clearly to him. "The grace of God be upon your head."

"To what do I owe this honor?" asked David, with tears streaming down his face in appreciation and awe. All his reading, praying, dreaming and wishing had come to this, a messenger from God.

"Chosen from among thousands, you are to be a spiritual leader. Your judgments will be respected, your pronouncements will be favored, and your name will be honored. But before all else, you will be an instrument of the Lord."

"How can I be of use?"

"You must warn everyone. Nairobi is a city lost to God. It will be destroyed. It will be leveled and all of the buildings and houses will be turned to dust and scattered to the wind."

"You say I must warn people. But when must I do this?"

"Now. Tonight. No time must be lost."

Suddenly the angel flew from its perch and disappeared into the night.

"My God," cried David as he rose from his knees. There in the darkened room, lit only by a night candle, his mind reeling, he felt he should rush out onto the street and confide in someone, anyone. Then he stopped to collect his thoughts. Whitehouse would never listen. That was the first thing to come to his mind. Who else would believe what he had just seen?

The door opened and Michael came in.

"Sorry," he said, as he made to close the door. "I thought you had finished, sir." He glanced at the coffee tray.

"No," said David. "Wait." He hesitated. "Go and get Memsab. Tell her to come quickly."

As soon as Michael closed the door, David had second thoughts. Was he acting too rashly? He reached for his glass and poured another neat brandy to steady his nerves. Isabelle was a formidable woman, but she was the only person he could think of at the moment who would trust him. It was then he regretted he really didn't have any friends other than Alice, and lately she had had little time for him. Taken up with her village work, he hadn't seen her in a while. But, no, he suddenly remembered, she's not a real friend, and I may have to sit in judgment of her yet. Not before long, he thought, she would have to be brought before him for infidelity.

Yes, he said to himself, as he poured another drink and waited for Isabelle, then another, as she seemed to be taking her time. His mind was calming considerably, though he had problems finding a chair to sit on, despite the fact that he was in a dining room that sat fifty people. He moved the decanter and his glass to the table and finally found a chair. Carefully brushing it off, he sat and poured yet another drink. He had just drained that glass when the door flew open and Isabelle appeared.

Disheveled, worried, with just a touch of hastily applied rouge, she was not pleased.

"It's you." She sounded disappointed. "I thought it was about Stephen. I heard some people talking."

"Sorry to say, he hasn't recovered," said David, who had trouble pronouncing the last word.

"Then what in heaven's name do you want?"

"It's something I've just learned," he said. "I'm very worried. It's something that bothers me a great deal." Isabelle had never seen him like this. He'd always appeared aloof when they had met previously. One cause of her animosity had been that she simply could not stand his religious carping and high-mindedness. Worse than Ian, she thought, with his politics and diplomatic nit picking. She missed Stephen, who never lifted his mind to any principles and in consequence was easily turned to her own needs, which were after all paramount.

But tonight she was attracted to David. Perhaps it came from his befuddled state, his innocence. He was handsome, and very young, and she was convinced he was a virgin. She suddenly became excited at the prospect of having him.

"I need you desperately," he said, and she felt it was almost as if he were reading her mind. She walked over to him and placed a gentle hand on his head.

"Oh, David, what a silly goose you are. And to think we've never gotten along."

"Until now," he murmured, looking up. He suddenly thought of her as Mary Magdalene. "I've known you only in my dreams." His hand went to her robe and parted the folds. Underneath he found a creamy white thigh so light and delicate, the veins stood out as soft blue tracings against her alabaster skin. He passed his hand along her thigh and his mind began racing as she responded by leaning toward him and kissing his neck.

Then brusquely, he pushed her aside, and jumped up.

"Stop!" he screamed.

"Why?" asked a now excited Isabelle.

"I'm a handmaiden of God. I'm a servant of the Lord."

Somewhat frightened, Isabelle shrunk from him. "You're drunk," she said. Drawing her robe close around her, she walked toward the door. "Either that, or unbalanced."

"But," he said, in a slurred voice, "when's Ian coming back?"

"I don't know," she said contemptuously, "and frankly, I don't care."

She slammed the door and stalked off to bed.

The sudden movement of the door blew out the only candle in the room and David sat down in the dark, rested his head on the table and went to sleep.

The Shimmers returned from the Coast to find mail waiting for them in Nairobi, including a letter from Kohl in code.

"He says Parliament is in an uproar over the railway and Dr. Peters has advised him that things may be coming to a head. Whitehouse is asking for an enormous supplement, and I don't think he has any support," said Albert as he pored over the letter. "The war in South Africa is making demands on the budget; also the new king is not as friendly with the Kaiser as his mother, Victoria."

"Maybe it's time to begin the last phase."

"I think you're right."

"And then on to Naivasha?"

"Yes, that's the best way."

In the morning, David was rudely awakened by Ian, who had returned earlier than planned.

"McCann," he said, as he waved a bulky file marked "confidential" at him. "What the hell's going on?"

David could hardly focus, let alone concentrate. He mumbled, "Must keep up."

"For God's sake, they've been passing me messages from the day I arrived in London. I had to cut my visit short to get back."

"Yes," said David, "it is serious, and I'm afraid I've not been able to keep up."

"You've been to the office?"

"Yes, every day."

"I looked in on my way up here," said Ian. "The bloody desk is piled high with all sorts of urgent business." He looked again at his protégé. "What the hell have you been doing? And what's wrong with Isabelle? She refuses to unlock her door."

David said nothing. He shook his head; he was still dressed in a dinner jacket and his head ached.

"Look at you. You stink of brandy," said Ian as he stood over him. "This is a hell of a thing to come back to. Stephen shot, Railway staff on strike, Kikuyus kidnapping bloody trains, Allen in jail and the countryside in an uproar."

"It does look bad, doesn't it, sir?"

"And did you know that someone named Jakoby has the Wakamba up in arms?" Ian asked. "And then the last straw, you sent me a memo in London asking why you haven't been given credit for a job well done!"

"An awful lot of it has to do with Nairobi," said David, trying to reconcile his visions and real life.

"Nairobi?" said Ian. "I'll say it's Nairobi, and that damned Allen, though Bagley's no better. I've told Whitehouse that I'm not going to sit by and watch them cock things up again. I'm taking over full control."

"But, sir, you don't understand."

"For God's sake, McCann, I do understand. It's serious—we're losing the colony. At this very moment, it's slipping away from us. Now, I don't want to be distracted again. By the way, where the hell is that African woman? Let's deal with her first. I want you to give her a pass or whatever it takes to make certain we're free of her. Might be best to provide an escort back to Nairobi or Machakos just to show the Wakamba we've actually released her."

"Can't do that, sir."

"You *what*?" yelled Ian, who was now really upset. "Can't do that? Why not?"

"Because she never arrived in Mombasa," said McCann. "The

train was stopped and she was taken off by some people. They threatened to shoot anyone who followed."

"Just as well," Ian said as he stood up and paced the large Turkish rug, a present from the Sultan. "Now, what about Kijabe?"

"Everything's back to normal. The tracks were cleared and the trains are running again."

"Trains!" yelled Ian. "Are you daft? I'm talking about the massacre. Have you forgotten, you're the district commissioner! What's being done about it?"

David shrugged his shoulders.

"I want you to form a commission to investigate immediately," said Ian. "We're going to Nairobi now, and the minute we arrive, I want you to take action."

He sat down as Michael came in with a large platter of breakfast.

Michael set out two plates and indicated with an ingratiating smile that David should have something to eat, but David turned his head away. The thought of food was repugnant to him, and he had not had a chance to tell Ian about the angel. But, he decided, that would have to wait, as he watched him dig into an enormous plateful of fried eggs, bacon and his favorite morning food, fried blood pudding.

"Would you believe it?" said Ian, laughing as Michael went out. "He says he saw you talking to a seagull last night."

Like a savage, thought David, as Ian shoveled another mouthful of the evil-looking sausage into his mouth and pointed to a piece of paper and a pencil.

Obedient functionary that he was, David started taking notes.

"Our main effort," said Ian, "must be to defuse the situation. For now, I want you to tell the Railway to arrange a special train and a company of sepoys. We leave in one hour. Tell them I'd prefer Whitehouse's personal coach. Then tell the army I'll need a ranking military officer with me. And for God's sake, man, go and put on a proper uniform."

The Lloyds had just returned from a long leave and were bewildered. They had heard along the way that Nairobi was falling apart and they expected chaos everywhere. But once they arrived, it all looked peaceful enough. Trains were still running, shops were open and the bars were full at midday.

The only change they could see was in the size of the town; it had grown significantly while they were away.

"This hotel looks almost deserted," said Dan.

He and Jenny were taking tea in the Palace Hotel with J.O. "Where is everybody?"

"I thought you knew," said J.O. "The Shimmers have gone. The staff was told to close the place down. But as I'm one of the few people who like the tea here, they still serve me."

"The Shimmers?" said Jenny. "Gone?"

"According to the waiter, they went south with supplies and a wagon."

"That's odd," said Dan.

"Maybe we'll bump into them on our way back to Naivasha," said Jenny.

"We leave this afternoon," explained Dan.

"First their Zulu maid decamps, then the husband and wife disappear. What about Franz?" asked Jenny.

"Bagley said they've put him to work on the railway."

"And where the hell has Alice got to?"

"I've heard she's out at Brian's place," said J.O., who turned slightly red underneath the tan of his weather-beaten face.

"Lucky girl," said Jenny.

Alice had left her wagon at the village and followed the two Somalis north on horseback. Their route took them through an extensive grassland in which trees, short and tall, leafless in the dry season, stood as lonely sentinels. She could hardly tell one from another, but the Somalis knew them, and they used them to keep on the right course toward the Athi River. She wondered how her father, George, the surveyor, would have responded to that.

More bosh, she supposed.

As she rode, she looked back across the countryside. She could almost see the dryness, which she felt in every bone of her body. In the vast tracts of open country facing them, the hot, dry winds raised dust devils that swirled up and floated over the plains, dancing over the emaciated bodies of thousands of cattle. Then swirling and whirling up into the dry hills and down again, the dust finally hurled itself against the dusty, sun-cracked walls of the shambas around Machakos region. Miles away, as the shimmering heat rose, her guides pointed out the paths of a few remaining game animals, marked by puffs of dust that rose from under their hoofs as they searched for grass.

It was then she realized that she could no longer remember what green grass looked like, though it had once covered miles and miles of the plains surrounding them. She couldn't help comparing the course of her life to this parched vista. Like the receding water table, each day seemed to take her further from her family and friends.

Brian was now the only male to whom she related emotionally. J.O. had helped considerably, by being what he was good at, a father figure, but her feelings toward Brian were of a different sort. Brian himself was an enigma, and she hated to put herself in a position where she would have to rely solely on him, because she still knew so little of him, and of his life and his remote lodge.

She knew that just riding out to his "castle" on her own was proof of her attraction, yet she had no idea what was so urgent about all of this.

What is it about him that makes me do such things?

He himself probably never has feelings of loneliness, because he has his concubines. Her thoughts were interrupted as the guides called out and pointed to more herds of animals on the move. Yes, she said to herself, we can see where the animals are going, the puffs of dust tell us. And me? Where am I going? All she could think about was that she had placed herself entirely in the hands of these two Somalis and Brian Stanford, the Recluse of the North.

After settling into his "castle of mud," as he called it, Brian had everything he needed to make his life comfortable, and, unlike what many thought, he had not yet gone "native." He continued to relish the comforts provided by a monthly hamper from Fortnum & Mason in London. Another of his extravagances was the band of Turkish musicians and dancers he had brought out from Istanbul, and even there he had asked the lead drummer to do double service.

A well-known artist in his native land, the drummer agreed to Brian's request to paint a miniature on a small flat piece of ivory. Why he wanted a miniature of Alice was a question never asked by this Turkish artist, who saw so many of the young Somali women in the household as much more desirable. Certainly more beautiful than this washed-out Western sprite. He also knew he felt that way because the Somalis were forbidden fruit; they were untouchable because the Somali guards kept them under watch night and day.

What a waste, he thought, as he saw Brian turn away from them.

In their place this mzungu now treasured a miniature! That in itself was a source of speculation and gossip among Brian's household. Was Bwana sick? Had his mind softened from a fever? Was it something they had done to turn him from a lusty animal into an introspective monk? It was beyond them why he sat for hours staring at this painting. Worse yet was the picture itself—Alice had been depicted as a young Turkish harlot. Her brown curly hair had been darkened and somewhat straightened, her lips had been reddened and made more full and her bosom had been lifted and expanded to an unseemly degree. The painter complained at the time that he needed more access to the subject, but Brian had forbidden any contact, other than an occasional often secret glimpse of his subject while Alice was there for Brian's birthday celebration.

Earlier at the Christmas party his world had been turned upside down. Driven by his fascination for Alice and her invitation to attend, Brian could not resist going to that party in Nairobi, and it proved a success, especially the cheetah cubs. But afterward it was more difficult because he hated the town and did not fit well into the local society. Too often he was afraid of a chance meeting between Alice and Beryl in his presence. He soon came up with the subterfuge of slipping into Kona's hut under one pretext or another, just to catch a glimpse of her or to invite her and J.O. off on a safari. After each short visit he found it difficult to readjust to life back in his lodge. He was confident that nothing was lacking here, and often reassured himself that he'd never tire of this. At least that was what he believed until this past month when he noticed a strong nagging feeling that made him feel that perhaps there was something missing after all. Try as he might, he could not decide what that might be, until the day he received a telegram that changed his life yet again.

Three days after he received that, Alice arrived. It was late. Night had fallen and a Somali guard, who had been posted at the gate for that expressed purpose, escorted her to the main sitting room. Along the way the guard handed her a letter from Dr. Sharpe. She opened it and hastily read through it as she came down the corridor and into the room where a light supper had been set out for her.

Brian rose to greet her. That's when she saw immediately that he looked like a sick cat.

"Brian, what's wrong?"

"I have to leave all of this," he said as he held out a telegram to her. "It's my father."

She glanced at it. It was from Brian's mother and said nothing more than that he was needed back in England to run the estate and take up his duties as fifth baron.

"I have to abandon what I started here," he said. "I can't carry on like this when I'm needed back home. And I've got to make some decisions immediately."

"But you needn't give it up entirely," she said as she sat and looked hungrily at the food. She was starving. Yet a thought ran through her mind, perhaps that's why he wanted to see her, he wanted her to manage things for him in his absence.

"What?" he asked, looking at her in a distracted way, his mind obviously miles away.

Thinking he was still trying to cope with the idea of farm management, she said, "I was about to suggest that you simply turn it over to the people here. Select some of the elders to act on a committee and let them run it as a cooperative."

"Alice...." He started to speak, then paused.

She thought that perhaps she had said something wrong, or at least something that had made him stop and think.

"Yes?"

"Then of course," he said, "there's Stanhope and my father's reputation, his involvement."

"Is this something you want to discuss?" Alice asked, because, at this point, she had no idea of what he was getting at. He had come full circle from managing a farm in Africa to perhaps some indelicate business regarding his father.

"Well," he said, smiling the way he did whenever he had something to say that would shock her, "unlike myself, he was no hedonist."

"Brian, what *are* you talking about?"

"My father, compared to me."

"Then you had best take another step back. I think you mean to say that *like* you he was no hedonist. Didn't we agree last time, you aren't. You can't be because no matter how hard you try you don't fit the mold."

"You're right, we did agree. But what I'm trying to say is that he never even claimed to be one. He was too involved in all sorts of activities, 'for the good of Man and for the glory of God,' as he used to say."

"Oh," said Alice, "you mean *that* sort of involvement."

"Yes," he said, again smiling. "The sort of man you'd like, Alice. A model husband, constant in his love for my mother, never played the field. Neither did she, and they both often wondered why I did."

"I hesitate to ask. Why did you?"

"Something I inherited I suppose. My forebears were a riotous bunch. Partly also I think it was youthful rebellion. But now I feel differently. In fact, just after I heard of his death, I thought how much I'd like to have been like him. He was so many things to so many people: philanthropist, leader of the church, farmer, amateur architect, naturalist, and yet he found time to lead the local hunt club. I won't be able to follow in his footsteps, let alone start."

"Obviously he could afford all this," said Alice.

"And more. His income was about £500,000 a year."

"Goodness," said Alice looking askance. "But then, why are *you* so worried? And what was the urgency all about?"

"Because if I go back to take up all of what the family wants, I'll lose what I want most."

"Which is?"

"You, Alice."

Her heart leapt when he said that, and her face flushed. But with those effects came a realization that this was an impossible conversation. And, she thought, this will all lead to some impossible proposals.

To forestall that she said, "I appreciate your feeling, Brian, and I feel the same way myself sometimes. Especially when I'm lonely. It's nice then to know a friend is near."

"I'm not talking about friendship, Alice."

She blushed and said, "I think you're simply overtaken by events. Why don't you try to get some sleep. We'll talk tomorrow about how you might cope with the situation here."

"Will you marry me?"

"No," said Alice.

"Why not?"

"There's still too much of a gap between us, Brian."

"In what way?" he asked.

"What we want in terms of life. I mean, here you are, wondering if you could ever follow in your father's footsteps, and yet I wonder how you'll ever be able to leave your Somali girlfriends and your snuffbox."

"You mean you don't believe I can change? Marry me anyway."

"I can't."

"Why not?"

"For God's sake Brian, think."

"Because I'm already married?"

"Yes."

"Easily fixed. Beryl wants a divorce."

"The answer is still no."

"Why?"

"You're a very independent and exotic person. I'm not like Beryl. I wouldn't be able to look the other way if you reverted to your old self."

"I can and will change."

"I doubt it," said Alice. "People always say that, and it does happen in novels, but not in real life. In reality it's very difficult for anyone to really change."

"Is there any way I can prove that I can become a different man, Alice?"

"That's just the point," she said. "I have a good feeling toward you now and much respect, but only because of the way you are at present. I'm not so sure I'd like you if you did change. Look at David. When I first met him he was a completely different person and easy to like. Now he's impossible to be near. Anyway," she sighed, "I have to go back to Nairobi, and very soon."

"Why?"

"This came from Dr. Sharpe." She handed him the letter and turned now to her supper. Love and friendship would have to wait; she was ravenous.

He read while she ate.

Alice,

Last week I went to your house and found you gone. I realize it is not my business to intrude in your affairs, but I think you'd better be aware of certain things for your own good. First off, your man, Kona (a rather strange bird if you ask me) said you could be reached either in Machakos or at this address, so I'm copying this letter to both places. Presumably, someone in authority has already told you that your brother-in-law, Stephen, was badly wounded during a massacre in Kijabe. Also, Major Curtis, who is I believe your step-uncle, was killed outright in the same action. I've been informed that the high commissioner's office has started an investigation and they've put me to work in my new capacity as medical officer assembling information and details. Also there was a telegram from Mombasa advising us that the major's body has arrived and they are preparing for a full military funeral with honors. I have sent a reply telling them that as you seem to be his only living relative, they must wait until they hear directly from you. Please let me know soon what you intend, and I will instruct everyone accordingly.

The second point involves Dorothy. On the basis of what you told me, and new information I gained from Allen's houseboy, Juma, I have asked the Railway Police for a warrant for Allen's arrest on a charge of manslaughter.

Now that I'm no longer with the Railway, I hope to crack down on a number of loose practices here, starting with Allen's case.

Best regards, Charley

"As you see, I have to get back. I've decided to leave early tomorrow morning."

"Is it even worth a try, Alice?"

"What?"

"What we were talking about just now. My changing, taking on a proper home life, children, a fire in the fireplace and 'a bun in the oven,' and all that."

"Brian, you're basically one of the best men I've ever met. And no one can fault your work with the Africans. But I think it might be better for you to take the next few steps on your own. Who knows, maybe someday you can even prove to the world that you can put aside your 'vacations.' Let's see if that happens first."

"Alice, tell me. What is it that you want? What is it you're looking for?"

"In a man?"

"Yes."

"Nothing more than a strong back and a courageous heart."

"Then I have a chance."

"We'll see," she said, as she returned to her supper and smiled as she thought of what Syonduku would say to all this.

The following morning Brian received by special messenger a pile of telegrams outlining sundry requests. They referred to memoranda, legal documents and financial papers, all of which were immediate and pressing. At the same time came a request for a baraza from the local people who felt he was losing touch.

As she rode away she felt sorry for him and wondered if she'd ever see him again.

Turning her thoughts now to what she had to face in Nairobi, she said to herself, maybe Syonduku was right, what I really need is a Hercules.

"So that's that," Roger said as he peered at John Allen in the candlelight. "They've caught a real killer, at last. Good for them."

"What are you going on about, Newcome?"

"You, the illustrious Mr. Allen. I presume they arrested you for the massacre, since you probably planned it."

"You presume wrong. Everything that happened in Kijabe was approved by the government beforehand, except you shooting Stephen."

"I didn't shoot him. But I don't expect you to believe that. What I'd like to know is why you're in here? Or do you normally spend your days and nights in a storehouse sitting on a bag of cornmeal."

"They made a mistake."

"Oh, I'll bet."

"Dr. Sharpe has accused me of Dorothy's death."

"I thought she killed herself?"

"She did." Allen's voice dropped to a whisper, and for a moment Roger felt a twinge of pity for him. He seemed genuinely sorry she had died. He remembered Allen had felt deeply about her, more so than Stephen had.

Of course, he thought, his opinion of Stephen had changed for the better when Stephen threw himself at Franz the way he did. That act alone had made Roger think, maybe, like Dorothy, he had judged too harshly. With Dorothy he now had to admit she knew a great deal more about life than he ever thought she did.

"So, she was right."

"How do you mean?"

"She thought men were the cause of most of the trouble in the world. I guess you turned out to be one of the best examples of that," said Roger. "Worse even then Stephen Hale."

"Don't compare me with that souse." Allen's voice had regained its harshness. "By the way, he's also your mistake—you shouldn't have shot him."

"I didn't," said Roger.

In the dim light of the candle Allen could just see Roger's face, which seemed now to lack the aggressive and temperamental tone he was famous for. He also could sense from Roger's voice that his temper was under control. Was he becoming mellower? Allen asked himself. Is that what happens to people when they catch sight of the gallows?

"Then who did?" he asked. "No one else had that much resentment toward him. According to Matthew, Franz was Hale's only friend."

"Idiots!" Roger's temper had returned with a vengeance. "You, Bagley, Matthew and the rest. Don't you see? The Shimmers are playing you all for fools. The Germans have been footing the bill for Jakoby and her activities, and I'll bet they're also behind this strike."

Allen laughed. "And I bet Dorothy didn't kill herself, the Germans did it."

"Who else would be behind the sabotage?"

"The bloody wogs, that's who. I can't help it if it's you and your friends who can't believe the truth. That doesn't help matters, especially yourself."

"Help matters?"

"For God's sake, man. Don't you see? Unless you help yourself no one else will."

"What are you talking about?"

"I talked to Bagley before they threw me in here. He said if you'll confess to collusion with the Kikuyus and agree to turn over your food stores to the Railway in compensation, he might be able to reduce the charge against you. It seems Franz could be persuaded to say he shot Stephen to prevent him from attacking you."

Roger stood up. He calculated that it must almost be almost midnight outside, yet the tin roof seemed quite hot. "What's that smell?"

"I don't smell anything. By the way, he gave me this envelope and a pencil. He said if you'd sign the contents, he'd revisit the charge."

Roger looked at him suspiciously. Then he opened the envelope and looked at the paper, which he read by the flickering light of the candle stub. "It's a confession and a release of the bulk of my food stores," he said.

"Yes, but not a confession for murder," said Allen. He placed the pencil close to the candle where Roger could see it.

"It's getting bloody hot in here," said Roger as he put down the paper and again felt the plank wall. "Maybe I'm wrong; it could be just the heat of the sun earlier today. It beats down on the walls and roof."

"These storehouses always get too hot," said Allen. "Well?"

"Well what?"

"Will you sign? If you do, Bagley said he'll let you out on your own recognizance."

"Are you certain?"

"That's the deal. He said the minute the guard sees it slide under the bottom of the door, you're a free man."

Roger walked over to the paper and picked it up. He read it through once more.

"Not much time to cogitate," said Allen. "That candle won't last."

Roger glanced at the stub, almost gone, then shrugged his shoulders and signed it.

"Now, what the hell is that noise?" he asked as he stepped back and listened against the warm wooden wall. "It sounds like a roar, like a bonfire."

Suddenly he smelled smoke. As Roger climbed back on the sack and held up the candle stub toward the ceiling, he could see thin wisps of smoke drifting through the cracks. He stepped further up onto several other sacks in order to feel the roof. It was red hot. When he turned to tell Allen, he heard a click. Allen stood with his back to the door, the signed confession in his pocket and a small revolver in his right hand. With his left hand he turned a key in the door.

"Stay right where you are."

Roger crouched to leap, but Allen fired at him, forcing him to jump behind a sack, blowing out the candle in the process. Roger looked out at the darkened room as the door opened. The bright light of a raging inferno briefly lit the doorway as Allen stepped out and paused. He laughed and yelled, "Here's a preview of where you'll be going, Newcome!" then he closed the door and locked it.

4

Most nights the railway club dining room tables were converted after dinner. They were turned into card tables to encourage the married officials to stay on. Their wives and daughters gladly paired off for whist while a few long-suffering bachelors sought out the sofas and chairs in the library. The bar crowd never varied; the young army and railway officers made up the backbone of the rustic nightlife in Nairobi. They roused themselves during the day only for horseracing and polo matches, or the occasional hunting safari, but somehow, as was always pointed out every Saturday night, "Bloody Africa's just not the same as Bloody India!" What was missing was the sympathetic audience, the posh 'almost equals,' the maharajahs and princes who permeated the social fabric of the subcontinent. In Nairobi the only audience was the settlers. Most of the Asian and Arab traders, and all Africans, were excluded from the club. Tonight they gathered around a group of army officers newly stationed in town who were still reveling in their Kijabe victory.

"This town's like a dead duck," said Lt. Geoff Bradshaw, known as Gerry, the leader of "Bradshaw's Animals."

"It's the railway strike," said Franz Shimmer, the next most popular member.

"But that's over."

"Yes, but people are still wary about coming out at night."

Lt. Smythe, who had just arrived by rickshaw from the station, confirmed what everyone had already observed: "It's dark and chilly out there, but at least it's quiet."

"Smitty's officer of the guard tonight."

"Didn't I hear from someone that you two lit a bonfire in downtown Delhi last year?" asked Franz.

"Smitty and I are famous for that one. Had an early Guy Fawkes' night, fat lot of good came from it. They sent us here as a reward!"

"Ah, but here we're not as narrow-minded as the Raj," said Franz. "Might even have the official blessing of the Railway." He winked at them.

"Christ, you've hit on it," said Gerry Bradshaw. "Here, DeCosta, another round."

"On my tab," added Franz, as the bar steward poured the drinks.

"That's what we need, damn it. We need a bonfire," said Gerry. "Here chaps. Old Franz tells me that the health people want to burn down Wogville, eh. What do you think of that? Anyone interested in raising the temperature a bit? Hell, we'd be doing a good deed."

One of the officers took out a cheroot and said to the barman, "Need a light here, boy."

All three laughed as Franz interceded. "Never mind the matches, DeCosta." He laughed with the others as he produced his own matchbox. "You can keep them, lads. I've got plenty more at home."

"Bring us two bottles of arrack," said Gerry as he turned back to the barman. "Might as well make a night of it."

On the road outside the club, Franz pointed to an alleyway. "See there," he said to Gerry, Smitty and two of their friends. "That will act as a fire break; that way it'll be confined to the bazaar."

"Not to worry, Franz, me boy. We can always piss it out if it gets too hot."

"Whoopee, or is it 'who pee,'" cried Smythe, fumbling in his pockets for the matches. "Who's got the bloody firewater, that's what we need."

They were now in an area known as the Savoy. The residents were milling about, sitting, talking by candlelight, cooking, dancing, drinking and having a lively time on a Saturday night, enjoying just the sort of thing Bradshaw felt was lacking in Nairobi. It upset the Animals to see that they did not respond even as the burning straw caught fire and spread from shack to shack. "Damn it, don't they know the danger they're in? Here, Shimmer, let 'em know."

"Diseases here," yelled Franz. "Have to move on, can't stay here!" And they began yelling and beating on the walls and doors. "Get up. Come on wake up. Have to get out!"

Several askaris came running, but soon realized that Bradshaw was an army officer.

In order to stop them, the askaris would have to find Veejay, who was acting for the DC. As they saw the drunken men racing through the alleys and lighting up more and more shacks, they knew the situation was hopeless.

"Lovely blaze, eh, Franz," said Smitty as he threw more matches onto another roof in another alley. He looked around and suddenly discovered that Franz was no longer there. He turned instead to Smythe. "Must be first-rate arrack; damned easy to start." He laced a wooden roof with it and tossed on another match. "Ah-hah, that's more like it!" He was pleased to see that now as the fire caught, the inhabitants, all light sleepers, were streaming out carrying their belongings.

Some were not so docile. They began yelling at Bradshaw, and started throwing stones. No one had reckoned with the dryness of the material, and the lack of ready water. In a short space of time the fire spread from shack to shack. Suddenly Bradshaw was afraid. He looked around for his colleagues. They had all left. In the distance he heard the alarm bell of the small fire wagon. Several askaris wheeled it down Victoria Street from behind the station. Once the alarm was given, residents from all over town became involved. The railroad and military staff turned out to stop the fire, but it was out of control. Soon the attitude developed that "It had to happen anyway, best to let it burn itself out."

On the road into town Alice whipped up her horse. She had started back early from Brian's lodge, but even now the sun had set and it was getting dark long before she came over the last rise in the road, where she was amazed to see a bright red glow. Too early for sunrise, she thought. Then it occurred to her that it might be grass on the farms in the hills above town being burnt in preparation for the rains. Can't be, she thought. That sort of burning had been given up a long time ago. As she rode further and saw smoke and sparks leaping, her fears were confirmed. Nairobi was in flames!

Franz ran around to the storeroom at the rear of Lowe's Hotel, the unofficial town jail. He broke off the padlock with the butt of his pistol then threw open the door. A lantern inside revealed Harry DeSuza lying on a blanket against the wall. "Hello, Harry."

"Oh, thank God! It's young Shimmer. I'd almost given up hope. Did you bring my money?"

"No," said Franz. "In fact, I was told to make certain that you were dead before I left Nairobi."

"Don't, for God's sake, man."

"Why not?"

DeSuza stared at the pistol and stammered out the first thing that came to his mind. "Franz, please, forget what I said about the money. I can pay for my freedom."

"You? Pay?"

"I know where she keeps her money."

"Who?"

"Jakoby."

"Good," said Franz. "I'm interested, but only if it's handy. I don't have time to waste."

"Just follow me," said DeSuza, as he sidled out the door under Franz's eagle eye.

"Where?"

"I'll show you," said DeSuza as they walked on. The alleys and streets on this side of town were dark and deserted. Most people were taken up with the fire, which now lit up the town center. They walked to Alice's house, where DeSuza pointed to an enclosure behind a fence.

"It's under the stone near the corner of that hut," he said. Franz looked carefully through the bush. He could see a flat stone in the moonlight. He pushed aside some of the thorn bushes to make an opening and suddenly heard DeSuza running off into the darkness. "Bastard," he muttered, then crouched down quickly as he saw John Allen run into the rear yard. Allen? he asked himself. What the hell's he doing here? He's after the same pot of gold, he concluded. He watched as Allen opened the top gate of the compound and slipped inside and hid behind a bush inside the enclosure. Suddenly the back door of Alice's house opened, and in the light from the kitchen Franz clearly saw Karegi look out before she turned and closed the door.

5

On the outskirts Alice whipped up her horse as she saw lightning flashes then heard thunder from the night sky above the town. Further on she saw sparks and cinders rising from the town center. They shot straight up, carried by the heat like tiny rockets into the black African night. Closer into town the smoke drifted down and across the road in front of her. She reached into her saddlebag and bunched up a black lace shawl that she held in front of her face as she rode on.

Surprisingly, the smell of rain was in the air as she reached the station yard and jumped off her horse. She handed her reins to the only person there, the station attendant. "*Wapi wageni*, where is everyone?"

"*Watakwenda*, they've all gone."

"But where? Where did they go?" she asked as she bounded up the steps.

Dan Lloyd came out of one of the station offices. "They're all out fighting the fire on the other side of town," he said. "This end of town's safe because the station yard acts as a break. Thank God for the rickshaw park," he said as he pointed to the broad empty space that lay between the station and the shanties.

"But what about the people; there must have been some burnt or injured."

"They've been taken out to the racecourse," he said. "Dr. Sharpe's out there with the army; they're helping set up tents."

"And the Railway?"

"Bagley and Matthew are standing by inside. They're waiting for a special train from Mombasa."

"What about the hospital?"

"It's not in the line of the fire. But Jenny's directing an evacuation anyway. I'm sure she could use help."

Alice ran across the yard and down the road to where Jenny and the hospital attendants were evacuating patients, many of whom could walk. A large wagon and driver were standing by to carry them to safety.

"Where's Stephen?" Alice asked.

"I don't know," said Jenny as she turned to a ward attendant. "*Wapi Bwana Stepheni*?"

He shook his head.

"I don't think he understood," said Alice and asked further, "*Kitanda ya Bwana*? Where's his bed?"

He pointed to the rear of the upper floor.

Suddenly a gust of wind blew smoke and cinders down the street. When she saw that, Jenny climbed up on the driver's seat. "The fire's shifting. I'd best get this last lot out of here. Can I leave you to check to make sure no one's left?"

Alice nodded and waved her on, then ran into the building.

The fire was one street away as she reached the lower corridor. The wind was blowing smoke through the open windows.

She stopped briefly at a pump to soak her black lace shawl in some water and held it to her face as she started up the stairs. Suddenly, somewhere close by, a kerosene barrel exploded and a fireball billowed down the alley behind the hospital, lighting up the whole back side of the building. A wave of heat, smoke and flames engulfed her as she fought her way to the second level and the room that the attendant had pointed out.

She turned as she saw a figure staggering through the smoke in the corridor behind her.

"Brian! What are you doing here?"

"I had second thoughts," he said, coughing as he handed her a wet handkerchief. She shook her head indicating she already had a wet shawl.

"Stanhope will have to wait," he said as they walked crouching down the corridor. They reached the last room at the rear of the building just as the wall started burning in earnest.

"Where is he?" asked Alice.

"Who?"

"Stephen. They said he'd be here."

"The bed's empty. It's already been stripped. They must have taken him out. Let's get the hell out of here!"

They started back down the corridor toward the stairs going down toward the front entrance when suddenly the roof supports began blazing. As the light timbers burned through, the heavy galvanized tin roof began falling in.

"Wait! There's someone in that last bed."

"Where?"

Alice pointed to a bed in the room before the stairs. Someone was lying with the sheets drawn up around their head. Brian ran in and grabbed the patient, sheets and all, and they managed to get through the front door just as the building was consumed in a complete and final roar, and with a great "whoosh" the roof collapsed.

They continued up Victoria Street to the station and mounted the steps. In the stationmaster's office they found J.O. "Alice! Brian!" he said, hardly recognizing the two soot-blackened people.

"Yes. It's us. Where's Dr. Sharpe?"

"Here," said the doctor, who came up the stairs behind them. He had followed them in from the yard.

"We've got the last patient," said Brian. "We couldn't find Stephen."

"But," said Dr. Sharpe, surprised, "all the patients have been accounted for. Jenny brought the last lot up to the racecourse just before I left. And as for Stephen Hale, he was released yesterday."

"Released?" said Alice. "I thought he was near death."

"The bullet hit the DC badge on his topi," said Sharpe. "It was deflected but it knocked him out. We treated him for a bruise, superficial bleeding and a slight concussion. This morning he headed for the Coast. He's going home. But who's that?" He pointed at the patient Brian was carrying.

"I don't know," said Brian. "This was the last one."

"Lay her down," said the doctor, noting it was a woman.

Brian laid her on a bench and Dr. Sharpe folded back the sheet. Alice leaned forward to see who it was.

"Oh, my God," cried Brian, turning away in horror.

He shook his head in dismay as he said to Alice, "It's Beryl, and she's dead."

"She was admitted last night," said Dr. Sharpe. He turned to Brian to comfort him. "We sent a messenger out to your place. He must have passed you along the way."

"But what happened?"

"Same thing as Dorothy," said Sharpe. "In her case, she thought she was sterile because for many years she'd never gotten pregnant. Then this past month it happened. The next thing, I had her houseboy at my door scared out of his wits. He thought we were going to arrest him for poisoning his Memsab. We rushed her to the hospital but it was too late. I gather John Allen gave her some pills. I'm sorry, Brian, in the chaos I forgot to tell them to put her in the morgue."

He turned to Dan Lloyd and handed him a telegram form. "Send this to Mombasa. It's urgent." He turned back to Brian and said, "I can't stay to help you sort this out. I'm sorry, but I've got to get back to the racecourse."

"And the fire?" Alice asked as Dr. Sharpe went running off.

"What about it?" asked J.O.

"How did that start?"

"God did it," said David as he walked into the waiting room. He had just arrived from Mombasa. Behind him they could see a troop of sepoys disembarking as officers and officials suddenly were everywhere.

A lightning bolt flashed across the sky above the train yard, followed by a terrific thunderclap. David with a pained look on his face pointed out the station window.

"See. He's angry with this town."

"Nonsense," said J.O. "The night guard said it was Franz Shimmer. He started it with the help of Bradshaw and his friends."

"And where's Roger?" asked Alice.

"The railway police are holding him," said Dan. "Bagley said they wanted to see if Stephen survived. If he died they'd be quite happy to charge him with murder."

"But Stephen's recovered," said Brian.

"And Roger? Where are they holding him?"

"He's probably still in the railway storehouse near Shantytown."

Alice ran back down the stairs. Disoriented by the pulsing glow of the inferno, she stopped at the head of the alley, unsure if that was the turn to the storehouse. As she peered through the smoky alleyway, she saw the figure of a short man. She froze when she heard the man's laughter—it was John Allen. He slammed a door, locked it, dropped the key, and ran off.

Brian had caught up with Alice in time to see Allen, and took off down the alleyway after the man who had killed Beryl.

Alice rushed up to the door and heard Roger pounding on the inside. The fire was closing in as surrounding wooden structures reached the kindling point and blazed up.

"Roger," she shouted through the door. "Stay calm, I'm looking for the key." She scrambled around on her knees as a nearby building collapsed in flames and fell against the storehouse. The thick wooden siding of the storehouse had caught fire and inside Roger saw smoke pouring under the heavy door as he yelled, "Help! Someone, help!"

He tried to kick the door down, then, gasping, he slumped to the floor. Thankfully he heard a key turning in the lock and the door opened to reveal Alice.

"Thank God!"

"Thank heaven he dropped the key close by," said Alice. "Quickly, this way!" She helped him toward the railway club where the railway staff was pumping water from a tanker onto the roof and walls.

Allen ran twisting and turning between the buildings, firing back at the shadow of Brian until his pistol started clicking. He threw the empty weapon aside. He ran on until he came to Alice's house where he opened a gate, slipped inside and crouched behind a bush.

Brian lost sight of him; it was pitch dark and he had no light. Allen seemed to have disappeared into an enclosure surrounded by thorn bushes, but the enclosure took up a large part of the area. It was impossible to see anything beyond that, so Brian pounded on the door of Kona's hut, which was close by.

"Ah-hah!" said Kona, as he angrily opened the door. He was not amused. He was upset at Brian because he always had a suspicion that he had come here often not to see himself, Kona, but to catch a glimpse of Memsab Alice. But this was too much; it was late, he had been disturbed earlier by people rushing about, but he needed his sleep. He was an old man, and this was disrespectful.

"So it's you, is it? *Unataka nini*? What do you want now?"

"I'm looking for someone," said Brian.

"Why are you here at this hour?"

"Kona, this is very important. Did you see someone come by?"

"Ah, so that's it. Yes, I heard the latch. Someone went into the compound."

"He must still be in there, but where?"

"I'll find him," said Kona who disappeared into the second hut, the one closer to the enclosure. There he pulled up a sliding door that opened directly into the cage where Lizzie and Jane slept. They were already awake and watching Kona's every move. Out on the savannah predators like them watched grass fires waiting for game to be flushed out. The pair sensed that a fire was in progress and instinct told them something was about to come their way.

"*Nenda*!" he yelled and the two animals dashed forward, coursing along the thorn bush until they converged snarling on John Allen.

Cornered, he yelled out, "Help!"

Brian and Kona ran up and stood near him. "You killed Dorothy and Beryl," said Brian.

"An accident," said Allen, gasping as the cheetahs stood over him growling. "I admit I gave them some pills, but who could have known? They worked before."

Brian reached down and grabbed Allen by the shirtfront. "You'll pay for this, you bastard. I'll see you hanged. Kona, tie him up and keep him here. I'm going back into town."

Even the elements seemed outraged, as following the lightning a torrential rain began. Sheet after sheet pelted down as Kona brandishing a sharp knife dragged and pushed Allen back toward the house.

The cheetahs sought out the shelter of their cage as the bone-dry soil of the compound turned to mud. The rain came down now in quantities not seen for years, chasing everyone off the streets and hissing as it hit the hot corrugated tin and the hot rubble of the shacks in town.

"Oh, I say," said Matthew, who had joined Bagley and Ian Burns in the supervisor's office, "here's a bit of luck."

The large raindrops had begun falling, spattering the dust and flooding the streets.

"We're getting some rain," said Bagley, not ready to commit himself further.

"Damn good," said Ian Burns. "That'll put it out. By the way, where the hell is John?"

"Don't know," Bagley said, as he watched Ian go charging off into the rain.

Then he winked at Matthew.

"Why didn't you tell him?" asked Matthew.

"Didn't want to complicate matters. Allen's got a signed confession from Newcome."

"So, it worked?"

"Oh, you mean Dr. Sharpe's summons? I knew it would be good for something. They'd never have convicted Allen. He's got the confession, now they'll drop the charges. It certainly helped to put him in with Newcome."

"Maybe you're right about this blaze," said Matthew. "It could all be for the best. Hell, no whites have been done in, and only a few of the Hindus and natives have gone under."

"Once Ian calms down and John makes peace with George, they'll see it in a more positive light," said Bagley.

George Whitehouse came out of the telegraph room.

"Ah, Bagley. What's the damage?" he asked.

"None of our buildings have been touched, sir, with the exception of the hospital, and they evacuated everyone from there," he reported. "It looks like there isn't much more to do tonight except wait until it cools down."

Brian walked rapidly back to the railway club. He was surprised at the number of people milling around. It was late at night and raining hard as he pushed his way through the crowd. In the main room he asked if anyone knew where Lt. Bradshaw was.

"Just saw him in the men's bar."

Brian made his way there, but the crowd puzzled him. It seemed everyone in Nairobi was in the room. As he approached the bar he saw Bradshaw with a brandy and soda toasting the new city of Nairobi, the one that would rise from the ashes.

"Oh yes, old Brian, is it?" he said, laughing as he saw him. "Too late, old man. Sorry to hear about Beryl. Allen always said she was a wild one." He winked at Smythe, who was standing beside him.

Brian looked at him for just one second, then his fist lashed out and hit him squarely in the face. The crowd became silent and pulled away from the scene. Bradshaw's glass fell from his hand and blood spurted from his nose as he slipped from the edge of the bar down onto the floor. Brian, frustrated and angry, stumbled backwards into the arms of J.O. just as a revolver shot exploded in the room.

Startled, he looked around. He thought Smythe had shot him until he noticed that the large room had gone silent and that no one was looking at him. They were all staring at the other end of the room where Ian Burns stood on a table, smoking revolver in hand. It dawned on him that Ian had actually called a meeting. Behind Ian and on either side were armed askaris, army men from Mombasa, as well as the head of the Railway, George Whitehouse. To one side he saw Alice and Roger Newcome holding hands. Then Roger did something that really upset Brian: he leaned over and kissed Alice on the cheek, and she turned her face up toward him and smiled.

Book Five

The Snake Out of Control

1

"Your complete attention, please, gentlemen!" Ian roared down the length of the room. "For those of you who don't know me, I am Ian Burns, and I have just received notice," here he held up what seemed to be a telegram, "from Whitehall. In addition to being High Commissioner of the Protectorate I've now been appointed Consul General. As of today, therefore, I am serving notice to everyone that, as the representative of His Majesty, King Edward VII, I will be the person solely responsible for the rule of law in this colony.

"I have called all of you here tonight to tell you that law and order have arrived in Nairobi. I will hold every one of you here personally responsible for any injury, damage, or death of His Majesty's subjects."

A murmur came from the crowd.

"As long as I am consul general, if any of His Majesty's subjects are harmed in any way whatsoever, the guilty party will be punished to the full extent of the law, and I mean hanging, if need be. Anyone, large or small, black or white, who is a subject in this protectorate, will now have our complete protection. The days of lawlessness in Nairobi are over, gentlemen, and any of you who cannot live here under these new conditions should leave immediately.

"I am directing Commandant Kirkpatrick," he nodded towards Big Billy on his right, "to arrest anyone connected with the unauthorized setting of the fire tonight. I would like Lt. Bradshaw, if he is here, to report immediately to the sergeant of the guard."

Several people at the bar looked down at the crumpled figure lying on the floor.

"Is Mr. Franz Shimmer here?" No one responded.

"As for the rest of you, please disperse. This meeting is finished. God save the King."

He turned and walked out.

Ian sat with David in George Whitehouse's private car on a siding in the Nairobi station. They both had brandy and sodas in front of them as Ian tried to inspire confidence in David.

"Your job now is to reassure these people, make friends with the Kikuyus, get to know the settlers and whoever else is important. Get them on our side," said Ian as he lay down the law. David sat across from him on the velvet-cushioned seat of the luxuriously appointed coach. He stared straight ahead as if he were in a trance. His black robe languished in a briefcase by his side. He sat on both his hands in order to keep them from trembling. He said nothing. He was not happy with what Ian was proposing.

"You're the DC of Nairobi, you're supposed to be in charge," said Ian. "Don't you understand? You're the only official left this side of Naivasha and the job of provincial commissioner is still vacant."

"Thank you for your confidence, Ian."

Ian looked at him and wondered if he was being sarcastic. But he didn't have time to waste. He continued with his pep talk. "Not to worry, David, old boy. Just remember, I'm counting on you. Get up to Kijabe. Start there and do what you have to do. As soon as you arrive, go around and search out the right people. Once you have them on your side, the rest is easy, a piece of cake."

"The right people, of course," said David, brightening somewhat. "I already have the army and railway staff with me," he added. "And they like me. I'll invite them to come with me to show the flag and all that." Maybe he'd get to use the gown yet, he thought.

"Like hell you will," roared Ian. "Keep them out of it! I'm talking about the natives and the settlers, the ones who have to do the work. They're the ones who are sitting on all that food. You have to calm them down and get to know them."

"But I don't know any, and I can't do this on my own."

"Yes, you can. It's simple. Call a meeting, assemble the facts. Wave around that report from Dr. Sharpe and tell everyone you're looking into the massacre. Then let them know that the right thing will be done." He smiled at David and winked. "It doesn't matter if anything's ever done, man, just as long as they have confidence in you."

He paused to see if David understood. David sighed.

"One thing you could do," said Ian, suddenly thoughtful, "is to hold a baraza."

"A baraza?"

"Cole said they're surprisingly effective in Naivasha. Even Stephen thought that was the final solution." David still appeared to be unconvinced.

"Now pull yourself together," said Ian as he got up and emptied his glass in one gulp. "It's getting late and I have things to do. I'll leave you to it."

"I can't do this on my own," David said as he reached out and took a stiff pull on his drink. For a minute Ian thought he actually saw tears in David's eyes.

"Why not?"

"When death and destruction are wrought by Him, there should be no interference."

"Now listen, David. This is your last chance. And if I were you, I wouldn't press that religious stuff on any of the locals. Come to think of it, why don't you take that American chap along. I've heard he's the one they trust."

"You mean the man who shot Stephen?" asked David, shocked at what Ian was proposing.

"Hold it. George told me Stephen was simply knocked out, he's alive. Newcome was falsely accused of that by Franz Shimmer. And since Franz has disappeared, I assume he really was the guilty party. Now that's an end to it."

"Ian, please tell me again why I'm going?"

"We need to show the world they can rely on us, man. The country is desperate for food. It's your job to convince the Kenyans to help. Make friends with Newcome, promise him a fair price and we're home free." He got up and went to the compartment door. "By the way, Rob MacGregor is sitting on a week's pay for the Railway. I have to get back to the station and find out where the hell he left it." As he stepped down from the train he added, "Matthew, Bagley and George have all gone to bed. They've taken me at my word, and left me in charge, so I can't complain. I'll find Newcome and send him along directly. Better tell the engineer to get the steam up and I'll expect you back here in two days."

2

Zaliwatena, Karegi's son, had had an eventful afternoon. He lay sleeping on his blanket, perhaps dreaming of tomorrow when Sarah would wake him. She always played with him in the morning, then Kona took him to his hut to watch the cheetahs and to play each day until his mother came home. Karegi, on her way to the racecourse to help Dr. Sharpe, had passed Sarah and Mary on their way into town to watch the fire. Karegi had no choice now but to stop and fix a quick supper for her son, even though she was in a hurry.

Ah, she said to herself, there's someone now. She heard footsteps in the house.

"Kona?" she inquired; she had seen him recently leaving the compound.

"Bwana?" she called out, thinking it might be Brian, whom Sarah had said was there earlier.

Suddenly the door opened and her question was answered. It was Franz. She drew back in horror.

"*Hayawani*!" she screamed, terrified. "Beast!"

"So my little friend," he said, waving his revolver, "again fate has thrown us together, eh." He ripped a curtain cord off a window.

"*Hapa*," he commanded, "come here." He grabbed her and pushed her in front of him, prodding her with his revolver. Then he tied her hands.

She was terrified with the remembrance of their last meeting in the slavers' camp.

"Bwana?" he said in a mocking voice. "Yes, your bwana has arrived." He looped the cord in a slipknot around her neck and walked her out the back door. It was pouring rain. Kona, like most other sensible people in Nairobi, had gone under cover for the night.

Rod MacGregor, a dark-bearded, large-bodied Scotsman, walked in the rain alongside the outline of the train that he had brought from Mombasa the day before. He had been awakened from his sleep by an askari, and told about the fire in town and that Bagley wanted to see him.

"It would be safer to go back to Mombasa," MacGregor had cautioned Bagley.

"No," said Bagley. "Whitehouse has decided, he wants to keep it here. He wants you to get some men and put that money into the station safe."

MacGregor reluctantly started back along the track ready to carry out that order, his mind taken up with how they would transfer the money, when without warning a man in the uniform of a railway security officer appeared out of the rainy shadows. He pointed a revolver at MacGregor. Behind him was a young African woman with her hands tied.

"Just continue walking," he said. "Make one false move and I'll blow your brains out."

MacGregor hesitated. His first reaction was to heave the lantern at the man and run, but he thought better of it as he remembered that although the sum of money on the train was large, it was in the form of small coins. They stopped at the open door of the paymaster's coach. Inside they could see the engine driver, Mr. Mehta, reclining on a blanket next to an enormous money chest, carefully reading a religious text by the light of the cabin lantern.

"Come out of there," said Franz.

Mr. Mehta looked up and saw a man with a gun with MacGregor. He put down his book and climbed down the stairs to the siding. MacGregor was smiling and Mr. Mehta thought he knew why. MacGregor was probably grinning at the thought of this slim young man struggling with a money chest that was heavier than himself. Shimmer prodded MacGregor and told him and Mehta to walk on to the engine compartment. There he boarded the platform and dragged Karegi up with him. The askaris standing by the engine backed away, amazed at this new development—they had never seen wazungus pitted against one another. Once on board, Shimmer waved his pistol and said to MacGregor, "Get up here and get the steam up. And tell the askaris to clear out."

As MacGregor mounted the steps, he suddenly realized that Shimmer had no intention of just taking some of the money. Damn him, he's going to steal my train, he thought. Once he reached the platform, he saw Shimmer's attention shift as he told Mehta to come up the stairs. MacGregor reached down for a length of firewood on the platform floor.

"To hell with you!" he yelled as he lunged at Shimmer, who promptly fired, wounding him in the shoulder. The impact knocked him back, crumpled at the feet of a horrified Karegi.

"You see, you British bastard, eh? I'm quite serious. And you're no match for me. Now crawl back into that corner and be quiet."

"You," he yelled at Mehta. "Get up here quick and start the train or you'll join him."

Brian had decided to go home, not to Ol Donyo Sabuk, but to his real home in Cheshire, outside Manchester. Forget about her, he said to himself. She was right, women always are. I had no business running after her. With that he shut the door to that part of his mind and walked away from the club. She's better off with Roger, he added; he's more her age. Part of his reaction he knew could be traced to the fact that he was still shocked by the death of Beryl. Her pallid face had brought back an image of a life full of waste, a life in which there had been no pleasant memories, only money in excess and drink spilt over lawns, wild reveries and early mornings lying on grassy lawns still wet with the vomit of his youth. He had left her corpse in the care of Dr. Sharpe and wandered off to the station where he found himself on the platform alone, absolutely so, as everyone had vanished from the rainy, sooty town center.

His first idea was to go to a hotel, but someone had mentioned they were full to capacity, and in his present state of mind he didn't feel like bunking down at the Settlers' Club, nor could he face going to Beryl's house, or to Alice's place. He had walked instead to the end of the platform and slumped down against the wall to take a nap. As he settled on the ground, he heard a train coming. He looked in the direction of the sound, but saw no light.

That's strange, he thought as he stood up to get a closer look. The train consisted of only an engine, a tender and one car. As it went by, going west out of the station, he had a brief glimpse of several figures in the engine compartment, but otherwise its dark form loomed up and looked very threatening as it went by. He still wondered why there were no lights, though he saw the dull glow of a lantern on the rear platform as the train passed and Brian's curiosity turned to panic. There against the wall on the rear of the train he saw Alice McConnell, waving her hands in a wild and urgent signal for help.

3

He stood amazed. The image of Alice clearly and vividly in his mind despite all he had done to forget her. He could still picture her as he stared into the darkness.

Was it a dream? he asked himself. He had been up all night and hadn't eaten anything in over twelve hours. He shook his head and decided he could not have seen what he had just seen. He had almost convinced himself it was a trick of his imagination as he turned again to sit slumped against the wall.

By chance, he looked down onto the roadbed. There, lying on the crushed gravel, was her black lace shawl.

He jumped down and retrieved it. It was still damp and smelled of smoke. Then he was startled by the noise of another train as he scrambled back up onto the platform.

This one, in contrast to the dark juggernaut that had just roared by, was as brightly lit as if a party were in progress. The headlamp flooded the track with light; the engine compartment was glowing as a driver and helper stoked the wide-open firebox. Behind followed a single luxurious coach that was bathed in light of every conceivable type. A sleek new train, it had just started out from somewhere in the station yard and had not yet reached full speed.

For a moment he thought it was simply an empty train being shunted to one side, an impression that was reinforced as he saw the empty seats go by. Then he saw two passengers, David and Roger, sitting alone in the well-lit coach. As the train passed, he jumped from the platform onto the rear step and climbed up into the car.

He threw the door open and watched as both men looked up, startled.

They appeared worried and angry at being disturbed. Almost, he thought, as if they had been caught in some sort of conspiracy.

"What the *hell* do you want?" asked an indignant Roger.

"This is a private train," said David, who had screwed down his eyebrows until he could hardly see.

"Sorry to intrude," said Brian. He still had no idea of why he was there, or what he should do next.

"Who invited you?" persisted Roger. He still remembered Brian sitting next to Alice on his first visit to Ol Donyo Sabuk, when he himself was relegated to second place on the other side of the campfire. He also recalled the way Brian had stolen the show with his two cheetah cubs at the Christmas party. Just the sort of cheap trick he's capable of, he thought. He'd do anything to get her attention.

"I'm sorry," said Brian, "but I need this train."

"We're on government business, old chap," said David. "Can't be diverted. Sorry. You'll have to look elsewhere."

That is exactly what's wrong with England today, thought David. He had heard all about Brian's former life and his racy adventures and close association with the Somalis. An aristocratic ragtag who had ignored his religious heritage. He reached for the emergency cord. Ian was right, he said to himself, he had to rise to the occasion. Take charge and show everyone who was boss. He'd have the train driver throw this man off well before they reached Kijabe.

"Keep your hand off that," said Brian as he leveled a pearl-handled Colt Dragoon revolver at David. "Both of you put your hands out where I can see them."

"But what the hell do you want?" asked Roger.

"Guilty conscience, Roger?" asked Brian, smiling.

"Are you mad?"

"Just a wild guess," said Brian. "Why else would you be on a train with David McCann on your way to Kikuyuland. It's obvious you're sucking up to the government. Everyone knows you want to make money off the natives. What better way to do it than sell their produce to the government and Railway at a huge profit? Now that Allen's out of the picture, it looks like a clear road for you. Somehow, I'd thought you were above all that. But it's clear I didn't know you that well."

Then he thought, poor Alice, does she truly know the real Roger? Here she was taking up with someone she thought was the ideal friend of the native. She had once referred to him as "The Last Mohican," the savior of the Kikuyu nation. Right now he looked like any ordinary salesman making a quick deal.

"It's none of your business," said Roger, blushing.

"This is government business," said David. "Everyone benefits from what Mr. Newcome and I are doing."

"Oh?"

"Don't say 'oh' like that," said Roger. "It's not just about food. McCann's going up there to look into the massacre. Something with which you and your settler friends seem to have very little concern."

"What exactly *do* you want?" asked David, with growing impatience.

"I'm not sure," said Brian, "but Alice was on the train that left just before yours."

"Alice?"

"She looked like she might be in trouble...."

He stopped talking as the train suddenly slowed.

"Now what?" he asked.

"We're coming into Dagoretti Station," said David.

The stationmaster was out on the platform waving them to stop.

"Roger, jump down and run up front," said Brian. "Tell the train driver to keep going or I'll shoot this little prig."

Roger did as he was told as Brian leaned out the window and yelled at the stationmaster, "We're in a hurry."

The stationmaster held up two telegrams as they passed. Roger grabbed them and jumped back in the coach.

He read the first one out loud:

FROM STATIONMASTER IN DAGORETTI STOP PAY TRAIN PASSED THROUGH WITH SEVERAL HOSTAGES AND ONE BWANA SHIMMER WHO

SAID HE WANTS ONE OXCART SIX HEALTHY OXEN FOOD WATER AND SPARE HORSE READY ON HIS ARRIVAL BELOW ESCARPMENT STOP MESSAGE JUST RECD FROM NAIROBI INSTRUCTS US TO ALLOW TRAIN TO CONTINUE UNMOLESTED IN WESTERLY DIRECTION END

"Bwana Shimmer?" asked David.

"It must be Franz," said Roger.

"He's stolen a pay train," said Brian, "and he's traveling to Kijabe."

"No one in their right mind would steal a Railway pay train," said David.

"Why not?"

"Because the Railway always pays the workers in rupee coins, which are numerous and heavy."

"Thirty thousand rupee coins is a hell of a load," said Roger.

"It's a backbreaking job just moving the pay chest on and off the train."

"If it's not the money, then what?"

"It must be political," said David.

"How so?"

"The junior staff and platelayers went back to work after the strike," said David, "but the situation is still tense. Especially so at the railhead in Naivasha. If they aren't paid, they'll go back on strike, or worse, riot."

"Then why the hell don't they just shoot this man?" yelled Brian, frustrated by what he saw unfolding.

"Look at the second telegram," said Roger.

HOSTAGES INCLUDE ROD MACGREGOR TRAIN DRIVER MEHTA AND ONE NATIVE RAILWAY HOSPITAL NURSE KAREGI STOP

"That's your answer," said David. "It's Rod MacGregor's train."

"What's so special about that?"

"He's an old friend of Ian Burns. That's why Ian sent a telegram from Nairobi, to warn them not to stop the train. He doesn't want MacGregor put in any danger."

"And Karegi," said Roger, as a pang of remorse shot through him. He recalled an earlier promise to Dorothy to look after her. Also he was reminded of the fact that he was a godfather to her son.

"Worse still, Alice is on that train," said Brian.

"Alice?" said Roger waving the telegram. "But she's not listed here."

"I think she must have jumped on as the train left. I saw her on the rear platform."

"Jesus in heaven," said Roger, "are you sure?"

"Absolutely."

The 0-6-0 F-Class engine rolled along, sparks streaming out of the stack as the lantern cut a swath through the rainy African night.

Brian held his head in his hands as he forced his mind to concentrate.

"Why this direction?" he asked.

"He obviously wants to cross the border into German East Africa," said Roger. "Once he's below Longonot he'll be in their territory."

"But he'd be easily recaptured at any point," said Brian. "The minute he camps overnight and goes to sleep, he's finished. And he has to sleep."

"I think it's his intention," said Roger, shaking his head, "to take the money chest and hostages by oxcart, up to a point. Then he'll get rid of them. He'll kill every one of them and ride off on the spare horse, leaving the oxcart behind."

"And the money?"

"He's probably planning on taking some of it with him to the border. The British rupee is accepted all over East Africa and is even preferred in Tanganyika. The rest he'll bury and come back for later. I'd wager within a few days he'll be a rich, free man, traveling in a colony where British court judgments don't apply."

Roger paused as he looked out the window into the night. "And we'll discover the hostages dead along the way."

They watched the stations pass.

At Limuru the stationmaster told them the stolen train had just left.

Within another thirty minutes they arrived at the last station, Kijabe.

The stationmaster, Mr. Gopal, came running to meet them as they left their train and ran with them to the winding drum that let the cars down the escarpment. It was still raining and dark; by the light of their lantern they saw the winding drum begin to turn.

"I am so sorry," said Gopal. "I couldn't hold them any longer," he said. "Mr. MacGregor was wounded and all of the hostages were tied together. He's even more dangerous now."

"Why?"

"He demanded twenty sticks of dynamite, fuses and caps."

"But does he know how to use such things?"

"He's a trained engineer," said Gopal. "On his record it says he received a diploma from a German university."

"It doesn't matter anyway," said David. "No one's going to interfere."

"Are you mad?" said Brian. "You can't let him escape."

"Alice may survive," said Roger, "since he probably doesn't know she's aboard, but he'll kill Karegi."

It was raining as they reached the platform on stage one and saw the paymaster's car just starting down the incline. Alice was visible on the rear platform of the car. She had flattened herself against the wall. Without even a pause, Brian ran down and leaped from the darkness onto the departing car, leaving Mr. Gopal standing there in the darkness.

Roger also tried to run forward, but David jumped on him and screamed, "Stop it. You can't do this."

They both tripped and fell heavily on the crossties.

"Damn it, Alice!" said Brian as he landed beside her. "What the hell are you doing?"

They pressed themselves tightly against the outside wall of the car as the door suddenly slammed opened and Franz looked out.

He laughed as he saw in the flickering light of the lantern Roger and David fighting on the tracks.

Roger broke free and bravely continued to hobble after the train, which had almost faded from his view.

Franz grabbed the lantern from its hook and disappeared into the car, slamming and locking the door behind him, leaving the two figures huddled in the rain.

Alice moved to the door and gently tried it; it was securely locked.

Brian, still holding his pistol, his birthday present from J.O., stared at her and whispered, "Now what are we going to do?"

Alice whispered back, "I haven't the foggiest."

"Why are you here?" he asked insistently. He still couldn't believe she would do such a thing.

"I saw you leave the club and I went searching for you at the station," she said. "When I got there, I saw Karegi being pushed onto a train and didn't think further. I just jumped on board. But where did you disappear to?"

"Nowhere," said Brian, who was reluctant to say anything more. He was still upset at the way she had announced her intentions, standing hand in hand with Newcome in front of the whole town. Worst of all, he was angry at her for letting Roger kiss her. Why didn't she just say she was in love with the man? he asked himself. Why string me along?

Then he remembered, in fairness to her, she had said no to him earlier.

He couldn't fault her for that. And he had to admit it was simply himself who couldn't let go; otherwise why was he here?

"You've changed," she said.

"Isn't that what you wanted?" he said coldly.

"But, why? Now you're so distant."

"I'd wager you'd want Roger here instead."

"I don't know what you're talking about."

"I saw you holding hands and kissing."

"Kissing?"

"I saw you. You let him kiss you."

"Of course I let him. You weren't close enough; if you had been, you'd have seen the tears of joy on his face."

"Naturally," said Brian in a wounded voice, "if you'd let me kiss you, I'd have tears of joy on my face as well!"

"Don't be an ass, Brian. I'd just saved his life. He was overjoyed."

"It's not just that. It's the way you looked at him. You must love him to act like that."

"I can't believe this," she said. "You're the one with the reputation for high living and playing loose with women. Why should a kiss on the cheek upset you?"

"As long as it's only that."

"Well," admitted Alice, "he did propose again."

"I knew it!" yelled Brian, and he turned away from her, but suddenly realized he had no place to go. They were in this together.

"Hold this," he said abruptly as he handed her the pistol and climbed up on the roof of the car. "Pass it up."

Alice dutifully passed up the pistol, then started to follow him up on the roof. He impatiently motioned her to stay behind. He seemed to be reaching the end of his patience.

"Don't you even know the meaning of the word 'no'?" he hissed. "Wait there!"

At the front end of the coach, Shimmer had opened the door and was standing looking down at the dark, rainy escarpment. He was waiting for something. Then he saw it, the counterbalance car for stage one coming up the incline. He turned back and looked at MacGregor, Mehta and Karegi. They were all tied together on the floor near the money chest. He cut a length of copper wire and wrapped several sticks of dynamite together. Then in one stick he placed a cap and fuse before he lit a cigar and stood ready.

The counterbalance car drew even; he lit the fuse, a long one, and threw the dynamite into the passing car.

Brian was scrambling along on top of the paymaster's car when after a few minutes he saw the counterbalance car explode with a roar.

The disintegrated car rained pieces all over the track. And the cable, now blown free of its connection, came whipping around the drum as the paymaster's car went flying down and rolled heavily onto the first carrier platform with a loud thud.

Franz had braced himself for the shock, but Brian was unprepared. His pistol went flying into the bush as he grabbed hold of the railing that ran the length of the car roof.

Alice was slammed against the outside wall, but was safe.

Franz then pointed his pistol at the brakeman on platform two. The brakeman was petrified. He had stoked up the steam engine as he had been ordered to do and was now standing in shock beside the winding drum.

"Set the clutch for a slow descent," Franz yelled at him from inside the paymaster's car, and watched like a hawk as he did that.

"Now walk back up the slope," he yelled.

Franz watched as the man started out on foot. "And tell your colleagues up there there'll be no salaries this month—I'm taking it all with me."

The brakeman scampered off as the paymaster's car descended slowly, positioned as it was on the first of the specially built carrier platforms.

Up on the roof of the car, Brian still clung to the rail as he crawled back to see if Alice was safe. He leaned over and whispered, "He's gone mad. He's blowing everything up."

"That's what Roger said he would do," she said. "He wants to ruin the whole railway system."

"We've got to stop him. I'll go back along the roof while you stay here and pound on the door."

It was easier now for him to walk because the carrier platform allowed the car to descend in a level fashion. He reached a place above the side door and waited until he heard Alice pounding on the rear door. Then he leaned over the edge, but suddenly he lost his hold and found himself dangling down into the doorway.

"Ah," said Franz. "A visitor. I thought I heard something." He covered him with his revolver as he reached up and pulled Brian down and in. Brian fell on his ankle, twisting it in the process. Shimmer laughed as saw him hobble to one side of the car.

"So! Bwana Brian. The Lord and Baron, eh? Well, look at you

now. You look like, how do you English say, a drowned rat. But a royal one."

He motioned him to sit to one side, then walked over to him and hit him across the face with his pistol. He watched him slump there before he abruptly turned and walked back to the rear door as he listened. "What was that? Another rat, eh?" He unlocked the rear door and looked out.

No one.

Alice was gone.

He looked up above the door; no one there.

He noted that the rain had stopped and dawn was breaking as he closed the door and went back to the front of the car.

They were approaching stationary platform three. The car they were on, carrier platform one, descended into a pit as the paymaster's car came to rest in front of the next stationary platform. "All change," he said and he kicked at Brian to wake him and motioned him out of the car.

"This is where you get off. If I don't have to, I'm not going to waste a bullet."

Brian limped onto the platform and joined the brakeman as Franz told them to push the paymaster's car onto the next carrier platform. Since the transfer track was slightly inclined it was not a difficult job for them, but the transfer was necessary in order for him to ride down to the next stage of the descent. As soon as they finished, Franz pointed his revolver at the brakeman and said, "Now start the engine, set the clutch for a slow descent, and leave."

The brakeman did as he was told, but Brian just stood there swaying.

"Well?" Franz said as he stared at him.

Brian saw no reason to leave. He had glanced up and saw Alice lying low on the roof of the car. In his mind he had decided to wait until Franz was just about to leave, then he'd jump back on the end of the car as he had done before.

He'd somehow rescue Alice. Then she couldn't resist his charms because he'd be a hero. And Roger, ha, poor Roger, he was still crawling around somewhere up above, possibly with a broken leg.

He watched the brakeman as the cable began paying out against the previously set clutch. Franz with his three hostages and the money chest now started down toward the fourth stationary platform where a counterweighted car was already in position three hundred feet further down the incline. That was the final leg and freedom.

"Oh," said Franz staring at Brian, "I almost forgot. Here's a parting gift."

He lit a short fuse on a stick of dynamite and threw it at him.

Now Brian moved! He hobbled down the tracks after the car. Then there was a hell of an explosion as the platform crumpled and Brian was blown to one side. The cable engine, which had been spared, continued to turn over as the carrier platform and its car slowed to a crawl, a slow but steady descent.

With nothing better to do until they reached the last stage, Franz looked at Karegi.

"My lovely little slave from safari days," he said. "Yes, I see you've changed, eh? A proper Christian, all dressed up." He reached over and ripped off her dress.

MacGregor yelled, "Don't touch her, you filthy bastard!"

Fraz laughed. "Oh, don't be so upset. I'm sure you must have wanted to do this yourself." He reached for Karegi's breast, but she reached forward with her mouth and bit him.

Cursing her, Shimmer pulled back his hand.

"Bitch! You shouldn't have done that. You animal!" He pulled out an ugly-looking switchblade knife and opened it with a click. His intention was clear; he was going to cut Karegi.

On the roof of the car Alice crawled along peering over the side. Hanging to the safety rail she let her feet dangle over the side until she came to a window. It was shuttered.

She shimmied further along and tried the next one. Also shuttered. Now she was desperate—the car was still moving and she was exhausted, but she shimmied along to the next one and again felt it with the toe of her boot. Here she found space on the top of the shutter that was not completely closed; there was a gap. But she was getting tired. She knew she couldn't keep this up, so she put all her weight onto that foot and suddenly the shutter fell straight down.

Her feet now resting on the windowsill, she let go of the roof railing and fell in a heap into the middle section of the car. She picked herself up and crept forward. Mr. Mehta saw her as she emerged from behind some benches and indicated with his eyes a flare pistol in a canvas holder, marked "Danger—for emergency use only."

She slipped it from the holder and pulled the safety pin, then aimed it with two hands just as Franz turned, knife in hand. She fired off a flare that slammed into Shimmer's side. It exploded in a fiery display of sparks and smoke, as he staggered back, tripping over MacGregor, who obligingly pushed him with his boot and sent Franz careening out the door of the car, where he bounced and rolled on the tracks before coming to rest in a smoking, glowing heap.

Almost simultaneously there was an enormous scraping and a thud as the carrier platform and paymaster car arrived at the last receiving platform, and Army personnel from the Naivasha garrison swarmed all over the car.

The early morning sun had come out and the rain had stopped. Sgt. Ross carefully lowered MacGregor to the siding as Karegi, wrapped in a blanket, climbed down on her own.

Alice looked back up the incline to see Brian, bruised and battered, staggering down the tracks. He finally reached her and she jumped down and caught hold of him just as he collapsed.

"It's you, Alice," he said, holding something up in his right hand.

She looked at it. It was a miniature painting on ivory.

"Who's that?" she asked with a worried look on her face. Another of his girlfriends, she thought.

"It's you," he insisted, and now seemed perfectly at home cradled in her arms.

She laughed as she looked at the picture, then hugged him closer.

"I'm sorry I ordered you not to go up on the roof," he said. "He would have gotten away entirely if you had obeyed me."

"And you, Brian," she said as she kissed his blood-smeared face. "You were right all along. I shouldn't set the bar so high. I thought it was best to start high, and then lower it as I went along. But that's all nonsense."

"Ah," said Brian. "You'll love Stanhope. It has high bars and low bars and everything in between."

Albert and Elise sat in the ox wagon in which they had been traveling for two days. First they had gone south to Magadi then north toward Lake Naivasha, where they now waited.

This was the culmination of their plan, the last phase.

"Where is he?" asked Elise, frantically scanning the early morning sky. "He should have been here hours ago."

"That must be him now," said Albert as he saw several horses approaching. Too late, he realized it was not their son on the lead horse, but Capt. Daniel Lloyd.

4

Alice's Diary (Stanhope, Cheshire, England, 1945)

There I was at nineteen, convinced I was at the end of my productive life. Perhaps that was why I accepted when Brian again proposed, or maybe it was the prospect of five hundred thousand a year, or the thought of owning fifteen thousand acres in Cheshire. In any event, I left Kenya and a life that strangely had prepared me for my new career, the wife of a peer.

I quickly learned that as the wife of a baron I ranked very low in the Table of Precedence. The spouses of a duke or a marquess demanded the respect I previously reserved for lions and elephants, while I was forced to take on the perspective of an antelope.

After a short visit with Rosmé, I traveled on by train with Brian and his mother to Manchester then to Stanhope by carriage. I'd often read in Jane Austen's books of the heroine's first glimpse of the mansion in which she would by one means or another live the remainder of her life. Still, it is never possible to prepare oneself. The bend in the road after driving through the estate grounds was to the right; Brian had skillfully engineered it so I was sitting on the left side in the carriage, and thus had a full and glorious view of Stanhope Hall.

Anchored by three massive, architectural blocks and surmounted by mansard roofs, it was decorated with many thin towers. Overall the three-storied hall has a French provincial look about it, yet everything below the roofline is Gothic, and acceptable to Brian's family, because that style has recently been declared both English and Christian. The remainder of the hall is filled out with about thirty rooms, each as large as a small ball-

room and joined on the southwest by a massive clock tower that rises 127 feet in the air. It has a carillon of twenty-five bells. The hall was earlier extended on the south side to provide a separate house of forty-three rooms in which our family lives, the hall being reserved for entertaining during the season.

As to income, it was a surprise to find that over half the family income goes toward charitable purposes, a pleasant surprise at that; still, the remainder allows for great leeway in the matter of entertainment. And Brian's mother, Lady Caroline Stanford, the daughter of an earl, demanded until her death that I keep up with Stanford tradition. She was a kind old lady who preferred me to Beryl, and who in many ways reminded me of Syonduku, especially in the way she used social occasions to put forward development plans. Both Brian and I deferred to her, and so did Rosmé when she eventually came to live with us. Rosmé had little to do at that point in her life until, as you might have guessed, she became a confidante of Lady Caroline's, which left me free to raise our five children.

I at first missed Lizzie and Jane; they had to be released into the wild. Now we have as many pets as gardeners, thirty each at last count, and an indoor staff of forty-two, which number includes Kona, whom we brought with us. Through the years he has taught a succession of housecats to hunt mice, leaving Stanhope one of the most rodent-free halls in the area.

I hear little news of Kenya. The intervening wars brought enormous changes in communications, but it also seems to have speeded up history to the point that everything I knew and loved out there quickly became obsolete, passé, and because of the risk of being boring, no longer the stuff of dinner table conversation. To top it off we missed out on the "Happy Valley" period, though Brian felt he could easily have joined in. In that respect, I think he has aged better than I, although that could have something to do with the fact that he never did give up his snuffbox. Certainly his "vacations" have gone a long way in allowing him to come to grips with all things modern.

ACKNOWLEDGEMENTS

No story of the Ugandan Railway could be written without acknowledging a debt, large in this case, to Charles Miller's *Lunatic Express*, a book that has gone through many printings and remains as fresh to the eye today as it was when first printed in the early 70s. Described by him as an "informal history," it captured everything, the spirit, history, tension, excitement and even the smell of that impossible feat, made possible by the sheer effort of the African, Indian and British workers and engineers, many of whom died in the process. Another valuable source was M. F. Hill's two volume series, *Permanent Way*, the official history of the railways in East Africa.

The suspicion by the Kenya colonists of the temperamental Wilhelm II, Emperor of Germany, was real and fueled by the antics of this eccentric man. For background information on his life and times, I am indebted to G. MacDonogh's *The Last Kaiser*. Under the German government's direction a parallel rail line was built in German East Africa, a development that worried the colonial government in Kenya from the beginning, and contributed to the bitter conflict that erupted fourteen years after the Iron Snake reached Nairobi. The resulting bizarre five year "mini-war," which featured Col. von Lettow-Vorbeck, who in Africa led Germany's only undefeated army in World War I and tied up 250,000 Allied troops during that period, is a story told in exquisite detail in Charles Miller's other tour de force, *Battle for the Bundu*.

Roger's experiences with the Kikuyus in the early days of the Kenya Colony are drawn from the autobiography of John Boyes, and the character of Brian is based in part on Lord Delamere, while much of the color and adventure of settler life is grounded in the autobiographical and other accounts found in Hobley's *Kenya*, Trzebinski's *The Kenya Pioneers*, and in *Pioneers' Scrapbook*, edited by Elspeth Huxley and Arnold Curtis. The hunting scenes of man-eating lions and African game are based on the experiences of Col. J. H. Patterson in *The Man-Eaters of Tsavo*, and several other books, including *Hunter*, by J. A. Hunter, my wife's grandfather, who also served as a model for J.O.

The African stories and myths are drawn from many sources, the most unusual of which are the colorful series called *Pichaditi*, a sort of "classic comics" sold on the streets in Nairobi during the 80s that are now, I hope, collectors' items. I also depended on Rebeka Njau and Gideon Mulaki's fascinating book, *Kenya Women Heroes and Their Mystical Powers*. Last, but not to be ignored, are all the graduate students, office workers, game wardens and men and women from sundry walks of life who made my life in East Africa a pleasant and thoughtfully rewarding experience.

I also acknowledge the help, advice and editorial comments made by Märta Bachman, Doreen McCall Smith, Coran Gaudet and Anne Sandlund, as well as my devoted wife. Portions of the text involving East African customs and traditions were reviewed by Mary Muiruri, whose comments were invaluable. Thanks, too, to my publisher, Robert Pruett, and editor, Annie Tobey, at Brandylane Publishers, as well as the many participants and leaders of workshops at the Writer's Center in Bethesda, Md., who offered ideas and suggestions, and the staff at Kramer's & Afterwards, who allowed me the use of the "back table," the local Cosi coffeehouses, and the staff of the Café Promenade in the Renaissance Mayflower Hotel, who provided innumerable coffee refills over the course of several years.